Mississippi
Brides

THREE-IN-ONE COLLECTION

DIANE T. ASHLEY
AARON McCARVER

BARBOUR
PUBLISHING

© 2010 *Across the Cotton Fields* by Diane T. Ashley and Aaron McCarver
© 2011 *Among the Magnolias* by Diane T. Ashley and Aaron McCarver
© 2011 *As the River Drifts Away* by Diane T. Ashley and Aaron McCarver

Print ISBN 978-1-62416-733-1

eBook Editions:
Adobe Digital Edition (.epub): 978-1-62836-311-1
Kindle and MobiPocket Edition (.prc): 978-1-62836-312-8

All scripture quotations, unless otherwise noted, are taken from the King James Version of the Bible.

This book is a work of fiction. Names, characters, places, and incidents are either products of the author's imagination or used fictitiously. Any similarity to actual people, organizations, and/or events is purely coincidental.

Cover image: Image Source

Published by Barbour Publishing, Inc., P.O. Box 719, Uhrichsville, Ohio 44683, www.barbourbooks.com

Our mission is to publish and distribute inspirational products offering exceptional value and biblical encouragement to the masses.

ecpa Member of the
Evangelical Christian
Publishers Association

Printed in the United States of America.

Dear Readers,

Welcome to this peek into the history of my (Diane's) home state. We enjoyed writing this series about three generations of one family living in Mississippi. If you read Tennessee Brides, you will run into several familiar characters. If not, don't worry. This series stands on its own. We enjoy creating characters who are connected in some way to other stories we've written, but everything you need to know is contained in the pages of the book you are holding.

Whenever we begin writing a new story, we set it in a specific time in our nation's history. The three stories in Mississippi Brides begin during the latter days of the War of 1812, and follow the events leading up to and during the Civil War, exploring the trials faced by those who lived during the deadliest time our country had seen. We strive to write realistic characters who struggle with such issues as slavery, women's roles within marriage, and the relevancy of faith. Some trust in God immediately—their faith as strong as a shining beacon. But for others it takes longer. Like so many of us today, they have to fall flat on their faces before they turn to the One who has every answer. We hope you'll be uplifted by these stories, and that they will ignite or reaffirm your faith as you follow each character's journey to romantic and spiritual fulfillment. After all, people haven't changed all that much, have they?

Thanks to the wonderful team at Barbour Publishing for sharing our vision. Without your hard work and dedication this book would not be possible. We love working with you and look forward to future projects.

To God be the glory.

Diane T. Ashley and Aaron McCarver

ACROSS THE COTTON FIELDS

Dedication

To my Wesley College family—from my years as a student through twenty years of ministry, God has used you all to enrich my life beyond measure. As our chorus says, "Wesley College, thou art owned of God. . . ." She is still a blessing to us all.

Aaron

For Mr. CJ and Mrs. Dorothy—thanks for trusting me to care for your oldest son and welcoming me into your family with such warmth and love. You are the best parents-in-law in the world.

Diane

Chapter 1

Nashville, Tennessee
August 1815

Alexandra Lewis sniffed and pressed a handkerchief against her dry lips. Would the tears ever stop? Or the pain? She wanted more than anything to go back to the time before. Before the world had changed. Before the sheriff had come to tell them about Papa's death. Before finding out the father she loved had been a liar, a thief...and a murderer.

How she wished she could just go to sleep and wake up to find the past week had been a terrible nightmare. But the sunlight pressing against her forehead and cheeks seemed real enough. Even though she didn't want to, Alexandra realized she would have to face the truth—their future was not going to be as easy as she had always imagined.

Tucking her handkerchief into the sleeve of her dress, Alexandra shifted her parasol to protect her face from the rays of the sun, then put her free arm around her mother. "It's okay, Mama. Everything is going to be okay."

Choked sobs answered her, but Mama leaned her head on Alexandra's shoulder. She sighed and patted her mother's back. Perhaps everything would be easier once they made it through the funeral service.

Not wanting to look toward the pine box that held her father's remains, Alexandra let her gaze roam across the grassy knoll on which she and her mother stood. No one else had come to support them in their grief, no one except the minister and his wife.

Alexandra lifted her chin and told herself they should be glad the whole town of Nashville was not here. As the townspeople had learned of the tragedy, they had taken pains to separate themselves from the Lewis ladies. Invitations no longer arrived, visitors no longer stopped by, and few notes of condolence found their way to the house.

It was not surprising given her father's actions, but Alexandra wished at least one or two of the people she considered particular friends had decided to come. Like Asher Landon, for example. He had been a frequent visitor in the weeks before...before the nightmare. But from what Mama was told, he was there the day Papa's villainy had been exposed. Perhaps he didn't want to be near her anymore.

If only Papa had not been so greedy, so anxious to enter the world of politics. His desire to be elected to a political position had led him to have a family of settlers murdered so he could obtain their land and fulfill the qualifications needed to run for office. He then covered up his atrocities by making it appear

7

the settlers had been attacked by an Indian living outside of Nashville. When his murderous actions were uncovered, he was killed in a shootout with Asher and Sheriff McGhee.

Did Asher think so little of her that he had no condolences to offer her and her mother? Or had he been influenced by Rebekah, the unsophisticated girl who wanted to drag him to the country? Alexandra lifted her chin. No matter. She didn't need the Landons or any of the other townspeople to survive.

The sound of a carriage coming toward them distracted her from her thoughts. Curiosity made her turn her head. Three people disembarked. She recognized the young woman as someone she'd met at parties. Dorothea? No, Dorcas. That was it—Dorcas Montgomery. A beanpole of a girl with blond hair and a pale complexion. Although they had met, she didn't really consider Dorcas a friend.

The girl nodded to her, and Alexandra tried to summon a smile. Perhaps she did have friends here in Nashville. Perhaps not everyone in town thought she and her mother were as guilty as Papa. Maybe the Montgomerys understood why his family mourned a man who had committed such awful deeds.

Of course no one knew Papa like she did. But even she couldn't understand why he had gotten involved. Had someone else forced him to take those dreadful actions? Or had he simply become a madman?

How could she reconcile his actions with the loving father she had grown up adoring? What had happened to the man who'd ordered a fancy officer's uniform and joined the ragged troops who defended New Orleans from British invasion? The man who had comforted and protected her for her whole life? When had he lost his way? And why hadn't she seen the truth when she could have helped him, perhaps even prevented his death?

"At a time such as this, many verses can bring comfort to a grieving heart." The minister, Roman Miller, opened his Bible and began to read from the book of Psalms. "'God is our refuge and strength, a very present help in trouble. Therefore will not we fear, though the earth be removed, and though the mountains be carried into the midst of the sea; though the waters thereof roar and be troubled, though the mountains shake with the swelling thereof. Selah.'"

He flipped through some pages and began reading again. "'Fear thou not; for I am with thee: be not dismayed; for I am thy God: I will strengthen thee; yea, I will help thee; yea, I will uphold thee with the right hand of my righteousness.'"

The words flowed around her, and something in Alexandra's chest eased a tiny bit. Perhaps she and Mama would recover from the disgrace, the shame, and the grief.

A voice, cold and heartless, seemed to whisper in her ear. People said God would provide for them. They said He was all powerful, all knowing. So why would He have let her father do something so horrible? Why hadn't He stopped all this from happening? Why was He punishing them?

The peaceful feeling slipped away, replaced by bitterness. The last few days had shown Alexandra the only one she could rely on was herself. She bowed her head when the minister said they should, but she blocked out his words. She didn't want to be lied to...not anymore. From now on, she only wanted to hear the whole, unvarnished truth.

"Alexandra?" Her mother's voice seemed to come from far away.

She looked up to see the others staring at her. "I'm sorry." She could feel a flush burning her cheeks. "It's...I..."

"Everything will be all right." Mrs. Miller smiled gently. "Getting lost in prayer is not a bad thing."

Mr. and Mrs. Montgomery offered their condolences to Mama, while Dorcas stepped over to her. Her hazel gaze speared Alexandra. "I'm so sorry for your loss."

Alexandra felt exposed, as if Dorcas was searching for some sign to report to her friends back in town. She could almost hear the whispered discussion—the exclamations of shock, the *tsk*s and titters of revulsion as Dorcas and the others in town analyzed every word she spoke, every action she made. She dug her fingernails into her clenched hands and managed a nod. "Thank you."

Mama reached for her arm. "We should get back home. People may have come by the house, and they'll wonder where we are."

Alexandra's heart dropped to her toes. Was her mother also losing her mind? Or was it grief that made her forget the lack of visitors? Should she agree? Or correct her mother?

While she was still trying to decide what to do, Pastor Miller held both arms out, one for his wife, one for Mama.

Alexandra followed them to the carriage, her eyes on the headstones of other men and women who had been buried in the cemetery. The beautiful setting was lost on her, even though she could hear the gurgle of a nearby stream. Instead of bringing comfort, its murmur seemed to reinforce her fear and loss. What would they do now that they had no man to lead the household?

❁

The busy waterfront streets of New Orleans gave way to tall trees and marsh grasses as Jeremiah LeGrand neared L'Hôpital des Pauvres de la Charité, the newly reconstructed charity hospital that first opened in 1736. Charity Hospital had originally been located in town at the intersection of Chartres and Bienville streets, but this was its fourth location since it outgrew its original building. The three-story structure was sturdy, with a line of wide, arched doorways at the ground level, but complaints had already been made about inadequate care and meager supplies because of the hospital's remote location. Jeremiah had his doubts about the decision to rebuild the hospital in the middle of the swamps, but he supposed the leaders knew what they were doing.

He stepped through wide double doors that stood open in hopes of capturing a cool breeze. It was only a few degrees cooler inside, but at least the sun no longer pounded on his shoulders. He nodded to a white-robed nun on his way to the ward on the second floor, glad he no longer had to explain his presence. Because of his frequent visits, the staff allowed him access without question.

He hoped to find his friend up and about this afternoon, practicing walking with his crutches, but Judah was still abed. Apparently the ceiling was filled with interesting designs. It certainly held his friend's total attention. Judah's arms were crossed beneath his head, and Jeremiah saw his light brown hair had been pulled back into an old-fashioned queue and tied with a strip of leather. His ruddy complexion had faded over the past months due to his inability to leave the hospital, but Jeremiah hoped that would change before long. The doctor had told them last week that the contagion was cured—Judah's leg had healed. All he needed now was a way home.

Removing his hat, Jeremiah tucked it under one arm. "Good afternoon." Sympathy washed through him as he watched his friend jerk a sheet over his legs. He tried to put himself in Judah's place, tried to imagine not having two strong legs to hold himself up. His stomach clenched, and he sent a silent thanks to God for blessing him with excellent health.

"Hi." Judah's greeting had a surly ring.

"I've brought you a surprise."

Judah's expression changed from a dissatisfied frown to a tentative smile. "Is it a letter from home?"

Jeremiah nodded, and his smile broadened. He held out several folded pieces of vellum that had been sealed with a blob of red wax.

The other man took them from him, but he didn't break the seal as Jeremiah had expected.

"Aren't you going to read it?"

"Later. I want to savor every word."

Jeremiah spied a wooden chair under one window and dragged it over to the cot. "How are you feeling?"

A sigh raised Judah's shoulders. "Sometimes it feels as if my leg is still there. But when I reach down. . .there's nothing."

"I'm so sorry. Is there anything I can do?"

"Give me back my leg."

Now it was Jeremiah's turn to sigh. "We've been through this so many times, Judah."

Judah turned his face away. "I know I should be happy to be alive, but how can I be? Here I am stuck in this steamy swamp for more than half a year while my wife is struggling to keep body and soul together at Magnolia Plantation. If I was any kind of real man, I'd have gotten back to Natchez long before now."

"I'm certain the note from your wife will hold no hint of censure."

"Of course not. My Susannah is an absolute angel. But she cannot run our plantation without my help."

"You've told me how good your overseer is. He will have helped her in your absence." Jeremiah shifted on the hard chair. "Judah, you must get past blaming yourself. It's not your fault that you were wounded. Nor is it your fault your leg didn't heal properly. I know it's been hard, but you should be able to go home soon."

A bitter laugh greeted his statement. "I can't even walk across the room. How can you expect me to get all the way to Natchez? I cannot ride a horse with only one good leg. Do you think I can paddle my way against the river currents?" He shook his head. "I need a job so I can earn the money for a carriage. I probably won't be able to make the trip home until after the end of the year. Susannah needs me now, not five months from now."

"You know I can help. I'll gladly loan you a carriage or the money to lease one. You can repay me whenever you get back on your feet."

Judah slapped his leg, the one that had been amputated below the knee. "That's just it. I'll never get back on my feet. I only have one."

Jeremiah winced at the anger in his friend's voice. "I cannot imagine how hard the past months have been for you, but if you will only turn your mind to the fact you still have so much. Look around you at the other men in this hospital. Most of them have no home to go to. Most of them would trade places with you in an instant."

Silence answered him. It drew longer and tighter as the seconds ticked by. Finally Judah nodded. "You're right, of course. I sometimes forget."

"I cannot blame you for that. You've had many trials."

"And a wonderful friend to keep me from becoming too morose."

Jeremiah ducked his head for a moment before meeting his friend's gaze. "If the situation was reversed, you would do the same for me." He hesitated for a moment before going on. "I promise you this, Judah. I won't insult you by offering you money, but I have an idea or two about how to help you get home before the harvest is over."

"An idea, huh?" Judah reached for the crutches leaning against the wall next to his bed. "If I'm to get home anytime soon, I'm going to have to become proficient on these things."

They spent the next two hours traversing the distance from one end of the hospital to the other. They stopped to talk to the other patients, dispensing hope and laughter as they went. By the time Jeremiah took his leave, he and his friend were laughing with the abandonment of young boys.

He still had no idea how to keep his promise to Judah, but he prayed God would show him a way.

Chapter 2

Visiting the hospital every day got more difficult as Mississippi River traffic increased. It seemed the growing number of boats appearing at the dock fueled the demand for goods instead of quenching it. And the few steamboats that traveled down and up the river so speedily could not handle all the demand. Every boat was filled, from the most rustic canoe to ocean-going schooners and brigantines. Trading was brisk and lucrative for everyone involved, but work filled almost every waking hour for Jeremiah and his uncle.

The shadows lengthened in the narrow streets, signaling the end to another day. Jeremiah locked the front door and leaned against it wearily.

"Eh, *neveu*, you are too young to be so tired." Uncle Emile stepped away from his desk. He was a short man, with a much darker head of hair and complexion than his nephew. He reminded Jeremiah very much of his father, who had died years ago during an outbreak of typhus. The same outbreak that took Jeremiah's mother. It had swept through New Orleans more than a decade ago, sparing neither the rich nor the poor. Then the following year, *Tante* Jeanne had died in childbirth along with the baby boy who would have been Uncle Emile's heir. Now there were only the two of them. The devastating losses they had faced had made them closer than many fathers and sons.

"It's been a busy week," Jeremiah stated the obvious. "Why don't you go upstairs and see what Marguerite has prepared for our dinner? The smells from up there have been making my mouth water for the past hour. I will put away the ledger and make sure we are ready for an early start tomorrow."

When Jeremiah finally climbed the stairs, his stomach was growling loudly enough to make someone think a bear was outside. He took his usual place at the dining table, at Uncle Emile's right hand.

Marguerite, the diminutive woman who cooked and cleaned for them, fussed with the soup tureen, ladling a fragrant stew onto his plate. "It's about time you got here, *petit*." She put a hand on her hip and frowned. "I was beginning to think you did not like *la cuisine* I have prepared."

Jeremiah let his mouth drop in surprise. "Have I ever not liked what you cook, tante?" He used the term of endearment even though Marguerite was not his aunt. From time to time he had even thought Uncle Emile might propose to her, but he never did. Would his uncle ever recover from the loss of his wife and child? It was a request he often took to the Lord, but so far, no result had been forthcoming.

Marguerite slapped him on the back with her serving cloth. "This is very true. You have a good appetite, not like your *oncle* who only picks at his food."

Uncle Emile huffed and patted his flat stomach. "I eat more than enough. I think you just want to fatten me up like a cow to be slaughtered."

All three of them laughed. It was a discussion often repeated at the dinner table. Marguerite shook her head and left them to their dinner. Uncle Emile blessed the food and tucked his napkin into the collar of his shirt.

Jeremiah tasted the savory stew, relishing the spicy blend of seafood and fresh vegetables. "Delicious."

"Yes, Marguerite has outdone herself." Uncle Emile picked up a plate of corn bread and passed it to Jeremiah.

The clock on the wall, an import from Germany, ticked loudly as the two men ate in companionable silence. Marguerite came back to remove the stew and serve a rich torte for dessert. Then she offered coffee, a rich, dark blend that complimented the sweet cake.

When they had both satisfied their hunger, Jeremiah and Uncle Emile retired to the parlor.

"You seem preoccupied tonight, Jeremiah. Is there something on your mind?"

Wondering how to express the general feeling of dissatisfaction that had been dogging him for the past week, Jeremiah sighed.

"I know." Uncle Emile clapped his knee and laughed. "Only a woman can bring such a sigh, neveu. Who is she? Why have I not heard of her?"

"Oh no, Uncle, it's not that at all." Jeremiah could feel his cheeks flush. "I just feel. . .I don't know. . .pointless, I guess."

His uncle steepled his hands under his chin. "Ah, I see." A frown drew his eyebrows together. "No, I do not see. You have a challenging job, an important one in my business, and more money than you care to spend. What is there to make you feel so aimless?"

Jeremiah nodded. "You're right, of course. I have many reasons to be thankful. God is faithful. He has filled my life with blessings."

"By the time I was your age, I already knew that I wanted to be a business magnate. Even as a young boy in Quebec City, I dreamed of marrying a special girl, bringing her to New Orleans, and running a successful enterprise."

"And you've accomplished all of that."

Uncle Emile closed his eyes for a moment before answering. "My only disappointment is that my beloved Jeanne did not live long enough to enjoy all this." He opened his eyes then and smiled at Jeremiah. "But *le bon Dieu* still arranged to give me a beloved son."

"Thank you, Uncle Emile." Jeremiah reached out a hand and gripped his relative's blunt fingers. "You've been wonderful to me."

"But. . ." Uncle Emile sighed and pulled his hand away. "It is not enough."

The words fell between them like boulders.

Jeremiah's stomach clenched. He didn't want to hurt his uncle, but the pull to do something more with his life was strong. He had prayed many times about the desire to break away from his uncle's business. New Orleans was an exciting place to live, filled with people from all walks of life, from different countries and different backgrounds. Many opportunities existed to help others here, but no matter what Jeremiah involved himself in, it was not enough. He wanted to do more. "I've been praying about this and looking for what God wants me to do, and I think I have an idea."

Uncle Emile sat back in his chair. "I don't know if I want to find out about this grand idea of yours, but I suppose I have no choice."

"That's not true." Jeremiah pushed back from the table. He had no wish to bring pain to the man who had raised him. He would continue looking until he found a way to follow God's calling without hurting his uncle. "I can keep my own counsel."

"Sit down." The older man did not raise his voice, but the command was obvious from his brisk tone. "I want to hear your ideas."

Jeremiah complied. He took a moment to pray for the right words to explain his dream to his relative. It was crucial to him to have Uncle Emile's blessing.

"You know how hard it was when *Maman* and Papa died. I. . .I was so lost." He swallowed hard. This explanation was more difficult than he had imagined it would be, but perhaps the only way to convince his uncle was to show his vulnerability. "Until you brought me to your home, I thought I would have to live on the streets."

"I would never have let that happen."

"I know that, Uncle Emile, and I will always be grateful. Please believe that. But not every child has a loving uncle to raise him. Some of those children do end up on the streets. Some of them starve, while others die of disease. Most often, the ones who do not perish become criminals. They are forced into hopelessness through no fault of their own. They become pickpockets and thieves—angry and lost because no one has offered them shelter or love."

He glanced up to see his uncle's reaction. The older man's face seemed to have become a mask. It was wiped clean of any emotion. What was he thinking? Was he offended by Jeremiah's desire to walk away from the family business? Would he support his nephew's desire? Or quash it?

Silence filled the room once again, like a third presence.

Jeremiah wished he had not been so honest, but the desire to explain his dream had been growing for months now.

"You wish to work with the Ursuline nuns at the orphan asylum?" The frown had returned to his uncle's face.

"No. I have no wish to interfere with the work of the Catholic Church, but the need is greater than even the nuns can meet." Jeremiah swallowed hard. "I want to establish a place—a home. I would like for it to be a large house in the country. That way, I could offer a safe haven to dozens of orphans. My dream is to offer them a refuge where the children can run and play and learn about the love of their heavenly Father."

"I see. So you are planning to leave New Orleans?"

"I don't know. I haven't gotten that far with my plans. But most of the land here is either fields for planters or swamps."

"You told me you have promised to help your friend return to Natchez, *n'est-ce pas?*"

Now it was Jeremiah's turn to frown. What did helping Judah have to do with any of this? "That trip will be only a matter of a few days if we can procure seats on one of the steamships going north."

Uncle Emile pushed his chair back from the table. He walked toward the fireplace, unlit at this time of year, and stood with his back to Jeremiah.

The silence returned.

Jeremiah picked up the linen napkin he had laid next to his plate earlier and twisted it in his hands. He wanted to say more, but something stopped him.

After a few moments, his uncle turned back to him. "I have an idea."

Jeremiah looked up at the man who had been a father to him for the majority of his life. Were the lines on his forehead deeper than they had been earlier? Was he hurting because Jeremiah had shared his dream, or was he just in deep thought?

"I have been thinking for some time of opening a new office up the river, but I do not have the time to explore for the best location and trustworthy employees. Perhaps you should plan to make your trip to Natchez more extended. Although the port may be similar to the area around New Orleans, who knows? If the area seems to have promise, perhaps you can build this house you dream of at the same time you establish a new office for our business. If trade continues to increase as I foresee, you should have more than enough money to build this orphanage and hire half the town of Natchez to watch over the children."

Jeremiah's heart soared. Why hadn't he thought of this solution already? "Uncle Emile, you are brilliant." Jeremiah stood and walked over to where his uncle stood, placing an arm around the shorter man's shoulders. "I can take Judah home, find land to build on, and not feel like I am deserting you. This is perfect. I can see the house now, big and comfortable and overlooking the river. You will have to come and stay with me as soon as it is built." Jeremiah grinned at his uncle. "I wish I had told you sooner."

"Let this be a lesson to you, *neveu.*"

Jeremiah knew his uncle well enough to know he was having a hard time keeping a smile from his face.

His uncle shook a finger at him. "Just because I am old does not mean I am senile. I still have a few good ideas left."

"You are the smartest man I know."

Emile inclined his head toward the door. "Go on, now. You have many plans to make if you are to accomplish your dreams."

Chapter 3

Jemma opened the door a few inches and slipped into the parlor. "Mr. McKinley has arrived, madam."

Alexandra's mother waved a handkerchief toward her daughter. In the six weeks since Papa's funeral, Mama had retreated further and further into a world of silence.

Alexandra sighed and wondered how she had become the one to make all the decisions. "Show him in, Jemma."

"Yes, miss."

As Jemma left the room, Alexandra couldn't help but wonder if this slave who had been a part of their household for as long as she could remember would still be with them given a chance to leave. Everyone else had deserted them.

Jemma quickly returned with the attorney, who had sent them a note requesting a meeting. He was about Papa's age, but the similarity stopped there. Where Papa had been somewhat rotund with a clean-shaven face, Mr. McKinley was tall and fit. He sported a neat mustache that matched his brown hair. He seemed to fill the room with his presence. From the shine on his square-toed shoes to his well-pressed suit, everything about the man screamed money. He walked to the table that took up one corner of the parlor and placed a large portfolio on it before turning and bowing to both of them. "I am sorry for your loss, Mrs. Lewis, Miss Lewis."

Mama pressed her handkerchief to her face, leaving Alexandra to acknowledge the man.

"Thank you, Mr. McKinley." The phrase was not as hard to voice now that a little time had passed. "It's a pleasure to meet you. Papa spoke highly of you."

"Thank you."

"We were a bit surprised at your note requesting a meeting." Alexandra softened her voice to make sure he would not take her comment as displeasure. "We would always be delighted to welcome you into our home."

"Yes." Mama's face reappeared for a moment. "Have you come to tell us the latest news of town? We do not hear any gossip these days."

The attorney looked a bit surprised at her mother's question, but he apparently found it impossible to disappoint her. "I did hear of a wedding last week of one of the town's most eligible bachelors. Nothing fancy, mind you. It was apparently a simple affair out in the country at the bride's home. Perhaps you know the couple—Asher Landon and Rebekah Taylor?"

Alexandra could feel the blood drain from her face. "Yes...I do know them." She pasted a smile on her face, but her heart, already torn from the scandal surrounding her father, shattered into a million tiny pieces. Everything fell into place. Asher had not attended the funeral or visited them because he'd been too busy courting his old sweetheart. He had toyed with her heart, led her on. Well, she hoped Rebekah would make him utterly miserable. A flash of guilt pierced her. Asher was an honorable man. She had been the one trying to draw his affections away from the woman he'd known all his life. But after all, Alexandra convinced herself, Asher would have been better off choosing her for a wife. She could have done more for his career in a month than that pale, simplistic woman could do in a year. "How nice for them."

"Yes, well. . ." Mr. McKinley cleared his throat. He must have realized his choice of topic was not a good one. "I am afraid the reason for my visit is not as pleasant." He stopped again. "I am sorry, but I have some rather bad news to share with you ladies."

Mama looked up, her hazel eyes damp. "Whatever do you mean, sir?"

"The news I have for you ladies is not going to help you recover from your grief."

Alexandra's heart started to pound. She didn't know how much more she could take. "Perhaps you should sit down, sir, and tell us this news. No matter how hard it is, we must know the truth."

Mr. McKinley nodded and took a seat in one of the chairs facing the settee. "I have paid all the bills your creditors have presented to me over the past three months, but I regret to tell you that I will not be able to do so any longer."

"Why is that, sir?" Alexandra was somewhat surprised by her aggressiveness. A year ago she never would have dreamed of questioning the family solicitor. But now she had little choice. "Are you retiring?"

He rubbed his mustache with one finger. "No, of course not."

"Have we done something to offend you?"

"No. I was shocked at the news of your father's doings, but I have never thought the worse of you ladies."

"Exactly what is the problem then?"

"To put it bluntly, miss, there is no money."

Her mother gasped and sank back, covering her whole face with her handkerchief and moaning.

"Mama, I think you should consider retiring. I can meet with Mr. McKinley and talk about our situation. I'm certain we can work something out." Alexandra stood up and walked across the room to pull the rope that would summon Jemma.

When the slave arrived, Alexandra directed her to escort her mother

17

upstairs and return with refreshments as soon as possible. The woman nodded and coaxed her mother up from the settee, cooing and murmuring to her as she helped her from the room.

After they departed, Alexandra took a deep breath. "I apologize, Mr. McKinley. Mama is not herself these days. Now, where were we?"

"I was telling you that the small amount of money your father deposited with me before. . .before he died. . .has been exhausted. Unless a large sum is available that I am not aware of, the two of you are near poverty."

Alexandra closed her eyes. When would the difficulties stop? She wanted to scream her frustration. She was barely a grown woman. Why must all this fall in her lap? What had happened to the easy life she had once enjoyed? Was it gone forever? Would things improve?

She looked at the stylish furniture she and her mother had selected for their home. She didn't want to give up everything. It was too hard to think of losing all of the things that made them comfortable.

Perhaps there was another way. It wouldn't be easy, but it might be less painful than giving up everything. "Could we sell this house? Perhaps we can buy or even lease a smaller one. If we are careful with our expenses, we should be able to get by."

Mr. McKinley shook his head, his eyes sorrowful. "Your father mortgaged the house."

"What?"

"Your father borrowed against the value of the house. I have to assume he was trying to amass money for some special purpose. But whatever his goal, I am afraid it will remain out of reach for his loved ones. You simply do not have sufficient money for the two of you to survive by yourselves."

Alexandra pushed herself up from the settee and wandered around the room, her mind spinning.

"Not everyone trusts banks to hold their money. Perhaps your father secreted a large amount of cash about the house? Perhaps in a safe?"

She considered the suggestion, hoping it might be valid, but shook her head after a few moments. "We've gone through P—my father's study, sorting through his papers. We have not found a safe or any appreciable amount of cash."

"I see." The lawyer walked over to the table and pulled papers out of the portfolio he had brought. He drew a pair of spectacles from the inside pocket of his coat and settled them on his nose. "Then I am afraid your situation is rather bleak."

He showed Alexandra lists of expenses and assets until her head was nearly spinning. She rubbed her temples to ease a throbbing pain there. "So if we sell everything, how much will we have?"

Mr. McKinley took in a deep breath. "Not much, I'm afraid. Do you have any family who can help you through this. . .difficult time?"

Alexandra looked out the window. "We do not have family in Tennessee." She watched the lazy downward journey of an oak leaf as an errant wind blew it loose from its limb. How nice it would be to have someone here to rely on. "Papa brought us here because General Jackson wanted him here. I once hoped I might marry into one of the local families, but after the trouble. . ." She let the words drift off. This man surely understood her meaning. Her social hopes had been dashed as soon as word had leaked out about her father's "indiscretion."

Alexandra knew what Papa had done was more than an indiscretion, but it was the only term she allowed herself to use when thinking of his actions. She wished more than anything that she could start afresh, but—

An idea came to her then. Why had she not thought of it sooner? She turned to look into the attorney's grave countenance. "Do you think we could amass enough money to pay for passage on one of the steamships?"

"Passage to what destination?"

"We have family in Natchez." Alexandra could feel her heart thumping. It was the answer to everything. She and Mama could move in with *Grand-mère*. No one down in the Mississippi territory would have heard about Papa's indiscretion. They would be able to start anew.

"I'm certain that can be arranged." The attorney smiled at her, relief apparent on his features.

"Everything really is going to be all right." She pushed back from the pile of confusing papers and stood up. Her mind began to imagine going to Tanner Plantation.

The attorney barely had time to get all his things together before she practically shoved him out the front door. He told her he thought he knew of a buyer for the house. That would relieve the greatest financial burden. And since they were going to leave anyway, it hardly mattered.

As soon as the man was gone, she skipped upstairs to tell her mother what they were going to do. The townspeople of Nashville were no longer of any concern. Even Asher. Let him have his Rebekah. Perhaps one of these days, she would return to Nashville on the arm of her wealthy, influential husband. Then they would see who had made the best of their circumstances.

Chapter 4

Fog wafted pale and cool over the brown river as the steamship churned its way into the port at Natchez. Alexandra clutched the edges of her cape and imagined that the mournful steamship whistle must sound like the cry of lost souls. She shivered, her gaze combing the bank ahead for a sign of one of her relatives.

Plenty of people scurried about even though the hour was advanced. The sun had not yet set, but she wasn't sure it would still be light by the time the steamship made landfall. Steamers might be the fastest vessels on the river, but this captain was very wary of snags and took a long time bringing his boat to shore. She supposed she ought to be grateful for his caution. They had experienced a very uneventful trip from Nashville to the Mississippi Territory.

The fog dampened her hair and clothing before sliding silently onto the bank. It obscured her view and gave an otherworldly feel to the late afternoon. Of course, it also softened the outlines of the ragged buildings, turning the shacks into hazy outlines that might have been fancy homes.

Alexandra could not see any sign of her relatives. She turned and headed back to the cabin she and her mother had shared for the past weeks. Jemma, the only slave who remained after they sold off their property, was folding their clothes and putting them away in one of the many trunks they had brought along. It was a good thing they had ordered new wardrobes before they found out about their financial situation or she and Mama would have been clothed in inappropriately bright colors.

Mama sat in one corner of the room, a kerosene lantern casting its yellow glow on her shoulders and the needlework in her lap. "Hi, dear."

"It's foggy and cool outside." Alexandra pulled her cloak off and dropped it on the bed that took up most of the room. "But we're almost there. Soon we'll be resting at Grand-mère's home."

"Yes." Mama's smile was shaky and seemed to be growing weaker with each day that passed, each mile that drew them closer to Natchez.

The mournful tones of the steamboat's whistle made all three women jump. Jemma closed the first chest and moved to another one. "Can't get off this boat soon enough fer me."

Alexandra put a hand out to keep herself upright as the steamboat lurched slightly. "Me either." She turned to look at her mother. "I didn't see anyone I know waiting for us, Mama. Do you think we'll have help when we disembark?"

Mama's smile disappeared. She wrung her hands. "Oh my. What will we do if they're not here? I don't know how we'll manage. Everything was so much easier when your father was alive."

"It will be all right, Mama." Alexandra shrugged. "I will find a carriage or a wagon. There must be someone who will be willing to take us to the plantation."

Mama grabbed her handkerchief, never far away, and started to cry.

Alexandra wanted to lash out at her, but she was so pitiful. Life would be much easier if Mama would take a little responsibility, but it seemed that was beyond her. Alexandra had arranged their passage with the help of the nice lawyer. She and Jemma had gone on board early to make certain the accommodations were acceptable. Then they had returned to the house and packed up the clothes and other meager belongings that had not been sold. All the while, Mama sat and stared out the window or wept into her handkerchief.

"Jemma, I have spoken to the captain about getting our things on shore. He assured me there would be no problem. We'll all go ashore, and I'll leave you to watch over Mama while I find a carriage or wagon, some kind of conveyance to get us home."

Jemma's eyes widened, but she nodded.

Alexandra sent her an encouraging smile. She had been a jewel during the trip. In fact, Alexandra didn't know if she could have made it without her help.

Alexandra grabbed Mama's cloak and coaxed her to stand and let it be draped around her shoulders. When she was certain Mama was suitably wrapped up, she pulled her own cloak on and helped her mother negotiate the steps leading to the deck. It only took a few more moments before the boat was secured and the loading plank was swung over to the bank.

"Let's go, Mama." Alexandra took a tentative step and flung her arms out for balance. "See how easy this is." She beckoned for Mama and Jemma to follow. All three of them made it safely to shore and looked around.

Natchez Under-the-Hill. Alexandra had heard stories of the area. It was a hiding place for gamblers, criminals, and lawless men, most of them running from New Orleans justice. It was no place for two ladies to spend any amount of time. Well, she'd better remedy that situation before it got any darker.

After repeating her instructions to Jemma and her mother, Alexandra walked toward the nearest building, hoping she would find it to be a livery stable. A woman who looked even more bedraggled than Alexandra felt stepped outside. When questioned, she pointed the way toward a stable a few blocks toward the east, away from the river.

The fog swirled around her legs as she walked, obscuring the ground and making it difficult for her to see where she was going. Hoping the woman had directed her correctly, Alexandra turned a corner and found herself in a quieter part of town. Buildings rose up on either side of her, their shadows lengthening as full dark began to settle on them.

A horseshoe hanging from a metal rod indicated that a building ahead was the one she sought. Intent on her destination, Alexandra hurried forward, hope singing through her. But disaster struck when she put her foot into an unseen rut and twisted her ankle. A shriek of pain and fear broke through her lips as she fell, landing with a jarring *thump*.

It took her a minute to recover her senses, and when she did, she groaned. She was covered in mud and dirt, her hat drooped to one side, and her cloak was torn in several places. She dragged herself up with some effort and leaned against the nearest wall, ignoring the bite of splinters that pierced her gloved hands. Her breath came in labored spurts, and the street seemed to move as though it had turned into the river.

Several minutes passed, but finally the street regained its solidity and her breathing settled into a more normal pace. She pushed away from the wall and put her full weight on her injured foot. Pain shot up her leg, causing her to fall back once more. At least this time the street did not waver, but she knew her situation was serious. Her mother was counting on her. She could not fail. She wanted to sink to the ground and sob, but crying would not help the situation. What was she going to do?

How many blocks had she walked in her search? She wasn't certain. She could no longer see the waterfront, or Mama and Jemma. And no one seemed to be around in this dark, narrow corridor. Alexandra closed her eyes. *God, help me.* The words formed in her mind even though she didn't really believe He would answer her plea.

A sound to her right made Alexandra's eyes fly open. Two men rounded the corner and lurched toward her. They appeared to be drunk, leaning on each other and weaving their way up the street. The drunker of the two was shorter, and he was moving in an odd hopping fashion while leaning against his taller companion.

"Come along, Judah," the taller one encouraged his companion. "We're almost at the stable where we're supposed to rendezvous with your lady."

Alexandra was surprised at the lack of slurring in the man's voice. At least he wasn't drunk. He must be helping his master home. She remembered seeing other boats at the landing. Perhaps this pair had arrived on one of them.

As they drew closer she realized the shorter man, a soldier by his garb, was moving oddly because he had lost the lower part of his right leg. She pressed a hand to her mouth, sympathy for his plight filling her. Suddenly her twisted ankle seemed a minor inconvenience.

The smaller man looked up and saw her. "What have we here? A lady in distress?"

The servant stared at her boldly, his gaze taking in her torn clothing and the spatters of mud on her face. "More likely a lady of the streets."

Alexandra's mouth fell open in shock. She closed it with a snap and directed her attention to the soldier. "You should teach your man to bridle his tongue. It will do neither of you any good to allow him to criticize his betters." She would have liked to turn her shoulder on both of them and stalk away, but the throbbing in her ankle halted her.

What the soldier's answer might have been was muffled by the sound of horses' hooves approaching. A carriage rounded the corner. Alexandra shrank back against her wall, biting her lip to keep from moaning as her leg throbbed once more.

The carriage came to an abrupt halt as it drew even with the two men, and a blond whirlwind emerged from it. The woman was even smaller than the soldier, but what she lacked in stature she made up for in energy. She ran to the soldier and threw her arms around him.

"Careful, or you'll overset him," the manservant warned.

"Praise God for bringing you home to me." The lady placed a kiss on the lame man's cheek before turning to his companion. "And Jeremiah, how can I ever thank you for your duty to my husband? He has written to me of your bravery and constancy. No amount of money could ever repay you for what you have done."

"It is my pleasure." The tall man smiled down at the blond woman, and Alexandra caught her breath. His features, which she had considered harsh, were transformed. His hair fell forward across his broad forehead, his lips curved upward and revealed a pair of dimples, and his warm gaze made her toes curl even though it was not directed at her.

"Oh, it is so good to see you both. Judah, my love, you cannot imagine how much I have missed you all these months. I cannot wait to get you home. You look so pale, dear. But we'll take care of that in a matter of days."

"Susannah, I have missed you so."

The words were filled with such emotion that Alexandra felt like an interloper. For a moment she wished someone missed her that much. Even though Asher Landon had been kind to her, he had never shown her the same depth of emotion. Suddenly she was truly glad he had decided to marry elsewhere. Perhaps one day she would meet a man who loved her as much as this man loved his wife. Alexandra shifted her weight to ease her discomfort, wishing once again for the ability to walk away.

The lady noticed her for the first time. "Who is this?"

The soldier shook his head. "I was about to find out if she needed our help when you arrived, dearest."

"I'm trying to find the livery stable. I need to hire someone to get me and my mother to Tanner Plantation."

"Tanner Plantation?" The blond lady peered up at her. "Are you a relative of the Tanners?"

Alexandra nodded. "My mother was a Tanner before she married. My. . . my father died recently and we—"

"Oh, you poor thing," the lady broke in on her explanation. She turned back to her husband. "We must help them, Judah."

Jeremiah shook his head. "You are too trusting. If she was who she claims, her family would be here to meet her and her mother. You should send her to the livery stable." He pointed to the horseshoe a few feet away.

The harsh words brought a rush of tears to Alexandra's eyes. If only she could slap this impertinent servant. What had the world come to that such as he was allowed to speak so to a lady?

No matter how badly it hurt, she would not stay here one moment longer. Setting her jaw, she pushed away from the wall. If she was very careful, surely she could make it. She ignored the threesome and stepped forward on her good foot, but when she took her next step, the pain overwhelmed her. The light from the carriage faded, as did the voices of the strangers, and she pitched forward once more.

❈

A pungent smell made Alexandra's head jerk back against a solid shoulder. Mama had burned a feather and was waving it under her nose.

"There, she's coming to now." A puff of air tickled her ear. The voice was unfamiliar, but the cadence of his words was not. For a moment she believed she was back in New Orleans right after the war. Papa was still alive, and everything else was naught but a strange dream.

Reality pushed her hopes aside as Alexandra opened her eyes to find herself inside a strange carriage. She was not in New Orleans; she was in Natchez. . . Natchez Under-the-Hill. She struggled against the arms holding her but could not break free. Horror stories of unwary victims being snatched from the streets and robbed—or worse—came to life in her mind. Her movements grew more frantic, but the arms were more like iron bonds than flesh and blood.

"Jeremiah, let go." A woman's voice came from the opposite bench. "Can't you see you're frightening her?"

Instantly she was free. Alexandra dragged herself as far away from him as she could manage and stared at the people inside the carriage.

The crippled soldier and his wife sat opposite her, while the rude servant sat on her side, his arms now folded across his wide chest.

"Where am I?"

The soldier smiled at her. "You blacked out, my dear. Jeremiah here caught you and transported you to safety."

Her fears faded somewhat. The couple's concern seemed genuine.

His wife leaned forward and placed a hand on her arm. "We would like to see you and your mother safely to your destination."

"I still think you should hire a separate wagon for them if you are so determined to be taken in by this woman's tale."

She could hear the censure in the servant's—Jeremiah's—voice. But he had a valid point. "Perhaps he's right."

"Nonsense, just tell us where to find your mother." The woman smiled at her. "We will take care of the rest."

Alexandra could not resist her friendliness. And she was so tired. And her foot was throbbing. So she directed them to the waterfront.

It took a few moments to find her mother, who had become distraught at Alexandra's long absence. But after explaining the chain of events and providing introductions all around, it was settled. Alexandra and her mother would ride inside the carriage with their new friends, Judah and Susannah Hughes. Jemma and Jeremiah would ride up front next to the driver as soon as he and Jeremiah stowed all of the luggage.

Their arrival at Tanner Plantation caused a flurry of activity. Uncle John and Aunt Patricia welcomed them as Grand-mère had already retired. Alexandra was hurting too badly to notice much. She thanked Mr. and Mrs. Hughes and allowed a slave to carry her inside and deposit her in the bedroom she was to use. Someone was summoned to wrap her ankle in bandages while someone else helped her undress and found a gown for her to sleep in. The pampering was a luxury she had not experienced since Papa's "indiscretion." Perhaps things were finally beginning to change back to what they should be.

As she drifted into slumber, a voice seemed to whisper in her mind. It didn't speak in words but in warmth. She felt loved.

A thought of her own drifted through and brought her crashing back into wakefulness. Was it a coincidence that Judah Hughes and his servant had found her right after she had pleaded for help from God? Or had the Almighty answered her prayer?

Chapter 5

Jeremiah finished dressing, picked up his Bible, and headed downstairs to break his fast. He was not surprised to find he was the first to rise. He'd had trouble sleeping, although he could not fault the feather mattress or cotton quilts his hosts had provided. No, it was the prickling of his conscience that had awakened him several times. Finding that the slaves were still preparing food, he decided to go outside and read from his Bible. Delving into the Word should help restore his peace of mind.

The morning was crisp and quite cool, not surprising since the end of the year was drawing close. He drank in the view of the river afforded by the wide porch, which faced in a westerly direction. Having met Judah in New Orleans, he'd had no idea his friend's home would be so breathtaking. It made him think of his dream home, the one he'd described to his uncle in the weeks prior to his departure, the one he hoped to build for the sake of orphaned children.

The river wound around the base of the bluff on which Magnolia Plantation stood, its waters as brown as a cup of chicory coffee. He could see no sign of civilization to the north or to the south. The opposite bank of the river was lowland swamp. To his right stood a dense pine forest, its tree trunks nearly as wide as he was tall. To his left were the cotton fields, acre after acre of white-studded plants that looked ready for the harvest.

When he'd arrived the evening before, he had barely been able to make out the vast cropland Judah and his wife grew. Susannah had told them a halting story of the past months while her husband had been convalescing in New Orleans. He had left her with a competent overseer, never realizing he would be away from home for more than a year.

The overseer had taken a new job a few weeks earlier, leaving Susannah without a man to help her supervise and direct the harvest. Some of their neighbors had leant assistance, but the result was not the same. Many of the fields had not been tended as they should have been. She had held out hope that the return of her husband would turn things around, but without an excellent yield from their cotton fields, they might not be able to meet their obligations. Seed had been purchased on credit last spring; the slaves needed clothing, shelter, and food; and the territorial government had recently sent a notice of taxes due.

A sense of purpose lifted Jeremiah's chin. He believed God had put him in this place for a specific reason. To help his friends regain their prosperity?

26

Maybe. Yet he had promised his uncle that he would establish a trading office in Natchez. How could he possibly accomplish both?

It would be nice to have someone to talk to, someone with whom he could be completely honest, someone who would help him see which path he should take. A vision of a bedraggled beauty danced through his mind. The damsel in distress? He had the feeling she had been pampered and spoiled all of her life. Even though she had been tired and dirty, her demeanor had reminded him of the simpering, self-centered debutantes to be found throughout the upper echelons of New Orleans society—empty-minded adornments purchased by wealthy dandies to produce heirs and embellish their elegant homes. Although he had never had the time or desire to attend fancy balls or court rich heiresses, he knew better than to think he could ever bare his soul to such as the woman he had rescued last night.

Yet if he closed his eyes, he could smell the lemony fragrance of her perfume. He could almost feel her in his arms. Her face had been streaked with dirt and mud, but it had still been beautiful. A grin lit his features as he remembered how she had cast him in the role of a cheeky servant. Somehow, he had failed to correct her. No matter, he would probably never see her again.

Jeremiah spied a wooden bench at the edge of the pine forest and headed for it. Brushing it free of pine needles, he sat down. He closed his eyes for a moment and prayed for the wisdom to make good decisions in the days ahead. He thanked God for forgiveness and asked for the grace to forgive others. Pledging his love, utter and complete, to his Maker, Jeremiah felt a sense of peace settle over him, and he sat still, caught up in wonder.

He opened his eyes and realized his Bible had fallen open while he prayed. The book of the prophet Jeremiah, his namesake. His eyes went straight to an underlined verse in chapter 29: *"For I know the thoughts that I think toward you, saith the Lord, thoughts of peace, and not of evil, to give you an expected end."* It was one of his favorite verses. The assurance that God sent His thoughts into Jeremiah's heart brought him great comfort. All he needed to do was be willing to follow God's lead. Everything else would follow in due course. He whispered his thanks to the Lord for the reminder. It settled his mind and gave him the strength to face whatever challenges might come his way. How could he have forgotten this truth?

A noise behind him indicated the other residents of the Hughes household were no longer abed. He turned to see Judah leaning against his crutches, standing in nearly the same spot Jeremiah had stood earlier. How would he adapt to the demands of running Magnolia Plantation? Would he and Susannah lose their home? Judah had told him it was an inheritance from a distant uncle. While Judah had never expected to be a planter, he had managed in the past. Now with only one good leg, would he be able to cope? Only time would tell.

Jeremiah pushed himself up from his bench and strode toward the porch. "You look very natural standing there."

"I don't know. Sometimes I think God is trying to tell me He intends something different for my life." Judah turned a troubled expression toward him. "There's so much to do. How can I—"

"That may be why I am here."

"Thank you, friend, but I cannot impose on your good nature. Both of us know why you're here."

"Have I ever told you how much I have always wanted to be a farmer?"

Judah's face registered his surprise. "You. . .a farmer? I don't believe it." He laughed and shook his head.

"I believe I'm offended." Jeremiah raised his eyebrows. "Do you think me incapable?"

"No, no." Judah lifted one of his crutches and pressed it against the banister that ringed his porch. "But I won't let you sacrifice your uncle's business for mine."

"I have been thinking about that, and I may have a solution."

"What do you mean?" Judah returned his crutch to the floor and leaned against it.

"I still have several things to work out before I present my idea to you. I only brought it up so you will not lose hope. In the meantime"—Jeremiah waggled his eyebrows—"I plan to roll up my sleeves and learn about your farming operation from the ground up."

Judah groaned. "What a clown."

"I know. I know." Jeremiah walked to the front door and held it open for his friend. "A wonderful aroma is emanating from your dining room. Shall we investigate its source?"

Chapter 6

Alexandra rested her weight on her foot with care, breathing a sigh of relief that the pain from last night had faded considerably. "The salve you put on my ankle has worked, Jemma."

"Yes, ma'am." The sparkle in Jemma's eyes bespoke her pleasure. "One of the grooms gave it to me."

"A groom?" A mental picture of a horse with a pulled fetlock entered her mind.

"After you were carried inside last night."

Heat bloomed in Alexandra's cheeks as she recalled being held so close to a man's chest that the thumping of his heart was all she could hear. Whatever was wrong with her? Was she daydreaming of a servant? Her mind must be addled by all the alarms and grief she had faced recently. She put a hand on her forehead but could not detect any fever. Perhaps she needed more rest.

Jemma flung open the velvet drapes that covered her bedroom window, and sunlight flooded the room.

The day was more advanced than Alexandra had realized. With a sigh, she put away the idea of returning to the refuge of her bed. Grand-mère was probably irritated already because she was not present at the breakfast table.

Jemma helped Alexandra exchange her sleeping gown for a day dress, which had been aired and pressed sometime after their arrival last night. It was black, of course, as befitted a grieving daughter, but the bodice clung to her figure almost like a second skin. Looking in the mirror as Jemma arranged her hair, Alexandra decided the dark material of her skirt contrasted nicely with the white skin of her chest and arms. Of course she was not on the lookout for a suitor since her heart had so recently been broken, but it was always better to be prepared for any circumstance.

She sallied forth from her bedroom some time later and negotiated the central staircase with caution. The dining hall was toward the rear of the house, closer to the kitchen out back. She entered the room, not surprised to see that everyone was still seated at the table. Alexandra put on her widest smile and bent to kiss the wrinkled face of Althea Tanner, her grandmother. "How nice it is to be home."

Grand-mère frowned as she turned her cheek up for Alexandra's kiss, her faded brown eyes as hard as acorns. "I'm not certain when *my* home became a sanctuary for wayward females."

Alexandra spotted her mother seated at the far end of the table, a further indication of Grand-mère's displeasure. The empty plate next to Mama was a sure sign of where she was to sit, so Alexandra moved in that direction, limping ever so slightly in an attempt to remind the others that she was not well.

Uncle John, as tall and thin as ever, stood and held her chair out for her. "It is good to see you, niece."

Her smile warmed. "Thank you, Uncle John." She hugged him before sliding into her chair.

Her mother reached for her hand under the table and squeezed it tightly. It was a warning to mind her tongue.

Alexandra returned the squeeze as her gaze roamed over the assembled family members. Aunt Patricia, Mama's older sister, was almost as tall and thin as her husband. Her smile, as kind and gentle as ever, reminded Alexandra that her aunt was the most charitable member of the Tanner family. Opposite Alexandra sat her cousin, Percival, Grand-mère's nephew who had lived with her since the death of his parents many years ago.

"Now that you are here"—Grand-mère's voice drew Alexandra's attention—"I will tell you the same thing I have been saying to your mother. I will not tolerate an indefinite stay." She pointed a gnarled finger at Alexandra. "You will find a husband. And I don't mean you will wait on the front porch for some suitor to appear. I sent untold amounts of money to your parents to make certain you would turn into an accomplished young lady."

"And we did as you instructed with your money." Mama showed an uncharacteristic willingness to challenge her strong-willed parent. "If you had been as willing to support James's aspirations, we would not be in this fix now."

"Don't you dare try to lay your husband's misdeeds at my door, Beatrice. Although I don't fault him for trying to take advantage of whatever situation arose, he should not have been caught. His actions severely limit your own daughter's prospects."

Having handily subdued her daughter, Grand-mère turned her attention to Alexandra once again. "You have been allowed to dillydally around for far too long. If you don't marry soon, you will be considered an old maid. And then there is the matter of your father's death. As soon as folks around here learn about the scandal surrounding my daughter's husband, they will think twice about letting their sons court you. I refuse to let you squander your chances to have a household of your own."

Alexandra's mouth dropped open. She had always known she would have to marry one day. In fact, she was looking forward to having a household of her own. But to be ordered to marry right away? Preposterous. She closed her mouth with a snap. "I suppose you have a candidate in mind. . ."

"As a matter of fact, I do."

Alexandra should not have been surprised. Grand-mère had probably been planning this since she and Mama had first written of their troubles. She had always pushed Alexandra toward the accomplishments that would assure her granddaughter's place in society, one of station and wealth. "Have I met this paragon?"

Grand-mère's eyes narrowed at the irony in Alexandra's tone. "Yes, he is Harvey and Marie Sheffield's oldest son. A fine catch. All the girls in the area are chasing him. You will have to work hard if you are to snare him."

Alexandra's lips folded into a straight line. She didn't like being told what to do. "You know the people here will want to know how Papa died. How do you suggest we suppress the truth?"

"I've thought of that, too." Her grandmother sat back in her chair and lifted a hand. The slave who had been standing in one corner of the dining room moved forward at the signal and pulled back the heavy chair on which she sat. Grand-mère grabbed the slave's arm and pulled herself upright, grabbing her cane for support. "We'll tell everyone your father died fighting Indians. We'll make sure they believe he was a hero."

Alexandra pushed back her untouched breakfast. Her stomach was roiling. Lie to everyone? Yet what choice did she have? Her grandmother's commands were not to be ignored. She controlled everyone in the family.

In that instant, Alexandra made up her mind. "Once we renew our acquaintance, Mr. Sheffield will not notice anyone else."

❈

Alexandra had the chance to prove her words faster than she had imagined. Grand-mère sent Uncle John and Aunt Patricia to the Sheffield home with a personal invitation to join them for dinner that evening to welcome Alexandra and her mother back home. Since the invitation was closer to a command, the Sheffields accepted and pledged they would bring their son along to renew his acquaintance with the ladies.

Alexandra had Jemma ready her fanciest dress, black of course, but its bodice was outlined with wispy black lace, and tiny gray rosettes were scattered across the slim skirt. It was a dress she would feel comfortable wearing to the fanciest ball in either Nashville or New Orleans. The only danger was appearing overdressed for a simple dinner, but she wanted to impress Mr. Sheffield from the start, and appearance was at least half the battle.

Jemma used an iron on her dark hair, coaxing it into a cascade of ringlets that outlined Alexandra's face, highlighting her cheekbones and making her appear sophisticated. A touch of citrus perfume dabbed at her wrists completed the toilette. Alexandra slipped the ribbon of her black lace fan around her wrist and glanced in the mirror to judge the impact. She looked awfully somber.

"Just think how nice it will be to have your own household," she lectured herself. "And how bad it will be if Grand-mère throws you out." She took a deep breath and practiced a wide smile. Much better. Lowell Sheffield would be bowled over.

The guests were already assembled in the front parlor when Alexandra made her grand entrance. She paused for a moment at the wide doorway to the room.

"Well, come in here, girl." Grand-mère waved her cane. "We've been waiting for your arrival for nigh on an hour."

Not the best introduction, but Alexandra made certain her smile did not falter. "Please forgive me." The men stood as she entered. Sweeping past everyone else, she bent over her grandmother and kissed the air next to the old woman's cheek.

"Humph." Her grandmother glared at her. "I suppose we'll survive." She turned to Mr. and Mrs. Sheffield. "This saucy thing is, of course, my granddaughter Alexandra."

"You've become quite the beauty, bound to turn our local girls green with envy." Harvey Sheffield was a barrel-chested man with a forehead that seemed inordinately high, likely an illusion caused by his receding hairline.

Marie Sheffield, as slender as her husband was wide, nodded from her seat on the sofa. "Yes, indeed. And the young men will buzz around her like bees in a flower garden."

Alexandra curtsied with all the grace she could muster and tried not to stare at the light reflecting from Mr. Sheffield's nearly bare pate. "You are too kind."

"My parents speak nothing but the truth." The man whom her grandmother had picked to become Alexandra's husband moved toward her, one hand covering his heart while the other reached for her hand. "I can hardly believe how stunning you've become since the last time I saw you." He bowed in front of her and placed a warm kiss on her wrist.

Her heart fluttered at the audacious move and warmth spread upward, burning her cheeks and ears. She pulled her hand from his and spread the ribs of her fan, using it to cool her face. "You have also changed since we were children, Mr. Sheffield."

Lowell Sheffield had filled out well in the intervening years. His naturally curly brown hair was pulled forward from the crown and framed his wide forehead in a most attractive manner. His shoulders, which she remembered as being rather narrow, had widened, and his chest was at least as deep as his father's. All in all, he was a passably attractive specimen. Becoming his wife would not be as dreadful as she had feared.

"I hope you are as pleased with my transformation as I am with yours, Miss Lewis."

His smile was handsome, too. Alexandra could understand why he was so popular with the single ladies. It had probably made him a bit overconfident. She used her fan to obscure the lower part of her face and studied him from head to toe. She took her time, as though she was uncertain of the answer she should give. After a moment, his smile wilted. Hers widened, but he could not see it because of the fan.

Alexandra bit her lip and lowered the fan. "Yes. . .of course you do." She put enough emphasis on the words to imply the opposite. Then she turned and sat next to his mother, complimenting the lady on her hair and dress. She listened with one ear as Mrs. Sheffield described in tedious detail the process of obtaining a seamstress who could copy patterns properly.

Alexandra's heart was beating like a kettledrum. Had her ploy worked? Only time would tell. She nodded at the appropriate places and eventually drew Mr. Sheffield, Lowell's father, into the conversation. By the time dinner was announced, she had at least two fervent supporters.

As soon as she stood, Lowell was at her side, his arm held out in invitation.

Alexandra put on her most innocent air and looked past him. "Grand-mère, do you have anyone to help you to the dinner table?"

Her grandmother snorted. "Your uncle will see to me. Go on with your young man."

With what she hoped was a convincing start, Alexandra turned to Lowell Sheffield. "Oh my, where did you come from?"

"I think you are toying with me, Miss Lewis." He offered his arm once again, a quizzical expression on his face. His eyes were a deep hazel color, reminding her of a shady woodland.

She put her hand on his arm, widening her eyes as she gazed up at him. "Me, sir? I am naught but a poor country girl. What makes you think I would dare tease someone as debonair as you, Mr. Sheffield?"

He smiled down at her as he led her to the dining room. "Because I don't believe you are blind."

Alexandra could not suppress the giggle that rose to her throat. Her heart fluttered once again as she caught his hazel gaze. His laughter mingled with hers, and they entered the dining room on an intimate note. It seemed Mr. Sheffield enjoyed a challenge. She would have to make certain she gave him one.

The only empty seats at the table, except for Grand-mère's and Uncle John's, were side by side. She wished her family had not made it quite so obvious they were throwing her at Lowell's head. It would have been smarter for someone to have arranged the table so that the two of them sat across from each other. Then he would have a front row seat for her bubbly personality. She could have flirted shamelessly with the elder Mr. Sheffield, further piquing the younger Mr. Sheffield's interest. But she would have to work with what she had been given.

During the first course, she was very attentive to her mother, who sat on her right. Mr. Sheffield was thus forced to converse with Cousin Percival, who always had more interest in his dinner than in dinner conversation.

"You cannot ignore me any longer," his breath whispered in her ear. "Etiquette demands that you converse with me a little."

Alexandra turned her head in his direction. He was leaning so close to her that their mouths nearly touched. Her gaze fastened on his lips. "I. . .I. . ." She forced herself to look up into his eyes. The specks of green in them seemed to have caught fire. Lowell Sheffield was definitely interested. And her tongue seemed to be stuck to the roof of her mouth.

Grand-mère cleared her throat, snapping the thread that seemed to have bound both of them. "Have you visited with the Hugheses to thank them for rescuing you and your mother?"

"Rescue?" Lowell sat back in his chair, but his eyes still seemed to devour Alexandra's face. "What happened that you needed to be rescued?"

Her mind whirled as she recounted the story of their arrival and her sprained ankle. She was pleased to have so easily secured Lowell's interest, but she wondered if her actions had started a fire that would scorch her. Yet the admiration in his gaze made her feel good. She and Mama had been social outcasts before their departure. It was wonderful to return to the status she had once enjoyed.

"If you could wait until the afternoon, I would be happy to escort you to Magnolia Plantation." Lowell's offer pierced her tumultuous thoughts.

She turned to her grandmother for permission, even though she knew it was a foregone conclusion.

"Of course you may go." Her grandmother's smile embraced everyone at the table. "I am very appreciative Mr. Sheffield can take time out of his busy day to escort you. Such a strong young man will be able to protect you no matter what may occur."

"It's all settled then." Lowell's shoulders had straightened at her grandmother's complimentary words. "I look forward to spending more time with you."

Alexandra's heart sped up at the look in his eyes. She had little doubt she would wring a proposal from this man in less than two weeks.

Chapter 7

B ut I love you." Susannah moved from her chair by the window and sat down next to her husband.

Jeremiah turned his head and wondered if he could get outside without drawing the attention of Judah and his wife. This conversation was much too personal for him to witness. And part of him wanted to chastise Judah again for focusing on his disability. God had given him so many blessings—not the least of which were a Christian wife who loved him dearly, a beautiful home, and the chance to fulfill whatever God's plan was for him. If only he would let himself see the truth.

"We're embarrassing our guest." Judah looked at Jeremiah, a martyred expression on his face. His cheeks were red with mortification, and his fingers plucked at the material of the sofa on which he sat.

His wife was sitting next to him, determination apparent in the tilt of her chin and the straight line of her shoulders. "Are you so proud you cannot listen to reason?"

Judah sighed and shook his head. "You and I can discuss this later. For now, we need to think about what is necessary for the plantation. We need someone to oversee the slaves."

"But the slave you selected to act as the overseer's captain, Oren, has been working as hard as he can to get the other slaves working." Susannah slid to the far end of the sofa and crossed her arms. "It's true he is not as effective as an overseer, but we have managed to get a few things done since Mr. Heidel left."

Jeremiah took a deep breath, glad he had not slinked away a few moments earlier. He had the answer if the two of them would only listen to reason. "I can do the work."

"That's out of the question." Judah's frown centered on him. "You're a guest here. I'm already beholden to you for bringing me home. I couldn't ask you to take on the responsibilities of an overseer."

"I didn't hear you asking me." Jeremiah leaned against the mantel and watched his friend. "I want to do this."

Susannah looked up at him, her eyes large and moist as if she was holding back tears. "We can't afford to pay you much."

Jeremiah held up a hand to stop her. "If you can put up with my ugly face for the next few months, that will be payment enough."

Sputtering laughter came from Judah. He looked at his wife, who nodded. "If you're serious. . ."

Jeremiah straightened and stepped toward the sofa. "I won't let you down."

"There's no doubt about that." Susannah reached for her husband's hand across the space she had put between them. "You've been an answer to our prayers."

"Where can I find this Oren you mentioned?"

Judah wrapped his large fingers around his wife's hand, pulling her toward him. "He'll probably be in the south field today."

Jeremiah nodded. "I'll be back before sunset."

"You'd better be back in time for tea." The loving glance Susannah had given her husband turned into resolve as she raised her chin and glared at Jeremiah. "I don't want to have to come get you from the fields."

"Yes, ma'am." Jeremiah rolled up his sleeves and headed out the door. "I'll see you for tea."

He strode across the front lawn, passing several outbuildings that had different functions. He recognized the grist mill, smokehouse, kitchen, and barns, but he made a mental note to investigate the other buildings. He arrived at the south field as the sun was reaching its zenith.

Oren, a tall, muscular black man, was directing the workers in the field, but to Jeremiah's eyes, little actual work was being done. Only a handful of men were trailing long sacks partially filled with white cotton bolls. The rest of the slaves were sitting or lying on the ground and watching.

"Oren!" As soon as Jeremiah called out the slave's name, a furor arose. The slaves who had been lolling about jumped to their feet and grabbed their cotton sacks. The ones who had been working stopped and gaped at him.

Oren walked toward him, a look of fear on his face.

Jeremiah held out his hand. "I understand you've been doing your best to get the crops in."

"Yessir." The slave looked at his outstretched hand and then back at Jeremiah's face. He didn't offer his hand. "Has Missus Hughes hired you to take over?"

"Not exactly." Jeremiah realized the man was too scared to shake his hand. He should have realized things would not be the same as they were in New Orleans. Although many people in his hometown owned slaves, many free blacks also lived there. But this man had probably never dreamed of such a world. "I am a friend of the family, and I hope to work with you and the others to make sure we catch up on the harvest."

The slave beamed at him. "I sure is glad yore here, sir."

"My name is Jeremiah."

"Yessir, Master Jeremiah."

"Just plain Jeremiah will do, Oren. I'm not your master. I don't know much about picking cotton, but I'm willing to work beside the men here. Is there a sack I can use?"

Oren's smile slipped, puzzlement plain on his face. "You want to work?"

"That's right. I believe in laboring alongside those who work for me." He looked toward the fields where all the hands had stopped. "So who's going to show me what y'all spend all your time doing?"

It didn't take the slaves long to realize Jeremiah was serious. He was given a sack and shown how to wear the long strap that was used to drag it behind him. He watched with curiosity as Oren showed him how to separate the fluffy cotton from its prickly casing.

After an hour in the sun, Jeremiah was hot, and his back was aching. He could not imagine how hard this work would be in the heat of summer and early autumn.

The other men avoided him, whispering to each other as they worked. To take his mind off his discomforts, Jeremiah began to hum his favorite song, "Love Divine, All Loves Excelling," breaking into words as he got to the final verse. He reached the end of a row and turned, starting his hymn all over again. This time he sang all the words, letting his voice broaden as spiritual joy filled him.

He didn't notice when another voice joined his, but soon, many voices were singing praises to God. He straightened and looked around him, humbled by the realization that these slaves knew Charles Wesley's hymn as well as he did. It was further proof that they were all God's children. In that moment, he knew he would have to do something to ease the burden of slavery until he could convince Judah and Susannah to free their slaves.

Chapter 8

"How do you expect me to captivate someone as handsome and interesting as Lowell Sheffield when I am limited to wearing nothing but black?" Alexandra twirled around, her skirts swirling with her. Her dress was cut in the newest style—empire waist, narrow skirt, and short sleeves—but the black cloth was only relieved by a narrow collar of lavender lace.

Her mother's eyebrows crowded together. "You can't flaunt tradition by abandoning your mourning colors so soon after your father's death. We will both have to dress in black for at least a year."

Alexandra collapsed on her bed. She put a hand under her chin and considered. "But it's not like we're living in Philadelphia or Boston. It's not even New Orleans. And you know how many compliments I receive from gentlemen when I wear brighter colors."

"I don't know, dear. . . ."

Part of Alexandra wished her mother would argue with her instead of sitting there, staring off into the distance. If only Papa had not—

She shook her head to clear it of the useless thought. Papa *had*, and the past could not be changed. The color of her dress seemed unimportant compared to the path she and her mother were being forced to take. "Come on, Mama. Let's go downstairs. It's too late to change, anyway. Mr. Sheffield will be here any moment."

Alexandra's gaze followed her mother's as it wandered around the room that had always been her special haven during visits. The pastel colors of the draperies and spread had faded a little over the years, but they brought her a sense of comfort nevertheless. To round out Alexandra's education, Grandmère had paid for an expensive teacher to come from New Orleans and instruct her in the art of watercolors. If her family was to be believed, she had some talent, so her landscapes were framed and hung in the room. Now they served as an ever-present reminder of happier times.

A knock on the door was followed by Jemma's voice. "You have a guest in the parlor, Miss Alexandra."

"Thank you." Alexandra bent over her mother and pressed a kiss on her cheek. "Are you coming downstairs?"

Mama patted her cheek. "Of course I'll come downstairs." She gathered her shawl and pulled it around her shoulders before drifting toward the door.

Mr. Sheffield whisked Alexandra out of the house in a matter of minutes, ushering her into his carriage with a flourish. It was a fancy vehicle with large wheels and a plush seat perched high above the ground. "I hope you are not afraid of my phaeton."

"Not at all." Alexandra looked out over the landscape, savoring the wide view. "I love the feeling of wind rushing past."

"You are so different than most of the girls around here." He picked up the reins and guided the horse toward the main road. "Eager to enjoy whatever comes your way."

Alexandra cast an admiring glance in his direction. "And you are a very astute man." She placed a gloved hand on his arm. "But I'm sure you hear that every day, Mr. Sheffield."

His ardent glance nearly scorched her. "I wish you would call me Lowell. All my closest acquaintances do."

Wondering if things might be progressing a little too fast, Alexandra removed her hand and shifted a few inches away from him. "We aren't children any longer."

"No, Alexandra, but I am beginning to think we may be destined for something more lasting than a childhood friendship."

She wasn't sure if it was the flirtatious tone of his voice, the usage of her first name, or the heady feeling of thundering across the countryside, but her heart seemed to be galloping faster than the horse in front of them.

The road was far enough from Natchez and the Mississippi River that they saw few other travelers, only rolling fields of hay, corn, or cotton. When they turned off the main road, she was surprised to see field after field of unpicked cotton. She had been in the area for less than a week, but the Hugheses seemed to be behind on their harvest. Grand-mère's fields were barren in comparison.

The carriage turned around a bend in the road, and she spotted a group of slaves who were working on the far side of a cotton field. She raised a hand to shade her gaze and realized a white man was working with the slaves. Alexandra frowned. She'd never seen an overseer who labored alongside the slaves. Was that why the Hugheses were so far behind their neighbors?

As if her gaze had disturbed the man, he straightened and stared in her direction. He looked familiar, but with the distance separating them, she could not recall where she might have seen him before. Then they were past the field, turning into the tree-shaded drive that led to the Hughes plantation home, and Alexandra pushed the thought away.

The Hughes plantation was impressive, although not as large as her grandmother's home. The two-story building had a deep porch running across the front, topped by a balcony that was equally long and deep. Old oaks shadowed a pond on one side of the front lawn. Alexandra spotted a white egret standing on the bank, watching the dark water, undisturbed by their arrival.

A slave ran toward them and grabbed their horse's halter. Lowell climbed down and tossed the reins to the boy before walking around to assist her.

Alexandra placed her slippered foot on the wooden step for dismounting and leaned forward into Lowell's raised hands. He swung her toward the ground with ease and set her on her feet. She thought of stumbling on purpose so he would have to catch her, but she decided at the last moment to step back. Sometimes it was good to be a little unattainable. "Thank you."

He raised an eyebrow, tucked his chin, and stared at her.

"Thank you. . .Lowell."

His smile was as attractive as any she'd ever seen. "It's my pleasure."

She brought up her parasol and opened it to protect her complexion from the autumn sunlight. The action also gave her time to quiet the butterflies fluttering in her stomach. Lowell was going to make a superb husband. Rich enough to grant her every wish and exciting enough to make any girl's heart trip. Alexandra had to admit her grandmother had chosen the perfect man for her.

A slave ushered them into the wide entry hall common to most plantation homes. Several doors opened onto this area, and the slave led them toward one on the right. Lowell gave her both of their names so the slave could announce their arrival to Judah and Susannah Hughes.

The room they entered was somewhat smaller than her grandmother's formal parlor, but it felt. . .cozy. The worn sofa on which Judah and his wife sat looked comfortable, if not fashionable. A scuffed, round table stood in front of it, a gleaming silver service atop it. On the far side of the table, three straight-backed chairs crowded each other, providing a place for guests to sit. Sheer curtains billowed around the tall, open windows. The breeze that moved them brushed her cheeks.

Mr. Hughes was struggling to get his crutches under his arm.

Alexandra's heart went out to him. "Please don't rise on my account, sir."

"Nonsense." He smiled at her as he pulled himself up. "What kind of man does not observe basic etiquette? Especially when visited by such a beautiful young lady."

His wife rose, too. "It's so nice to see you, Miss Lewis, Mr. Sheffield. Welcome to our home."

"Thank you." Alexandra curtsied to both of them before sinking into one of the chairs.

Mrs. Hughes sat back down, waiting until both of the gentlemen had also taken their seats. "How is your foot?"

"I am fully recovered, thanks to your kindness in rescuing me."

Mr. Hughes shook his head. "All we did was offer a ride. It was Jeremiah who rescued you."

Alexandra was about to answer him when the door to the parlor opened once more. She turned to see the subject of her host's pronouncement enter. Of course! He was the man she had just seen across the cotton fields. No wonder he looked so familiar. But what was he doing in the parlor? Did he have some message for his master?

He had apparently taken a moment to rinse his face, although his cheekbones were flushed from his time in the bright sunlight. His sleeves were rolled up to his elbows, and her gaze seemed caught by the muscles in his lower arms. Her mind flashed to the first night she'd seen him. She could almost feel those strong arms supporting her shoulders and knees.

The butterflies Lowell had caused earlier became more insistent, beating against her chest as though trying to escape. What had happened to the breeze? The air seemed to have been sucked out as this Jeremiah entered the room.

"Jeremiah." Susannah raised a hand and the servant bowed over it. "We were just speaking of you."

The butterflies got caught in Alexandra's throat as the man turned his blue gaze in her direction. Unable to speak, she nodded at him, expecting him to turn from her and give some note or information to Mr. Hughes.

But he didn't. Instead he seated himself in the chair next to hers. Whatever was the world coming to when a servant sat down to partake of tea? Her shocked gaze swept from him to the Hugheses. Neither of them looked as though anything was out of place.

"Miss Lewis, isn't it? Are you and your mother recovered from your journey?" His voice curled around her, setting the butterflies loose once more.

Before Alexandra could voice her astonishment at his breach of manners, Mr. Hughes leaned forward. "That's right. The two of you have not even been properly introduced. Miss Lewis, please allow me to introduce Jeremiah LeGrand, a man who has proven himself to be a courageous and devoted friend."

As Mr. Hughes continued the introduction, Alexandra pinned a fake smile on her lips. She didn't care if the man had single-handedly defeated the whole British Navy; he was a servant. He must be taking advantage of his master's gratitude to insinuate himself into the society of his betters. It should not be allowed. She drew away from him, practically moving into Lowell's lap. Not that the latter would mind.

She wished Mr. and Mrs. Hughes had not put her in this position. She wished she had not twisted her foot in Natchez Under-the-Hill. She wished this Jeremiah LeGrand had not helped her. Or that Grand-mère had sent someone to meet them. Only one of those little details would have made this afternoon unnecessary.

"Mr. . . LeGrand. You seem to be in the habit of rescuing others. Is that why you were working in the fields a little while ago?" She wondered if anyone else in the room noticed the frost in her voice. A quick glance at Mr. LeGrand's stiff features gave her the answer. If he wanted to push his way into higher society, he would need to develop thicker skin.

"I try to follow the Lord's bidding." His voice didn't sound angry, but she felt the sting of his words.

She lifted her chin and shot him an angry glance. "As do all good Christians."

"Would you care for tea, Miss Lewis?" Susannah Hughes's voice interrupted the staring contest between them.

Alexandra turned to her hostess and nodded, accepting the china being offered. She balanced the delicate saucer on her knee and sipped from the matching cup.

Mrs. Hughes served tea to the others in the room and the conversation became more general.

Lowell was the perfect gentleman, answering questions about his parents and sharing amusing anecdotes of local parties and hostesses. Then he coughed and leaned forward. "I regret my parents would not allow me to join you fellows in New Orleans. I would have enjoyed fighting next to Old Hickory."

The man on the other side of her grimaced. "I thought General Jackson had an impossible task, but God stepped in."

"What do you mean?" Alexandra couldn't stay out of the conversation. "I was in New Orleans. General Jackson was nothing short of brilliant. My papa said he was everywhere, tireless even though he was not well."

Judah Hughes put his teacup on the table in front of him. "I don't think Jeremiah would disagree with you, would you?" He waited until Jeremiah nodded before continuing. "Very few people would dare disparage the Hero of New Orleans."

The smile that turned up the corners of her mouth was so brittle she was surprised it did not shatter. "In that case I apologize, Mr. LeGrand." She also placed her teacup on the table, glancing at Lowell as she did so.

He followed suit, standing and holding a hand out to her. "I believe we should take our leave, Miss Lewis. We have taken up too much of the Hugheses' time."

Alexandra stood up and put her hand on his arm. The other two men stood up, too.

Susannah reached for the bell pull. "It was so kind of you to come and see us. I hope you will visit again soon."

"And you must come to Tanner Plantation. Grand-mère mentioned it specifically when I told her my destination. She said you have not been to visit in quite some time."

"Yes, I have been rather busy, what with the harvest and then the arrival of my wonderful husband." Susannah glanced toward him, her love written plainly across her face.

For a moment, Alexandra was jealous of the woman. As handsome as Lowell was, she could not see herself experiencing the kind of devotion Susannah felt for Judah. Then she caught herself. This poor woman was tied to a cripple, a man who would always struggle to climb stairs, a husband who could never again partner her at a ball. It was a tragedy. Susannah was a woman to be pitied, not envied.

Judah smiled at his wife. "Now that things are returning to normal, I'm certain we can arrange for you to spend some time visiting families here. If we can keep Jeremiah out of the fields, all three of us can go."

"I doubt I'll have much time for that."

A shiver ran up Alexandra's spine as his deep growl sounded behind her. "What a shame." She swung around wondering what game he might be playing now. "I'm surprised you do not see the advantage of being introduced to my family. But perhaps as a servant, you are not aware they are some of the most prominent people in the territory."

Susannah gasped at her words. "What?"

Jeremiah's gaze narrowed on Alexandra's face. "Don't tell me you still think I'm a servant?"

Alexandra could feel the blush starting somewhere in the vicinity of her heart. It rose with all the insistence of an incoming tide, heating her face and ears as if someone was holding a hot iron to them. "What do you mean?"

Judah moved awkwardly toward her. "Jeremiah is not a servant. His uncle is one of the wealthiest men in the country. He has no need of any acquaintance to make his way in our society, here or anywhere else for that matter."

She closed her eyes for a moment and wished the floor would swallow her up. But then her anger turned against the man who had deceived her. Why had he let it go this far? He knew, but he said nothing. Now she would have to apologize. "I am sorry, Mr. LeGrand."

"It's my fault." His blue eyes, so lacking in condemnation, eased her shame. "I should have told you the truth on the night we first met." He shrugged. "But you seemed to have so many more important issues to deal with that evening, and I didn't think I'd ever see you again."

Alexandra was as embarrassed as the day she had discovered she was being shunned by Nashville's elite because of her father's actions. She was relieved when Lowell offered his arm, but she could feel Jeremiah's blue gaze piercing the back of her neck as she was escorted out of the house and long after they had left the Hugheses' land.

The ride home was quiet. She supposed that was her fault. She couldn't think of much to say. Her mind was spinning from the implications of what she had learned. What kind of man worked when he did not have to? What kind of man had so little concern for his reputation that he would allow her to continue misjudging him? She could make no sense of it. Jeremiah was not like any other man she'd ever met.

She filed away her questions for consideration later and turned her attention to Lowell. Perhaps he would appreciate her reticence. He was probably much more used to women who gushed, giggled, and prattled endlessly.

They had almost arrived at her home before she thought to compliment his driving skills. "You are very kind to spend your afternoon squiring me around."

His gaze was so different from the irritating man they had left at the Hughes plantation. His hazel eyes were warm, kind, and intelligent. Although there had been warmth in Mr. LeGrand's eyes, they held none of the eagerness she saw in Lowell's. "Spending time with you is quite pleasant."

The words were spoken with as much ardency as she could wish. But where were the butterflies? Had her time in Mr. LeGrand's presence killed the budding romance? Nonsense. All she had to do was concentrate and they would return. Wouldn't they?

Chapter 9

Facing a disapproving relative was not one of Alexandra's favorite pastimes. But it seemed that was what her life had been reduced to. She raised her chin and stared at her aunt's bunched features.

"You should not go visiting by yourself." Aunt Patricia's high-pitched complaint made Alexandra want to stamp her foot.

"And who would you suggest as an escort? Uncle John? Cousin Percival?" The latter was dozing in one corner of the parlor. He didn't even rouse when she said his name. A fine escort he would be. And her uncle had left before daybreak to accompany a large shipment of cotton to the dock in Natchez. He would not return until after dark.

"Your mother could go with you."

Grand-mère shook her head. "She is upstairs abed. It seems she has a sick headache."

"So you see, no one is available." Alexandra pulled on her gloves. "I will take the gig. It has enough room for me to carry them my painting."

Her aunt was still not satisfied. "I don't see why you cannot wait until tomorrow."

"Leave her alone, Patricia," Grand-mère came to her rescue. "No one can blame her for wanting some younger company. Susannah Hughes is an unexceptionable young woman. Exactly the type of matron she should emulate."

"Thank you, Grand-mère." Alexandra kissed the old woman and made her escape.

It was another beautiful day, with a slight chill to the air to presage colder weather. The warm autumn was much more to her liking than the colder weather of Nashville. Frost would probably not dust the ground before Christmas. Alexandra settled herself in the seat and checked to make certain her gift was secure. She hoped Susannah would like the representation of her home. Alexandra had painted it from memory after her visit, including the oak-shaded pond and attractive home. She had even included the white-feathered egret.

It took her longer to reach the Hugheses' home than when she had ridden with Lowell since she was not as daring a driver as he. And the horse pulling her gig was more content to plod than gallop. But she arrived at last to find Susannah, Mr. Hughes, and the fascinating Mr. LeGrand sitting on the front porch.

Susannah met her at the top of the stairs. "What a pleasure to see you again."

Alexandra removed her hat and gloves and handed them to the slave who stood nearby. "I really should have waited until you returned my call last week, but I have a gift for you and could not wait to bring it."

"What a thoughtful gesture." Judah looked stronger than he had before, rising and putting the crutches under his arms with little trouble. He moved to his wife's side and smiled at Alexandra.

"Yes, indeed." Was that irony she heard in Jeremiah's voice?

A flush entered her cheeks. Did he realize he was the real reason for her visit? She glanced in his direction, caught once more by the bright blue of his eyes. Those eyes had haunted her as she worked on her landscape. She had even outlined the planes of his face in her sketchbook—from his broad forehead to the square edges of his chin—but she had not been able to capture the exact color of his eyes. They seemed to be lit from within, inviting her to fall into their depths.

What was the matter with her? Alexandra shook herself mentally and turned from the man. Susannah was looking at her oddly. Had she missed something? The painting. It was still in her hands. She thrust it toward Susannah.

It took the smaller woman only a moment to unwrap the artwork. Her mouth formed a large O, and she held it so her husband could see it. "It's beautiful, Alexandra."

"You are very talented." Judah added his praise to that of his wife. He turned to Jeremiah. "Come and see. She has painted our front lawn. She even included the egret."

Jeremiah walked over to them, his gaze moving from the painting to her face. "It's excellent, Miss Lewis. God has graced you with a special gift."

Alexandra's pleasure slipped away. What did God have to do with this? She had worked hard to learn the rudiments of color and perspective. God had not graced her at all. She opened her mouth to answer him, but Susannah forestalled her.

"Let's go inside and decide where it should be displayed."

Judah nodded. "I think we should start in the parlor. I've never liked that portrait of your great-uncle over our fireplace. He seems to watch every move I make."

"That is supposed to be the mark of a master, is it not, Miss Lewis?"

Jeremiah's question caught her off guard. Was she supposed to agree with him and discourage the Hugheses from placing her art in a prominent position? Her landscape would be more fitting than the portrait of some dead, forgotten relative.

"I don't care if it's a masterpiece or not," Judah answered. "I would much rather gaze at this landscape while enjoying my tea."

"I will leave the three of you to decide then." Jeremiah bowed in her general direction. "I have work to see to."

Disappointment shot through Alexandra as she watched him stride away. She laughed at some remark Judah made, but her mind was consumed with thoughts of Jeremiah. What had happened to her ability to attract a man's attention? She seemed doomed to failure where Mr. LeGrand was concerned. He was not interested in her at all. Was it because she had mistaken him for a servant?

As she watched the proud set of his shoulders, she wondered how she ever could have thought him anything other than a gentleman. Would she never learn to look beneath surface appearance? She had been misled by his casual dress and failed to see his intelligence and refinement. Perhaps he would one day forgive her for her mistake.

※

Jeremiah could hear her laughter as he walked toward the building that housed the cotton gin. Was she laughing at him? And why should the thought disturb him so much? She was nothing to him. He didn't even like the type of woman she represented. Hadn't he read just this morning about the dangers of linking his future with a shallow woman?

The urge to return to his bedchamber and open his Bible was nearly irresistible. He wanted to reacquaint himself with the chapter in Proverbs that described the value of a virtuous woman. Perhaps he could take a few moments during the lunch hour for reading. In the meantime, he needed to focus on the task ahead of him.

During the past week, he had instituted several changes in the way work was accomplished on Judah and Susannah's plantation. The first improvement he had made was to remove the female slaves from the field. They were better suited to work in the smokehouse, gin, sewing room, or kitchens. He had also implemented work breaks for the men in the field. They were allowed two half-hour breaks for eating and several smaller breaks for sitting in the shade and cooling off with water from the nearby stream. The result was a better harvest as the workers were no longer pushed to the limits of their endurance.

Jeremiah entered the wooden building that had been reserved for use in ginning cotton. Judah and Susannah had made the decision to invest in the hand-cranked apparatus when they first came to Magnolia Plantation. He had read about the invention that separated cotton seed from the fiber but had never seen it working until he came here. It still boggled his mind to see how much cotton could be processed in a single day's time. The cleaned fiber was packed into bales for shipment back east, where it would be turned into the strong cloth that seemed to be more in demand with each passing day.

He watched the process for a little while, making certain the machinery was working properly and the slaves inside were not having any problems. Seeing their shy smiles was rewarding. Even though he did not have the power to free them, he could make certain their circumstances were as humane as possible.

After leaving the cotton gin, he poked his head in the sewing room to find a roomful of women sitting in a circle of chairs, their fingers flying as they worked on making everything from tablecloths to shifts and trousers for the slaves. Young girls worked next to the older women, concentrating on making straight stitches with the same speed and skill. He was again reminded of the verses in Proverbs.

God seemed to be tapping him on the shoulder, pushing him to return to the house. He hoped Alexandra would be gone by now, but even if she was still there, perhaps he could avoid seeing her if he was very quiet. He cast a longing glance at the vacant overseer's house as he walked. He had wanted to move into it, but Judah and Susannah would not hear of it. They insisted he stay in the big house with them.

Alexandra's gig was still out front, so Jeremiah circled around to a side entrance. Using the back stairs, he climbed to the second floor. The slave who was sweeping and dusting in his room hurried out as he entered, leaving the door wide open.

Jeremiah found himself stretching his hearing to try and make out what was being discussed in the parlor on the first floor and thought he heard his name. Were they discussing him? Were Susannah and Judah telling her what he was doing with the slaves? Was she impressed with his progressive ideas, or did she think he was being foolhardy? And what did it matter anyway?

Disgusted at the direction of his thoughts, Jeremiah closed the bedroom door with a snap and turned to his bedside table. The black leather Bible sitting on it drew him. He sat on the edge of his bed and grabbed it, opening it to Proverbs. He found the thirty-first chapter and his finger ran down the page to verse 10: *"Who can find a virtuous woman? for her price is far above rubies."*

He stopped and considered the words. They still held true today. He had met many women in his lifetime, but most of the ones considered a good match were calculating and manipulative. Alexandra Lewis was a good example. Yet something about her captured his imagination. Perhaps it was her weakness the first time they had met. In spite of her evident pain, Alexandra had been more concerned about her mother and her slave than her own comfort.

He closed his Bible with a sigh and sank to his knees next to the bed. "Lord, You know my heart belongs to You. I am content to remain single if it is Your will, but if not, please lead me to a straightforward and honest woman who loves You with the same love and devotion I feel. A part of me would like someone who loves me in the same way Susannah loves Judah, but that is secondary to living the life You direct." A feeling of peace settled on him. He basked in the privilege of serving God even though he was only a man. "God, thank You for sacrificing Your Son for my sake. For providing the way to eternal life in Your presence. Help me to always keep You first in all my ways. Amen."

He pushed himself up and returned the Bible to its place on the table. It was time to get back outside. He had a lot of work to accomplish before his day was over. His uneasiness banished, Jeremiah felt ready to tackle whatever problems lay ahead.

Chapter 10

The Christmas season was especially hard without Papa.

The family continued to follow their holiday traditions. On Christmas Eve, a tree was brought into the parlor. The ladies strung berries to decorate it while Uncle John read the account of Christ's birth from Luke. Alexandra gave each member of the family a miniature she had painted, a project that had kept her busy in the weeks leading to Christmas. So busy she almost didn't notice Lowell's absence...almost.

He had not been back to see her since the day he took her to Magnolia Plantation to visit the Hugheses. Had he heard something? No, that was silly. She had attended a small dinner last week and learned the Sheffields were out of town on business. Surely Lowell would visit once they returned.

Alexandra bid her relatives good night and sought her bedchamber, trying to ignore the pervading gloom. It seemed she could feel the passage of time in her very bones. What would she do if Lowell did not return? Could she find another suitable candidate among the local families? She tried to imagine flirting with some of the men she had met. Would they be as responsive as Lowell? Or would they spurn her efforts with the same haughty attitude Mr. LeGrand had adopted?

She rolled over and punched her pillow as she relived his rejection. How dare he? And why was it his blue gaze followed her into her dreams?

❀

Soft, cold rain pattered against Alexandra's windowsill on Christmas morning. The gray drops drained the countryside of the remnants of color. The grass was hidden under a carpet of brown leaves, and even the green pine needles drooped under the weight of the raindrops. Alexandra felt as sad as they looked. Would she ever experience unadulterated happiness again? Or would her father's death overshadow every joy? She felt broken, lost. And she didn't know where to turn to find herself again.

She walked to the mirror above her washbasin and pointed a finger at the reflection. "You will stop pitying yourself. No man likes a female who cannot brighten his day." She hardly recognized the woman who looked back. Large dark eyes, narrow nose, and wide mouth. Her ebony hair gleamed in the yellow light of a kerosene lamp. With an impatient hand, she twisted it back and pinned it into a hasty knot. Was she beautiful? Most men seemed to think so. But was beauty enough?

She thought of her mother and grandmother who had both been vivacious when they were younger. Her mother, however, seemed to be fading as quickly as the grass outside. And while her grandmother had not faded away, Alexandra wasn't certain she wanted to be as domineering as the matriarch of the family. Was there some way to avoid either future?

She turned from the mirror and grabbed a shawl. Tanner Plantation was draftier than she remembered. She hurried downstairs to the dining room and took her place. Mama drifted in soon after, followed by Aunt Patricia, Uncle John, and Cousin Percival.

Grand-mère entered last, taking her seat at the head of the table. "I have received a note from Mrs. Sheffield."

Grand-mère's announcement caught Alexandra by surprise. She looked up from the plate of coddled eggs and met the older woman's gaze. "She's returned to Natchez?"

"Yes." Grand-mère helped herself to several slices of bacon and a piece of toast. "She will be visiting this afternoon. I expect you to be present."

Alexandra nodded. "Did she say whether Lowell will accompany her?"

"Such a nice young man." The comment came from her mother. "I look forward to renewing our acquaintance."

"She did not say," her grandmother responded before turning to Aunt Patricia. "Will you be here?"

Aunt Patricia shook her head. "You know I always visit the poor on Mondays. I consider it my Christian duty to take care of those who are not as fortunate as you and me." She turned and stared at Alexandra. "I had hoped to convince you to join me today."

Alexandra was relieved to have a valid excuse. She had gone with her aunt a few weeks earlier and found it depressing. They visited families who lived in single-room hovels with dirt floors. The people were grateful for the baskets of herbs, fruits, and vegetables—and Alexandra was grateful to bid them good-bye. She shrugged and made a mental note to have another pressing engagement before Monday rolled around again.

"She will be here with me awaiting our visitors." Grand-mère looked back toward Alexandra. "And I trust you will look a great deal more presentable. Whether your young man is present or not, you need to remember to always put forth your best efforts."

Anger flashed through her, but Alexandra pressed her lips together. She was not some child to be reminded of such things. Her eggs suddenly lost all appeal. She pushed the plate away and stood up. "Then I suppose I should start getting ready now."

She heard her mother gasp but ignored the sound. Righteous anger carried her out of the room and up the stairs. But it dissipated as she considered the long hours before she could expect Mrs. Sheffield to arrive. She went back to the window and stared out at the rain.

❁

Although Alexandra had had plenty of time to get ready for the Sheffield's visit, she followed society's dictates and arrived downstairs "fashionably late." She entered the parlor, a smile of welcome on her face. At least the winter chill was being held at bay by the cheerful fire. Her gaze traveled around the room, coming to rest on the handsome countenance of Lowell Sheffield.

He stood when she entered and stepped forward as she dropped a curtsy. The warm kiss he pressed into the palm of her hand should have made her heart race, but it was cold and wet.

She shivered and pulled her hand free.

"How nice to see you, Miss Lewis."

"And you, Mr. Sheffield." She stepped past him to speak to his mother. "Welcome home, Mrs. Sheffield. I trust you had a pleasant Christmas."

The older lady inclined her head. "It was quiet."

"Too quiet." Lowell's voice tickled the curls at the nape of her neck. "I missed having our usual celebration."

"Yes, but there simply wasn't enough time to plan anything," said his mother.

Lowell put a hand under Alexandra's elbow and guided her toward a pair of chairs somewhat removed from the older ladies. "I have something to tell you."

All of Alexandra's doubt about his feelings disappeared. Lowell Sheffield was showing all the signs of a smitten suitor. "What is it?"

He shook his head. "You will have to come to a party my parents are hosting to find out."

"A party? Have you forgotten I am in mourning?"

"No, but I hope you can make an exception."

Mrs. Sheffield raised her voice slightly to include them in her conversation. "I was telling your grandmother of my plan to host a small party. Nothing large, just a few of the young people—"

"Will there be dancing?" Her grandmother did not wait for Mrs. Sheffield to complete her explanation. "You know she is still observing the proper mourning period."

"I will sit out any dances with your granddaughter," Lowell offered.

"And cause everyone to gossip about the two of you? I don't think that would be wise."

Disappointment hit Alexandra with the force of a blow, but she knew better than to argue with her strong-willed grandparent. "Perhaps you can come over the next day and tell me all about it."

Grand-mère made a tsking sound. "Did I say you could not go?" She turned to Mrs. Sheffield. "I don't know what to do with young people these days. They never listen."

"But I thought—"

A frown stopped her words. "I said Mr. Sheffield would start tongues wagging if he sat next to you for every dance. As long as I can rely on you to act circumspectly, I see no reason why you should not go."

"I'm glad you trust her to us." Mrs. Sheffield's smile was radiant. "I'll make sure she is taken care of."

Her grandmother nodded. "I know you will. When is this party taking place?"

"A week from today," Lowell answered for his mother. He leaned back against his chair, the picture of a wealthy young man in control of his destiny.

"Do you mean I have to wait a whole week to find out your surprise?" Alexandra gazed up at him and fluttered her eyelashes, a move that generally helped her get her way.

Lowell put a finger to his lips. "I have promised not to tell you yet."

Alexandra pouted at him but to no avail. He would not budge.

All too soon, his mother rose to her feet and gestured to him to join her.

"Until next week." He bowed over Alexandra's hand before escorting his mother from the parlor.

As they left, she could not help comparing Lowell Sheffield with the very different man who was residing at the Hugheses' home. Lowell would never be caught in public in his shirtsleeves. He was much too aware of his dignity. It was an attitude shared by most of the men she knew, an attitude she had always accepted as normal until she met Jeremiah LeGrand, a man who had no care for the cut of his clothing or the style of his hair.

Was that why Lowell Sheffield, who had once seemed so attractive, now appeared superficial and shallow to her?

Chapter 11

I still don't understand why you think I should attend this dinner." Jeremiah pulled on the cuff of his coat. It felt odd to wear formal clothing after so much time in the field.

"You have been working far too hard." Susannah's curls bounced as the carriage hit a rut. She turned to her husband. "Tell him, Judah."

"You've been working far too hard."

Jeremiah groaned and met his friend's gaze. "Traitor."

Judah spread his hands. "You should know by now you cannot win this argument."

A sigh from Susannah's corner of the carriage was long-suffering. "I don't know why I even try to help the two of you."

"Does that mean we can go back home?" Jeremiah raised his hand as if to knock on the wall separating his seat from the driver's bench.

"Don't you dare. We are going to this dinner. And you are going to enjoy yourself." Susannah's voice contained a note of exasperation. "I'll not have you telling your friends in New Orleans that we don't know anything about entertainment."

Jeremiah grunted. "I don't know when I've enjoyed myself more than the past months."

"I am glad to hear it." Judah shifted slightly. "But if you truly want to be a landowner, you should consider evenings like this one to be part of your duties. You never can tell who you will meet and what you will learn."

"It's not like this is my first dinner party."

"Excellent." Susannah patted his knee. "Then we won't have to worry about your ability to make civilized conversation."

"I have to talk, too? I thought all I had to do was eat."

Their laughter filled the carriage as they pulled up at the Sheffields' home. Jeremiah exited the carriage first and offered his hand to Susannah. Then he waited patiently as Judah maneuvered his crutches. This was Judah's first party since coming back to Natchez. Jeremiah would have to watch out for his friend in the crowd.

Torches cast flickering light on the sidewalk leading to the graceful mansion. As they entered through the double doors, unobtrusive slaves took their wraps and disappeared. Jeremiah followed Susannah and Judah to the older couple who were waiting to welcome their guests. The Sheffields were typical hosts—well dressed, charming, wealthy. He exchanged greetings with them and walked into the parlor to meet the other guests.

These were the cream of Natchez society, the simpering debutantes and cosseted sons who would eventually lead the Mississippi territory into its future as a state. Lord, help them all. They made him feel old.

Susannah introduced him to several young women, but he forgot the previous girl's name as soon as the next one was brought forward. Some were prettier than others, some more graceful, but not one of them stirred the slightest bit of interest.

The room was beginning to grow crowded, and Jeremiah pulled at the starched collar that grew scratchier with each passing minute. Would they never sit down to their meal?

He glanced toward the door as another guest entered, her black dress in sharp contrast to all the other girls in the room. Alexandra.

She hesitated a moment, her dark eyes scanning the guests. When her gaze met his, something clicked in his mind, like a bolt being shot home. Or was something inside him being unbolted?

His mind went back to the first time he'd seen Alexandra. Her bravery had touched him then, and he had enjoyed being able to help her. But then he'd seen her in a different light, a more coquettish side of her which he found hard and unattractive. Which one was the real Alexandra?

He had to know the answer. He stepped forward, holding her gaze, trying to read the thoughts in her head. Those eyes of hers—soft as velvet and endless as the night sky—spoke to him. In them he read sadness and fear. She looked so lost for a moment, rousing his desire to rescue her once more.

Before he reached her side, it was gone. The connection between them was broken by the arrival of Lowell Sheffield at her side. Jeremiah watched as the other man, much more charming and urbane than he would ever be, bent over her hand and kissed it before tucking it into the crook of his elbow. He acted more like a suitor than a friend. His possessive attitude made Jeremiah's jaw clench, but he knew he couldn't pull her away from her escort without making a scene.

"So it really is Alexandra Lewis." A tall blond girl he was probably supposed to remember was standing next to him. "I couldn't believe it when Mrs. Sheffield said she would be attending tonight, but there she is. As bold as Jezebel."

Before he could decide whether or not to ask her what she meant, dinner was announced and another young man elbowed himself between them. "Miss Montgomery, I would be honored if you would allow me to escort you to the dining room."

Jeremiah bowed and left the two of them, going in search of the couple who had brought him here. He was going to wring a promise from Susannah never again to accept an invitation on his behalf. He would much rather spend the evening at home with a good book. Or even a bad one. Either way, the "conversation" would be more intelligent than what he was experiencing now.

❀

As much as she had looked forward to this evening, all Alexandra could think of was escape. She smiled at Lowell and allowed him to monopolize her attention. Obtaining his offer of marriage was her goal, after all.

She glanced at him and wondered again why he no longer seemed appealing. He was handsome, rich, and kind, three things she valued most highly.

Lowell caught her staring and tilted his head toward hers. "What has put that frown between your eyes? Is something wrong with your food?"

"What?" She looked down at the untouched plate. "Oh no, of course not. The food is delicious." To prove the point she picked up her fork and speared a long bean, raising it to her mouth and nibbling at it in spite of the unsettled feeling in her stomach.

"Then it must be my presence that has put that sour look on your face."

"I apologize for my manners, Mr. Sheffield."

"Lowell, remember?"

"I apologize, Lowell. You must think my parents raised a very ungrateful child." She put down her fork and reached for her goblet. She lifted the crystal to her mouth and cool water rushed down her throat. She hoped it would settle her stomach, a stomach that had been churning since she realized that Dorcas Montgomery of Nashville was attending the party. Dorcas was the surprise Lowell had promised her.

A scornful smile turned up the corners of her lips. Some surprise. A friend from Nashville and one who knew the truth about her father's death. Would Dorcas share her knowledge with the Sheffields? She glanced down the table at the willowy blond. At least Dorcas was not one of the ones who had shunned her and her mother. Maybe her secret was safe.

"Not at all." He took the goblet of water from her hand and returned it to the table. "I think you are worried about something. Please trust me enough to tell me what is wrong."

"It's nothing." She grasped for an excuse that would satisfy him. "I'm a little worried about my mother. She is so sad in the evenings since Papa. . .died."

Lowell took her hand in his and raised it to his lips. "Your concern does you credit. You have a woman's tender heart."

Shame washed through her at his words. If only he knew how deceitful she really was. She had thought of her mother some this evening, but much more of her attention had gone to the girl sitting a few chairs down from them. "How do you know Dorcas?"

"My father and her father have done business in the past." He nodded toward Dorcas. "You probably know her family grows tobacco, and I'm sure you've heard how prices have fallen since the end of the war. Mr. Montgomery is thinking of trying to switch over to cotton. He wanted to purchase some of our seed and get my father's opinion on his chances of success. When we got ready to return, Ma asked Dorcas to come with us."

"I see."

"I've known Dorcas for years." He winked at her. "At one time, my parents and her parents thought we ought to make a match of it. But my taste doesn't run to blonds."

Normally, Alexandra would have dredged up some witty response to his comment, but her heart wasn't in it any longer. What had happened to her in the past weeks? She glanced away from Lowell and straight into the blue eyes that had haunted her dreams far too often. But in her dreams, the eyes were kind and caring. The gaze that skewered her now, however, was full of loathing. It took her back to her final weeks in Nashville and the hard-hearted people who had condemned her. Alexandra wanted to jump up from the table and run away, but she could not move.

Lowell had turned from her to answer a question from the person sitting on his other side.

Someone removed her plate and replaced it with a bowl of berries topped with fresh cream. She wondered where Mrs. Sheffield had procured fresh fruit at this time of year. It was surely an extravagance in the middle of winter.

Lowell had turned his attention to his dessert and wolfed it down in a few large bites before turning his attention back to her. "Are you ready to move to the ballroom?"

She put her spoon back on the pristine tablecloth, her dessert untouched. "Yes." Pushing back her chair and resting her hand on Lowell's arm, she lifted her chin and walked out of the room with all of the grace she could muster. The evening could not end soon enough for her.

The orchestra launched into their first piece as she and Lowell entered the ballroom. The polished floor would soon be scuffed by the movements of the eager dancers, but for now, it gleamed in the candlelight. Alexandra longed to throw off convention and let Lowell sweep her across the room in his arms.

Instead, she was engulfed in perfume as someone came up behind her and put her hands over Alexandra's eyes. "I bet you can't guess who this is."

Dorcas's accent, with its mountain twang, gave her away.

"It can be none other than the guest of honor." Alexandra pulled on the hands and turned around to see the golden-haired girl smiling at her oddly.

Dorcas giggled and hugged her. "Aren't you sweet? I've been waiting all night to get to say hello."

"It's nice to see you, Dorcas. How are you enjoying your stay in Natchez?"

"The Sheffields have been so considerate of my comfort that I feel like one of the family." She glanced toward Lowell, who was smiling at both of them. "But I have such good news for you, Alexandra."

Something in the tone of the other woman's voice put her on alert. She studied Dorcas's face, forcibly reminded of the content expression of a well-fed house cat. The room was filling up now as the rest of the dinner guests caught up with them. "Is that right?"

"Yes." Dorcas clasped her hands together and spoke a little louder. "The scandal about your father's death is dying down now. Hardly anyone is talking about the way he murdered that poor, innocent family. And the sheriff has fully recovered from the gunshot wound. I imagine you could even come back to Nashville and be received again."

Silence fell in the room. Heads turned toward them.

"Whatever are you talking about, Dorcas?" Lowell sounded as shocked as Alexandra felt.

"Oh no." Dorcas's eyes widened convincingly, but her smug grin told the true story. "Don't tell me I've spoken out of turn. I just assumed everyone knew. . . ."

"Knew what?" Now Lowell sounded exasperated.

"Please don't be angry with me, Lowell." She turned her gaze away from him, and Alexandra saw her eyes were moist. "How was I to know?"

Alexandra might have fallen for the ruse if she had not used it herself from time to time to convince others of her own innocence. "Dorcas is referring to the manner in which my father died last year."

Lowell took a step away from her, leaving Alexandra standing all alone in the crowded room. No one else was talking; even the orchestra had stopped playing as the musicians realized some drama was being played out.

"My father died under a cloud of suspicion." She glared at Dorcas, daring her to say anything more. "He was apparently involved in a plot to seize some valuable farm land from a family in the area."

"But I thought he was killed in an Indian raid?" Lowell's voice had hardened. He would probably blame her just like all those self-righteous people in Nashville.

"You are mistaken, Lowell." Alexandra took a deep breath. The words boiled around in her head, words that would condemn her to a life of shame. Her mouth was wobbly, making it hard for her to form the words properly, but she refused to let these people intimidate her. She clenched her jaw and forced the syllables out, one by one. "My father was killed in a shootout with the sheriff. Had he lived, he would most likely have been hung for his crimes."

A girl behind her gasped. Someone farther away asked what she had said. The buzz began slowly but gained momentum as her words were repeated to those who had not been able to hear for themselves.

Alexandra ignored all of them, even Dorcas, her attention centered on Lowell. Would he condemn her, too? Would he slip away from her as Asher had done? Was she doomed to lose each candidate she deemed suitable?

She saw the answer in his eyes and closed her own to hide the pain. She should have known better. She had been through this before. No one cared that she was innocent of the crimes her father had committed. She was guilty because she was his daughter. And the ironic thing about it was that she understood. She was one of these people. In the past, she would have separated herself from anyone with the barest hint of scandal, earned or not.

Alexandra pushed her way past Lowell and ran into the hallway. Tears swam in her eyes and overflowed onto her cheeks. Unable to see clearly, she barreled into someone. "Ex–excuse me."

"Alexandra. . .Miss Lewis. . .whatever is wrong?" The concerned voice made the tears flow harder.

"I. . .I have to g–get out of h–here."

A strong arm wrapped around her.

Alexandra burrowed into the reassuring warmth of a muscular chest. She was beyond caring who was holding her. All she knew was that her world had ended. . .again.

Chapter 12

Jeremiah sent one of the hovering slaves to ready the Hugheses' carriage. "Don't worry. I'll see you safely home."

He frowned a warning at any of the guests who approached them. He had no idea what calamity had occurred before his arrival in the ballroom, but it didn't matter. What mattered was the crushed girl who was clinging to him like a half-drowned kitten. He stroked her back and murmured soft words of understanding and encouragement. He had no idea where the words came from, only that they were what she needed to hear right now.

Harvey Sheffield approached them warily. "The carriage is ready. Do you want me to get one of the slaves to accompany her?"

"I'll do it." Jeremiah wasn't going to let her be hurt anymore tonight. He was tempted to pick her up as he had that first night, but he decided to see if she could walk with his support. He helped her stand up and, keeping an arm around her, guided her to the front door.

It took a minute to sort out their wraps, but once they were both bundled up, he helped her into the carriage and took the seat opposite her, his back to the coachman. She seemed calmer now, only sniffling from time to time. Without comment, he gave her his handkerchief.

"Thank you."

"You're welcome."

She pushed herself into the far corner of the carriage. "Why are you being so nice to me?"

Jeremiah had been asking himself the same question. He didn't even know what she had done or what had been done to her. But he needed to get her mind off her troubles. "A tent meeting has been going on across the river at Lake Concordia. I went to hear the preacher on Sunday. Do you know what book of the Bible he preached on?"

"No. How would I know?"

His eyes were growing accustomed to the darkness in the carriage. He could see her face now even though he could not make out her features. He imagined her brows were drawn together in a frown. "He spoke on John's first letter to his fellow Christians, specifically on John's instruction to love each other. *'Whosoever doeth not righteousness is not of God, neither he that loveth not his brother.'* That verse really struck me. Our attempts to be honest and righteous are no more important than the love we show to each other."

The silence went on so long after he stopped speaking that Jeremiah wondered if she had fallen asleep. But then her husky voice answered him. "So you're seeing me home because it's your Christian duty?"

"I am ministering to a sister in Christ. I'm doing what I can to help someone God loves."

"I don't feel very lovable."

The heartrending catch in her voice made Jeremiah's eyes sting. "But you are so precious to God. Don't ever doubt it. He created you. He knew you even before you were born, and He loved you so much that He let His Son die on the cross for you."

Another silence.

"If that's true, then why did God let my father commit those terrible deeds? Why didn't He stop it from happening? Why didn't He protect me and my mother from the consequences of Papa's indiscretion?"

Jeremiah prayed for an answer that would heal the hurt in her heart. "People aren't reliable, Alexandra. Only God is. If you put your faith in another human being, you will always be disappointed. But if you turn to God, He will comfort you no matter what happens."

He could feel her gaze on him, but she didn't comment.

When the carriage pulled up at her family home, she stopped him from rising with a shake of her head. "I appreciate your kindness, but you should go back to the Sheffields'. Your friends will be worried about you."

Jeremiah nodded. He reached for her hand, squeezing it gently. "I'll be praying for you, Alexandra."

The party was ending by the time he returned, but Jeremiah heard all about what had happened from his friends on the ride home. It was a shame about Alexandra's father. A part of him could understand why her family had made up the story about Mr. Lewis dying a hero's death. But they must have known the truth would come out eventually. Now Alexandra and her mother would be forced to deal with the consequences. For their sakes, he hoped the scandal would blow over quickly. But if it didn't, at least they had family here who would stand by them.

Judah took a more conservative view of the evening's events. "I don't think it's a good idea for you to accept Alexandra any longer, Susannah."

The darkness of the carriage seemed to close in on Jeremiah. "You can't mean that."

"I have to protect my family's reputation."

"And what about your Christian duty to love others?"

"Jeremiah"—he could make out Susannah's blond curls as she leaned forward and shook her head—"don't be so hard on my husband. He's just a little confused. But don't worry. I'm not going to ostracize your Alexandra."

What was this? Had Susannah misunderstood his concern? "She's not my

Alexandra. She's just a young woman who deserves our sympathy."

"Of course she is." Susannah's voice sounded a little choked, making him wonder if she was laughing at him. "And she shall get it. I promise you that."

Chapter 13

A shaft of sunlight woke Alexandra the next morning. No one had come in to light the fireplace in her room yet, so it must still be early. She burrowed deeper into the covers and tried to go back to sleep, but her mind wouldn't stop replaying the previous night's debacle.

She kept seeing Dorcas's face. She had known exactly what she was doing. But why? Did she harbor some grudge against Alexandra? She remembered the day they buried Papa and the feeling she'd had that Dorcas was looking for a reason to spread gossip about her. Perhaps it was simply her nature.

She pulled her knees up toward her chin. Gossip had always been a part of her world. She could remember the thrill of learning about one of her acquaintances in Nashville who had been caught embracing a man who was not her fiancé. It had been the talk at all the parties for several weeks. The whispers had grown to head shakes, and soon everyone was turning away from the indiscreet girl and her family.

Eventually the young man had asked to be released from the betrothal. At the time, Alexandra had joined the rest of her peers in condemning the girl's behavior. She deserved the treatment she had received. Didn't the Bible say people reaped what they sowed? The whole town had been in agreement. They had been united in their condemnation. No member of the family was exempted. Even the younger daughters were looked upon with suspicion.

At the time, it had never occurred to Alexandra to consider another interpretation of the events. She had never considered the pain they might be experiencing. Pain similar to what she felt this morning. But she had been innocent. She didn't deserve the treatment she would surely receive now that the truth was known.

Someone, probably Jemma, entered the room. She listened to the scrape of the iron poker stirring the warm coals, followed by the rhythmic *whoosh* of the bellows and the soft crackle of the fire. With a sigh she flipped back the counterpane.

"Good morning, Miss Alexandra." Jemma moved around the room, opening the curtains to allow more light to enter. "It's a pretty day."

"Not to me." Breakfast loomed in her mind like a towering thundercloud. She would have to tell her relatives that the scandal had caught up with them. "I wish I could sleep until noon."

Jemma's brown eyes widened. "Whatever is the matter?"

Alexandra supposed she might as well start practicing her story now. She swung her legs over the edge of the bed, her toes searching for her slippers. "An acquaintance of ours from Nashville was at the party last night. In fact, she was the reason for the party. And she kindly suggested that I could soon return to Nashville since Papa's scandal was no longer being discussed."

"Here you go." Jemma picked up her slipper and helped Alexandra ease her foot into it. "I suppose that's why you was crying last night."

A sigh of remorse filled her. Lowell would never want to marry her now. "What am I going to do?"

"Don't you worry none, miss. Things'll be all right."

"No they won't. No one will receive me anymore. It will be exactly like Nashville. The invitations will stop, and no one will come to visit. I'll never catch a husband like Grand-mère wants."

"Don't you be talking like that." Jemma pulled Alexandra's nightgown over her head and replaced it with a black cotton chemise. "You got so many blessings. Maybe this is God's way of getting you to share them."

Alexandra picked up her corset and stepped into it, tugging upward until the stays enfolded her rib cage. She held it still while Jemma laced up the back. "What do you mean?"

The next layer of clothing was a dark petticoat, followed by a black overdress with long sleeves to protect her arms from the cold temperatures.

"There's lots of folks in Natchez who need help." Jemma shrugged and led her to the dressing table so she could fix Alexandra's hair. "Maybe God is freeing up your time so you can visit with them."

Preposterous. Spend her time helping the poor? Accompanying her aunt Patricia on more depressing visits? Yet what was the alternative? She could not stand the idea of sitting in the parlor, waiting for visitors who never arrived. Jeremiah's words from the evening before came back to her. He had shown her such kindness, coming to her rescue without question or concern for his own dignity. She opened her eyes and met Jemma's gaze in the mirror. "Maybe you're right."

Jemma beamed. "Once you show those people who you really are, they'll forget all about the past. You wait and see. They'll be knocking on your grandma's front door in no time. Nobody can resist a young lady with an open heart."

Alexandra left her and joined her family for breakfast. The gloom that had seemed so impenetrable earlier lifted a little. Once they saw the new Alexandra Lewis, her friends would be ashamed of their actions. And if they weren't, well, that was all right, too. She had no need of false friends. Like Jeremiah had told her last night, depending on human beings always brought disappointment. She was done with relying on others. She could count only on herself.

A thought struck her, and she turned on the staircase to look back at her bedroom door. Had God used Jemma to make her feel better this morning?

Did He really care enough to involve Himself in her life? A spark of excitement warmed her, but then it faded. How ridiculous to think such foolishness. If He cared that much, why hadn't He been there when she really needed His help? Why had He been so silent during those days and weeks right after Papa's death? And why hadn't He stopped Papa from going down the wrong path?

No, believing in a caring, loving God was for children and old people. They needed to believe someone would protect them, be there for them. But she was young and healthy. She could make her own way in the world. She didn't need God or anyone else.

Neither Aunt Patricia nor Uncle John was present for breakfast. Alexandra had been so caught up in her own worries she had forgotten they were visiting his relatives and would be gone all day. Her plans to devote her time helping her aunt minister to the needy were dashed. What would she do with her day?

Grand-mère entered the dining room, leaning heavily on her cane. After she was seated and served, she turned to Alexandra. "How was your party last night?"

"It did not go as well as I had hoped."

Her mother, sitting across from her, looked up. "What happened?"

Alexandra wrung her napkin as if she could squeeze composure from it. "Do you remember the Montgomerys from Nashville?"

A wrinkle appeared in her mother's forehead.

"Well, no matter." Alexandra took a deep breath. "It seems Mr. Montgomery and Lowell's father have done business together for years. They went to Nashville—"

"Oh no." Mama's hand went to her mouth.

Alexandra nodded. "They brought Dorcas Montgomery back with them for a visit, and she announced to all the guests that Papa had been involved in a scandal. She was quite ingenuous, telling me we can most likely move back to Nashville now that all the talk has died down."

Her grandmother grunted. "At least no one knows the particulars."

"I'm fairly certain Dorcas gave them every scintillating detail once I left."

"Then you should have stayed and faced all of them down." Her grandmother pointed a gnarled finger toward her. "That's what's wrong with this world today. None of you young people have any gumption. Back when I was a young girl, I would have stood up to the lot of them. Made sure no one talked about me behind my back. If you'd have squared your shoulders and looked down your nose at this Dorcas, it would have all blown over by now."

"You weren't there, Grand-mère. Everyone was so shocked. Even Lowell couldn't look at me."

Her mother made a soft sound of sympathy.

The sharp knock of her grandmother's cane on the pine floor made Alexandra jump. "That young man will not go against the wishes of his family.

And they know well enough that a marriage to the Tanner family will be advantageous. I have more than three times the acreage Harvey Sheffield can lay claim to."

Alexandra twisted her napkin in the other direction. "It's not always about money, Grand-mère. The Sheffields must look to their reputation."

Her grandmother looked toward her daughter. "Didn't you teach this girl anything, Beatrice?" She glared at Alexandra. "It's always, always, always about money. Money can polish any reputation, fulfill every dream, and buy every item your heart desires. As long as the Sheffields think they will benefit financially from a marriage with my family, they will make certain Lowell does not waver in his pursuit."

No sooner had her grandmother concluded her diatribe than the dining-room door opened, and one of the slaves entered. "You have visitors, Mrs. Tanner. Are you able to receive them?"

Her grandmother nodded. "Show them to the front parlor." The slave retreated to do her bidding, and Grand-mère returned her attention to Alexandra. "Now do you believe me?"

Alexandra pushed her chair back from the table. She felt a little sick. All this time she'd thought Lowell was interested in her. To find that he was only interested in her family's money was quite a blow to her ego. Only an hour earlier, she would have rejoiced in his appearance at her home. Now she only wanted to retreat to her bedroom and hide from the world.

Chapter 14

I t's really too early to be making a morning call." Jeremiah shook his head at Susannah. "I tried to warn you that we would be kept waiting until the Tanners break their fast."

"I only wanted to make sure none of them was upset about last night. Miss Lewis seemed so distraught."

Jeremiah glanced toward her husband and shook his head.

"I don't care what you say. I know you care about her, too." Susannah's glance was smug.

Judah moved his crutches to one side and put his free hand on Jeremiah's shoulder. "How many times is it that you've rescued Miss Lewis?"

"Actually it was your carriage that rescued her the first time." Jeremiah twisted his lips into a slight smile. "Come to think of it, your carriage was the rescuer last night, too."

Susannah laughed. "And I suppose you had absolutely nothing to do with it?"

"I'm not saying that. I was there at the right time to lend a hand. God has been kind enough to use me to aid a Christian sister in need."

The door opened and the ladies of the Tanner household entered. Mrs. Tanner led the way, leaning heavily on her cane, followed by Alexandra's mother and then Alexandra herself. Her face seemed so pale, and smudges under her eyes bespoke a restless night. His heart went out to her. She seemed so fragile, nothing like the aristocratic belle who had treated him as if he was inconsequential when she first saw him. Even though he would not have wished this pain on her, perhaps God would use it to mold her into a woman who cared about the needs of those outside her immediate family.

Once they had all exchanged greetings, Mrs. Tanner told them all where to sit. Judah and Susannah were relegated to a pair of delicate chairs while he was told to take a seat on the far side of the fireplace, opposite the sofa on which Alexandra and her mother sat.

Mrs. Tanner took up her seat, an oversized chair with cushions that made him think of a throne. "To what do we owe this pleasure?" The older lady went straight to the point.

Susannah leaned forward and caught Alexandra's gaze. "We just wanted to check on you after the party and make certain you know you have friends here."

Mrs. Tanner stamped her cane on the floor. "Of course the girl has friends. She's an accomplished young lady with an outstanding pedigree. She's the most eligible female in Adams County, maybe in the Mississippi Territory."

Jeremiah hid a smile. It was fitting for her to defend Alexandra. She reminded him of Uncle Emile. He'd never allow any slur against his nephew.

A glance at Alexandra showed her discomfort with the direction of the conversation. Time to introduce a new subject. "What do you think of the talk of statehood?"

Alexandra's mother looked out the window, obviously unwilling to join the discussion. Or maybe she had no opinion on the matter of politics.

Mrs. Tanner, however, did not share her daughter's diffidence. "I think it's a load of hogwash."

"What about the protection of the army?" Susannah folded her hands in her lap. "And so many immigrants are arriving now that the war is over. We need law and order or we risk falling into chaos."

Judah nodded, smiling at his wife. "I agree. One thing the politicians in Washington should have learned is how important this part of our continent is. If the British had taken New Orleans, no treaty would have stopped their advance up the river. Every settlement, including Natchez, would have been raided. The men would have been impressed into the British services and the crops would have been seized to support the invaders."

"So they should know enough to protect us whether we remain a state or a territory." Mrs. Tanner's smug gaze traveled the room.

"But wouldn't you like to have some say in who is running the territory?" Alexandra entered the conversation. "You always say President Madison should not have the power to decide who will govern us. If we become a state, we will have the right to elect our leaders."

Jeremiah was impressed with Alexandra's comments. She might be pampered, but she was not empty-headed. "Do you think the territory should be made into one state or two?"

A frown appeared in her brow as Alexandra considered his question. "Since the Indian lands were included in the territory, it has become a huge square, much larger than any of the other states."

"But we don't have many people living in that area, especially on the eastern side of the territory."

"As Susannah said, immigrants seem to be pouring into the territory in ever-growing numbers. Who knows where it will end?" Alexandra shrugged. "Of course I could be wrong. I have never traveled to the eastern portion of the territory. Perhaps it should be one state."

"Well, one advantage of making two states is the increased number of senators who would represent the area."

An arrested look entered her face. "I see. That makes a great deal of sense. So do you think there should be two states?"

"I don't think it much matters what any of us in this room thinks." Judah spoke before Jeremiah could answer. "We won't be involved in the decision-making process."

"Too true, dear." Susannah accepted a cup of tea from Alexandra. "And perhaps that is best."

Alexandra continued pouring cups of the strong brew and passing them out. Jeremiah took a tentative swallow of his drink. The dark liquid stung the inside of his mouth, but it wasn't too bitter for his taste.

"Are you still working in the cotton fields, Mr. LeGrand?" Alexandra's face looked more relaxed than it had when she first entered the parlor.

Susannah stirred a lump of sugar into her tea. "He's single-handedly brought things back from the edge of disaster. Thanks to his hard work, we'll be able to pay our taxes and buy seed for the spring planting."

Now it was Jeremiah's turn to squirm. He did not like to brag about what he'd been doing.

"Yes, I've heard about things over at Magnolia Plantation." Mrs. Tanner refused a cup of tea. "And not all of it is good."

"What do you mean?" asked Judah.

"My granddaughter told me about his penchant for working next to the slaves. It's not good to coddle them. It leads to dissatisfaction and perhaps even a slave revolt."

Jeremiah nodded. He could understand that his way of doing things might seem odd, even threatening to the other landowners. A large number of black slaves lived in the territory. Most whites believed the only way to maintain control was to keep their slaves too exhausted and too detached to foment rebellion. He disagreed. To him it made more sense to give the slaves land of their own to work and chances to earn their freedom if they wished to do so. He had a lot of plans that would not meet with the approbation of people like Mrs. Tanner. He wished he could openly discuss his ideas. Maybe one day. But for now, he should concentrate on the young lady they'd come to see. "I'm sure you have more experience than I do, Mrs. Tanner."

"Jeremiah is very humble." Susannah's voice held a note of censure. Jeremiah wondered if it was aimed at him or at Mrs. Tanner. "He is a successful businessman in his own right. Did you know he and his uncle have one of the most successful shipping businesses in New Orleans? And he has postponed his plans because of his insistence on helping us get back on our feet."

Jeremiah frowned at Susannah. He didn't need anyone to defend him. "I believe in helping others when I can. God has blessed me greatly so that I can pass blessings on to others in His name."

"That's easy for you to say." The anger in Alexandra's voice was hard to miss. "What do you know about losing a parent?"

Judah's mouth dropped open, and silence invaded the room.

Jeremiah folded his arms across his chest. "You're quite right, Miss Lewis.

I don't remember my parents at all. You see, they died when I was a child."

The look on her face, a combination of horror, shame, and sympathy, was something he would never forget. It was hard to suppress the smile trying to curl his lips. A laugh fought its way up his throat, but Jeremiah pushed it back down.

"I'm so sorry." She was the picture of remorse, her hands folded in her lap, her eyes trained on the tips of her feet.

Jeremiah was ashamed of himself. He should have let her words stand. Why had he felt it necessary to embarrass her? He was usually much more circumspect. "You could not have known."

She glanced up at him, and he was surprised to see the sheen of tears in her eyes. "That doesn't excuse my tantrum. Please say you forgive me."

"Forgiven and forgotten." He smiled at her to show her his words were true.

"Good for you, young man. My granddaughter is a pretty thing, but she's easily provoked to anger—a trait her parents should have rid her of many years ago."

Jeremiah had turned to give his attention to Mrs. Tanner, but he saw Alexandra's chin lift from the corner of his vision.

"Please, Grand-mère." Her voice was strained.

He wished he'd never defended himself. When he'd agreed to come with his friends, it was with the hope of making her feel better, not to add to her discomfort.

He looked at Susannah, who nodded and put her cup on the table at her elbow. "I am hoping to get you ladies to come to my house on Thursday for some of my special mint tea and a few hours of quilting."

Jeremiah had expected Susannah to announce their departure, not invite Alexandra and her family for a visit.

"I don't—"

Alexandra's refusal was overridden by her grandmother. "They would love to. Both my daughters and Alexandra accept your kind offer."

"Excellent." Susannah stood.

Judah and Jeremiah followed suit, bowing to the women and taking their leave as usual. As they gathered their wraps and headed out the door, Jeremiah could hear Mrs. Tanner telling Alexandra and her mother why they would be visiting the Hugheses' home on Thursday. He needed to make sure he was not at the house at that time. Maybe he and Judah could look for a place to house Uncle Emile's new office. It was about time for him to concentrate on his other reason for coming to Natchez.

He nodded to himself. It was the perfect excuse for avoiding further contact with Alexandra.

Chapter 15

It was raining when Jeremiah awoke on Thursday morning. He groaned and dressed with more care than usual. His excuse for not being available when the visitors arrived had disappeared when the weather turned inclement. He couldn't even go out and work with the slaves. Or could he? As he headed downstairs, plans began to evolve in his head. He would need to time things right if he was going to avoid Miss Alexandra Lewis. And avoiding her was of paramount importance to him.

Breakfast was a hurried affair. He ignored Susannah's pointed comments and headed outside. The rain beat steadily on the barn's roof as Jeremiah checked the tack for wear.

Noise outside indicated when she arrived. Jeremiah's heart beat a rapid tattoo in response. What was Alexandra wearing today? Would her hair be pulled back in a tight bun? Or would it be styled in ringlets to frame her face? He shook his head to clear it. Why did it matter?

The easy answer was that it shouldn't matter to him at all. But Jeremiah was not in the habit of accepting easy answers. The subject would take some serious soul searching. Nothing about Alexandra should affect him beyond the consideration he would offer to any sister in Christ. But the rat-a-tat of his heart told a different story. What was it about her that made him feel so. . .so agitated? Jeremiah knew he could not be falling in love with her.

His mind rejected the idea before it was fully formed. In the first place, he did not know Alexandra. He'd only been around her a few times, and their conversation had been limited. She *was* more than the shallow debutante he'd first thought her to be. She was beautiful and smart, but that didn't mean she was the woman God intended for his mate.

Which brought up the most important reason he could *not* have feelings for Alexandra: She depended on others for happiness and acceptance, not on the Lord. She might be the sweetest, most unassuming young woman in the territory, but if she didn't love the Lord with all her heart, she was not a woman he could share—

The sound of the barn doors opening and closing brought him out of the tack room. There she stood, dressed in black, her hair loosely pulled back and pinned at the nape of her neck. Her hands were folded in front of her, and she was looking around the shadowy barn with all the innocence of a baby bird.

"What do you want, Miss Lewis?"

She jumped at the sound of his voice and put one hand up to her throat. "Oh, you gave me a fright, Mr. LeGrand. Susannah sent me to remind you that tea will be served in a few minutes."

He could feel heat rising to his cheeks. Susannah shouldn't be playing the matchmaker. How aggravating. He would have to talk with her later. But for now, he needed to rid himself of the beauteous Miss Lewis. "I won't be taking tea with you today. I have too much work to do."

She walked to where he stood outside the tack room. The fresh scent of her lemony perfume seemed to flow over him like warm bathwater. "Why do you dislike me so much? Have you not forgiven me for mistaking you for a servant? I am very sorry for offending you."

"What?" He looked down at her in surprise. "What makes you think I dislike you?"

She shrugged and twisted her hands together. "You seem to make it a point to avoid me whenever I come to visit."

"I have a great deal of responsibility these days and very little time for social visits." He tugged at the collar of his shirt, which had suddenly grown uncomfortably snug. He knew he was not being completely truthful with her, but how could he be? How could he admit he was no stronger than any of the other men who chased after her? That some part of him wanted to protect her from all danger? How could he tell her that his heart was pounding even now because he wanted to reach out and touch her soft hair?

"I see." She glanced up at him, a wounded look in her eyes. "I suppose I should go back inside."

"I suppose so." He didn't move, and neither did she. He felt like an idiot, but he couldn't think of a thing to say to her. All he wanted to do was stare into those dark brown eyes.

After what seemed an eternity, though it couldn't have been more than a minute or two, she sighed and turned away. "It was nice to see you again."

He didn't answer. His throat worked, but he couldn't get any words to come out. He watched as she moved away from him and wished he could say something to stop her. But what was the point? He'd already gone over this. He didn't—couldn't—care for Alexandra Lewis.

Chapter 16

Aunt Patricia was delighted when Alexandra asked to accompany her as she made her rounds. The first place they stopped was a small shack just north of the plantation grounds.

"Who lives here?" Alexandra avoided a clucking chicken as she helped carry several baskets of warm food toward the shack.

"An old black man, Tobias Jenkins. His master died a few years back, and he and the other slaves were set free by the widow. John wanted to give him some land, but your grand-mère refused. So John and I bought a little parcel off the plantation grounds and gave it to him. He started off fine but caught the croup last winter. Since then, it's been difficult for him to keep body and soul together."

"Doesn't he have any family or friends to help him?"

Aunt Patricia shook her head. "He had a wife, a woman he jumped the broom with, but she died shortly after they were freed. There's no one else." She slid the wicker handle of her basket toward her elbow and reached out with the other hand to knock on the door.

"Who's there?"

Alexandra could hear hacking coughs coming from the little house.

"It's Mrs. Patricia and my niece Alexandra. We've come with some stew for you and medication to ease that cough."

The door swung open slowly, creaking on its hinges. A small man with the darkest face Alexandra had ever seen looked out at them.

Aunt Patricia performed quick introductions, and they went inside, placing their baskets on the hearth in front of a roaring fire.

The interior of the small home was much cozier than the exterior indicated. A quilt covered the mattress of a narrow bed, its bright colors giving a cheerful feel to the room. A rocking chair stood next to the fireplace, obviously the seat the old man used. A small table was nestled in the corner of the large open space, two chairs pulled up to it.

Tobias pointed to the chairs. "Why don't you turn those around and have a seat next to the fire." He moved slowly toward the table and held up a knife over a loaf of dark bread. "Would you care for a slice? I made this two days ago."

Aunt Patricia shook her head as she settled into one of the chairs. "We ate before we came, Tobias."

72

He began coughing as he put the knife back on the table.

The hacking sounded awful to Alexandra's ears. She stood and helped the man walk across the room and sit down in his rocker. "Can I fetch some water for you?"

Tobias shook his head. It took a few moments, but he finally got the coughing back under control. "You're a kind young lady." His face had lost some of its color, taking on the hue of river mud. "It seems to come natural in your family."

His words stung her conscience like tiny barbs. "I haven't been very much interested in helping until now."

"It doesn't matter when you start." Aunt Patricia smiled at her. "Only that you do." She turned to Tobias. "How have you been doing?"

He shrugged, wiping his mouth with a white handkerchief. "Not too bad."

"I worry about whether or not you're eating regularly."

"It doesn't take much to feed a lazy old man." He grinned at them, showing both of the teeth he had. "Now come spring, when I get to planting my garden, it may take something more to keep up my energy, but I've saved a little money. I'll be able to barter with the merchants in Natchez to buy what I need."

Aunt Patricia rolled her eyes. "Don't try to fool me. You haven't been able to work since last winter. I doubt you have more than fifty cents to your name."

Alexandra watched as her aunt, the daughter of a wealthy landowner, bantered with the friendly man. The woman she'd thought of as starchy and uninteresting was showing a completely different side of herself. She was smiling and laughing and looked a decade younger than she had as they rode over to the cabin. It was as though she was gaining as much from this visit as Tobias was.

"I suppose we had best get on our way, Alexandra." Aunt Patricia stood and picked up the cloak she had laid across the back of her chair. "We have several stops to make before dinner."

Even though the cold air nipped at her nose as Alexandra followed her aunt back out to the carriage, contentment warmed her through and through. Maybe she would actually enjoy dispensing goods to the needy.

After several similar stops, her aunt instructed the coachman to take them home. "We need to get back. A lot of work is waiting for us there."

Alexandra settled into a corner of the coach opposite her aunt. "What kind of things do you have in mind?"

"Your uncle and I were down at Natchez Under-the-Hill last week, and we saw many poor, tired immigrants passing through on their way to who knows where. You should have seen them. Exhausted and scared, ragged and hungry. The children were so thin their little arms looked like knobby sticks, and their parents were not in much better shape. They need everything from warm meals to cloaks and blankets. Most of them sold all their belongings just to get to America."

Her memory dredged up a dreary picture of the waterfront, and Alexandra's heart melted. "What a wonderful idea. It sounds as if they need our help."

"Yes, they do. I found a whole stack of blankets we no longer use because they have holes in them. So we are going to mend them and take them to the waterfront for those poor souls."

Anticipation made her toes curl. Alexandra could hardly wait to get started. "I hope you know you have changed my outlook. I mean. . ." She paused, searching for the right words to express her thoughts.

Aunt Patricia reached across the carriage and patted her hand. "I know what you mean, dear. There's nothing like ministering to others to remind us of the many blessings we have."

Chapter 17

I have an idea." Jeremiah's statement elicited a groan from his friend. He looked out of the carriage as it traveled the road to town. He and Judah had been planning this trip for several days. A piece of property was being offered for sale that should make an excellent shipping office, and Jeremiah wanted to purchase it if the building was in good shape and the price was fair.

"The last time you said that to me, we ended up spending the whole day across the river at that tent meeting."

"You have to admit the minister was a great speaker. The Spirit was using him to deliver a message we needed to hear."

Judah laughed. "He was good, but it's a wonder we didn't catch colds after all that time out in the open. Ferriday Plantation may not be that far away, but crossing the river at this time of year exposed us to some raw weather."

"I still think it was worth the trouble." Jeremiah remembered the hours spent hanging on every word the minister delivered. A part of him wished he had the talent to teach the Word, but he had not been gifted in that way. He was able to share the Gospel with people one-on-one and even sometimes in a group of five or so, but he was not an orator. "But back to my idea. What would you think of ordering slate tablets and pencils?"

"Whatever for? Who are you planning to teach?"

Jeremiah turned his attention away from the landscape. "I was thinking about showing your slaves the rudiments of reading and writing."

Judah crossed his arms over his chest and grunted. "You can forget your revolutionary ideas. I know things were different where you grew up, but here slaves are the labor force that makes our crops profitable. If we teach the slaves to read, they will clamor for freedom. How do you think things would go at home if I freed all the slaves?"

"I believe you could hire them to work for you instead of forcing them to do so. Can't you see enslavement is wrong? The men and women you 'own' are precious in the Lord's sight."

"They are precious to me, too. . .precious to the smooth operation of the plantation." Judah frowned at him. "You'd better keep your ideas to yourself. Many people in this county would lynch you for the ideas you've espoused to me."

"Do I need to fear a vicious mob attack?"

"No, but you may get a very chilly reception if you start ordering school supplies for slaves. It's not legal. If word got out, you would go to jail. The people around here don't take kindly to newcomers messing with the system that's been in use for decades."

Jeremiah considered the advice. His friend had grown up here and knew the people. But that didn't mean Jeremiah's plan was doomed to failure. It would simply be placed on a back shelf for now. As soon as he got the shipping business up and running, he could use his uncle's contacts. It shouldn't be a problem to have a few dozen tablets and pencils ordered.

"It's a nice day." Judah leaned forward to look out of the window. "Spring will be upon us soon."

"Indeed." As Jeremiah watched the passing scenery, his mind wandered back to the idea for a school. He could have a new building raised on the plantation grounds. That way, few of the planters would realize his plans until they were underway. It could be about the same size as the sewing house, unpretentious and simple, with several desks and a tablet for each person in attendance. He could start with the children who were too young to be put to work. Then they could go home every day and show their parents and older siblings what they had learned.

The coach passed a wide road leading west into a dense forest. "Is that the drive to a plantation home?" Jeremiah asked.

Judah glanced past him and shook his head. "That's Liberty Road."

"Good name." He encouraged his friend to elaborate with a nod.

"Several hunting lodges down that road are owned by some of the most prosperous planters around here. They don't get down there very often, but they have slaves on duty all the time. As long as the masters are not in residence and the lodges are cared for, the slaves are free to do what they will with their time. They have much more liberty than you would expect."

"Why don't they run away?"

A shrug answered him. "I guess they are comfortable."

Jeremiah couldn't imagine living in a half-world of slavery. "Until the master comes. Then they have to give up their freedom again. It seems to me that would be a painful process."

"Not as painful as being whipped or branded if they are caught without papers. Since our neighbors up north have been threatening to shackle the Southland by outlawing slavery, things have gotten much more tense. Catching a runaway slave has always been serious business, but it's even more so since slaves who make it to certain states or territories in the North are considered free."

"I wonder where it will end."

"From what we've learned since returning to Natchez, the price of cotton is rising daily. Our economy strengthens with each shipment." Judah shifted his position on the cushioned bench. "The system works because our slaves work."

Jeremiah couldn't agree with Judah. "There must be a way to make plantations successful without the enslavement of human beings."

"Maybe so." Judah's expression had drawn into a frown. "I've never purchased a slave myself."

"But you've not considered freeing the ones you inherited."

"I'm not as wealthy as you, Jeremiah. If I freed the slaves, Susannah and I would lose everything."

Jeremiah recognized the fear in his friend's voice. "It wouldn't be easy, but you and your wife should consider other ways to make the plantation profitable. Perhaps you could free a few at a time to make it easier on you."

"I'll think about it."

They arrived in town and found the property Jeremiah wished to inspect. It was a brick building clinging to the edge of the bluff overlooking Natchez Under-the-Hill. They went inside and found a pair of small rooms in the front of the building that could be used as office space and a set of rooms upstairs that could be updated for a living space.

"I can see a large desk in that room, and you with your feet up on it while you count all the money you earn." Judah's teasing words made Jeremiah laugh.

"I'm much more likely to be down at the waterfront making sure the shipments find their way to the correct boats."

"Once you get this place fixed up, I cannot imagine wanting to leave it. I can almost hear the deals being made between your business and the local farmers." Judah hobbled across the room and looked out a dirt-streaked window. "They'll be lining up outside to sell you their cotton."

Jeremiah watched his friend, glad to see the liveliness in his expression. It was good to see Judah animated. He seemed to have forgotten his infirmity for a few moments. If only Judah could stay here and run things. . . It would give Jeremiah more time to do what he wanted to do—work the land and make meaningful changes.

Inspiration struck as suddenly as a summer storm. "What would you think of managing the business for me?"

Judah turned so quickly he almost fell over. "I. . .I don't know the least thing about the shipping business."

"I can teach you what you'll need to know." Jeremiah's voice grew more certain as the details fell into place in his mind. "You can start by making inquiries in town for the furniture we'll need."

"That's ridiculous. I'm a farmer. If it wasn't for this leg. . ." He waved a hand downward as his voice faded.

Jeremiah dropped his chin and raised an eyebrow. "Instead of focusing on your problems, you should consider my suggestion. You would be a natural." Certainty flooded him. He knew this was right. All he had to do was convince his friend.

Judah's serious gaze wandered around the room. "I don't know. . . ."

Silence invaded the room as Jeremiah waited for his hesitant friend to think about his idea. A prayer filled his heart. Would this be the right path for Judah? And what about Susannah?

Judah turned back to him, excitement animating his face. "Hickman O'Grady made a couple of the pieces we have at home. He has a shop a few blocks away. We can go see what he might have to offer in the way of furnishings."

"I'll leave that up to you. I need to go by the bank and make a few other stops." Jeremiah withdrew his pocket watch. "I'll meet you back here in a couple of hours."

Judah nodded and made his way to the door.

Jeremiah could hear his friend's excited voice directing the coachman. He glanced toward the ceiling, the grateful outpouring of David's Psalm 103 filling his heart. " *'Bless the Lord, O my soul: and all that is within me, bless his holy name.'* Thank You, Lord. You are so faithful to Judah and to me."

The future opened up in front of him, stunning him with its possibilities. God had blessed him beyond his greatest imaginings.

Chapter 18

Alexandra gazed at the dresses comprising her wardrobe. Should she choose the black silk with gray rosettes? Or the black bombazine with its gray fichu? Or maybe the black taffeta skirt unrelieved by any hint of color. She looked toward Jemma. "You pick one of them."

Jemma shook her head. "Now, Miss Alexandra, you're too partic'lar for that."

She raised her gaze to the ceiling and blew out a breath of disgust. "They're all black, so what does it matter?"

The way her slave stared at her made Alexandra's cheeks flush. She looked at the faded brown homespun dress Jemma always wore. She knew she ought to be grateful for what she had. Things could be worse—she and Mama could be homeless, working their fingers to the bone washing clothes or making soap. Then she wouldn't have to worry what to wear because, like Jemma, she would own only one dress.

She finally pointed to the dress with the nice fichu. "I want to look my best in church without overdoing it."

Jemma picked up the dress and helped her get it over her petticoat, tugging and fussing until each fold of material was hanging just so. Then she tweaked a few strands of hair that had been mussed. "Will you be wearing your hat, or did you want the lace scarf?"

Alexandra considered a moment before choosing the gray scarf and sitting down in front of her dressing table. Jemma fastened the delicate material over her hair with several pins. When it was secure, Alexandra rose and picked up her fan and the black reticule that would hold her handkerchief and a few hairpins. "I believe I am ready."

"Yes, ma'am. You look real nice."

"Thank you, Jemma." Alexandra went downstairs to meet the other members of her family.

"Put on your cloak so we can get started." Grand-mère rose slowly and looked her over with a discerning gaze. "And remember to hold your head high. The way to deal with burgeoning scandal is to face it head on."

Alexandra wanted to run back upstairs and refuse to come out, but she knew her grandmother would never allow such behavior. She didn't want to face anyone, not with the memory of Lowell's frozen features so clear in her mind. What if he cut her? She glanced at her grandmother and decided with a lift of her chin that she would never let them see her discomfiture.

"That's the spirit, girl." Her grandmother allowed a cloak to be settled across her bent shoulders. "Don't ever forget you're as good as any of them. Your grandfather and I settled in this area long before most of the upstarts we'll see this morning. You have nothing to hang your head about."

The carriage ride was bumpy. And crowded. Squeezed between Aunt Patricia's generous curves and her mother's angular bones, Alexandra wished she could have sat outside with the driver. At least then she could see the ruts ahead and brace herself. She was certain she would be black and blue before evening.

Their arrival caused a bit of a stir, probably because the service had already begun by the time they entered the church. Alexandra could feel the weight of curious gazes as they walked down the central aisle in search of available seats. She knew her grandmother had wanted them to arrive late as if in defiance of anyone's disapprobation.

The pastor halted in the middle of leading a congregational hymn. "Welcome, Mrs. Tanner. I'm glad you and your family could join us."

Grand-mère inclined her head before waving her hand. "You may continue, Preacher."

A wave of giggles swept the congregation. The pastor's cheeks reddened. He cleared his throat, adjusted his spectacles, and resumed the hymn. When he had finished leading the congregation in singing, he began his sermon by reading the Sermon on the Mount from Matthew's Gospel. " 'Blessed are they that mourn: for they shall be comforted.' "

Alexandra wanted to get up and walk out. Jesus' promises were empty. When Papa died, no one was there to comfort her or Mama. She reached for her mother's hand and squeezed. *Never mind,* she wanted to tell her mother. *I am here for you even if God is not.*

Her mother's hand was so cold. She seemed to be fading away right in front of her family. She went through the motions of living—needlework in the parlor, eating meals in the dining room, responding when she was asked a question. But Alexandra could not think of a single conversation her mother had initiated since their arrival in Natchez. She remembered how much she had hoped coming home would help her mother cope with the grief, but nothing seemed to pierce the fog that surrounded her.

How Alexandra wished she could make things better. Would marriage to Lowell make a difference? She looked around surreptitiously for his familiar features, and her gaze locked with Dorcas Montgomery's. She was reduced in an instant to the level of a child. She wanted to stick out her tongue at the woman or scrunch her face into an ugly expression. Instead, she smiled sweetly. The look on Dorcas's face turned as sour as old milk. Alexandra's smile widened. Keeping her composure had its benefits.

She turned her head in the other direction and wondered how she could have missed the fiery reddish-blond hair and broad shoulders of the man sitting at the far end of their pew. Jeremiah LeGrand was studying his Bible as if it held the answer to all of life's difficulties. She could feel her nostrils flaring. Did he really believe what the pastor was saying? Apparently so.

He was quite the conundrum to her. He'd been so kind on the ride home in the carriage after the disaster at Lowell's home, yet he had not hesitated to reprimand her when she'd been rude. And then in the Hugheses' barn, for a moment she thought she saw attraction in his gaze. But when she'd tried to let him know she was receptive, he had retreated behind an impenetrable wall.

Her grandmother cleared her throat and shook her head at Alexandra. Chastened, the young woman returned her attention to the pulpit.

The pastor had apparently finished with the New Testament. "When Job heard he had lost all of his cattle and children, he mourned greatly, but he refused to turn from God. His wife told him he should, but Job held onto his faith, and even though he had to face many trials and doubts before God restored him, he was restored." He flipped through the pages of his Bible. "The Bible says he was blessed to receive even more than he had lost, including livestock, three beautiful daughters, and seven sons."

Alexandra wondered if God would return her to the prosperity, hope, and happiness she had once enjoyed. She didn't see how it was possible. Not after what had happened at Lowell's house. Neither he nor anyone else was going to want to marry her. She would probably end up an old maid living off Grand-mère's generosity. Or maybe there was some old widower who would marry her in spite of the scandal. She shuddered at the thought and hoped things would not get that desperate.

Perhaps Uncle John and Aunt Patricia would give her some land like they had done for Tobias. But then how would she manage? She couldn't imagine washing her own clothes, growing her own food, or even trying to keep her house clean. No, she needed to find a husband. Someone who would care for her and give her back the things she used to have.

"I think one of the lessons of Job is to trust God to have our best interests at heart. God sometimes allows us to be tested, but He is always there waiting for us to turn to Him. Once we do, He is faithful to deliver us."

Alexandra considered the man's words as he prayed to end the service. She followed her family out of the church, waving to Susannah and Judah. She was unable to get close enough to them to speak because of the crush of the people in the aisle.

Grand-mère took her time, making sure to stop and speak to anyone who was anyone.

Someone's elbow dug into her side, nearly oversetting Alexandra, and a large hand wrapped around her waist.

"Excuse me." She glanced up to see who had saved her from an embarrassing tumble. Jeremiah's face was only inches from her own, causing her heart to flutter. Her breath caught, and for an instant, it seemed they were the only ones in the room. He smiled at her, showing those intriguing dimples, and her lips trembled into a weak smile. But then reality intruded. What must this man think of her? That she was always in need of rescuing? She pulled away from him. "Let me go."

"Pardon me." His hand fell away. "I was worried you would fall."

Someone else jostled her, and Alexandra was pushed back against his broad chest with a soft *oof*. His hand captured her elbow, his arm warm across her back. Perhaps she did need someone to keep her safe. But why did his touch send her heart climbing up her throat?

Safe in the shelter of his strength, Alexandra allowed herself to be guided to the front door. She barely noticed when her grandmother stopped to speak to Governor Holmes, the affable man chosen by President Jefferson, when he was still in office, to govern the territory. Everyone said he would make a good governor if Mississippi ever gained statehood. She smiled and curtsied when Grand-mère introduced her. The governor bowed and turned to greet the man standing next to her. Her mind was too preoccupied with her reaction to Jeremiah's closeness to pay attention to the conversation.

Another voice, one that sounded petulant in contrast to Jeremiah's deep tones, called her name. Alexandra turned and felt her heart thump back into place. "Lowell, h–how are you doing?"

He looked as handsome as ever, and was that contrition she saw in his gaze? "I'm so glad to see you this morning. I've wanted to talk to you about what happened. . .you know, about what Dorcas said."

Now her traveling heart moved further downward, apparently reaching toward her toes. She realized Jeremiah had stopped talking. She could feel both men's gazes on her. Both listening intently. Alexandra licked her lips and raised her chin. "If you wanted to apologize for your boorish behavior in not defending my reputation, all you had to do was come to visit, something you've done any number of times since my arrival." How amazing that she had managed to get all those words out without the slightest stumble.

Dorcas came out of the church then and walked toward them.

Not wanting to hear anything that woman had to say, Alexandra turned away. . .and met Jeremiah's intense gaze. What was he thinking? Was he sympathetic to her dilemma? Or appalled at her outspokenness?

Her heart clenched at the possibility of his disapproval. Before he could confirm her worst fear, Alexandra hurried to her grandmother's carriage. She'd better have her relatives send for the doctor. Something was definitely wrong with her heart.

Chapter 19

Sunday luncheon was an interminable affair. Alexandra pushed her food around on her plate while her grandmother relived every moment of the church service, including Alexandra's tirade at Lowell Sheffield.

"You did very well, my dear." The gray-haired woman pointed a finger at Alexandra. "You administered quite the set down. I don't doubt that young man will come by before the day is over."

Alexandra could not dredge up any excitement over the idea of entertaining Lowell. Why did she wish it was Jeremiah who would be coming to visit instead of Lowell? "You may be right, Grand-mère. But it's amazing how little I care."

Mama looked up at her rebellious tone. "Alexandra, whatever is wrong with you? You know what you must do."

Now her mother wanted to rejoin them? And why did she have to align herself with Grand-mère? Why wouldn't anyone take her part? Would she spend the rest of her life defending herself from attack? She pushed back from the table and swept out of the room before the tears could escape.

The door to her grandfather's study beckoned. It had been a refuge when she was growing up, a place where she felt unconditional acceptance. Alexandra's tears disappeared, replaced by a crushing weight. She was so weary, so drained.

She opened the study door and went in, her gaze traveling from the tall, book-filled shelves to her grandfather's wide, walnut desk. It looked exactly as it had in her childhood. If she closed her eyes, she could almost hear his deep voice barking orders for the day's work. Walking to the nearest bookcase, she saw the worn cover of his Bible. She pulled the book out of its place and went to a large leather chair near the cold fireplace, glad the room was warm enough that a fire was not necessary.

She slipped off her shoes and curled up in the chair, holding the large volume in her lap and wondering why it was not used more often by her relatives. She could not remember ever seeing Grand-mère read from a Bible. When Alexandra was a child, her mother had talked about her own parents' faith. What had happened to make Grand-mère turn from the faith that had once sustained her? Or had she merely pretended to believe to appease Grandpapa?

She opened the Bible with a sigh. Perhaps things would have turned out differently if this book had not been tucked away in his study.

Isaiah, the prophet. Not a very good place to start. Maybe she could find the verses about comforting the mournful. Underlined words stayed her hand: *"But Zion said, The Lord hath forsaken me, and my Lord hath forgotten me."*

The words resounded with her. If God really was there, He had forgotten all about her. But the underlining didn't stop there.

"Can a woman forget her sucking child, that she should not have compassion on the son of her womb? yea, they may forget, yet will I not forget thee. Behold, I have graven thee upon the palms of my hands; thy walls are continually before me."

The promise in the underlined verses was impossible to miss. She opened up her hand and looked at the palm. According to these words, God had written—no, *engraved*—her in the palms of His hands. A tear slipped down her cheek. Engraved in His hand. The truth was almost impossible to believe. Yet there it was. His answer to her complaint. God had not forgotten her after all.

Alexandra closed the book and slipped out of the chair to her knees. She steepled her hands and closed her eyes. Words seemed unnecessary as God's love filled the silent room. Her heart, her very soul, writhed as she confessed her doubt and sin. Then it was gone, and she knew. Christ had interceded for her. With boundless love, He had given His best for her. His blood had washed away her sin. The wonder of His truth washed over her, and peace settled on her shoulders. Never again would she have to wonder if He cared. She knew it with every fiber of her being.

Alexandra would have spent the rest of the afternoon in her grandfather's study if she hadn't heard someone calling her name. She rose with a contented sigh. She was a different person than the one who had sought solace here. When she opened the door, she came face-to-face with Aunt Patricia.

"What on earth have you been doing, Alexandra?"

She glanced back over her shoulder before answering. "I was talking to God."

A smile creased Aunt Patricia's face. She gave Alexandra a hug. "What a perfect thing to do on the Sabbath."

"I. . .I have been ignoring Him ever since Papa's death. But today He got my attention in the most wonderful way. Did you know our names are engraved on His hand?"

Aunt Patricia laughed and hugged her again. "Of course. Isn't it wonderful?"

Alexandra nodded. "Were you looking for me?"

"Oh my, yes." Aunt Patricia stepped back. "I almost forgot. Young Sheffield has arrived as my mother predicted. He seems full of remorse and quite eager to see you."

A shrug lifted Alexandra's shoulders. "I am not sure he and I have anything to say to each other."

"I know he must have hurt your feelings terribly, Alexandra, but you cannot hold a grudge against him, not when you have so recently been reminded of God's grace. How many times do you think you have disappointed Him?"

Remorse filled her heart. "When you put it that way, I have to agree." Now it was Alexandra's turn to offer a hug. "It's disconcerting how quickly I can forget what I just learned."

"Yes, that is why we should seek out the company of other Christians. They help us stay accountable."

Alexandra's mouth turned up in a smile. "Thank you."

"That's quite all right, dear. Now go in there and visit that anxious young man."

When she opened the door to the parlor, Lowell's back was turned toward her. His head was bent as though he was depressed. She must have made some sound because he twisted around to face her.

She smiled, feeling God's peace inside her as warm and bright as a candelabra. "I'm so glad to see you, Lowell."

Chapter 20

The harvest is almost finished." Jeremiah looked over the fields with satisfaction. The white bolls of cotton had been picked, and most of them had been ginned to separate the seeds from the usable fibers. He strode to a nearby barn and pulled open the wide doors, waiting for Judah to catch up to him.

"It's hard for me to believe all you've managed to get done." Judah's voice was full of appreciation. "And it's something I can never repay."

Jeremiah rolled his eyes and flung a hand out to indicate the stacks of tightly packed bales. "We haven't turned all this into money yet."

"Jeremiah, Master Judah." Oren, the slave who had been so valuable to him for the past several weeks, walked over to them. "We's about to start piling the cotton into wagons."

"That's good." Jeremiah smiled at the man. "You've done a great job. I've been telling Judah how much help you've been."

"Yes." Judah leaned against the wall. "I am so pleased with all the work you've done."

A wide smile split the man's face. He bent the upper part of his body in a partial bow. "Thank you, sir. I was worried 'bout things for a while, but Jeremiah here, he got things working real smooth. He's been good to all us slaves. We would do anything for him, and you and the missus, o' course."

"Thank you, Oren. It was a real pleasure to work with you and the others." Jeremiah could feel Judah's surprised gaze on him. He shrugged. He hadn't done anything miraculous, just treated the slaves like men instead of property. He supposed he'd earned their respect because he'd worked right alongside them, refusing to quit until the work was done. It had been a backbreaking but rewarding exercise. A part of him wished it was not over.

The sound of a wagon trundling toward them made Jeremiah step back. "How many loads do you think it will take, Oren?"

Oren looked at the wagon and then at the stacks of bales. "I guess we can get about a hun'erd bales to a load. And there's the two wagons." He squeezed his face tightly as he considered. "Mebbe three or four trips to town will do 'er."

Jeremiah nodded. "That's what I was thinking. It will take us half a day for each load, so we won't be done until tomorrow or maybe Wednesday." He turned to Judah. "What do you think about using the storehouse in the back of my new shipping office? That way we won't be forced to sell to the first captain who offers us a price."

Judah nodded. "A sound suggestion. What are you going to charge for storing the bales?"

"Nothing at all."

"Jeremiah, I cannot continue letting you shoulder all of my responsibility. You've done more than I ever dreamed. It's time to let me start repaying my debt."

"I've been thinking about that. . . ." Jeremiah let the words drift off.

"Don't tell me." Judah laughed so hard his shoulders shook. "You've got an idea."

Jeremiah joined him. It felt good to laugh. To enjoy the bounty of this day.

Oren looked from one to the other of them, a tentative smile on his face.

It took a few moments, but the laughter finally came to an end. Jeremiah clapped his friend on the shoulder. "Yes, I do. But why don't we let Oren get started working out here? I want to explain my idea to both you and Susannah at the same time."

He gathered up the slaves who would load and transport the cotton, explaining what needed to be done before leaving Oren in charge. Then he and Judah walked back to the main house. "I cannot tell you how much I've enjoyed these days."

"You are a different man from the one I knew in New Orleans."

Jeremiah considered the statement as he helped Judah negotiate the steps to the front porch. "I feel different, too. It's almost like being closer to God to bring the crops to maturity and harvest them."

The two men went inside and found Susannah in the parlor, cutting out squares for a quilt. She glanced up as they entered. "What are the pair of you up to? You look as though you've been involved in some mischief."

Judah sat next to her on the sofa and leaned his crutches against the wall. "We were out checking the cotton, but Jeremiah says he has something he wants to talk to us about."

Jeremiah went to the fireplace and held his hands out toward the dancing flames. He closed his eyes and prayed for the right words to explain his hopes to these friends. If they agreed, he believed things would go more smoothly for all three of them, but he wanted more than anything to follow God's will. Taking a deep breath, he turned to the couple. "First of all, I'd like to say how much I appreciate your letting me work on the cotton harvest these past weeks. It has always been a dream of mine to farm, and you've helped me realize that dream."

Judah opened his mouth, but Jeremiah forestalled him with a shake of his head. "I don't want to get bogged down in compliments and comparisons this morning, so please hear me out. You did an excellent job getting the new office ready for business, Judah. I couldn't believe how much you accomplished in such a short time. The apartment upstairs still needs work, but I think it could be made livable, even for a couple."

He glanced toward his friends and let a smile bend his mouth upward. "I also purchased several acres behind the office that are currently vacant. My idea is to build a home on that property, one large enough to house the owner and his family. That way, he will be close to his family even when he's working. I don't think it will take long to build the house as there seems to be an abundance of capable workers in town. I am hoping it will be finished and the owner can take up residence before next autumn."

"I don't understand, Jeremiah." Susannah put down her mending and frowned at him. "You sound like you are not planning to stay here and run your shipping business."

Jeremiah nodded. "That's right. I have never enjoyed the business like my uncle does. I have already written to him telling him I didn't relish the idea of returning to the shipping industry and asking if he would consider allowing a young couple I know to join his business." Jeremiah reached into his pocket and pulled out a folded note. "He wrote back that he likes the idea of incorporating another family into LeGrand Shipping, and he is delighted to have a war hero for a business partner." He waited for the meaning of his words to sink in.

Susannah looked at her husband. "It's the answer to our prayers."

Judah looked at each of them, clearly torn. "I don't know. . . ."

A glance upward accompanied Jeremiah's prayer for the right words. "I know this will be a big change for you, so I'd like for you to take your time and discuss it thoroughly. If you have any doubts at all, we can talk it over beforehand."

It seemed to be the reassurance his friend needed. "I don't think there's any need for that." Judah glanced toward his wife and received a nod. "Susannah and I would be foolish to reject your offer." He picked up his crutches and pulled himself up. Leaning his weight against them, he held out his right hand.

Jeremiah crossed the distance to the sofa in two strides. He gripped Judah's hand firmly. "You don't know what this means to me."

Susannah stood up next to them. "You don't know what it means to us, either. I don't know why we didn't think of it ourselves. It makes so much sense. Your talent in running a plantation is obvious from the work you've managed to accomplish. And living in town is the perfect answer for me and Judah." She leaned up and placed a kiss on Jeremiah's cheek. "Sometimes I think you are an angel sent from God."

"Maybe not an angel." Judah put an arm around his wife. "But he does remind me of Abraham, who walked without question the path God set out before him."

While Jeremiah felt uncomfortable with their lavish praise, he did feel God's hand at work and could only praise Him for His loving guidance on all their lives.

Chapter 21

Jeremiah's fingers tangled in the folds of his cravat. He seemed to have lost the ability to dress himself. He could not be nervous about hosting his first party as the owner of Magnolia Plantation. His gaze fell on the folded papers he and Judah had signed to formalize their exchange and thanked God for working things out to both their benefits over the past month.

Someone knocked at the door to the master bedroom.

"I'll be down in a few minutes." He walked over and jerked the door open as he spoke, expecting that Susannah had sent someone to hustle him downstairs.

He was not surprised to find Ezekiel standing there. "I come to see if you need help, master." The weathered face of the former slave whom he now employed as a butler/valet focused at a point somewhere behind him.

Jeremiah stepped back. "Ezekiel, haven't I asked you not to call me master? You are a free man now. I am your employer. The Lord is your only Master."

"Yessir, mas—I mean Mister Jeremiah." A smile of pleasure split the man's face. "I guess I'm het up over all the excitement downstairs. What with Miss Susannah worrying 'bout you getting downstairs before yore guests start arriving..."

"If you can, help me with this cravat. I can't seem to make the silly thing cooperate." He turned back to the mirror and tugged on his shirt collars, which were beginning to droop a little.

Ezekiel clucked his tongue. "Let me see that."

Jeremiah sighed and raised his chin.

It only took a moment or two before Ezekiel stepped back. "Is that better?"

A glance in the mirror confirmed that he had chosen his valet well. "Perfect. I don't know what I'd do without you, Ezekiel."

The other man chuckled. He picked up the frock coat lying across Jeremiah's bed and held it up. "It's good to have a little help here and there."

Jeremiah eased his arms into the coat and waited while Ezekiel smoothed the material over his shoulders. "I feel like a trussed up chicken."

Ezekiel shook his head. "You look nice. Like the gentleman you are. Now why don't you get on downstairs before Miss Susannah comes up here to find you."

The look that passed between them was full of understanding. All the people working for him at Magnolia Plantation knew Jeremiah did not relish social gatherings. He headed toward the entrance hall with a sigh and prayed the evening would end quickly.

Judah was waiting for him at the foot of the stairs. "Susannah was beginning to fear you weren't going to be here in time to greet your guests."

"Where is your lovely wife?" He glanced around him. Candles and flowers seemed to fill every corner and surface of the vestibule, but he saw no sign of Susannah.

"She's gone to see about a trunk of items your housekeeper has collected for shipment to our apart—"

"If I never move again it will be too soon." Susannah's voice interrupted him. She moved gracefully toward them, her blond curls bobbing as she shook her head. "I never realized how much we had accumulated since moving here. And I don't know where we're going to put it until our new house is finished."

Jeremiah bowed to her. "You are most welcome to store everything here until you have more room. I know you and Judah must be cramped in your rooms above the shipping office."

"Nonsense." She reached up and patted his cheek. "I've no doubt you will soon settle down with a wife and family and will need every inch of space for them."

He grimaced. "Don't be so certain. I am content with things as they are for now."

Judah winked at him. "Susannah can't help herself. She's a born matchmaker."

The diminutive woman smiled toward her husband. "Can I help wanting others to experience the happiness we have?"

The loving look they shared made Jeremiah feel like an outsider. Would he ever find a woman to share his life? The arrival of the first guests ended his speculation. He waited while Judah performed the introductions, spoke to the couple briefly, and gestured toward the ballroom as the next visitors entered.

He recognized many of the guests from church, including the pastor and Mr. and Mrs. Sheffield, who arrived with their son, Lowell. But there were others he had never met previously. There was a pause in the flow of guests after the arrival of one such family.

"I cannot believe the Osbournes came." Judah leaned against the oak balustrade behind him.

Susannah frowned at him. "Why wouldn't they come? I made sure to include them. I am sorry their oldest daughter ran away from home, but that is no reason to exclude the rest of the family. And their youngest girl, Felicity, is of marriageable age."

"I didn't say you should not have invited them." Judah straightened and stepped toward his wife. Jeremiah could not help but compare his friend's animation and energy against the bitterness and defeat that had once ruled Judah. Running the shipping business in town had given his friend a reason to believe in himself once more. "I am just surprised they ventured out. This is the first party they've attended since the scandal became common knowledge."

The rest of the conversation was cut off as the front door opened once more for the Tanner family. The matriarch, Mrs. Tanner, entered first, her cane tapping the marble floor. She was followed by the rest of the family— John and Patricia Bass, Mrs. Lewis, and finally the beautiful Alexandra Lewis. Jeremiah found himself unable to tear his eyes away from her. She looked so elegant in her finery, her dark hair piled high on her head, her eyes glowing in the reflected light of the candles.

"Have the Sheffields already arrived?" Mrs. Tanner's question brought his attention back to her.

"Yes, ma'am." He bowed over her hand even though her question cut through him like a sword thrust. "Welcome to Magnolia. I hope you and your family enjoy yourselves this evening."

"That remains to be seen." She moved away, followed by her daughter and son-in-law.

Alexandra's mother was next, her whispered greeting barely reaching his ears before she followed her relatives into the ballroom.

Alexandra dropped a curtsy and held out her hand, encased in a black glove. As Jeremiah took it, he wished he could think of something witty to say. Something that would impress her. But his brain turned to mush. He barely managed to get out the necessary greeting before watching her enter the ballroom.

"I imagine most everyone has arrived." Susannah held a hand out to her husband. "Let's join them in the ballroom."

The orchestra had been playing for some time now, and the ballroom floor had become crowded with couples of all ages. His gaze rested on a lone young woman who stood a little apart from the rest of the young, single ladies hoping to be partnered for the next dance. He recognized her as Miss Osbourne, the girl whose older sister had caused a scandal. Perhaps he should ask her to dance.

He headed toward her but was cut off by a group of talkative debutantes who moved in her direction. Miss Osbourne looked up at their approach, an expression of hope on her face. One of the young women pointed at her and giggled, another put a hand to her mouth, while the third girl simply turned her face away. It was the cut direct. His heart went out to her. Another innocent condemned by the narrow dictates of local society.

Miss Osbourne's face crumpled, and she ran toward the nearest exit which he knew led to the library. He started to follow her, wanting to reassure her, but before he could take a single step, someone brushed past him. The scent of lemons filled the air. Alexandra Lewis. She hurried out the same door Miss Osbourne had taken. Was she intent on comforting the girl? His heart warmed. What better person to speak to her than someone who had endured a similar experience? He turned back to the ballroom and assumed his responsibilities as host.

Jeremiah smiled and made his way around the room, speaking to everyone and answering whatever questions came his way. Yes, he had freed his slaves. Yes, he had supplied land and seed for those eager to support themselves, as well as hiring many of the former slaves to help him on the plantation. No, he had no fear of being murdered in his own bed. He made it a point to speak to Mr. and Mrs. Osbourne, hoping his actions would be copied by his other guests.

He was about to go in search of Miss Osbourne and Alexandra when they returned to the ballroom. Alexandra beckoned toward Lowell Sheffield, who moved toward her. Even though he was several feet away, Jeremiah could hear her as she introduced her beau to the shy young woman at her side. Lowell dutifully asked the girl to dance, and the pair of them left Alexandra standing alone.

A desire to thank Alexandra for her thoughtfulness overwhelmed him, and he moved toward her. "May I have this dance?"

Her dark gaze met his own. "I am flattered, sir."

Jeremiah led her to the center of the room as the orchestra began playing a minuet. He had to concentrate on the steps and therefore did not get to speak his mind. But as soon as the music died away, he took her by the arm. "I'd like a word with you if you have a moment."

Color rose in her cheeks, but she nodded and allowed him to lead her through one of the arched doorways onto the wide balcony outside.

"What did you wish to say to me?" Even though there was little light out here, he could see that her shoulders were squared and her chin was high.

"I am very impressed that you left the party to comfort Miss Osbourne." He wished he could see the expression on her face as she absorbed his words. But all he could see was the shrug of her shoulders.

"Jeremiah, you are the one who taught me to reach out to others when they are hurting. How could I do less for that poor young woman than you did for me? She just needed someone to remind her of God's love."

Her lemony perfume enveloped him once again, making him think of warm breezes and long summer afternoons. He couldn't stop himself from leaning toward her. She was so sweet, so sincere in her explanation. Even though he would never have wished such pain on her, he could see how much maturity it had brought her. She was no longer the self-centered girl he had met in Natchez Under-the-Hill. And he found himself falling in love with the young woman she had become.

His heart pounded. Falling in love? With Alexandra Lewis? He cleared his throat and tried to marshal his thoughts. "Alexandra. . .I—"

"Alexandra, there you are." Light seemed to flood their corner of the balcony as Lowell pulled back a curtain and stepped toward them. "Your grandmother told me to come find you. She wants to see us dancing together."

Jeremiah could not think of a way to prevent the young man from inserting himself between them. He watched as she smiled up at Lowell. Was that relief on her face? Or were the shadows playing tricks with him? Yet she never looked back as Sheffield led her to the ballroom.

And why should she? Her future had already been set for her. Her kindness this evening had probably been nothing more than a performance for the benefit of Lowell and his family. Why else would she choose to return with him to the dancing?

He was a fool for thinking she had changed. Without God's intervention, she would never be anything more than a shallow girl intent on securing her place in local society.

Chapter 22

Sadness filled Alexandra as Lowell helped her into his carriage. She glanced back at Jeremiah LeGrand, so tall and straight, standing alone on the steps of the church. Last night's party did not appear to have endeared him to the townspeople. He looked like a boulder in a rushing stream, untouched by the men and women who brushed past him.

Lowell climbed up next to her and grabbed the reins. "What are you looking at?"

She turned and offered him a smile. "Nothing. I was just wondering if what I heard about Jeremiah LeGrand was true. Has he really bought Magnolia Plantation?"

"Yes. It's a disgrace. Pa says he's making a mockery of all the other planters. Did you know he's freed all of his slaves?" Lowell slapped the reins. "Claims he can make his plantation work by paying his laborers and allowing them to grow their own crops." Alexandra did not much care for the sneer he wore as he continued. "Several of our neighbors say it's going to lead to rebellion and maybe worse. We've instructed our overseers to report any suspicious activities among our own slaves."

Alexandra looked at the set face of the man beside her. "Is there any chance Mr. LeGrand is right? Slavery seems so terrible to me."

"Slavery is not terrible. It's been around for a long time. It's a biblical concept. Even the Jews used slaves to get their work done. In more than one place, the Bible warns slaves to work hard for their masters. Paul said they should do their best work like they are working for the Lord."

"But what about the farmer who paid wages to his workers in Jesus' parable?"

"You don't understand the least thing on this subject, Alexandra. If I set my slaves free, they wouldn't be able to fend for themselves. They would probably end up dead from starvation or become criminals who rob others of what they have."

Alexandra wanted to argue they could be taught skills. On her grandmother's plantation, many of the slaves worked as carpenters, blacksmiths, and bricklayers. They even had a cabinetmaker. Obviously these men were skilled. But Lowell did not give her a chance as he warmed up to his theme.

"I can't agree with people who mistreat their slaves, but as long as we feed and clothe them, they are better off than if they were free and had to deal with all the problems Pa and I have to solve. They're much like little children, happier when they are told where to go and what to do. In turn, their work makes it possible to produce the cotton the rest of the world wants. Without slaves, I would not be able to turn a profit."

"But what if Mr. LeGrand teaches his slaves a trade? Wouldn't that be a better solution for them and for him?"

The glance Lowell tossed at her was full of scorn. "I suppose it speaks well of your tender heart to be so concerned with the welfare of others, but you should leave such things to men."

Disbelief flashed through Alexandra. In previous days, she might have lashed out at Lowell for his attitude, but those days were gone. Her faith would not let her continue challenging Lowell's stance. She would pray for a change of heart for the man sitting beside her. Lowell was an intelligent, well-educated man. Surely he would eventually be open to new ideas.

A long, mournful whistle gained her attention. "That sounds like a steamboat." She put a hand on Lowell's arm. "Can we go to the waterfront and watch it come in?"

He glanced down at her hand and then into her eyes. She could tell by his gaze that Lowell was smitten. Alexandra's cheeks warmed at the message she read in his hazel eyes. She removed her hand as if it had been burned.

"Of course, I'll take you if you think your family won't mind."

Alexandra considered. "We won't stay long. I love seeing the paddlewheels churning through the water, and the people are so interesting."

"Pa says most of them are riffraff and wastrels looking for an easy life."

The flush drained out of her cheeks. "Lowell"—she could not keep the disappointment from her voice—"I cannot believe you said that. Many of those people have sold everything they own for passage here. They deserve our sympathy, not our scorn."

He didn't answer her as he maneuvered the carriage around to comply with her request, but the set of his chin told her he was not happy with her point of view. Another difference.

Alexandra was beginning to wonder if they had anything in common. They should have seen eye-to-eye on any number of topics, but the more they were together, the more she realized they did not. It was ironic. Lowell would probably ask for her hand in marriage in the next few days, but she wanted more than anything to tell him they would not suit.

He guided the carriage to the edge of a bluff between a pair of towering, leafless oak trees. The wind pulled at her scarf and cloak, burning her cheeks as it whipped around them. The discomfort disappeared, however, when she spotted the twin chimneys of the steamship coming around the bend. "Look, there it is."

"Careful, Alexandra." Lowell jumped down from the carriage and looped the reins around one of the lower limbs of the tree on his side of the carriage. He strode around to her side and held his arms up.

Alexandra put a hand in one of his, expecting him to steady her as she dismounted. Instead, he circled her waist with both hands and lifted her out of her seat, swinging her around before he allowed her feet to touch the ground. She was caught off guard by his move and a nervous giggle tried to escape from her throat. Not wishing to encourage his behavior, she clamped her lips together. She stepped away from him and faced the river. "Can you read the boat's name?"

"No." Lowell's voice sounded choked, but Alexandra refused to turn around. "I have something more interesting to watch."

"Really, what's that?" She glanced back over her shoulder for a moment. If his gaze had been ardent before, it was a raging fire now. A fire that threatened to consume her. She had to face him or risk losing control of the situation.

"You are so beautiful, Alexandra."

It was too soon. She wasn't ready. She didn't have her answer ready. She had to stop him from going further. "You are very sweet, Lowell, but I think you were right after all. We need to get back home. Everyone will be sitting down to dinner, and they'll wonder where I am." She met his gaze, hoping he would read the plea in hers.

A long moment of silence stretched between them. His breathing was labored, as if he'd run all the way up the bluff instead of driving. His gaze dropped to her mouth. Alexandra knew he was about to embrace her. What should she do? Let him have his way?

She felt his hands on her shoulders, pulling her closer. Her heart was thumping like an Indian drum. But was the feeling coursing through her anticipation or dread?

His eyes drifted closed, and he pursed his lips, making her want to giggle once more. He looked like a hooked fish. At the last minute she turned her head and his lips landed somewhere near the base of her ear.

"Lowell, stop." She pushed him away.

Ever the gentleman, Lowell allowed her to put some distance between them. "Alexandra, I have something I'd like to ask you about."

"Not now, Lowell. There's no time." She scrambled back into the carriage without any help, drew her cloak around her shoulders, and tapped her foot. "I have to get home."

He sighed and nodded. "Have it your way, Alexandra. But this cannot wait forever."

She chattered about every subject that came to mind all the way home, hardly allowing Lowell to insert a comment. She started with the sermon—an uplifting message based on Psalm 33—and ended with a one-sided discussion on the advantages of statehood. By the time they arrived at the house, she was winded.

Lowell looked confused. She could understand why. She felt the same way. That was why she had to postpone his proposal. She needed to pray for an answer about what to do.

Grand-mère still expected her to marry. Mama was counting on her to provide a home through an advantageous union. But could she truthfully repeat the oaths that would bind her to Lowell for the rest of their lives? Could she promise to honor and obey him? What about the differences that were becoming more obvious with each day that passed?

On the other hand, Lowell had decided to proceed with his courtship despite the scandal revealed during Dorcas's visit. But his loyalty was only a result of his family's respect for her grandmother's wealth. If she found herself as poor as she'd been in Nashville, she had no doubt Lowell would disappear.

So she smiled and thanked him for escorting her home. Then she left him standing on the porch and went inside to have Sunday dinner with her family. Perhaps she would figure out what to do before too much longer.

Chapter 23

Going to town felt like a terrible waste of time. Jeremiah had begun working with the blacksmith, a burly former slave who now received a wage for his craft. The horses and mules needed to be reshod, the plows needed to be sharpened and straightened, and rusty scythes needed to be replaced. The planting season was almost upon them, and Jeremiah was far from prepared.

But he could not turn down the request from his friends. Susannah wanted to show off the improvements they'd made to the building. Judah wanted his opinion on a problem with a shipment. And both accused him of becoming a hermit. So he left the blacksmith with detailed instructions, saddled his horse, and rode to town. Perhaps he would get back before sunset and do a little work.

Jeremiah arrived at the shipping office before mid-morning. The scene inside was hectic, with boat captains, farmers, and planters all vying for Judah's attention. His friend was methodical in his work, however, proving he was the right choice for this job. After haggling over prices, he posted a large sign with the day's rate for the available commodities and began to take orders and set up delivery dates and times.

The office eventually emptied out, and Judah sat back with a long sigh. "I can't believe I let you talk me into this work."

Jeremiah laughed. "I can't believe you are so good at it. My uncle had better watch out, or you'll soon own his whole company."

The smile on Judah's face was as wide as the river outside. He looked content. "I have a confession to make though. I don't really have a problem for you to help with."

"I'm not surprised, not after watching you this morning. You are so much more competent than I ever was. You could probably teach me a thing or two."

Judah grabbed his crutches and stood up. "Let's go upstairs. I'm certain Susannah has lunch ready by now. Then I want to take you down to the docks. There's a group down there I think you'll be interested in seeing."

"What kind of group?" Jeremiah waited while Judah locked the office door.

"You'll see."

The two men climbed the narrow staircase that led to the renovated apartment above the office and joined Susannah in the dining room. She was as full of energy as ever, pointing out all the items she'd purchased since his last visit and sharing her plans for flower and vegetable gardens as soon as their new house was completed. The talk between them was lively and fun. Jeremiah had forgotten what it was like to take his meals with friends. Maybe he was getting too reclusive.

"Are you ready, dear?" asked Judah when they finished eating.

Susannah pushed back from the table and nodded. "The carriage should be waiting." She winked at her husband. "You didn't tell him, did you?"

"Not a word."

"Hey." Jeremiah raised a hand. "The two of you are talking like I'm in another room. I'm right here."

Susannah glanced in his direction, a sly smile on her face. "So you are. Let's get our cloaks and be on our way."

The road that separated Natchez Under-the-Hill from the main part of town was steep but not difficult to negotiate. Jeremiah looked out of the window at the line of dugout canoes, keelboats, and steamboats vying for space along the banks of the river. He had forgotten how noisy it was, the mix of languages and accents, the shouts of vendors, and the sweet chorus of familiar hymns.

Hymns? Who would be singing hymns down here? He turned a startled glance toward his hosts, whose faces held identical, knowing smiles.

The carriage drew to a halt, and Jeremiah pushed the door open, jumping out before the coachman had time to let down the step. Ignoring his friends, he walked toward the sound of the singing.

" 'Through many dangers, toils, and snares. . .' "

His steps hastened. He rounded a corner. A crowd of immigrants, mostly children, lifted their voices to praise God. The sound filled the very air around him, almost angelic in its power and beauty. He could not resist joining them, adding his baritone to the wonderful mix of voices. When the last note drifted out over the surface of the water, he finally looked to the front to see who was leading this group. A trio of ladies stood together, dressed in fancy cloaks and hats.

His mouth dropped open. Alexandra? Was this the young woman he'd judged to be too conscious of her social standing? Too caught up in worldly matters? Yes, he'd seen a change in her during church services, but Jeremiah had never dreamed she could have come so far as to spend her time here. Yet there she stood, her aunt on one side, her mother on the other. She leaned over and whispered something to her mother, who nodded.

"Thank you so much for joining us." Alexandra's voice was not loud, but it carried well, even out here in the open. "It surely pleased God to hear our voices joined in praise. We have one other song that I think most of you will have heard. After that, please follow us to the green house down to your right where we will have a warm meal for everyone."

Her mother began singing first. " 'Eternal depth of love divine, in Jesus, God with us, displayed.' "

Alexandra and her aunt added their voices, and soon the crowd was singing again. He heard Susannah's soprano and Judah's bass behind him, but his attention centered on the girl who stood so calmly up front and brought hope to these tired and weary people.

The woman who had dismissed him as nothing more than a servant was now ministering to those less fortunate than she, while treating them with the same love Christ would have shown. She saw souls in need, not servants to meet her needs. How could he do anything except love her? He had always found Alexandra devastatingly beautiful, but now she had exceeded any notions he once held of the ideal wife.

As soon as the song was finished, he eased his way through the dispersing crowd. He wanted—no needed—to talk to her. "Alexandra!"

Her head turned, and their gazes met. Something passed between them, something wordless, spiritual, and loving. It was as though their souls embraced. Her eyes widened, and he knew she felt it, too. He reached her side and held out an arm.

She placed her hand on it. "Mr. LeGrand, you are looking well. Have you come to help us distribute food and blankets?"

He shook his head. . .then nodded.

Alexandra laughed. "Well, which is it? Yes or no?"

He swallowed hard. "I came with Judah and his wife. They didn't tell me you would be here."

Her velvet brown eyes darkened. "I don't know how I'm to take that. Are you saying you would not have come if you'd known?"

Jeremiah felt tongue-tied. He wasn't very adept at talking to women, but he'd never been quite this abysmal. "Not at all." He decided to try another tack. "Your singing was wonderful. I know the people here were blessed by it. You are providing them with the hope they need to continue their journeys."

A blush rose in her cheeks, and she broke eye contact. "It was my aunt's idea. She is so eager to share God's love. All I do is help where I can."

They were walking among the immigrants and dock-workers now, and he glanced around at the happy faces. "Don't diminish your contribution. Whenever you give of your time and the talents God has graced you with, you are doing His will, walking in the path He set for you."

Jeremiah would have continued, but they arrived at the house where the food would be handed out.

Alexandra broke away from him with a smile of thanks. "I have to go help the others. Thank you for escorting me here."

He bowed and let her be swept away from him. But he stayed to help, handing out what they had prepared. From time to time, he found himself standing close to her. But then they were separated once again. He hoped to escort her and her mother and aunt back to Tanner Plantation, but Susannah and Judah dragged him away before the women were ready to depart.

"Did you enjoy yourself this afternoon?" Susannah asked as the carriage climbed back up the hill.

"It was one of the best days I've had since I came to Natchez."

Judah groaned.

His wife laughed. "I told my husband you were in love with Alexandra Lewis. He didn't believe me. But I've known it for a long time now."

Heat climbed up Jeremiah's throat. How was it that Susannah had understood what he had been too blind to see? Women just seemed to know these things. What about Alexandra? How long had she known? "She is a fascinating young lady."

Judah wrapped his hand around his wife's. "Maybe so, but she is not nearly as fascinating nor as wise as the beauty I am married to."

"How can I argue with that statement?" Jeremiah was glad to have the attention removed from him. "Your wife is indeed a woman of integrity and charm, even if she is a little devious at times."

All three of them laughed and then began to talk of the people they had met that day. The sun was beginning to set by the time they made it back to the shipping office.

Even though they pressed him to stay for a while, Jeremiah refused. He had a lot to think and pray over this evening, and he needed solitude to do it.

Chapter 24

Dorcas Montgomery was on her way back to Nashville. Grand-mère had delivered the information with relish. "Now there's no reason not to bring young Sheffield to the point."

Alexandra swallowed hard. "I'm not sure that's going to work." They were sitting in the parlor, taking tea. At least they didn't have any visitors. Yet.

"Don't start that nonsense again, girl." Her grandmother slapped the arm of her chair. "You will smile prettily and say yes when he asks for your hand in marriage. If you don't, you will invite my extreme displeasure."

"Come, now." Aunt Patricia's tones were as phlegmatic as ever. "It's not as if you can put Beatrice and Alexandra out of your home."

Alexandra cast a thankful glance in her aunt's direction. "I promise to work very hard, Grand-mère. I don't like being a burden to you, but I don't want to link my future with a man I do not love."

"Love!" Her grandmother spat the word. "Love is for commoners. You have a duty to your family. To all the children you will one day have. A duty you—will—not—forsake." The last three words were said with such emphasis that Alexandra winced.

Before she could answer, however, the door opened, and the subject of their argument was announced. Lowell looked very fine, dressed in a cropped riding coat, his dark breeches tucked into polished black boots. He still held his hat and gloves in one hand but gave them to the maid before entering the room. "Good afternoon, ladies." He bowed to them and advanced toward Alexandra's grandmother. "You are looking very well, Mrs. Tanner."

"Thank you, Mr. Sheffield." She grabbed her cane. "Help me up, young man. I trust you won't be too disappointed to learn my daughter and I have business to see to upstairs."

Alexandra rose, too, but her grandmother shook her head. "You should stay here and entertain our guest."

Wishing the floor would swallow her up, Alexandra returned to her seat and watched as both of her relatives deserted her.

Lowell did not sit down as she expected. Instead, he took a turn about the room. "Alexandra, I'm sure you know why I've come today." He turned toward her, an expectant look on his charming features.

She leaned back against her chair and wished she'd thought to bring her fan to the parlor. "I. . .I suppose you wanted to see me."

He came to sit next to her on the sofa and reached for her hands. "Yes, but I have a very specific reason for doing so this afternoon." His palms were damp and cold, once again reminding her of a fish.

How could she ever say yes to him? Yet how could she say no? Alexandra withdrew her hands from his grasp and pushed herself up. She walked to the piano in one corner of the room and ran a finger across the keys. The sound was forlorn, echoing the sadness in her heart. She turned around and practically buried her nose in Lowell's chest.

He took a step back and captured her hands once again. Then he sank to one knee. "Alexandra Lewis, I adore you. Ever since you came back to Natchez, you have captured my imagination, my every waking thought. You are the perfect woman to become my wife. You will add charm and beauty to my home. Please say you'll marry me."

As proposals went, she supposed it was a good one. Alexandra was flattered by his declaration, but her heart was not touched. Everything in her screamed for escape. But Lowell was a good man, and she was supposed to obey her mother. Although the commandments did not mention grandparents, she felt that was a minor point. Grand-mère was providing for her and should be accorded the same respect. Her heart thumped unpleasantly. "Yes."

Lowell looked stunned for a moment, but then he recovered. He stood up and swept her into his embrace. "Thank you, dearest." He pulled away, bent at the waist, and pressed a fervent kiss on her hand. "You've made me the happiest of men."

Alexandra stared at the ruffle on his shirt, unable to relax. What had she done?

Chapter 25

The local newspaper had been folded next to Jeremiah's breakfast plate. He removed the domed cover to display a hearty breakfast of eggs, sausage, grits, and biscuits. After saying grace, he dug in and opened the paper to read the headlines. His eyes swept past a discussion of the evils of statehood and landed on an announcement.

His fork clattered to the table. He grabbed the paper and looked more closely. The words swam before his gaze. It could not be. But there it was in black-and-white. Alexandra Lewis had accepted a proposal from Lowell Sheffield. The woman he loved was in love with someone else. His heart shattered. The room darkened around him.

He looked again at the date. They were to be married in a month's time, at the end of April. Why the unseemly rush? Not that he would hesitate if he had secured her agreement. In fact, he would have pressed for an even earlier date. Lowell probably realized as well as he did that many men would like to call Alexandra theirs.

He threw the paper down on the table and pushed his chair back. His stomach roiled. He would never be able to finish his breakfast. The sustenance he needed could only come from turning to his Master. God would lend him wisdom and strength as He always had.

❀

Jeremiah saw Alexandra again at church the following Sunday. He thought he was prepared for the pain, but seeing young Sheffield standing so near her took his breath away.

Susannah and Judah stayed close to him, their expressions full of sympathy and sadness.

"You're a better man than he is." Judah's whisper took his attention away from Alexandra.

He shrugged and pushed his hands down into his pockets as they left the church.

"My husband is right, you know." Susannah's voice exposed her concern. "She is making a bad decision. You should go to her, tell her how you feel—"

"Stop right there." Jeremiah knew they meant their words for the best, but if they continued, he might lose his sanity and run screaming down the street. "I will be fine. She will be fine. I'm certain she is following God's lead.

Now let me go and congratulate them."

He strode away from them to face the couple. "Let me add my best wishes to those of the rest of the town."

Alexandra looked up at him, her eyes dark and fathomless. For a moment he thought he saw panic in their depths, but it must have been his imagination. "Thank you, Mr. LeGrand." Her smile was as bright as the first rays of the rising sun. "I trust you will be able to attend our wedding. My grandmother is planning the ceremony. We're inviting family and all of our friends."

Pain swept through him at her words, and he realized that he'd been hoping the betrothal announcement was a mistake. Or perhaps that Alexandra needed to be rescued from her overbearing grandmother. But she seemed to have embraced a future as the wife of Lowell Sheffield, a man who was his exact opposite.

This then was the real Alexandra Lewis. The woman he thought he'd seen glimpses of, the one he was in love with, must be a figment of his imagination. "I thought you were someone different, but I was obviously mistaken." He let his gaze sweep from her dark, perfectly coiffed curls to the tips of her pointed leather boots. She was no more than an empty-headed girl eager to enjoy the luxuries of her station. "I'm sure it will be everything you plan and exactly what you deserve."

He clamped his jaws shut when he saw the tiny frown between her brows. What was it about this woman that affected him so? Shame replaced his disgust at her choice. Why had he ever thought someone like Alexandra Lewis could change?

When did I become so harsh?

Sheffield put a possessive arm around her waist and sent a pointed gaze in his direction. "Did Mr. LeGrand say something to disturb you, my dear?"

She shook her head and turned to the next person in line.

Jeremiah realized he'd been dismissed. Without another word, he retrieved his horse, climbed into the saddle, and cantered back to the plantation. Once there, he threw himself into his usual chores with determination. Perhaps he could work himself free of the shame and regret eating at him.

❀

Alexandra ran up the stairs to her room and threw herself across her bed. Tears soaked her pillow, the same tears that had threatened ever since Jeremiah's scornful remarks after church this morning. He was right, of course. She was nothing but a shallow, spineless mouse who could not stand up for what she knew was right.

Some time later, when her tears were exhausted, a knock on her door made Alexandra sit up. "Come in."

Her mother peeked around the edge of the door. "Am I disturbing you, dear?"

Alexandra slid off her bed and rubbed at her hot eyes. "N–no."

"Oh, my darling daughter." Her mother stepped inside, closed the door behind her, and held out her arms. "Come here and tell me all about it."

With a sob, Alexandra complied, falling into her mother's embrace. She had only thought the tears were dried up. They gushed from some vast well inside her and slipped around the corners of her eyes. She felt like a child as her mother stroked her back and murmured comforting words in her ear. After all they had been through, it seemed their relationship had come full circle.

Alexandra finally pulled away, sniffing.

Mama pulled a handkerchief from the pocket of her skirt and patted her daughter's wet cheeks with it. Then she looped her arm through one of Alexandra's and led her to a chair. "Sit down and let's see if we can sort this out."

Alexandra took a deep breath, still feeling the hitch in her chest from all the crying she'd done. She watched as her mother pulled another chair around to face her. "I don't know what to say."

Her mother raised an eyebrow at her. "Let's start with the problem that is making you cry your heart out. This is a very special time in your life. A time when you should be happy and excited, looking forward to your nuptials and setting up your own household."

"I know. And I am happy. It's just that. . .just that I don't want to be shallow and uncaring." She stopped to consider her words. "I have only recently realized what it means to be a Christian. I want to do the Lord's work."

Her mother tilted her head. "And you don't think you can do that once you marry Lowell?"

Alexandra sighed. How could she explain the problem without exposing the real reason for her sorrow? Jeremiah's pointed words had pierced her deeply. Every line of his face had screamed disdain. She shouldn't care. He was practically a stranger, but somehow she wanted to earn his approbation. She wanted to see his blue eyes glow with appreciation the way they had last week when she'd seen him on the riverfront. It mattered more to her than she could have ever imagined.

Knowing she could not give her mother the real reason for her tears, she finally settled on something that would be understood. "Lowell and I don't always see eye-to-eye on matters."

"Oh." Her mother dragged the syllable out. "So you've had a tiff with your betrothed?"

"No. Lowell is very understanding, but he doesn't think I should worry about things like business and commerce."

"Alexandra, when have you ever cared about such things?"

She looked across at her mother, unable to argue the point. Mama was right. She had never cared about the topics men seemed to spend so much time discussing. Never wondered about slavery or politics. She had always focused on clothes and parties, flirting and gossip.

But her tongue was tied by her inability to fully reveal what was in her heart. She could hardly admit to Mama her feelings for a man to whom she was not betrothed. So she shook her head and twisted the handkerchief she was still holding. "I don't know."

"Well then, I guess we'll have to put it down to youthful dithering." Her mother sighed. "Perhaps your father and I did not raise you as we should have. My mother certainly thinks we allowed you too much freedom."

Too much freedom? When she couldn't even choose her own husband? She had no freedom at all. But now was not the time to make a complaint. Now was the time to do her duty for her family. "Don't worry." She turned to face her mother. "I won't let you down, Mama."

And she would not. Her mother was counting on her to make an advantageous marriage. "Everything is all right. Thank you for coming to talk to me. I'm feeling better now." Putting on her best smile, she pushed aside her doubts and her feelings for Jeremiah LeGrand.

Her mother stared at her for a few moments before nodding. "Just remember how much you've dreamed of having a husband and a home of your own. Lowell is the answer to your prayers." She stood up, gave Alexandra one last hug, and left her alone.

Even if her own life was falling apart, Alexandra was comforted to see her mother beginning to resume her life. For a while, she had thought Mama would never recover from Papa's death. At least that fear had proved to be groundless.

Perhaps her fears that she was marrying the wrong man would also turn out to be groundless.

Chapter 26

Jeremiah wiped sweat from his brow and shaded his eyes against the sun. A carriage and a pair of men on horses were riding up the lane toward his home. The gatekeeper, one of the freed slaves, came running to him. "Master Jeremiah, you got some fancy visitors comin' to see you."

He dropped the sledgehammer he'd been using to pound new fence posts into the ground. "Mark, didn't I tell you to stop calling me master?"

"Yessir. I'm sorry." The young man dug a toe in the ground.

Jeremiah put a hand on his shoulder. "It's okay. Now tell me what the men said."

Mark's eyes widened. "They said fo' me to come git you and tell you they was comin'."

He squeezed the boy's shoulder. "Okay, you've done what they asked. Now go on back to the gatehouse."

The young man, boy really, ran off.

Jeremiah walked to the well and raised a bucket of cool water, using it to wash his face and hands. Then he strode to the house, unrolling his sleeves as he walked. Too bad he didn't have time to change into fresh clothing, but it would be rude to keep his guests waiting that long.

He stopped to tell the cook to prepare scones and coffee before going to meet the men in his parlor. The tentative smile on his face disappeared when he saw Mr. Sheffield and his son, Lowell, standing to one side of the parlor, apparently discussing some divisive matter. A stocky, gray-haired man was staring into the fireplace. Randolph Fournier. Jeremiah recognized the man although he did not know him well. "What can I do for you gentlemen?"

Mr. Sheffield started as if Jeremiah had shot at him. Lowell shuffled his feet and looked at the floor. Mr. Fournier turned around and sketched a shallow bow before clearing his throat. "We've come on a very serious errand, I'm afraid."

The housekeeper entered the room with the tray he had ordered. Jeremiah thanked her and invited his guests to sit down. None of them spoke until she left the room.

Pouring the coffee carefully, he passed the brimming cups to each of them. "Please forgive my clumsiness. I am an awkward host."

Mr. Fournier took a sip from his cup, made a face, and set it down. "Your manners, or the lack of them, are not the reason we're here."

Mr. Sheffield turned down the coffee but took one of the scones from the tray. "Yes, we have heard a troubling rumor about how you're running this place. But instead of condemning you outright, we came to find out the truth of the matter."

Sitting back against the sofa, Jeremiah forced his fists to relax. He understood exactly why these men were here. They were going to try to force him to follow their rules. He crossed his arms over his chest. "Go ahead."

This time, Lowell spoke up. "Is it true you are paying your slaves—"

"Former slaves."

Lowell grimaced at the interruption. "Are you paying them for the crops they are raising on your land?"

"Yes." Jeremiah did not elaborate. The way he saw it, these men had no right to question the way he ran things at Magnolia. And if they thought they could stop him from doing what he thought was right, they would soon learn their mistake. He would never try to tell any of them how to run their estates, and he expected the same consideration from them.

"Preposterous." Mr. Fournier raised a white handkerchief to his nose and sniffed. "You come in here from who knows where and stir things up with your radical ideas. You may not realize how much trouble you're causing, but the whole town is in an uproar. Even the slaves. Don't think they haven't learned about what you've done. It's a wonder we haven't all been murdered in our beds. You have put all of us in danger. We will not allow anarchy to rule here."

"Mr. Fournier, Mr. Sheffield, Lowell"—he nodded to each man as he spoke their names, praying for temperance—"while I realize each of you is an experienced planter, you must realize that you do not have all the answers. This is my plantation, my home. And I will run it in the way I see best."

The older men looked shocked.

Lowell had a sneer on his face. "What did I tell you, Pa? This visit is a waste of time. He'll never listen to reason." His cup and saucer hit the table with a clatter. "We may as well be on our way."

"Please don't let me stop you." Jeremiah stood. "I wouldn't want to keep any of you from your busy lives."

"Well, I never." Mr. Fournier stood up and brushed his coat lapel free of crumbs with his handkerchief. "I suppose it's also true you're teaching your slaves to read and write?"

Jeremiah nodded.

"That is against the law, sir."

Jeremiah took a deep breath to steady himself. "As I said earlier, they are no longer slaves, and it is not against the law to educate free people."

The older man shook his head, his expression showing disgust. "You mark my words, LeGrand. You will not be allowed to continue flaunting our traditions. Don't make the mistake of ignoring our advice."

"I wouldn't dream of ignoring you, sir." Jeremiah opened the door and swept his hand in a wide arc. "But I will not be intimidated by someone just because he doesn't agree with my views." He called for the carriage and horses to be brought around and escorted his guests to the front porch. "Now if you will excuse me, gentlemen." He rolled up his sleeves and brushed past them, taking the front steps two at a time. "I have several jobs to finish before the day is over. Thank you for your visit."

Jeremiah knew his guests seethed as they departed, but he was determined to stand firm in what he truly felt God was leading him to do. No matter what any of them said or did.

Chapter 27

And I'm not sure about inviting the Anderson family, my dear." Mrs. Sheffield's hazel eyes sharpened, reminding Alexandra of her betrothed.

Alexandra took her pen and carefully inscribed the name on the list. "I'm not sure I know them."

"That's not surprising. They do not have any children your age. Their oldest son, Charles, went to sea when he was just a lad. He doesn't come home often. And their girls, Catherine and Christine, married Kaintuck boatmen." She shook her head. "It was a terrible scandal because they chose husbands so far beneath them. I don't think their poor parents ever recovered."

Wondering if she'd been caught up in a nightmare, Alexandra pushed back an errant curl with one hand and held down the list of families with the other. She wanted to run away, but there was nowhere to go. So she sighed and turned her attention back to Lowell's mother. "I don't want to exclude anyone because of something in the past. I know only too well how hurtful that can be."

Mrs. Sheffield's eyes widened. "Oh, my dear, I'm sorry. I didn't think—" The older woman's cheeks reddened. "Of course we will invite them." She cleared her throat. "Is the wind getting too brisk? Perhaps we should move inside."

Alexandra accepted the change of subject in deference to Mrs. Sheffield's obvious dismay and glanced around. The gardens and the front lawn were beginning to come to life as spring chased away the freezing temperatures of winter. "I am enjoying the sunshine and the chirp of the birds."

Galloping hooves drowned out the sounds as Lowell and his father thundered down the lane toward the house and around to a side entrance without stopping. Mrs. Sheffield raised a hand in welcome, but neither man acknowledged her greeting.

Mrs. Sheffield looked at Alexandra, a forlorn smile on her face. "Mr. Sheffield and Lowell have been preoccupied of late."

"Should we go inside and find out what has happened?"

"Oh no, dear. You will find it's much better to leave the men alone at times like this. They would not appreciate our meddling. They will rush hither and yon making plans and devising strategies. And then the crisis will pass, and they will once again devote their time to us." She patted Alexandra's hand. "In the meantime, we have each other. Now, where were we?"

Alexandra looked down at the list, but her mind clanged a warning. Was this why Lowell did not seek or value her opinion in certain matters?

The front door opened, and she turned, a relieved smile on her face. Lowell must have decided to come out and greet her. But it was only the housekeeper wringing her hands on her apron. "Missus Sheffield, I need you inside, ma'am."

"What's wrong, Sally?" Mrs. Sheffield pushed back her chair. Alexandra started to rise, but she shook her head. "You stay out here. I'm sure I'll only be a minute or two."

Sitting back in her chair, Alexandra tried to recapture the peacefulness she had felt during her morning prayer, but it was impossible. She thought back to the days before her father had died. If she had not ignored his rushing hither and yon, things might have turned out differently. But with her awakened faith she knew she could not impose her own will on her father. God had lovingly given each person the right to choose whether to follow Him.

Yet she still could not rid herself of the notion that she might have been able to protect the victims of his crimes if she had just paid attention to the choices her father was making. She stood. She had no idea what was going on with the Sheffield men, but she would find out. She was determined not to make the same mistake again.

Raised voices drew her attention to one of the large windows. It must be coming from Mr. Sheffield's study. She was about to sweep past it when a name brought her up short.

"He is a menace to all of us." She recognized Lowell's voice. "Jeremiah LeGrand must be stopped. We tried it your way, Pa, but now you must see he will not listen to reason. He believes that freeing his slaves will not endanger the rest of us."

"There has to be a less violent way to convince him."

"It's either him or us." Someone pounded a fist on the wall next to the window where she was standing.

Alexandra jumped back, her heart hammering against her chest. After a moment, she forced herself back to the glass panes. She had to know what Lowell was proposing.

"Late tonight, when all of them are asleep. If we burn down the house, he'll have no choice but to leave. It's his own fault. If he would only have agreed with us, we wouldn't be forced to take such extreme measures."

"Some people can't help being stubborn." Mr. Sheffield answered. "Just make sure you don't get caught."

"I won't, Pa."

Alexandra backed away from the window, a hand over her mouth. She wanted to march right into that study and tell both of the Sheffield men what she thought of their plans. But they would not listen. She could almost hear

Lowell's condescending tones as he sent her back to his mother. No one else would listen to her, either, not until it was too late. It would be just like what happened to Papa. She had come full circle.

Frustration made her want to stomp her foot. What could she do? Threaten them with exposure? End her betrothal before disaster struck? Or was there something else she could do? Some way to stop them from succeeding? An idea popped into her mind, but Alexandra rejected it. It was too daring, too risky. But it might be the only way to avert disaster.

❈

The work he had accomplished today put him well ahead of his plans. Jeremiah was pleased. He was certain this season would be the best one ever at Magnolia Plantation, and with the steady increases in the price of cotton, all of his people should make a tidy profit. He put down the almanac he had been perusing, blew out the candle on his bedside table, and pulled the quilt up to his chin.

Sleep eluded him as he considered the next plan he wanted to implement. He could just imagine what the townspeople would say if they knew he planned to turn his plantation into an orphanage. But it was a dream God had given him, and now he had the perfect place to take care of children who would otherwise have nothing. He could almost hear their shouts and laughter as the orphans played and worked together. He would build a large classroom in the second floor of the main house, and he would hire a tutor or two to help with the instruction.

Excitement coursed through Jeremiah as he dreamed of his plans. He turned over and plumped his pillow before settling back down against it. Thanking God once again for the bounty, he closed his eyes and drifted to sleep.

The noise that woke him seemed to be an echo from his dreams. But then he heard it again—the whinny of a horse outside. The newly finished corral was too far from the house for him to hear those horses. He had a visitor. And most likely a visitor bent on mischief.

Jeremiah pushed the covers back and reached for his clothes. He dressed quickly and slipped out of the bedroom. He couldn't see much as he negotiated the staircase. Clouds had appeared in the sky as the sun set this evening, and now they played hide-and-seek with the moon. But he could hear the scrape of a window being raised. He followed the sound into the parlor at the same time as a shadowy figure stepped through and entered the room.

Instinct took over, and he launched himself at the miscreant, tackling him before he could use whatever weapon he held. His aim was true. His head contacted the intruder's torso at the waist and both of them went down in a tangle of skirts.

Skirts? Jeremiah's startled gaze fell on a delicate face ringed by dark curls. "Alexandra?" He rolled off her and bounded to his feet. "What is the meaning of this?"

She moaned and rolled into a ball.

Anger immediately turned into concern. "Are you hurt?"

"No." Her answer was muffled but emphatic.

"Have you become a burglar?" Another thought occurred to him. "Or are you so enamored of me that you cannot help yourself?"

Alexandra hissed and pulled herself into a sitting position. Cold moonlight illuminated her disdain. "Of course not. I came to warn you."

Jeremiah raised his eyebrows at her and crossed his arms over his chest. "Warn me? In the middle of the night? And of what? And sneaking around like some kind of thief. . .whatever the warning is, could you not have sent me a message?" He held out a hand to help her rise. "You're not carrying a weapon, are you?"

After a slight hesitation she put her hand in his. "Please try to refrain from idiotic questions. This is a serious matter."

Her glare made him grin. Now that she was on her feet, only a hairsbreadth separated them. Her perfume seemed to surround both of them. Suddenly his questions disappeared. All he could think of was how Alexandra reminded him of a ruffled kitten, soft and prickly and oh so appealing.

He wanted nothing more than to take her in his arms and kiss her until the glare in her eyes was replaced by a much more intimate look. What an inappropriate thought! It must be the enveloping darkness leading his mind down the wrong path.

Jeremiah backed away and looked toward the mantel for a tinderbox. "Let's get a little light in here."

"No!" She put her hand on his arm. "If you do, they might see us."

"Who?" He looked out of the window she had just come through. "What are you talking about, Alexandra?"

"Lowell. He and some of the other planters are coming over here tonight to set your house on fire. I heard them talking this afternoon. They said it's the only way to control you."

It took him a moment to absorb the meaning of her words. "Are you sure?"

She nodded. "What are we going to do?"

Jeremiah caught her chin between his thumb and fore-finger. She was so intent on helping him, but he could not allow her to put herself in danger. "*We* are not going to do anything. *You* are going to go back home, climb into your bed, and forget all about my problems. I will handle Lowell Sheffield."

When she opened her mouth to object, he swooped down and captured her lips with his own. He knew he shouldn't do it, knew he would regret it, but he couldn't resist the temptation. He would never again find himself alone with Alexandra.

For a brief instant, surprise held her still, but then she melted into him. It was the most miraculous thing he had ever experienced. The very air around them seemed to crackle with the emotions unleashed by their embrace.

It took him a moment to realize the crackling noise was coming from outside. He looked out of the window and saw gray smoke curling toward the house. Fear struck him like a bolt of lightning. "They must have set the hay barn on fire."

Jeremiah released her and ran out to the front porch. He could hear them now, whooping and hollering like a band of Indian warriors. He couldn't see the faces of the men as they rode off into the night, but he would worry about their identities later. For now, he had enough problems on his hands.

He prayed no one would get hurt as he rushed toward the well and released the bucket. It filled quickly, and he hoisted it upward. Pulling it from its hook, he ran toward the barn and tossed the water at the hungry flames. Then back to the well to start all over again.

Alexandra ran to the cast-iron bell on the far side of the house and jerked on its rope to set it ringing. The sound alerted the men and women who worked for him, and he soon found himself surrounded by eager hands. They formed a line from the well to the barn and passed bucket after bucket along. Jeremiah had no idea how long it took before the flames began to die back. He only knew that his hands were blistered and his shoulders ached.

As the sun began to rise in the eastern sky, the extent of the damage became obvious. He had lost the hay barn and the gin, and the weeds in one of the smaller fields had been scorched. He knew it could have been much worse. Would have been if not for the daring of a brave young woman.

He looked around until he spotted her helping some of the women and children search for hot cinders. Her dark hair cascaded around her shoulders, which drooped from exhaustion. Jeremiah thought she had never looked more beautiful.

He accepted a cup of cool water from a young girl and drank deeply. It tasted as sweet as honey to his parched lips. Taking a second cup from her, he strode to Alexandra. "It's time for you to stop." He thrust the cup toward her. "You've done more than enough."

She looked up at him, her face streaked with soot. "I'm so sorry, Jeremiah. I wish I'd gotten here sooner."

Jeremiah shook his head. "If not for you, I would have lost the whole place. And perhaps my life. You don't know how much I appreciate your willingness to put your reputation at risk by coming to warn me."

An odd look crossed her face. She took the cup and sipped from it. "God would not let me do any less."

Her words nearly brought him to his knees. He could not believe how badly he had misjudged this woman. The immature, spoiled debutante was an illusion. Alexandra Lewis was a woman of excellence. She epitomized all the qualities of the perfect helpmeet—intelligence, beauty, and faithfulness. Never mind her singed clothing and mussed hair, Jeremiah could not imagine any woman being more beautiful than Alexandra. Or more unattainable.

He clamped his jaws together. He'd better get her out of here right now before he decided he couldn't let her leave at all. Jeremiah turned away and waved to Oren. "See to it Miss Lewis gets home safely."

He walked away without a backward glance. She was not his to claim. She was betrothed to another.

Chapter 28

"Wake up." An unseen hand pulled back her quilt, and cool air swept over Alexandra. It was like being doused in cold water. Alexandra sat up and rubbed at her eyes.

"Mama?" She stared at the woman standing next to her bed, trying to sort through the fog of her tired mind. "What's wrong?"

"Your betrothed is downstairs demanding to see you right away."

"Lowell is here?" She pushed herself out of the bed, groaning when her aching feet hit the floor. She felt as though she'd been beaten. Every muscle in her body screamed abuse.

"Yes." Her mother pulled Alexandra's gown over her head and pushed her into a fresh petticoat. "Your grandmother sent me up here to help you get dressed, but we must hurry."

The clothes she had worn yesterday were piled in a corner of the room, a malodorous heap she would never again wear. Her mother tossed a questioning glance her way, but Alexandra had nothing to say. She didn't want to talk about what had happened last night. At least not until she'd had a chance to decide how to explain her actions.

With a sigh, her mother dragged a dress from her trunk, shaking it to release the wrinkles and hoisting it up over Alexandra's head.

As limp as a rag, Alexandra let her mother lace up the back of her dress and push her down onto the stool in front of her dressing table. "Ouch! Mama, slow down. What is so important?"

Her mother's mouth dropped open. "What's so important? Didn't you hear me? Lowell wants to see you right away."

Alexandra didn't protest further. Jemma came in and dressed her hair. Alexandra was glad she had taken time to wash it out before climbing into bed last night. Even though it meant more tangles now, at least it no longer smelled of smoke. She endured the pulling and tugging of the brush as she considered what to say to Lowell. It was a good thing he was here so early. They could straighten out a few things right away.

"He's waiting for you in your grandfather's study." Mama led her downstairs and waved a hand in that direction. "Don't forget how much we're counting on him."

Alexandra pushed open the door, surprised to see Lowell ensconced behind her grandfather's desk. She let his effrontery slide, however. They had more important things to discuss.

"It's high time you got down here." Lowell's handsome face was a harsh mask. "Once we're married, I don't expect you to lie about in your bedchamber until mid-afternoon."

Alexandra marched to the front of the desk and stared down at him. "Is that so? Well, I have a thing—"

He interrupted her words. "Sit down. The reason I'm here is because I've received a report that you were seen coming home alone in another man's carriage, and I want an explanation."

Even if she had wanted to sit, Alexandra didn't think her rigid legs would allow it. She was appalled. "I'll stand, thank you. And as to my whereabouts, that should concern you since it's your fault I was not at home."

He stood up and came around to the front of the desk. "I'm listening." He took a stance directly in front of her, his hazel eyes as hard as marble.

Alexandra refused to back down in the face of his anger. She lifted her chin and squared her shoulders. "I was at Magnolia Plantation helping Jeremiah LeGrand put out the fire you and your cronies started."

Lowell's face paled as his expression changed from anger to shock. "Are you telling me you spent the night alone with an unmarried man?"

Jeremiah's embrace flashed through her mind. But she pushed it away. She had not gone to his house for that reason. "You are not listening to me, Lowell. I know you set that fire."

He snorted. "Of course I did, and I'm not ashamed to admit it to you, as I know you would not betray me. LeGrand needed to learn a lesson. The real question here is whether or not I should end our betrothal."

Alexandra drew herself up, ignoring the tender muscles in her back. "In that case, you have nothing to be concerned about. I won't marry you even if it means I have to scrub floors for the rest of my life."

Lowell's head snapped back as if she'd struck him. "You can't mean that. Not after my family supported you in spite of the scandal surrounding your father."

Alexandra raised her chin defiantly. "I apologize for any distress our association may have caused, but I promise you we will never be married. And if it were up to me, you would be facing the sheriff right now on a charge of arson." She sailed to the far side of the room, buoyed by the peace and strength surrounding her. "I'll be happy to call for your horse."

"I can't believe it." Lowell's voice reflected his shock as he stumbled across the room.

Alexandra almost felt sorry for him. He probably had never dreamed anyone would flout his family's money and influence.

At one time, he would have been right, but that time was behind her. Now she followed a Higher Power. She would rest in the knowledge God loved her and had a wonderful plan for her future.

Chapter 29

Jeremiah knocked on the Sheffields' front door and waited for it to swing open. The tall, thin, black man who opened the door accepted his card and left Jeremiah in the hallway. A clock ticked the minutes away while he waited.

Finally the black man returned. "Right this way, Master LeGrand."

Jeremiah followed him to a large library where both Sheffield and his son sat. After the greetings, he was invited to take a seat.

"Have you reconsidered your position, Mr. LeGrand?" Lowell sprawled across a horsehair sofa.

"Not at all." Jeremiah's eyes narrowed, and he reached for the man's right hand. "Is that a burn?"

Lowell jerked his hand away. "I burned myself putting a log on the fire this morning."

Jeremiah nodded and turned to his father. "I'm sure you understand that I can ruin your family if I go to the sheriff. While I may not have seen exactly who was at my house last night, after I report the conversation we had, he will be looking at you and your son very closely for evidence of wrongdoing."

Father and son exchanged a glance. "What do you want?" Mr. Sheffield was the one to ask the question.

"I want a formal, written confession from your son. Rest assured that it will never see the light of day as long as nothing like this ever happens again."

Mr. Sheffield opened a drawer in front of him and pulled out a piece of stationery that he shoved toward his son.

"Pa! You know the sheriff won't listen to the likes of him."

"That may be true, Lowell, but I told you not to get caught. You're too hotheaded, too certain your good looks and connections will get you free of any problems. That little Lewis gal knows it, too. That's probably why she broke off your engagement. You should be glad Mr. LeGrand is giving you this chance. I would hate for a son of mine to risk being branded a criminal."

Jeremiah kept his gaze fixed on an intricate silver candelabrum, but his mind was whirling. Alexandra had ended her betrothal? Was it because of last night? Because of their embrace? His heart thudded in his chest. Suddenly the confession young Sheffield was penning seemed insignificant.

Mr. Sheffield continued to harangue his son, recounting every failure and setback in Lowell's life. By the time Lowell was done writing, Jeremiah almost felt sorry for him. But then he looked at the blisters on his own hands. He had to protect himself and those who depended on him.

Lowell signed the sheet with a flourish and handed it to Jeremiah, who glanced at it briefly before folding the document and placing it in his coat pocket. "Thank you, gentlemen." He stood up. "I'll find my own way out."

He flung himself onto the back of his horse and galloped away from the Sheffields' home as though enemy soldiers were chasing him. All he could think of was seeing Alexandra. He had to find out why she had ended her engagement. He had to know if he had a chance.

❈

Alexandra sat on the piano bench and stared blindly at the sheet music perched in front of her. She had told her family her marriage plans had been cancelled, but she had not offered any reason.

Grand-mère had blasted her with threats, but when Alexandra refused to be cowered, she had finally given up and retired to her bedroom. Aunt Patricia and Uncle John had congratulated her on standing her ground and told her they would help if she needed it. Mama had cried a little, but then she had hugged Alexandra and confessed that Lowell was a bit overbearing. Cousin Percival harrumphed twice and toddled off.

Now she sought time alone to gather her thoughts and seek God's guidance.

"Your hands must not be as sore as mine if you can play a song." The deep drawl made her gasp.

The piano bench squeaked as she pivoted.

There he stood, tall as a cedar and immovable as stone. A lock of his thick hair had drifted across his forehead, and her fingers longed to comb it back. His blue eyes burned with the heat of summer, igniting an answering fire in her soul.

"Jeremiah—I mean, Mr. LeGrand. It's good to see you."

He turned from her, and Alexandra's heart plummeted. Did he despise her so? She had been very forward in going to his home. But what else could she have done? "Did you lose much in the fire?"

He twisted back to face her, and Alexandra's gaze searched his expression for a clue to his feelings.

"No, thank God. Nothing that cannot be replaced." His voice was rough. He cleared his throat. "I went to see Lowell and his father."

Alexandra tipped her head to one side. "Why would you do that?"

"I wanted to make certain my home would be safe in the future." A smile made the dimples in his cheeks appear. "I didn't want you having to rush to my rescue again."

"I didn't do much." Alexandra hid her blistered hands behind her skirt. "No more than anyone else would have done."

He stepped toward her, a strange light in his eyes. "I don't know anyone who would have been as brave as you were."

The air seemed to leave the room in a rush. Alexandra put a hand to her chest. "You give me too much credit."

"Alexandra, this is not what I came to talk about."

She took a shallow breath. "It's not?"

He shook his head and more hair fell across his forehead. "I. . ." His voice faltered.

Alexandra watched his throat work, wishing she could think of something to say to ease his discomfort. Was he going to apologize for embracing her? Or was some other matter troubling him?

"You may have heard about the changes at Magnolia Plantation."

She nodded and watched him pace across the room before returning to stand in front of her.

"I have so many ideas I still want to implement, but I've realized lately I need help in doing that. A helpmeet who shares my enthusiasm for reaching out to others." He stopped and looked up at the ceiling. "Besides offering opportunities to the people working at the plantation, I've always dreamed of creating a haven for orphaned children who have no one else to care for them." His gaze returned to her face. "How would you feel about being a part of those changes?"

A gasp of pleasure filled Alexandra. "I'd love to be a part of—" The squeakiness in her voice surprised her. Suddenly her throat didn't want to work. She swallowed hard and started again. "I've changed greatly over the past months. I've learned about the importance of giving to others, caring for those who are not as blessed as I."

His dimples peeked out as his lips curved upward. "I've seen firsthand how much you've changed. You are the one I want to share my life with. Please tell me it's not too late. Tell me you don't love Lowell Sheffield."

She flew off the bench and into his arms, burrowing into his shoulder with a sob. Jeremiah's arms wrapped around her, drawing her close and making her feel safe. All of her concerns and doubts melted away. "I don't love him, Jeremiah. How could I when you hold my heart in your hands?"

"Are you sure you can be happy with a simple farmer?"

"Only if his name is Jeremiah LeGrand." She lifted her face then and let him see the love she felt. How had she ever entertained marriage to anyone else? As their lips met, she sent a prayer of thanksgiving to God. What a joyous thing to follow His bidding.

Epilogue

Magnolia Plantation, December 1817

B e careful, Charlotte." Alexandra admonished Judah and Susannah's toddler as she lurched toward the tall Christmas tree. "We don't want you to scratch that beautiful face of yours." Alexandra caught up with the little girl before she could reach the other children and led her in the opposite direction, across the ballroom floor to where Susannah sat.

"Thank you." Susannah pushed herself up from the sofa with one hand, the other cradling her slumbering newborn. "I don't know how Charlotte gets away from me so easily."

Judah and Jeremiah emerged from the far side of the tree, where they had been engaged in keeping the large fir steady while it was being decorated by orphaned boys and girls from ages three to six. Alexandra and Jeremiah had taken them in when an epidemic of yellow fever swept through Natchez and were taking care of them until permanent homes for them could be found.

"It's not as if you don't have your hands full." Judah smiled at his wife and took the infant from her, cradling the little girl in the crook of his arm. Alexandra was glad he no longer needed his crutches. The wooden leg he used allowed him so much more freedom to move about.

Her attention was caught when three-year-old Katie, the youngest of the orphan children, plopped down in the middle of the floor and began to cry.

"Whatever is the matter, Katie?" She glanced at the other five children, who were still running back and forth with strands of berries and homemade decorations for the tree. "Did someone push her down?"

Deborah Trent, the oldest of the children, stepped forward. A very serious little girl, she mothered the rest of the youngsters, none of whom were related to her. She put her arms around Katie and whispered in her ear until the little girl stopped crying.

Alexandra was thankful Deborah was so good with the children. It seemed she had so little energy herself these days.

The year had been hard for Natchez, but they still had a lot to celebrate. On December 10, Mississippi had become the twentieth state to enter the union, the new government meeting in the nearby town of Washington until the epidemic left Natchez, now the state capital. Their neighbors were beginning to tolerate her husband's progressive ideas about sharecropping, if not adopting the practice itself. And they had been able to make Jeremiah's dream of providing for orphaned children come true. She smiled across the room at him and thanked God once again for uniting them. She could hardly wait to see his face when she gave him his gift this year.

He walked over to her and dropped a kiss on her forehead. "I love you, dearest."

"I love you, too, my darling husband." The look in his eyes still had the power to make her heart flutter. She was the most blessed woman in the world. Thankfulness filled her. She had come so close to allowing her grandmother to bully her into the wrong marriage. Only by following God's will had she managed to find the true path to happiness. "Will you read the Christmas story to us now? Or after we exchange gifts?"

He pointed his chin at the large Bible that rested in a place of honor on top of her writing table. "Let's remind our children of the real reason for this celebration."

They gathered everyone around, the children, their friends, and all of the people who worked for and with them. The large ballroom was quite crowded, but there was no noise as everyone listened to her husband read from the second chapter of Luke.

After the reading was finished, everyone received a gift, from the youngest sharecropper's child to Ezekiel, the oldest member of the household. Alexandra received a pair of gloves and a shawl from the Hugheses, as well as several hand-drawn pictures from the children.

When the rest of the gifts were distributed, Jeremiah moved toward her, his hands behind his back. "I have a special gift for you, my love."

He brought his hands around, and she saw what appeared to be a scroll tied with a black ribbon. "What is it?" She took the roll from him and loosened the string. Smoothing the papers in her lap, she glanced at the opening paragraphs. "Is this a deed?"

"Yes." His smile widened, making his dimples appear. "Do you remember the house in town that we looked at a few weeks back?"

Excitement coursed through her. "You bought it?" The papers slid to the floor when she jumped up and threw her arms around his neck, thinking of the Georgian mansion with expansive grounds that could be converted into a homey and comfortable orphanage to house a dozen unfortunate children. "You are undoubtedly the most splendid husband in the world."

"How can I not be when I have such a wonderful wife?" He held her in a tight hug. "I still cannot believe how much God has blessed us, Alexandra. Beyond my fondest dreams."

"Mine, too, my dearest." She smiled up at him. "I have a gift for you."

He let her go long enough to reach for the small package on the side table next to the sofa where she had been sitting. "That looks too small to be for me."

The others in the room seemed to fade away as Alexandra watched him unwrap the paper to uncover a tiny knitted cap. "It is too small for you."

Recognition like the first rays of dawn filled his face. "A baby?"

A blush filled her face as she nodded. "Yes."

"Should you be standing up?" Concern replaced the wonder in his expression. "Shouldn't you be resting? Here, sit down."

Judah's laughter drew a frown from Jeremiah. "She's not quite that delicate yet."

"Leave him alone." Susannah elbowed her husband. "I still remember when you were that attentive to me."

Judah stroked his chin. "That was just yesterday, wasn't it?"

They all laughed.

Alexandra felt as light as a puff of air. She never would have dreamed her life could be so filled with joy and laughter, hope and happiness. As her husband raised her hand to his lips, she knew that no matter what the future held God would see her and her faith-filled husband through it all.

AMONG THE MAGNOLIAS

Dedication

For my church family at Victory Congregational Methodist Church. Your love and support have always upheld me when I needed it most. I am thankful to be part of such a loving congregation.

Aaron

For John and Pat Bass—You are the inspiration for the characters I named after you. Thanks for the love you have lavished on your nieces and nephews. Sorry that I never quite developed a taste for tuna fish casserole.

Diane

Prologue

November 1839

C hattanooga. . ." Nathan Pierce let the syllables roll around in his mouth as he strode down the street toward the tavern at the crossroads. He liked the name of his newly incorporated town. Many others had been suggested, but he felt the Indian word suited the area best. A reminder of the original inhabitants of Tennessee, the people who had been removed to make way for the expansion of the United States. He had done what he could to make their removal easier—giving them food and blankets in an attempt to make their trek easier. But so many had died.

With a heavy sigh, Nathan hunched his shoulders against the cool November air as dusk crept over the town. Drawing even with three women, apparently a mother and her two daughters, he tugged on the brim of his hat. "Good evening."

A chorus of giggles, shushed by the older woman, was the only answer he received from them. They looked vaguely familiar, but Nathan could not recall their names, not an unusual circumstance these days with the flood of settlers coming into the area. Everything was changing. But he couldn't complain too much. Business at Pierce's Dry Goods had become so demanding he had hired two men to help him at the counter, as well as a young boy who swept the floors and dusted the shelves to keep his store gleaming.

Poe's Crossroads was no longer the meeting place for the town council, but it was still a good place to visit to catch up on whatever was happening in the community. And Margaret still performed there nightly. He liked visiting with the lively redhead. She had offered a sympathetic ear back in the days when his heart had been broken by Iris Landon—no, Iris Stuart.

Margaret was playing a lively tune on her piano as he entered the large room. Card games had already started at a couple of tables, and the bar was crowded with eager patrons. He ignored the odor of unwashed bodies and stale beer as he made his way across the room to an empty table near the piano, avoiding wet spots where the sawdust had failed to absorb spills.

Margaret finished playing with a flourish and turned on the piano bench. "You're here early this evening, Nathan."

He nodded. "Charles is going to close up, so I thought I'd come get some supper and see how you're doing."

Her lips turned up. "I'm flattered." She waved at one of the waitresses and held up two fingers before taking a seat at his table. Two cups of coffee were

127

plunked down on the table between them, followed quickly by two plates of meat and potatoes. Margaret folded her hands in her lap and bowed her head, encouraging Nathan to bless the food.

He looked down at his lap. "Lord, thanks for good company and good food. Amen." Raising his head, he picked up his napkin and placed it in his lap. "Let's eat."

It was loud in the room, but they ate in silence. Nathan cleaned every bite of food from his plate and sat back with a contented sigh. "Poe's cook cannot be outdone." He looked toward Margaret's plate and watched as she pushed her food around with her fork. "Is something wrong with your dinner?"

"No," she answered him, shaking her head. "I guess I'm not very hungry."

He stared at her face. Margaret could not be called beautiful in the strictest sense of the word. Her mouth was a little too generous, her nose a tad too long, and freckles covered every inch of her face. But her bright blue eyes and carrot-colored hair made most men look twice. Her personality is what made him seek her out. Margaret was a good friend—undemanding and nonjudgmental. "What's wrong?"

She sighed and put her fork down. "I've been thinking about making a change."

"What kind of change are you talking about?"

Her shoulders lifted in a shrug. "Having more people here makes things complicated."

Nathan frowned. "But you've lived here most of your life."

Everyone knew Margaret's history. Her parents had brought her west on the Tennessee River but perished of disease, leaving her without any knowledge of existing family. Her only connection to her past was the piano she now played for customers here at the crossroads.

"I want to do something more with my life than this." She spread her hands to indicate the tavern. "I'm tired of waiting for something good to happen. I'm ready to make my own future. Do something important with my life."

"Do you have something in mind?"

"Not really. All I know is I'm tired of coming into this place. Tired of being importuned by men who have the wrong idea about me. Tired of being shunned by the women in town."

"They don't know you like I do." He reached out to take her hand in his. "If they did, they'd be proud to call you friend."

Her smile seemed sad to him. Nathan wished he could do something for her. He thought of his bank account. He had enough money to give Margaret a new start no matter where she wanted to go. He opened his mouth to tell her his idea when his chair was bumped. Hard.

He wrinkled his nose as an offensive odor of sweat and grime washed over him. A beefy arm reached across the table and grabbed Margaret's arm, pulling her hand from Nathan's grasp as she was hauled out of her chair. "Whatta' we have here?" His words were slurred, indicating he'd been imbibing freely. "Ye tol' me ye had no time fer bein' friendly. Yet I sees yer holding hands wit' Mr. Fancypants here."

For a split second, Nathan was frozen by shock. How dare someone accost Margaret?

"Let go of me, you oaf." Margaret tried to pull away, but the big man had a tight grip on her arm.

Nathan surged up from his seat. "Let her go." He reached out and grabbed the man's arm, a part of him noticing a puff of dust while the majority of his mind registered the rock-hard muscles of the stranger's biceps.

A rush of energy pumped into his arm, and he swung the stranger around to face him, causing the man to lose his grip on Margaret's arm. Margaret stumbled into the table, knocking it and its contents onto the floor.

"You shouldna' have done that, mister." The drunken man focused his close-set eyes on Nathan. He swung his free hand up and landed a hard blow on Nathan's chin.

Seeing stars for a moment, Nathan lost his grip on the man's arm. He swallowed against the pain and balled his fists. "I don't want a fight."

"Too late." The other man took another swing at him.

This time Nathan saw the move and managed to duck. His opponent stumbled forward, carried by his own weight. Nathan straightened his legs and twisted to follow the other man's movements. He raised his fists to protect his face, knowing there would be no other way out but to defeat the man. Although he would have much preferred a peaceful end to this confrontation, he knew how to fight. His uncle had made certain of that.

As the man turned to continue the attack, Nathan moved forward and landed two heavy jabs—one on his opponent's stomach and another on his chin. The man stumbled back and Nathan followed him, his blood boiling. Another blow to the stomach, followed by a swift uppercut, doubled the man over. Nathan stepped back, panting slightly from his exertion. He glanced around to make certain Margaret was okay, and his foot skidded through a puddle of coffee.

"Look out!" Margaret's cry brought his attention back to the man in time to see the glint of a knife headed in a deadly arc toward his chest.

Time seemed to slow to a crawl. He reached out both hands to stop the hand holding the weapon. It was like trying to stop a wall from falling down on him. His arms shook with the effort. The knife inched closer, slowly taking over his whole field of vision. He was no longer aware of anyone. . .only the honed edge of the blade that now almost tore through his shirt.

Failure loomed, as did the death he had no doubt would swiftly follow the knife's plunge into his chest. In a desperate move, he stepped forward, placing his right leg between the other man's feet, and twisted hard. Caught off guard, the man leaned his upper body forward.

In an instant the situation changed. Nathan felt his opponent's foot slip. The larger man lost his balance and his momentum doomed him. The knife between them resisted briefly before sliding deep into the man's body.

Horrified, Nathan released his tight grip on the man's hand and tried to catch him before he hit the ground. It was a futile effort. The stranger outweighed him by at least two stone. When he hit the floor, he groaned loudly, rolled over. . .and died.

Nathan fell to the floor beside him, uncertain of what to do but wanting to help the man if at all possible. He reached for the knife, whose hilt was protruding from the man's chest, but before he could pull it free, someone grabbed him from behind and lifted him away. Suddenly he was aware of other voices, some frantic, others excited.

Someone came running in and knelt where Nathan had just been. Dr. Robinson. He watched with fading hope as the doctor checked for a pulse, put his ear next to the fallen man's mouth, and finally straightened with a single head shake. "He's dead."

"Good riddance." The voice was Margaret's, but he heard the other men crowded around the body echo the sentiment.

"But I. . .it was an accident." Nathan looked down at his shirt, splattered with blood, and shuddered. He was a murderer. He had taken another man's life. "He slipped and the knife. . ." He felt again the sensation as the knife hesitated then plunged to its hilt, scraping past a bone on its deadly journey. He shuddered, his hands shaking like leaves in a strong wind. "He can't be dead."

Someone patted his shoulder. "It's okay, Nathan. Everyone knows it was self-defense."

"That's right," another man chimed in. "I saw him attack you. It was a fair fight until he pulled out his Arkansas toothpick."

Dr. Robinson stood up and looked at him. "Are you hurt?"

Nathan shook his head.

"Then I'm going back home to my supper." He pointed to the body on the floor. "Only the undertaker can help him now."

The man patting his shoulder spoke again. "God rest his soul."

Nathan turned and pushed his way past the knot of men. The words echoed in his mind. . .*God rest his soul*. . .*God rest his soul.* He wondered exactly where the slain man's soul was at this instant. Had his untimely death doomed him to eternity in hell? And what would happen to Nathan now? God would surely condemn him for taking another man's life. Why hadn't he found another way out of the situation? Why had he allowed the man's violent nature to rule?

The questions dogged him all the way back to his home. They echoed as he washed away the dead man's blood. They followed him into his bedroom, robbing him of sleep. When he did finally manage to close his eyes, all he could see was the stranger's surprised face, all he could remember was the feel of the knife biting into the other man's flesh. He was as guilty as Cain and deserved whatever punishment God meted out to him.

❋

Christmas was supposed to be a time of love and celebration, but Nathan could find no joy at all. He should not have accepted Iris Stuart's invitation for Christmas dinner.

He glanced around the room at the other guests—Wayha Spencer and his two granddaughters were here. He ought to be glad that they had not lost their home like so many of the other Indians in the area. If not for Iris and Adam's intervention, they would probably not be here.

Lance and Camie Sherer were here, too. They had also brought their children. Just being around such nice families ought to make him feel better—but it didn't.

Adam Stuart walked over to him. "I've got something I need to talk to you about." He inclined his head toward the door. "Let's go to my study for a minute."

Nathan followed him to the quieter room and waited for Adam to speak. "I'm worried about you, Nathan."

With a sigh, Nathan walked to the window and looked out at the scenery. Last week's snow had mostly disappeared, leaving patches of white here and there in the shadiest parts of the Stuarts' grounds. "Is that why you and Iris invited me?"

"Of course not." Adam's easy chuckle filled the room. "You and I have been friends for years, Nathan. Which is why I feel I need to say something. You haven't been the same since the accident."

"Accident?" Nathan didn't even try to keep the derision out of his voice. "You mean murder. Although it may not have been intentional, I murdered Ira Watson."

Adam walked up behind him and put a hand on Nathan's shoulder. "The Bible speaks to the difference between homicide and accidental death. You know you held no enmity against that man. He attacked you—"

"Not until I stepped between him and Margaret."

"So you are condemning yourself for protecting a lady? A woman who has been your friend for longer than we have? Who could not protect herself from his brute strength?" Adam's hand tightened on his shoulder. "God would not condemn you for protecting the weak."

"How can you speak for God?" Nathan let his anger escape. "How can you say what He thinks? He created Ira Watson and died for his salvation as much as He died for mine."

"That's true, but sadly not all men choose to embrace God. Some refuse to listen until it's too late."

Nathan knew his friend was speaking the truth. He wanted to embrace it, but he could not. "I wish I hadn't gone to eat supper there that night. I wish I'd gone home and eaten alone. I wish someone had stepped in when the fight first broke out. I wish any number of things had happened that night. But they didn't. And—I—killed—Ira Watson."

"If you were guilty, don't you think the sheriff would have arrested you?"

He lifted his shoulders in a shrug. "No one liked the man. He hadn't been here long, so he didn't have anyone to defend him. I couldn't even find any family connections."

"All of that is beside the point. The sheriff is a fair man. When he learned the circumstances surrounding Mr. Watson's death, he knew no reason existed for him to arrest you."

"He's only a man. He should have arrested me. He wasn't inside my head that evening. He didn't know how angry I was. How could he? Only God knows what was in my mind, and I feel the weight of His judgment."

"Listen to me, Nathan." A new tone had come into Adam's voice now. A sound of command. "You have got to find a way to forgive yourself and put that unfortunate episode behind you. Believe me, I know the danger of holding on to the past. I almost waited too long. Every day I thank God for bringing me out of my bitterness. He can heal you, too, if you'll let Him."

Knowing Adam was right, Nathan pinned a smile on his face. "I've been thinking about that."

"I'm glad to hear it." Adam returned his smile. "If there's anything I can do to help, please don't hesitate."

"Just pray for me."

"Always." Adam led the way back to the parlor.

Nathan watched as his friends laughed and talked, wishing he could join in. But an invisible wall seemed to separate them, a wall he didn't know how to break through. Maybe if he had the right tool. . . maybe if he studied his Bible more. . .maybe if he dedicated himself completely to doing the Lord's work. . .

The idea took root. He could study more and understand God's Word better if he let go of all his worldly considerations and devoted himself to the Lord's service.

The more he thought of it, the more he liked the idea. He would become a preacher. He'd sell everything he owned—the store and its inventory, his land, his home—everything. He'd go wherever the church sent him. He'd face any hardship with fortitude. And once God saw how devoted he was, maybe He would erase the guilt of Nathan's evil deed.

He said good night to his hosts and assured them he would be better in the days ahead. He watched as a look of relief passed between Iris and Adam. He felt humbled to know he had such good friends. They truly cared about him. He wanted to tell them of the plan he'd come up with after his talk with Adam, but it was too new, too precious. He did not want to risk having anyone put a stumbling block in his way. He knew this was the right thing to do.

Nathan climbed onto his horse and rode home, feeling more hopeful than he'd felt in a month. He glanced up at the clear night sky, thinking of that night more than eighteen hundred years earlier, when God had become a man. He was determined to find his way back to the upright man he'd once been.

He would study hard, learn every verse, memorize the whole Bible if he had to. He would show God how penitent he was. He would become worthy again, even if it took him the rest of his life.

Chapter 1

May 1841

Nathan leaned forward in the saddle. "It won't be long now, Lazarus. We should arrive in Natchez before noon."

The horse nodded as if excited by the promise. Nathan straightened and looked around him. The terrain was so different on the southern section of the Natchez Road. Pine trees crowded in on either side and formed a canopy above horse and rider, offering welcome shade in the warm spring temperatures. Although Nathan was acclimated to warm temperatures—it already felt like summer here in Mississippi even though it was only midmorning—he was already sweating. He supposed many things would be different here.

Should he stay in a hotel in Natchez On-the-Hill before appearing at Magnolia Plantation? He was several days ahead of his scheduled arrival, and he did not want to inconvenience his hosts. Or should he proceed directly to the plantation, which would serve as his home base for the next few years? At least he hoped he would be stationed here for that long before the church decided to give him a new circuit.

He could not wait to see the accommodations being provided by Mr. and Mrs. LeGrand. A separate home for his own use. It would be quite a change from the past year apprenticing under Douglas Feazell. He was looking forward to hours of quiet without the interruption of Pastor Feazell's three rambunctious children.

By all accounts, Mr. and Mrs. Jeremiah LeGrand were a couple with but one child, a young woman with intellectual, rather than family, pursuits. He had no doubt she would be plain, outspoken, or terribly spoiled by doting parents—perhaps all three. But at least she would not pull on his coat to get his attention or try to climb in his lap with sticky fingers.

Nathan's stomach clenched. He did not understand why children were so ill-behaved. He had been a model of propriety from the time he could walk. Everyone said so. Why did other children have to run and romp, scream at nothing, and shout when a whisper was more appropriate?

Nathan took several deep breaths and urged his horse to a canter as the dense foliage began to give way to cultivated fields. He passed an inn and waved to a man sitting on the front porch in a rocking chair. He traveled another mile before seeing a large house in the distance that must be one of the plantation homes. Was it Magnolia Plantation? He had no way of knowing, so he stayed on the road that would take him into town. He would find someone there to give him specific directions.

The bustling port city came into view as he crested a hill. People hurried along wooden boardwalks on errands, and the streets were clogged with wagons, carts, horses, and carriages. The sights and sounds were nearly overwhelming to him. Banks and millinery stores vied for space next to grocers and livery stables. On his left, he caught the shouts and laughter of children running on the lawn of what appeared to be a school or orphanage. He shuddered and moved on as quickly as he could manage.

He allowed his horse to follow other riders moving in a westerly direction and was eventually rewarded by a stunning vista—the wide ribbon of the Mississippi lay at the bottom of a precipice, her muddy waters rushing southward with a flotilla of cargo-laden boats.

Not wanting to actually go down to Natchez Under-the-Hill, he moved out of the flow of foot and horse traffic, choosing a grassy park bordering the main road. The park must have been created for visitors such as him, offering several benches and a hitching post. Nathan dismounted and tethered his horse before walking to one of the benches that overlooked the river below. He breathed deeply of the warm air, removed his hat, leaned back, and closed his eyes to thank God for a safe journey.

A young girl's voice interrupted his prayer. "Hey, mister, are you asleep?"

Nathan opened his eyes to see a girl with hair as blond as his own wearing an oversized dress. She could have been anywhere between the ages of toddler and debutante. "I am not."

The girl pursed her lips and nodded. "Too much to drink?"

He looked around for rescue. The girl must have a nanny or mother somewhere in the vicinity.

"My uncle Freddy used to drink in the morning." She sat down beside him on the bench and swung her feet to and fro. "But then he got mashed by a hotel." The girl smacked one hand down on the other with a loud sound.

"He what?"

She nodded and fixed him with a blue-eyed stare. "A big tormato came here last year and killed lots of people. Uncle Freddy was eating his dinner at the Steamboat and it fell down on him. That's why I had to go to Mercy House and live with the other orphans."

Nathan's mouth dropped open. He ran his hand through his hair, a sure sign of anxiety, and immediately tried to straighten it. "Did you come here alone?"

"Ummm." The girl sneaked a glance past him. "Nooo. But Miss Deborah is busy."

He swiveled his head to see a group of children being gathered up by a tall woman who was frantically looking around. He could understand her concern. His desire to ease her fear overcame his own anxiety. "I think you've been missed."

The girl tried to hide behind his shoulder. "I wanted to see if you were okay."

"Well now that you know I am, why don't you let me return you to your friends?" Nathan stood up and held out a hand to her. He didn't know why he didn't send her on her way, but he could not ignore the sadness in the child's eyes. "Come along. I'll take you back."

"You look like Uncle Freddy. Maybe you could say you're his brother and Miss Deborah would let me come live with you."

"I have many reasons to reject such a suggestion." Nathan tried to keep the horror from his voice. "The first is that it would be a lie. I'm a pastor. Would you have me break one of God's commandments?"

Her eyes widened, and she shook her head.

"Good. Come along, then, Miss. . ."

"Mishal Carpenter, but everyone calls me Mia." She stood up and brushed a leaf from her skirt.

"Miss Carpenter." Feeling a little like he'd been run over by a team of horses, Nathan escorted the precocious child back to her guardian. As he walked away, he could hear the children asking about his identity. He didn't hear what Mia's answer was, but he hoped it had nothing to do with "tormatos" or uncles.

Nathan collected his horse and decided to stop at the land office he'd passed on his way through town. After winding his way through the steady stream of townspeople, he arrived at the glass-fronted building that advertised the business within and the owner, Silas Ward. He dismounted and entered the front door, setting off the tinkling of a bell.

"Hello, what can I do for you?" An olive-complexioned man with dark eyes and darker hair smiled at him from behind a tall counter.

"I need to find out how to get to Magnolia Plantation." Nathan removed his hat and held out a hand to the merchant he imagined to be Mr. Ward. "I'm new to these parts, and I thought you might be able to help me."

The man on the far side of the counter frowned, and his mustache twitched.

Nathan wondered if he had broken some local custom. Back home he could have stopped at any number of businesses to make a similar inquiry, but this was not Tennessee.

"What's your business with the LeGrands?"

Nathan let his hand fall to his side. "I'm the new itinerant pastor, and the LeGrands have graciously offered me a place to stay while I'm holding church meetings here in Natchez."

The man's expression lightened a degree or two. "So you're the new pastor. And here I was thinking you might be a customer."

"Sorry to disappoint you, sir, but I have no need for land." Nathan stretched his mouth in a smile. "I hope that won't keep you from attending church once

I am able to take the pulpit."

"Of course it won't." The man extended his hand across the counter. "My name's Silas Ward. Pleased to make your acquaintance, Pastor."

Nathan returned the firm handshake. "Likewise, Mr. Ward." He watched the features on the other man's face, amazed at the transformation. From professional courtesy to distrust to friendliness. Mr. Ward would make a fine actor. But was his ability to modify his temperament at lightning speed an indication of imbalance?

As Mr. Ward described the route he should follow to Magnolia Plantation, Nathan tried to quash his misgivings. It was not his place to judge others. That much he had surely learned in the past year.

He assumed a pleasant smile, thanked the merchant, and escaped with a sigh of relief. His dislike for Mr. Silas Ward was disturbing. He would have to pray for understanding and acceptance. His future as a pastor depended on his ability to relate to all the people in the community.

Chapter 2

W hat's that on your cheek?"

Abigail LeGrand rubbed at her face and sneezed. "Probably dust."

"Let me." Her mother pulled a handkerchief from the pocket of her skirt and stepped close. "You're only making matters worse."

Abigail tapped her foot but submitted to her mother's ministrations. Why wasn't she covered in dust, too? But then no amount of grime would ever take away from her mother's beauty. From the top of her gleaming black tresses to the toes of her fashionable slippers, Mama always looked as though she'd stepped from the covers of a ladies' magazine.

"I don't see why you're so concerned, Mama. We still have a lot to do this afternoon to get the cottage ready for the new minister." She pointed at the pile of dust covers she and her mother had removed from the furniture. "Those need to be washed and stored, and I still have to cut the magnolia blossoms you wanted."

Her mother sighed and looked around. "I always forget what all has to be done, but we need to hurry. The new preacher will be here any day now, and I want everything to be right for him."

"It will be, Mama. You are the perfect hostess, and I'm certain you'll soon have the new pastor eating out of your hand."

"As could you if you would only apply yourself."

"Mother!" Abigail used the tone of voice she reserved for indicating disdain. "I have no desire to endear myself to any man, pastor or not."

"Sometimes I think your papa and I did you a disservice when we let you talk us into sending you to Elizabeth Female Academy."

Abigail frowned at her. "How can you even think such a thing? Would you have preferred someone like Violeta Sheffield, a simpering debutante with no accomplishments beyond needlework and watercolors?"

"Of course not, but you should not be so patronizing about Lowell and Dorcas's daughter. She is a sweet girl whether she has earned a degree or not."

Her cheeks heated up at the criticism. Abigail knew her mother was right. "I'm sorry, but I get so tired of hearing everyone talk about how accomplished and biddable she is. Does no one in this town appreciate a female who has a little sense?"

Her mother's dark eyes flashed. "You outshine Violeta in every respect. Never doubt that for a moment. But as your mother, I have the right to be concerned about whether or not you will experience firsthand the joy of having a family of your own."

"I spend enough time at the orphanage to give me a good idea of what it's like to provide guidance for children. Besides, you are the one who has always cautioned me to avoid placing all my dependence on a man." Abigail grabbed a cloth and attacked the dust scattered across a rosewood accent table.

Her mother picked up a broom and began sweeping. "I didn't want you to make the mistake of thinking marriage is the only goal a female should have. Your first dependence should always be on God, then on the talents He gave you—"

"Exactly. So why should I want to bury my talents in order to be subservient to some man?" A strand of hair loosed itself from Abigail's tight bun. She pushed it back with one finger as she continued her work. "Besides, most of the men in Natchez would think I'd lost my mind if I tried to talk them into freeing their slaves and adopting the sharecropping methods we use here."

"That's true, dear, and perhaps that is why the Lord is sending us a young pastor." Her mother stopped sweeping and looked into the distance, a tender smile on her face. "A godly man who will see you as the treasure you are."

"I don't understand why you feel it incumbent on me to marry at all. I am perfectly content to live here with you and Papa."

"That's because you don't know how wonderful marriage to the right man can be."

Her mother's words struck a chord in Abigail's heart. She had ample evidence of the joys of a successful marriage, but she didn't think any man as perfect as her father existed. Jeremiah LeGrand was smart, hardworking, thoughtful, and loving—a kind father and a good provider. But most of all, he was a man who put Christ first in his life. She knew her parents had faced hard times because of their beliefs. Even now, some in Natchez chose not to associate with the LeGrand family. But her parents had never seemed to care what others thought. They did as their faith dictated.

"Everything looks very nice." Mama surveyed the gleaming parlor with a smile of approval. "I hope Brother Pierce will be happy here."

"I'm sure he will be, Mama. No one has ever been disappointed here."

"There's always a first time. And this pastor is so much younger than most of the men we have hosted in the past. He might prefer to live closer to town."

Abigail rolled her eyes. "What man in his right mind would prefer the noise and dust of town to all of this?"

"I pray you're right."

"You worry too much." After giving her mother an affectionate hug, Abigail picked up her gardening shears and a shallow basket. "I'll be back in a few minutes with enough magnolia blossoms to freshen every room in the cottage."

"Be careful, dear. Some of those blooms may be too high for you to reach."

"Yes, Mother." Abigail sighed. Would her parents never cease treating her as a child? She was a full-grown woman, a confirmed old maid by most people's estimation. At the ripe old age of twenty-three, Abigail believed she had learned how to rely on herself.

Shaking off her irritation, Abigail concentrated on her self-appointed task. Spring was her favorite time of the year. Dozens of magnolia trees surrounded the grounds, their large, dark green leaves the perfect background for the fragrant white blossoms that had begun to flower in the past weeks. As she moved from tree to tree, selecting the prettiest flowers to scent the pastor's cottage, thoughts of God filled her mind. What a beautiful world He had created. And she was blessed to have the leisure to appreciate it. Why would she ever want to leave Magnolia Plantation? The answer was simple: She wouldn't.

She filled her basket and wandered back across the shade-dappled grounds toward the cottage. It looked exactly like the main house, only smaller. The corners and sides of the cottage were red brick broken by wide windows that let light and cooling breezes into the front parlor. Steps led up to a shady verandah supported by a pair of white columns. The front door was almost wide enough to drive a carriage through and framed by sidelight windows and a transom. Besides the front parlor, the cottage boasted two bedrooms, a dining room, and a small study. Perfect for a single minister or one with a small family.

Abigail climbed the steps and pushed the door open. "I'm back, Mama."

"We're here in the parlor, dearest."

We? Who was in the parlor with her mother? A groan escaped her as she realized the probable identity of the visitor. She put a hand to her hair. Working outside had done nothing for her coiffure. It probably resembled a rat's nest. So much for making a good impression on the new pastor.

Abigail took a deep breath and pinned a welcoming smile on her face. At least her mother wouldn't pester her anymore about trying to make a match with the man.

※

Nathan stood as a young woman entered the room. At first glance he might have mistaken her for a scullery maid. Her dress was dirty and torn, her auburn-hued hair was tangled, and she was carrying a large basket of white flowers. Yet something in her carriage, some look in her wide, dark eyes drew his attention.

"Brother Pierce, I would like you to meet my daughter, Abigail." His hostess retained her seat on the sofa, nodding toward the woman who was putting her basket on a table that stood inside the door.

He stepped forward with a bow. "It's a pleasure to meet you, Miss LeGrand. Your mother has been saying some nice things about you."

She looked past him with a frown. "I see." She executed a graceful bow in spite of her appearance. "I hope you will make room for a parent's bias as I doubt I can ever measure up to whatever she has told you."

Nathan's mouth dropped open. So much for the demure young woman he'd pictured. While Mrs. LeGrand was the epitome of grace and refinement, it was obvious to him that she had failed to instill the same qualities in her offspring. Even though he had been raised in a far more rustic environment than this young woman, he was surprised by Abigail LeGrand's lack of sophistication. Or was she merely flouting parental control? She was certainly old enough to have a household of her own. The Shakespearean tale of the shrew came to mind. Perhaps all she needed was a strong man to take her in hand as Petruchio had done with his Katherine. He wished the man the best of luck.

"Come sit down, Abigail," her mother admonished her rude daughter. "All I told the pastor was how much we were looking forward to making his acquaintance and that we were ready to do whatever we could to make his stay here more comfortable."

Nathan waited until she did as her mother requested before he returned to his seat in a padded chair next to the fireplace. "Perhaps you ladies would be so kind as to tell me a little about the people in the area I will be expected to reach. Are there many lost souls hereabouts?"

"I'm sure we have our fair share of nonbelievers, Pastor." Mrs. LeGrand answered his query, so he turned his attention to her. "But we also have several ministries in the area that try to reach out to them."

Nathan was eager to get started. The more people he baptized, the more worthy he felt. Perhaps he could eventually wash away the sin he'd once committed. He rubbed his hands together. "I can hardly wait."

Mrs. LeGrand smiled at him. "Perhaps Abigail can introduce you around to some of the townspeople."

A snort from the daughter let him know how she felt about her mother's suggestion. "All you have to do is visit Natchez Under-the-Hill, Brother Pierce. You will find enough lost souls there to keep you busy for quite some time."

Nathan waited for her mother to once again reprimand Abigail, so he was surprised when she nodded.

"Yes indeed." Mrs. LeGrand's words held a note of approval. "Natchez Under-the-Hill is almost a separate town and offers many opportunities for evangelism. We are all involved in a ministry to give aid, hot meals, and blankets to the immigrants and others in need. Perhaps you'd like to join us on Saturday afternoon?"

"It sounds like a wonderful idea, but I suppose I should speak with the church prior to committing my time."

Abigail raised her eyebrows, making Nathan wonder if she ever asked for permission before plunging into a project. He rather doubted it.

Well, part of his duties as a pastor was to provide a good example to the members of the community. He might as well start now by driving home his meaning. "I have an interview with the bishop in Jackson on Wednesday. I should be able to give you a more definitive answer by Thursday."

"Where do you come from, Pastor?" Abigail changed the subject.

"I studied under Pastor Douglas Feazell in Indiana for the past year, but I was born and raised in the southeastern corner of Tennessee. The town's now called Chattanooga."

"I've heard of Chattanooga. And of the poor Indians who were driven away from their homes because gold was discovered nearby. Tell me, Pastor, is it as wild an area as the newspapers report?" Abigail's question had an edge to it. "I have read of gunfights and lawlessness to rival anything that happens in Natchez Under-the-Hill."

Nathan's stomach clenched. Had she heard something of his past? His heart beat so hard he was surprised his shirt was not moving. How could he have dreamed someone so far away would have heard of his crime? He didn't know how to answer the girl. Should he admit his guilt? Or gloss over the past? After all, the people who were there that day had proclaimed him innocent of murder. The silence in the room lengthened as his mind bounced back and forth like an out-of-control stagecoach.

Mrs. LeGrand must have realized how uncomfortable he was. She stood up and straightened her skirts. "Why don't we leave Mr. Pierce alone, Abigail. I'm sure he'd like some time to wash off the dust of the road and settle into his new home."

Abigail hesitated a moment before nodding her agreement.

Mrs. LeGrand walked toward the door but turned back to him before she exited. "I'll ask John to bring you some hot water for a nice bath. He's Mr. LeGrand's personal gentleman, and he'll know exactly what to do to make you more comfortable."

"That's not necessary." He didn't want to be a burden to the LeGrands. "I haven't been waited on in a long time."

She smiled at him. "Then I have no doubt you will enjoy his help. Oh, and don't worry about being late for dinner. We never sit down before eight o'clock to give my husband time to wash after he returns from the fields."

"Dinner?" Nathan shook his head. "I'd not thought to dine with you—"

"You might as well acquiesce gracefully, Brother Pierce." When Abigail smiled, he could see the family resemblance. "I assure you my mother will not take no for an answer."

Nathan sighed as he followed the ladies to the front door. He had the feeling life here at Magnolia Plantation would not be without its challenges. He only hoped he could navigate his way through the choppy waters of the LeGrand family relationships. As an only child, he didn't have a lot of experience in such matters. Perhaps he would be best served to avoid the members of the family altogether.

With a nod he made his decision. He would spend most of his time at other communities in his circuit. After dinner tonight, the LeGrands would hardly ever see him.

Chapter 3

"I wish my hair was as thick as Mama's. It would make it so much easier to style." Abigail looked at Jemma's reflection in the mirror. Jemma had been part of the LeGrand household since Abigail's parents got married. Even though she could have left early on, when they gave her her freedom, she had opted to remain here and work as a lady's maid. Although the housekeeper was supposed to be the manager of the household staff, everyone turned to Jemma to solve household problems.

Jemma had dressed her mother's hair for as long as Abigail could remember, and she also helped Abigail on special occasions. Not that this was a special occasion. It was only dinner, after all. The same meal she took with her parents every evening. The only difference would be the presence of the new pastor.

"It's not like you to envy others, Abby." The pet name Jemma had given her since she was born gave her a feeling of familiarity and calmed her nervousness. "But never fear. Your hair looks quite nice. See how it gleams in the light of the candles. Everyone at dinner will notice."

Abigail caught the look in the family servant's gaze and blushed. She was grateful Jemma didn't comment on how out of character it was for her to request help to dress for a family dinner.

She cleared her throat and turned her head this way and that to marvel at the hairstyle. Jemma had swept her hair back and up, forming intricate swirls and weaving into them a strand of emerald beads to match Abigail's dress. "You are a genius, Jemma." She stood up and hugged her. "I don't think anyone else could do as good a job as you."

"Go on with you." The maid returned her hug and stepped back. "Let me help you with your dress."

"No thank you." Abigail waved her away. "I appreciate your offer, but I'll be fine."

After Jemma left, Abigail walked over to the bed and stared at the green dress lying across it. She'd had a hard time striking the perfect balance between an informal family dinner and a dinner party with guests. The last time she wore this particular dress, her dinner partner had remarked on the way it enhanced the color of her eyes.

She wandered back to the mirror to stare at her face. Reddish brown hair, brown eyes. She wrinkled her nose and stuck out her tongue at the dull reflection. She looked like a washed-out copy of her mother. Expelling a sigh, she clipped a pair of emerald earrings to her earlobes and removed her wrapper. Then Abigail returned to the bed and slipped her dress over her head. After twisting this way and that, she managed to fasten most of the buttons. Perhaps she should not have sent Jemma out so quickly, but it was too late to call her back now.

The casement clock in the hall chimed the quarter hour, reminding Abigail of the time. She tugged at the full sleeves to bring them down to her wrists and tied them quickly, hoping they were secure enough to stay out of her soup bowl. Something about her dress felt odd, but she didn't have time to check for problems. Instead she searched in her bureau for a shawl which she draped over her shoulders to hide any imperfections and made her way to the dining room.

As she reached the doorway, she heard her father's deep voice welcoming the new pastor. She hesitated a moment in the hall and put a hand to her chest. Why was her heart beating so? "It's only a family dinner," she whispered to herself. "No reason to be nervous. He's a man like any other. His opinion means nothing to you." After a few deep breaths, she pinned a smile to her lips and stepped inside the room.

Her father turned and opened his arms. "Good evening, daughter."

Abigail walked into his embrace. "Hi, Papa. How has your day been?"

"Excellent. I trust yours was as well." He stepped back and looked down at her. "Are you cold? I see you are wearing a shawl. Do you think I should light a fire?"

"Oh no, Papa. It was a bit cool in my bedroom and I thought I'd better bring my shawl to ward off any drafts."

"If you're sure."

Abigail wished she was not the center of attention. "Tell me about your day, Papa."

He shrugged. "I was telling Brother Pierce here about my idea for cultivating a new strain of peas."

Abigail turned to him. "I didn't realize you were a farmer."

His look turned sheepish. "I'm not, but I have some friends who are well versed in planting and harvesting crops."

"I see." She glanced upward and wondered how tall Nathan Pierce was. He easily topped her father, who was nearly six feet tall. She wondered why such a handsome man had not married. Was he so devoted to God that he'd not found time to court? Or had his heart been broken in the past by some coldhearted debutante, causing him to avoid romantic entanglements?

"What did you do prior to answering the Lord's call to the ministry?" her father asked.

"I owned a dry goods store back home."

Abigail's mother walked in. "I apologize for my tardiness."

"Don't worry about it, my dear." Abigail's father left her standing next to Nathan and kissed her mother on the cheek. "You are always worth waiting for."

"And you are ever the gentleman, dearest." She turned her attention to their guest. "I am so glad you were able to join us, Brother Pierce. We would have been devastated if you had not, wouldn't we, Abigail?"

Abigail looked up at the pastor. His cheeks had darkened at her mother's words. How she longed to say something that would ease his discomfort. But nothing came to mind, so she simply nodded.

"Since we are all arrived, why don't we take our places?" Abigail's mother put her hand on her husband's arm and allowed him to lead her to her seat at the foot of the table.

Nathan bowed to Abigail and held out his arm. "Miss LeGrand?"

She put her hand on his arm. The contact, even through the material of his coat, made her fingers tremble.

"You *are* cold." He placed his hand over hers.

Abigail could feel her mother's concerned gaze. "I'm fine." The words were for both of them.

Nathan led her to a chair and pulled it out for her.

She sat down with a sigh of relief. How foolish to have worn the heavy woolen shawl. She could even feel a prickle of heat where it covered her back. Feeling trapped, she squirmed in the chair and tried to ease the shawl away from her arms so she could cool off a little.

He sat opposite her and spoke easily to both her parents. Abigail offered little to the conversation, but she enjoyed watching the expressions cross the new pastor's face. He was not as rustic as one might have thought for a man raised in an untamed corner of Tennessee. She learned that he'd sold all his worldly goods before leaving to work under an itinerant pastor for a year. She admired his ability to walk away from all that was familiar to him and put his faith in God. Abigail wished she had that much courage.

"Don't you agree, Abigail?" Papa's voice garnered her attention.

What was the question? She glanced from one of the faces to the other. "I. . .uh. . .yes, I agree."

From the shocked look on her mother's face, her answer was wrong. Papa coughed and hid his mouth behind his napkin for a moment, apparently laughing at her. When he put it back down in his lap, his expression was matter of fact. "Well, since that's settled, we'll see you the first thing in the morning, Nathan. I know you and Abigail will have a good time on your outing."

Her mother pushed back her chair. "Why don't we retire to the parlor, Abigail, and leave the men to join us in a few minutes."

Abigail nodded and pushed back her own chair, relieved the meal was over but concerned about what she had gotten herself into by not attending the conversation more closely. The material of her dress tautened at the waist, squeezing her stomach as she rose from the table. Then she felt a pop and the material loosened. With a gasp, she grabbed her shawl and pulled it back up to her shoulders. Would the evening never end?

"I am pleased you agreed to take Nathan to town tomorrow. He'll probably want to visit his new church, and I'm sure he'll be interested in seeing the orphanage. He has such a good heart. I know he'll want to work with them like Pastor Ogden used to do." Her mother took her usual place on the horsehair sofa and patted the space next to her. "Is something wrong, dear? You didn't seem your usual self at dinner. Are you feeling poorly?" She laid her hand on Abigail's forehead. "You're burning up!"

Abigail stopped her mother from raising an alarm by grabbing her hand. "I'm fine. I just had a little trouble getting dressed."

Her mother sat back against the sofa. "I thought Jemma helped you. I know she did your hair."

"Yes, but I was so. . .so wrapped up in daydreams that I sent her away too soon." Abigail bit her lip. She'd almost admitted her distraction. Where was her mind tonight? She needed to pull herself together. "I. . .I must not have gotten the back buttoned up properly."

Her mother choked back a laugh. "So that's why you are wearing your winter shawl."

Abigail's face flushed. "Yes, ma'am. I feel like such an idiot, but I couldn't explain."

"I can see you were in a quandary." Mama's eyes danced, increasing Abigail's misery. "Let me see if I can fix it before the men come in."

"I can't."

"Why not?"

"When I got up from the table, I'm pretty sure one of the buttons broke off and rolled under the table. I only hope Na—Brother Pierce—doesn't find it."

This time her mother could not control her laughter. She giggled, snorted, and hooted.

At first Abigail wanted to be offended, but then the humor of the situation got through to her. She joined her mother, and soon they were holding onto each other, tears streaming down their faces.

❧

Nathan wondered what could possibly be so hilarious to Mrs. LeGrand and her daughter. Had they been laughing at him? He shrugged off the thought. They surely had more interesting topics of conversation than the habits of a newcomer.

"What are the two of you laughing about?" His host asked the question he would have liked to ask.

"It's nothing." Mrs. LeGrand took out a handkerchief and dried her eyes. "Only a discussion about la—ladies' fashions." A giggle threatened to choke her words. "I'm sure it would bore you men."

Nathan followed Mrs. LeGrand's gaze to Abigail's face, which had turned bright red. He felt like an interloper within this intimate family gathering. The closeness of the LeGrand family set off a feeling of loneliness inside him. He had no idea why.

Wait. Hadn't he decided to devote his time and energy to the Lord? Wasn't it essential for him to do so because of his past actions? His future did not include a family, so he'd better get his mind focused on what really mattered.

A silver service dominated the table in front of the sofa, and the rich aroma of fresh coffee filled the air. He took one of the two chairs facing the sofa on the far side of the table while Mr. LeGrand seated himself in the other. Mrs. LeGrand poured a cup of the dark brew and handed it to him. He waited to sample the coffee until she had finished serving everyone.

Mr. LeGrand swallowed a mouthful of his coffee and sat back with a sigh. "Excellent, Alexandra."

"Thank you, dear." She turned her dark gaze on Nathan. "Why don't you tell us what things are like in Chattanooga. I know it must have been awful to witness the trials of the Cherokee."

"Yes." His cup rattled as he put it back in its saucer. "The loss of life was most unfortunate."

Abigail's eyes opened wide. "Unfortunate?"

He could feel his cheeks burning. Apparently he had not been forceful enough in his description. While he had never condoned the removal, he had understood President Jackson's reason for doing so.

Mr. LeGrand cleared his throat and shook his head at Abigail as soon as she looked in his direction. "Yes, it was terrible. Forcing people to leave their homes is a harsh solution."

Mrs. LeGrand nodded her agreement before turning to him. "Do you keep in touch with your relatives, Brother Pierce?"

"I'm afraid I have no relatives left. My parents died when I was a young boy. I was raised by my aunt and uncle and inherited their store after they passed away." Although he was grateful for the change of subject, Nathan didn't want to go into any detail about Uncle Richard's demise. His death in prison after the conviction of kidnapping was not something the LeGrands needed to know. "Why don't you tell me more about Magnolia Plantation? Has it been in your family for generations?"

Mr. LeGrand laughed. "Actually I purchased Magnolia about twenty-five years ago, after I arrived in Natchez."

"Is that right? I cannot imagine anyone wanting to leave such a beautiful home."

"It's a long story, but the short version is that Judah Hughes and I came to a mutually beneficial agreement. You'll meet him before long. He and his wife, Susannah, manage a very successful shipping business in town."

"My husband is being modest, as usual." Mrs. LeGrand tossed a fond look at her spouse. "He brought Magnolia Plantation back from the edge of ruin after Judah was wounded in the Battle of New Orleans. If not for him, Judah might not have made it back to Natchez. When they did arrive, my husband rolled up his sleeves and joined the slaves out in the fields."

"In the Lord's eyes, I'm no better than any other man."

"Papa set all of our slaves free as soon as he bought the plantation." Abigail's face showed her pride.

"That's interesting." Nathan's brows furrowed. "I thought all the planters here depended on slave labor to harvest their crops."

"Yes, but I felt setting the slaves free and paying them for their services was a better and more humane way to run this plantation," Mr. LeGrand said. "And you can see for yourself that we have a comfortable lifestyle."

"You supply the land?"

Mr. LeGrand nodded. "And comfortable housing, as well as some of the seed."

"Jeremiah is careful to make sure all of our tenants have everything they need, and then he takes a very small percentage of the proceeds from them," Mrs. LeGrand added.

"What do your neighbors think of your system?"

Abigail leaned forward and put her cup and saucer on the table. "They don't much like it, but it's hard to argue with success. Everyone in Natchez knows about our sharecroppers. They'd like nothing better than for Magnolia Plantation to fail, but every year we do better than before."

"The Lord has blessed us." Mrs. LeGrand dropped a lump of sugar into her coffee and stirred. "So how can we hold a grudge against those who do not agree with us?"

Nathan sensed the LeGrands were not telling the whole story. Slavery was an issue many people felt strongly about. This family had probably had to endure snubs and slurs for their stance, if not worse. They were to be admired.

He wondered if that was why Abigail was unmarried. She certainly had a keen mind. He found himself watching her as she spoke to her parents. Except for a tendency to fidget, she seemed an excellent choice for some lucky suitor. And she would obviously inherit this beautiful estate. She probably had a multitude of young men pursuing her and her family's wealth. Perhaps she even enjoyed their attention and encouraged them to vie against each other. He ran a finger under the collar of his shirt and wondered why the idea of her flirting with a string of hopeful beaus made him feel uncomfortable.

He shook off the feeling and smiled at Mr. and Mrs. LeGrand. "This has been a pleasant evening, but I believe it's time for me to return to my new home. Thank you for inviting me for dinner." He pushed himself up with an effort. The long wearisome trip had apparently caught up with him. Every muscle in his body ached, and he felt like he was at least one hundred years old.

"We are so excited to have you here." Mrs. LeGrand's eyes sparkled in the candlelight. "I hope you will join us for meals whenever you are here. Even though the cottage has a kitchen, you'll probably find it easier to simply show up here. There's always plenty to go around."

Mr. LeGrand stood up. "Yes, there is." He patted his flat stomach. "And I need help to keep from getting so heavy I can't work out in the fields."

Nathan laughed. "I'm sure you can outwork me any day of the week."

"Get a good night's sleep, Pastor." Abigail folded her hands in her lap. "We can leave right after breakfast."

He bowed to her and her mother. "Thank you for your warm welcome, ladies. I never dreamed I would enjoy such luxury as all of this. And thank you, especially, Miss LeGrand, for making time for me tomorrow. Good night."

Nathan left the plantation home and walked across the manicured lawn to his new home, enjoying the serenade of the crickets. What a peaceful place this was. He glanced up at the twinkling stars in the velvety sky above. "Thank You, God."

Weariness settled on his shoulders as he opened the front door and lit a lamp with the tinder box he found on the mantel. He made his way to a bedroom, stripped off his clothing, and fell into the feathery softness of his bed. His eyes were nearly shut by the time his head settled on the pillow, and as Nathan drifted into slumber, he thought life as an itinerant pastor was far easier than he'd ever dreamed it could be.

Chapter 4

Birdsong awoke Abigail the next morning. She stretched her arms above her head and yawned. A feeling of euphoria filled her for no apparent reason. Why did she feel so. . .expectant? As though something wonderful was about to happen. Was it the birds outside her window? Although her mother had often told her night air was bad for her constitution, Abigail often raised her window after everyone else had retired. She breathed deeply of the early morning air that was cool with a bare hint of the warmth that would come later.

She did love springtime. She enjoyed watching the bees buzz from one bloom to another before using their tiny wings to lift their cumbersome, fuzzy bodies into the air. As a young girl, she had often followed the bees across the plantation grounds and into the woods, amazed to watch them enter a hive and deposit their load of nectar before heading out once more on their never-ending search.

Rolling over to prop herself on her elbows, Abigail breathed a prayer of appreciation for the natural beauty God had created. The large oak tree outside her window seemed to have leafed out overnight. It never ceased to amaze her how everything seemed to turn green at once. Movement drew her attention, and she watched a pair of gray squirrels chase each other around the upper trunk of the tree. They disappeared after a moment or two, and her gaze traveled farther across the lawn to the roof of the guest cottage.

Brother Pierce. . .Nathan. Her breath caught. Her heart skipped a beat. She was supposed to take him to town this morning and show him the sights. She jumped out of bed with a renewed sense of energy. Not that she was looking forward to seeing him. She was excited to be able to share the town she loved with someone new, someone who didn't yet know all the nooks and crannies of her home.

As she dressed in her riding habit, this time waiting for Jemma's help to get her buttons properly fastened, Abigail wondered where they should start. Should she introduce him to the waterfront missionaries? As a minister, she felt sure he would want to be involved with those who offered food, blankets, and the Word of God to the immigrants and dockworkers. Or maybe she should take him by the church where he would soon be preaching.

Walking into the dining room, she found her mother still breaking her fast. "Has Papa already gone outside?"

Her mother put down her cup and nodded. "You just missed him."

Abigail bent to kiss her mother's cheek. "I admit I spent some time admiring nature from my bedroom window instead of getting dressed and coming downstairs right away."

"You look very nice this morning." Mama picked up a piece of toast and lavished it with blackberry jelly as Abigail moved to her chair. "But why are you wearing your riding habit? I thought you would take the pastor to town in the buggy so you could tell him all about Natchez during the ride."

She shook her head. "I'd rather gallop across the fields on a day like today. It's too pretty to be confined to the roadways."

"And that's why you are still single, my dear." Her mother handed Abigail a plate of scrambled eggs. "You cannot engage a gentleman's attention unless you are close enough to converse with him. Besides, I get the feeling our new pastor is quite refined. He reminds me of the young men I used to know in New Orleans. He would probably rather not be on horseback since he is going to have such a beautiful companion."

Abigail rolled her eyes. "Only you would call me beautiful, Mama. Some might have considered me attractive when I was younger, but I am far too old for any man to be interested in courting me."

"I'll admit you're not a simpering debutante, but you have many admirable qualities." Mama frowned at her. "And at twenty-three years of age, I don't think you are quite at your last prayers."

"I will be twenty-four next month, and then next year I will be a quarter of a century old." Abigail unfolded the linen napkin next to her plate and placed it in her lap. "Far too old for marriage and children. Not that I am complaining. I am very content with my work at the orphanage in town. God has given me so many opportunities to care for those in need. He knows I do not need a man to be happy with my life."

The words came easily to Abigail. She had said them many times before. And they were true. She leaned on the Lord's strength and had no desire to submit to the will of a husband.

The frown on her mother's face deepened. "Sometimes I think your father and I raised you wrong. We wanted to make sure you had the freedom to wait for the right man to marry, but we may have made you too independent." She reached across the table.

Abigail put down her fork and placed her hand in her mother's. "How can you say such things, Mama? Are you so unhappy with my living here?"

"Not at all." Her mother's grip tightened around Abigail's hand. "But I want you to experience the joys of marriage and motherhood."

Surprised to see a sheen of tears in her mother's eyes, Abigail pulled her hand away and stood up. She rushed to the other side of the table and put her arms around her mother's shoulders. "Do not worry so, Mama. I love you very much, and I'm grateful for the upbringing you and Papa gave me. Perhaps one of these days God will send a special man I can marry, but isn't it better to wait on His provision than to rush into marriage with the wrong spouse?"

"Of course you are right." Her mother put her arms around Abigail's waist and squeezed her tightly. "I want you to have as fulfilling a marriage as your father and I have."

"I don't know how I could be any happier than I am living here with you and Papa." Abigail stood next to her mother for several minutes before moving back to her side of the table. "But if the right man comes along, don't worry. I'll snap him up faster than a hungry alligator could."

Mama's face relaxed as she laughed at Abigail's words. "I do believe you would."

They went on to talk about plans for the day. Soon her mother excused herself and left Abigail to finish her breakfast. She considered her mother's suggestion to take a carriage to town but rejected it. The day was far too glorious. Besides, she wasn't interested in making a match with the new pastor.

Would there ever be a man she would feel comfortable enough with to marry? Abigail didn't know, but she did know one thing—Pastor Nathan Pierce might be attractive, but he was not the man for her. She would never marry an itinerant pastor. The thought of being separated from her home and family was too unbearable.

❦

Nathan felt he had entered a foreign country. Never in his life had he heard so many dialects being spoken. It reminded him of the story in Genesis. Was this what Babel had sounded like when God confounded the speech of the tower builders?

"And this is our new pastor, Nathan Pierce." Miss LeGrand glanced in his direction after introducing him to the ladies working in the soup line.

What was he supposed to say to them? He let his glance move from one expectant face to another. Black and white, young and old, they were waiting to hear what he had to say. "I commend you for your work here."

Smiles answered his first statement. Buoyed by their approval, Nathan breathed more easily. "In the Good Book, the Lamb of God gave us instructions to clothe and feed those in need. You are following His guidance, and I know He is smiling down on all of you. When the time of winnowing comes, you can be confident you will receive His thanks and the richest rewards of heaven."

Miss LeGrand touched his elbow. "We should let them get back to work."

"Yes, of course." He glanced down at her face and wondered if she approved of his words to the ladies. Then he wondered why he cared. He followed her through the rows of cots on which the immigrants sat or lay and watched as she greeted them with warmth and concern. She must come often judging by the way these people responded to her questions about their health and families.

Nathan was impressed by the waterfront facility. He hadn't known what to expect, but after walking through the mean streets of Natchez Under-the-Hill, he had been pleasantly surprised by the large building that was used as dining room by day and dormitory at night. Several windows in the square room allowed natural sunlight in and provided a commanding view of the busy waterfront outside. In a far corner of the room, he could see a man talking to a group of young people. "Who is that?"

Abigail looked in that direction. "That is my uncle John. His wife is my grandmother's sister. They are the ones who started the mission." She walked toward the older gentleman as she explained.

Uncle John stood up and hugged her before turning his gaze on Nathan. "Are you our new preacher?" He held out his right hand.

"Nathan Pierce, at your service, sir." Nathan immediately liked the man whose hand he was shaking. Tall, with a head full of snowy white hair, he was the type of man one knew immediately could be counted on.

"John Bass." The older man's blue eyes twinkled. "My wife and I are eager to hear your sermons, Pastor."

"I pray they will meet your expectations, sir."

Mr. Bass nodded. "I'm sure they will. What brings the two of you down to the waterfront today?"

"Papa wanted me to show the pastor around town," said Abigail. "But we need to get going, Uncle John. We have several other stops to make."

"It was a pleasure to meet you, Mr. Bass."

"I'm sure we'll see each other often, Pastor. We welcome your guidance as we try to do our Christian duty."

As they left the mission, Nathan wondered if he would be able to offer the guidance Abigail's uncle spoke of. Suddenly he felt unworthy of the position he'd been given. He didn't know enough to lead others. What had he been thinking? Panic seized his throat, and fear nearly brought him to his knees. He stumbled a bit before catching himself.

You have no other choice. Not if you want to wash away your sins. Not if you want to earn God's forgiveness. And what other option is there? Do you want to burn in hell for your misdeeds? Of course not. So you will go forward.

He felt slightly better after giving himself the mental lecture. He was a grown man, and he had studied under one of the best itinerant pastors. He was ready. He had to be ready. Taking a deep breath and shading his eyes from the bright sunlight, he followed Abigail back through the warren of streets.

A man lay facedown in the middle of the road ahead of them, and Nathan reached out a hand to capture Abigail's elbow. He might not be certain of his ability to shepherd others, but he did know how to handle this situation. "Please stand behind me while I check on him."

He could see the surprise in her glance, but she did not pull away from him. "You should not bother the man. He's probably sleeping off a night of excessive alcohol consumption."

Nathan ignored her advice as he bent over the unconscious man. A snore from the prostrate form proved Abigail's advice was sound. He flipped the man over with careful hands. "I don't want someone to run over him."

"Not likely. Not here. There's probably a drunk asleep on nearly every corner of Natchez Under-the-Hill. The saloons fill them with cheap alcohol before robbing them of their money and kicking them out to make room for the next target."

He dragged the man out of the street and into the shade of the livery stable. "Maybe he'll be safe here until he wakes." He reached inside his pants pocket and withdrew the pouch that held his money. It was much slenderer than when he'd started his journey, but he still had enough to help this poor fellow. He withdrew a couple of coins and stuck them inside the pocket of the man's waistcoat. "Maybe you can afford better accommodations with this."

When he straightened it was to find her looking at him with a quizzical expression in her intelligent dark eyes. Nathan wondered if he had broken some local taboo. But hadn't she brought him down here to show him the mission work being done on the riverfront? Or did her sympathy only lie with those who sought shelter in the facility behind them?

"I admire your kindness, Pastor. Your instincts may need some work, but the desire to help others is the first mark of a worthy minister." She waited until he reached her side before moving on.

All morning she had been leading the way, but now she allowed him to tuck her hand under his elbow. Nathan felt taller as she looked up at him. Had he finally won her approval? Ever since meeting Miss Abigail LeGrand, he had felt he was being carefully measured and tested. Her current approving attitude was a distinct change and one he welcomed. He would need all the support he could muster to succeed. "What all do your aunt and uncle do at the mission?"

She nodded to the riverbank where a hodgepodge of boats, from multi-storied steamboats to flat-bottom keelboats and narrow dugout canoes, vied for space. "Those boats bring immigrants streaming into the area. People who have nothing but the clothes they are wearing. They get here so hungry and frightened, so unsure of what the future holds. All we do is offer them a hot meal, a couple of blankets, and a safe place to spend the night."

"That sounds like a lot to me." Nathan compared this waterfront to his home in Tennessee. The people who had been traveling on those boats generally had possessions. Except for the Indians who had been removed from their homelands. "We had a similar group back in Chattanooga. They gave food and blankets to the Indians who were being moved out West."

He saw Abigail's shoulders rise and heard her sigh. "What a sad time for them."

"Yes, but I find myself agreeing with the actual relocation."

She pulled away from him. "How can you say such a thing?"

Now he sighed. "I don't know what it's been like for the Indians and the white people in this part of the country, but where I'm from, there has always been a great deal of friction. Friction that caused pain and death on both sides. There was simply not enough room for both peoples to coexist. I cannot say I agree with the forced march that killed so many of the Indians—"

"How progressive of you."

He ignored her interruption. Miss LeGrand was very outspoken, but she seemed to be very intelligent. Perhaps if he explained the real situation she would understand. "But I do think President Jackson was right giving them their own land west of the river."

Abigail faced him, her fists resting on her hips. "And I suppose you also think it is a good idea to enslave Africans and force them to work their whole lives to provide luxuries for planters."

"Of course not."

"That's a relief."

Nathan ran a finger between his collar and his throat. "No one could condone tearing innocent people from their homes and families and bringing them across the world to work for uncaring landowners."

"Do I hear a hesitation in your voice?"

He cleared his throat and nodded. "Once they have been brought here, without money or training, how can they be expected to stand on their own feet and make a living for themselves? They need kind, considerate landowners to provide for them." He could see her eyebrows drawing together. "In exchange, they provide the labor the landowners need to produce crops. As long as they aren't abused, I don't see anything particularly wrong with the system."

Abigail's mouth dropped open. Her eyes had grown as large as saucers. "You don't see anything wrong with one human being *owning* another?"

He shook his head. "I take it you disagree with my opinion."

"Brother Pierce, that is a gross understatement." She marched off in a huff, leaving him standing alone on the sidewalk.

Passersby looked at him curiously, but no one stopped. Nathan wondered whether he should catch up with her and apologize for expressing his honest opinion. But she had asked, after all. He took a deep breath and followed her. If she could not abide an opposing viewpoint, perhaps she was not as intelligent as she first appeared.

Chapter 5

Abigail could not wait to tell her mama their new pastor's position on slavery. How could he even call himself a pastor? How could he read the Bible, see the love that Jesus held for His fellow men, and look favorably on the enslavement of human beings? So deep was her disgust that she marched all the way up the hill to Natchez On-the-Hill without slowing.

When she reached the hitching post where they'd tethered their horses, she finally thought to look back to see if he had followed her. She was almost disappointed to see his tall figure marching toward her, his blond hair blown by a fresh breeze from the river's currents. She would have liked to abandon him here, but she supposed she would have to wait.

"Abigail!" A voice drew her attention back to the park. She recognized the Thorntons' carriage and Charlotte's brown curls bobbing as she waved enthusiastically. "Abigail!"

"Hi, Charlotte." She did not have to force the smile raising her lips as the carriage drew near. "Where are Eli and Sarah?"

"I left them at the shop with my parents. Mama insisted, although I'm not sure Papa was as pleased."

"If I know Uncle Judah, he is as happy as a new puppy. He's probably showing little Eli all the secrets of the shipping business."

Charlotte giggled. "You're right. But since Mama is most likely spoiling my daughter with cookies and fresh-baked cake, it only seems fair."

Both of them laughed. Having grown up spending nearly as much time in the Hugheses' home as she had at Magnolia Plantation, Abigail knew her friend was right. "I may have to go and visit your mother."

"She would love to see you. She was saying the other day that you do not come by as often as you used to."

"I know, but my children take so much of my time." Abigail stopped speaking as she felt a presence behind her. She turned around and looked up into the pastor's face. The pastor's shocked face. "I didn't mean—"

"Who is your companion?" Charlotte's query interrupted her explanation.

Reminded of her manners, Abigail decided to drop the matter. Let the silly man believe what he wanted. She performed the introductions and stood silently while Charlotte and the pastor spoke briefly.

"I suppose I'd better get back to my shopping." Charlotte smiled at both of them. "It's a pleasure to welcome you to Natchez. You are in very good hands. Abigail knows everyone."

Brother Pierce bowed and nodded his head. "I'm sure you are right."

Abigail wondered why she didn't believe him. She glanced toward the carriage, surprised to see the lack of understanding in her friend's expression. How could Charlotte miss the irony in his voice? She unhitched her horse and walked toward a nearby mounting block. She swung herself up and looked back at him. "Shall we continue?"

"Am I keeping you from other duties, Miss LeGrand?"

Her cheeks burned. She lifted her chin. "My children? Not at all. I'm about to take you to meet them."

He swung onto his horse and turned its head toward her mount. "I really don't—"

She touched her heels to the horse's flanks and cantered off. Judgmental boor. How dare he take that condescending tone with her?

She fumed as they traveled through the bustling streets of town. Several people hailed her, but she waved at them without slowing down. She was much too irritated to make polite conversation. Besides, she could hardly wait to see what the arrogant pastor would think when he saw her children. Stopping in front of a two-story home that was separated from the traffic by a whitewashed fence, she dismounted and tied her horse to a ring in one of a pair of cast-iron hitching posts shaped like the heads of eagles.

"Miss Abigail." A chorus of voices greeted her entrance into the yard. In only a few seconds, she was surrounded by a group of eager children.

She laughed at them and pulled pieces of hard candy from her reticule. She never came here without treats for them. Her ire melted away as she watched their faces. These children were so thrilled by small things.

"So these are your children?" His voice was not as cold as it had been when they left the park. "I thought—"

"You don't have to tell me what you thought." She frowned at him and indicated the youngsters who still encircled her. "I could hear it in your voice."

One of the younger boys tugged on her skirt. "We have company, Miss Abigail."

She ruffled the boy's hair, aware that he thought himself too old for hugs or kisses. "This is Pastor Nathan Pierce, Joseph."

"No." He looked solemnly at the tall man beside her. "We have more company."

She could hear a choked sound behind her. Was Brother Pierce laughing at Joseph? If he had seen the frightened little tyke when he was first delivered here by one of the boat captains he would not laugh so hard. Joseph's parents died on the journey upriver. Abigail turned around to give the man a piece of her mind and found that he was not even paying any attention to her conversation with Joseph.

He had acquired an admirer. Mia Carpenter had wrapped her arms around one of his legs and was holding on with all her might. "Did you come to get me?"

"No." The man looked like he thought he was about to be skinned. His cheeks had flushed, and he was trying to pry the child's hands away from his pants. "I came with Miss Abigail."

Abigail felt Mia's questioning glance and nodded. "We need to go inside, dear. Let go of him."

Although the young girl's lower lip trembled, she complied. Satisfied, Abigail turned and led the way onto the shaded porch. A breeze lifted the corners of her hat, and she raised one hand to hold it secure while she opened the front door.

"Deborah, it's Abigail and the new pastor," she called out to the woman who was the matron of the orphanage as she stepped into the entry hall. The parlor was the first door to the left, but she waited for Brother Pierce to join her before entering.

His shoulders filled the doorway, and for a moment Abigail forgot her aggravation. Who would have thought a preacher could be so. . .handsome? The word popped into her head unbidden.

"Hello there."

Abigail told herself the thumping of her heart was because Deborah had surprised her. It had nothing to do with the pastor. He was a man. No different from dozens she had met in the past. And no different from dozens more she would meet in the future. She shook off the thoughts and turned to her friend.

A wide smile and sparkling brown gaze belied the austerity of Deborah's coiffure. Pulled back tightly from her face and twisted into a bun at the base of her neck, the red-gold strands had begun to dull with age. She was dressed in her usual uniform—a serviceable black skirt and matching waist.

"Where's your apron?" Abigail gave her a hug.

Deborah smoothed a hand over her collar. "I took it off because we have a guest, a new benefactor I'd like you to meet."

"I can't wait to meet him." Abigail's eyebrows rose. "And I've brought another guest with me."

She turned back to the tall, blond minister. "Brother Pierce, this is one of the hardest working women in Natchez, Deborah Trent. She is older sister, mother, and caretaker of all the children here. Deborah, meet Nathan Pierce, our new minister."

They greeted each other as one of the older boys dashed into the house, waved at them, and rushed up the staircase.

Deborah turned from Brother Pierce and frowned toward the young man. "Slow down, Micah. Unless there's a fire upstairs, you need to demonstrate more decorum for the younger children."

"Yes, ma'am." The boy slowed his headlong progress to a trot as he disappeared from sight.

With a smile and a shrug, Deborah led the way into the parlor. "Please excuse me for deserting you, Mr. Ward."

A swarthy stranger stood as they filed into the parlor. The first thing Abigail noticed about him was the mustache he stroked with one long finger. He was well dressed and well groomed, from the careful styling of his dark hair and starched perfection of his shirt collar to the gloss on his black, square-toed boots. All the matrons in town would be pushing their marriageable daughters in his direction.

As Deborah introduced them, Abigail dropped into a reflexive curtsy. He bowed over her hand and pressed a warm kiss on it. The hairs on her arm prickled and she jerked her hand away. She was more accustomed to men kissing the air above her hand.

"It's a pleasure to see you again, Pastor." Mr. Ward's statement made Abigail's jaw drop.

The two men shook hands.

"You two have already met?" Deborah asked the question uppermost in Abigail's mind as she took her place on the horsehair sofa.

Abigail sat on the other end of the sofa and folded her hands in her lap.

"I had no idea how to find your home, so I stepped into the land office to get directions." Brother Pierce explained the circumstances as Deborah poured cups of tea for each of them.

Conversation languished when he finished talking. Abigail sipped her luke-warm tea and wracked her brain for something to ask Mr. Ward about his business in the land office. She glanced in his direction and their gazes clashed. She remembered the way he'd kissed her hand and felt her cheeks warming.

"Mr. Ward has dropped by nearly every day since his arrival last week." Deborah smiled at the man and Abigail breathed a sigh of relief when she felt his gaze move away.

After blotting his mouth and mustache with a linen napkin, Mr. Ward returned his attention to her. "It's the children that I love to see. Their energy and enthusiasm reminds me of my own youth."

"Is that right, Mr. Ward?" Abigail's curiosity blossomed. "Were you an orphan?"

He nodded slowly and steepled his hands under his chin. "My parents died when I was very young, but I was taken in by a distant cousin. If not, I might have been dependent on an establishment like this one." He smiled in her direction. "Of course I once thought orphanages were dreary, harsh places, but since coming to Natchez, I have discovered my mistake. And Miss Trent sings your praises all the time. She tells me you donate large portions of your time here."

"I have not been here nearly as much as I should lately." Abigail balanced her cup and saucer on her knees. "Mama and Papa have kept me busy at home."

"It's always that way during springtime." Deborah smiled at both of the men. "Especially at Magnolia Plantation, since Abigail and her family do not rely on slaves."

"How commendable." Mr. Ward's smile was directed toward her. "My cousin and I have never agreed with slavery."

Perhaps Mr. Ward deserved more consideration. "I've never understood why so many think slavery is necessary. Papa has never relied on slaves. The moment he purchased Magnolia, he freed all the people there and offered to help them get established on their own farms. We pay living wages to our help, and Magnolia still prospers."

Abigail looked toward Brother Pierce. His gaze seemed focused on the tea in his cup. But then he glanced up. His expression was cloaked, his mouth forming a straight line as he studied her. She straightened her posture, a defensive reaction.

"I only wish more plantation owners agreed with you and your father." Mr. Ward's comment drew her attention away from the noncommittal pastor. "Perhaps others will follow your lead."

Her heart warmed at his supportive words. Abigail smiled at Mr. Ward. "We can only pray for that result."

Deborah stirred a lump of sugar into her tea and leaned forward. "Very true. I have always admired your parents' stand on abolition. And that of your great-aunt and great-uncle. They freed all of the slaves at Tanner Plantation after your parents proved it was possible. Who can say what effect their successful operations will have on other planters? Perhaps one day all of Natchez will turn from slavery."

"I am amazed to find such heartfelt abolitionist leanings here." Brother Pierce entered the conversation. "Before coming to Natchez, I had believed everyone here supported slavery. In eastern Tennessee, slavery is almost nonexistent. The people work their own farms. But of course, we do not have such massive operations as here."

Abigail looked at him out of the corner of her eye. Was that why he had no firm opinion on such matters? Perhaps she should not be so quick to judge him. If she traveled to Chattanooga, she would surely run into many things that were different. Things she had no opinion about because she didn't have enough information. Shame pricked her. But slavery? Should that be condoned in any circumstance? She didn't think so. Perhaps it was time to change the subject to something less contentious. "What's new here? It seems so long since I came by."

"As a matter of fact, before you arrived Mr. Ward and I were discussing a rather strange occurrence. I don't know exactly what to make of it." Deborah put her spoon on the service tray, and a small frown drew her eyebrows together. "I don't believe in such things, but some of the children have become convinced we have a ghost."

The hairs on the back of Abigail's neck lifted. "A ghost?" She looked from her friend to the newcomer. Both were nodding. "Are you sure it's not a jest?"

"Oh no." Deborah's frown deepened. "A couple of nights ago, several of the girls came screaming out of their bedroom. They were terrified."

"Exactly what frightened them?"

"One of the girls was awakened by a noise. She's frightened of mice and thought that was what she was hearing. She woke up another girl, and they got out of their beds to investigate. Both of them saw a weird green light shining under the door. Their screams woke the others, and they stampeded from the room en masse."

Brother Pierce shifted in his chair. "Who was in the hallway?"

"No one."

Deborah's quiet words made Abigail's eyes widen. She could feel her discomfort increasing with every second ticking by. "What do you suppose it was?"

A shrug answered her question. "I hope it was nothing more than a bad dream and a vivid imagination. I don't like the idea of someone wandering around the house at night."

"Perhaps you should contact the sheriff." Brother Pierce's voice was gentle and restored Abigail's equilibrium.

"That's a good idea." She reached over and patted Deborah's hand. "I can stop by his office on my way home."

"Thank you for your concern, but I don't really think it's necessary." Deborah squeezed Abigail's hand. "But I promise to contact him myself if anything else happens. I will not put the children in danger."

Mr. Ward cleared his throat. "I think you have the right idea, Miss Trent. But you must not forget to contact the authorities if you have any further trouble."

Abigail put her teacup back on the serving tray and stood up. "I suppose we should get back to Magnolia."

The other three also stood. After saying good-bye and promising to come back soon, Abigail and Brother Pierce left the large house. As they walked across the front lawn, she glanced up at the tall man. "You are a man of surprises."

He settled his hat on his head. "What do you mean?"

"I am amazed you have met both Mia and Mr. Ward."

A slow chuckle rumbled through his chest. "It was a matter of happenstance. The little girl found me. She seems to have confused me with her uncle."

"Yes, it is very sad. Mia lost all of her family. We have sent out inquiries for grandparents or cousins but no one has answered them. But she doesn't usually show such affection to strangers. You must have made quite an impression on her."

"I don't know about that." He opened the gate for her.

Abigail waited as he latched it behind them. She could see why the little girl might be attracted to him. Brother Pierce was nothing like most pastors she had met. He was methodical and quiet, a man one could rely upon. She wondered if he was quiet when he preached, too. That would be a change. Most of the pastors in this part of the world were fiery and loud when they took the pulpit. It would be interesting to listen to his sermons.

On the ride back to Magnolia Plantation, Abigail pointed out some of the larger plantations and told him the story of how her father had come to Natchez from New Orleans. She loved the story of his bringing Mr. Hughes home after the battle against the British at New Orleans. He was a good listener, easy to talk to because of the interesting questions he asked about those times. By the time they turned into the winding lane that led to the plantation house, she was feeling much more kindly toward him. "Please make plans to dine with us again this evening."

His blue eyes studied her so long that Abigail began to wonder if her hat was askew. She resisted the urge to check and waited for his answer.

"I do appreciate the invitation, Miss LeGrand, but I must refuse. I have several chores that must be completed. Letters and unpacking and such. Please give my regrets to your estimable parents."

The sting of his refusal made her cheeks burn. With a curt nod, she turned her horse's head and cantered away. Abigail knew she shouldn't care if he would rather eat alone than join her at the family dinner table. So why did she?

Chapter 6

Thank you for giving me a ride to the church." A drop of water slipped down Nathan's back, and he wondered if the dreary weather was a statement from God about his sermon.

"It's no trouble at all." Mrs. LeGrand smiled at him.

Mr. LeGrand tucked his wife's hand under his elbow. "We didn't want you to arrive drenched."

"At least the worst of the storm has passed." Sitting to his right, Abigail was the picture of spring. Her dress was as green as spring leaves, and her perfume tantalized him. Sweet with a hint of spice. Nathan wanted to savor the scent. She was so pretty, and this morning she was the picture of maidenly innocence. He wondered why she had not been snapped up by some handsome, rich swain. Perhaps all the men in this part of the world were blind. . .or more likely intimidated by her intelligence and independent spirit.

If he was looking for a wife, she would be the perfect candidate. Of course he was not. The last thing he wanted was to fall in love and marry. He had more important tasks to complete. And he never wanted to be in the position of again having to use his physical strength against a human being. He shuddered.

"Are you cold, Pastor?" Abigail looked over at him.

Prickles of heat broke out on his forehead. "No, I was thinking of something." He hoped none of the other occupants could see how hot he had grown.

Mr. LeGrand glanced his way. "You don't need to be nervous about your sermon, Brother Pierce."

"That's right." Mrs. LeGrand leaned forward and patted his knee.

Her motherly concern wrapped him in a cocoon. It had been so long since anyone fussed over him. He hadn't realized the lack until this very minute. Since the death of his aunt a decade earlier, he and his uncle had lived without a caring, feminine touch.

The coach lurched through a rut, and Abigail fell against him. "I'm sorry."

Their bodies were pressed together from knee to shoulder. Her hair tickled his nose, and her perfume filled his senses. Part of him wanted the contact to linger, but he helped her sit back up. "It wasn't your fault."

For the rest of the trip to town, he listened to Mr. LeGrand talk about the effect today's rain would have on crops. The older man obviously loved growing things. But Nathan found it hard to concentrate on the fine points of germination and cultivation. His mind was still preoccupied with the past. And the fateful night when everything changed. His hand jerked as for a brief instant he relived the feel of the sharp knife sliding into another man's body.

"Are you okay?" Abigail's concerned gaze combed his face. "You look pale."

He cleared his throat and straightened his shoulders. "I'm fine. I'm trying to get my thoughts in order."

"I'm sure you'll do a wonderful job."

Nathan appreciated her kindness and the supportive nods of her parents. But as the carriage drew up to the church, he wondered if he had made a terrible mistake to become a pastor. What did he know of such things? He was as guilty as anyone else.

They entered the church to find it only half full. But that didn't stop Mrs. LeGrand from introducing him to everyone who had preceded them. The first couple was Mr. and Mrs. Hughes, the managers of Natchez's most successful shipping business. The second couple, Mr. and Mrs. Sheffield, were not as welcoming. He suspected there might be an interesting story behind their attitudes.

He renewed his acquaintance with Abigail's great-aunt and great-uncle whom he had first met at the waterfront mission. Several other couples and families went out of their way to make him feel welcome.

By the time he began the sermon, his trepidation had eased. He retold the story of Noah, a man who had listened to God's whispers and ignored the opinions of his neighbors. He warned them to focus on the world to come and reminded them that they were all sojourners in this world. Then he concluded by reading to them from Paul's epistle to the Philippians: "*'For to me to live is Christ, and to die is gain.'*"

When he stepped down from the pulpit, the townspeople crowded around him. He received their congratulations with a feeling of accomplishment. He had survived the first sermon in his circuit.

"That was a wonderful sermon, Brother Pierce." Somehow he heard her voice above all the other people in the church.

"Thank you, Miss LeGrand. I'm pleased you enjoyed it."

"Yes, Brother Pierce." Her father clapped him on the back. "You have the makings of a fine pastor. I can see why you were chosen to be a circuit rider. God is going to use you in a very powerful way."

Nathan ducked his head. He wasn't sure if the older man's words were true or not, nor was he certain he wanted to be used in a powerful way. He'd rather serve God quietly, pay for his sins, and maybe make a difference in a few people's lives. He had no desire to set the world on fire.

"Come, come." Mrs. LeGrand's voice interrupted his thoughts. "I've been telling everyone about the ball we'll be having in a week to make certain you get the chance to meet everyone."

"A ball?" The words struck terror in his heart. "I don't know if that's a good idea."

Mrs. LeGrand put a hand on his arm. "Of course it's a good idea. Wait and see. Everyone in the county will attend. It will be a great deal of fun. And you can dance with all the pretty girls. A handsome man like you, and one with such a commanding air, all the girls will be eager to have you partner with them. And who knows? Perhaps we'll even manage to find you someone special. Someone you can spend the rest of your life with."

Feeling like a leaf caught in a maelstrom, he followed her back out of the church. Surely there would be a way to halt her matchmaking plans. The last thing he needed was a wife.

Chapter 7

Abigail, you look lovelier than usual this evening." Her father beamed as he watched her descend the central staircase. "You'll be the belle of the ball."

She rolled her eyes as she reached the first floor. "There will be a dozen young ladies who have a better claim to that title than I."

Papa hugged her and dropped a kiss on her cheek. "They cannot begin to compare." He stepped back. "Is that a new dress?"

"Oh, Papa. Of course it's not new." She laughed. "I've been much too busy to go for a fitting."

Her mother joined them. "Sometimes I wonder if you keep yourself so busy so you can avoid having a family of your own."

Abigail had heard this speech before. She dropped a curtsy. "I'm trying to emulate you, Mama. Remember telling me how close you once came to marrying the wrong man?"

"Twice." Papa winked at her. "She didn't tell you about the soldier she met in New Orleans."

Wrinkling her brow in confusion, Abigail turned to her mother. "I thought you were engaged for a short time to Lowell Sheffield because your family pushed you to marry."

Her mother cleared her throat. "Yes, but that was a couple of years later."

"Wait, I have to hear this story. You met someone in New Orleans?"

Was that a flush in her mother's cheeks?

Abigail's head swiveled back to her father. "Weren't you a soldier in New Orleans?"

"Yes, but I wasn't the type to spend my nights at the local balls, so sadly, I never met your mother until I moved here."

She couldn't believe her mother had never told her about falling in love with a soldier. Was she still in love with him? Or had Papa turned her head? "Who was he?"

Her mother put her hands on her hips. "He's no one important. I once fancied myself interested in Asher Landon because I thought we could make an advantageous match. But he was in love with someone else. And I thank God for that. If he had not given me the cold shoulder, I might never have come home to Natchez. And I might never have met your papa."

"And then I would have spent my life alone." Her father put an arm around her mother's waist and hugged her briefly.

The front knocker sounded, and he relinquished his hold to answer the door. Abigail stood next to her mother as their guests arrived, her mind captivated by the glimpse into her parents' past. She tried to imagine them young and in love, but it was beyond her ability.

A pang of some emotion tightened her chest. She was determined to remain single until God arranged for her to meet the right man, someone who would not try to curtail her dreams. He would have to live here with her in Natchez so she could continue helping at the orphanage and working in the waterfront mission. He would be accommodating and thoughtful, a man who listened to her ideas and supported her efforts—

Brother Pierce stepped into the foyer, and her galloping thoughts came to a sudden halt. While he shook hands with her father and bowed to her mother, Abigail reached a hand up to check her coiffure even though she knew it was secure. Jemma had outdone herself, winding Abigail's long hair into dips and swirls and securing it with ribbons and diamond-studded pins. And although her dress was not new, it was one of her favorites, made of pale pink jonquil, with deep flounces and wide sleeves. She liked the way it swirled around her ankles as she danced.

"You're looking especially lovely this evening, Miss LeGrand." Brother Pierce took her outstretched hand in his own.

The light reflected off of his thick hair, like molten gold, as he bowed. Her heart stuttered as his large fingers squeezed her hand gently before straightening. "Th–thank you, sir. I. . .It. . ." Why wouldn't her mouth work properly? She took a quick breath and prayed to regain her composure. "We haven't seen you much this week."

"I have been preparing for my first trip to some of the surrounding areas."

A feeling not unlike emptiness filled the pit of her stomach. He was leaving? "How long will you be gone?"

He shrugged. "I don't really know. I have met with my predecessor several times this week. He says he generally spent ten days to two weeks on the circuit, but he suggested I curtail this trek and return in time for Sunday services."

Abigail realized her shoulders had drooped at some time in their conversation. She straightened them with an effort and forced her mouth up in a smile. She was not some young girl to moon over the handsome pastor. "Then I'll wish you Godspeed."

He nodded and turned to go into the ballroom.

Even as she greeted other guests, she had a difficult time concentrating on their conversations, her gaze often straying to the people in the ballroom as though she was trying to catch a glimpse of a certain tall, blond minister.

When her parents deemed it time, they joined the others. As soon as she entered the ballroom, Silas Ward stepped forward. Had he been watching for her?

His dark eyes glowed in the light of the chandelier. "You look so beautiful this evening. The color of your apparel is only eclipsed by the bloom of your cheeks."

Raising an eyebrow at his effusiveness, Abigail looked past his right shoulder and met Brother Pierce's serious gaze. "Thank you, Mr. Ward. You are most kind. I trust you are making yourself at home in our busy town."

"Yes, yes. Natchez is a beautiful and interesting town. From the muddy banks and saloons of Under-the-Hill to the stately mansions like your home, I have found this town to be welcoming." He stroked his mustache.

"I'm glad you like our little piece of the world. Things are not perfect in Natchez, not by any means. But for the most part, all of these people have their redeeming qualities."

She turned to slip past him, but Mr. Ward put a hand on her arm. "I was wondering if you would honor me with a dance."

Although she had planned to make a quick round of the people in the room, she could not resist the plea in his dark brown eyes. "Yes, of course, Mr. Ward."

As if on cue, the musicians began playing a waltz. Mr. Ward held out an arm and escorted her to the center of the room. His arm went around her waist, and Abigail assumed the proper position as he swept her into the dance. At first she found it a little difficult to follow his lead, but then the music caught her. Abigail forgot the awkwardness and allowed him to twirl her around the room to the strains of Johann Strauss's "Viennese Carnival."

"I have not seen you at the orphanage this week." His voice tickled her ear.

Abigail pulled away a little. "I generally go by there in the morning. Deborah always needs help with the youngest children while she is teaching the others reading and arithmetic."

"I see. Perhaps I should make it a habit to drop by and help you."

She concentrated on the lapel of his coat. "I'm not certain that's a good idea. Deborah has been telling me how much she appreciates your afternoon visits. She says you are very good with the older boys."

"I don't do much."

She could not fault his modesty. Deborah said Silas had been teaching the boys how to whittle. "At least what you're teaching them will keep them occupied and out of trouble. At best they could learn skills for future employment." Abigail glanced up at his face, surprised to see that his cheeks had flushed. "I hope I have not spoken out of turn."

His hand tightened around her waist. "Of course not. I appreciate your compliments. I would be quite disturbed if I thought you did not approve of my feeble efforts to make a difference. Those poor boys. At the risk of losing your good opinion, I must admit that their circumstances disturb me greatly."

Her eyebrows climbed up toward her scalp. She stiffened in his arms. "Are you saying Deborah's not doing a good job?"

"Oh no." His jaw dropped open. "That's not what I meant at all. In fact, the orphanage is exemplary. And Miss Trent is a capable matron. If all orphanages were as well run as this one, our world would be a much happier place."

The waltz drew to a close, and Abigail stepped away from him. "I enjoyed our dance, Mr. Ward, but I fear I must leave you to attend my duties as hostess."

He bowed. "Of course. But I hope to speak with you again on this matter. I cannot have you thinking I do not approve of the orphanage."

"That's not necessary, Mr. Ward. You have explained yourself quite admirably. I appreciate your kindness to the children and your compliments concerning Miss Trent." She felt his gaze on her as she crossed the room and could not decide if she liked the attention or not.

Charlotte Thornton stood next to her mother, Susannah Hughes, and Abigail's mother. She joined them and spent the next hour listening to their discussion of the trials and joys of motherhood. Charlotte had a way of giving a humorous bent to her children's escapades. Soon they were all laughing as she described her daughter's attempts to whistle back at a yellow warbler perched on a tree near her bedroom window.

Standing with her back to the ballroom, Abigail felt rather than saw someone standing close to her. She turned and almost buried her nose in a starched shirt. Her breath caught as she looked up into the new minister's blue gaze. His eyes reminded her of summertime—long, warm afternoons spent rocking in the shade of the front porch and watching the boats pass by on the ribbon of river at the base of their bluff. Heat from her memories might be the reason her cheeks were so flushed.

"Can I tear you away from your friends long enough for a dance?"

"She would love to dance with you, Brother Pierce." Her mother answered his question for her.

It wasn't that she didn't want to dance with him. The problem was feeling as though she was being pushed in that direction. Abigail held herself stiffly during the opening bars of yet another waltz. Did this orchestra know any other types of songs?

"Thank you for agreeing to dance with me, Miss LeGrand."

"The honor is mine, Brother Pierce." She gave the acceptable response although what she really wanted to do was slip away. How dare her mother put her in this predicament. Brother Pierce probably thought she was desperate for a husband. Bad enough that every time he showed up her tongue tied itself in knots.

He cleared his throat, causing her to look up into his eyes once more. The whole room seemed to disappear around her as she fell into their blue depths. Why did his eyes have to be such an arresting color?

"I wish you would not call me Brother Pierce." He smiled down at her, and the blue color deepened. "It makes me feel so old. . .and responsible for giving the right answer all of the time."

Abigail's heart melted at the vulnerability exposed by his words. She had never considered what it might mean to be a pastor. Of course she knew he would have to prepare sermons and visit the sick. Her mind went back to the days when she was a child and the pastor visited. Her parents had turned to him for reassurance and advice on any number of topics. Sometimes they had even sent her from the room so she would not be privy to the more adult problems they faced. "All right, Nathan. But I have a couple of conditions."

"What conditions?" His smile wavered.

"First, you must call me Abigail."

He nodded. "Agreed, Abigail."

"And the second is that you must help me at the orphanage whenever you are in town."

He hesitated a moment and almost stumbled. "I suppose so."

"Good. Strange things are occurring there, and Deborah and I would like to talk to someone about them."

The music stopped before she could elaborate further. He escorted her back to her mother. "I don't know if I'll see you before I leave tomorrow, Abigail, Mrs. LeGrand. But please rest assured you will all be in my prayers."

"That's very kind of you, Nathan." She could feel her mother's approving glance on her as he strode across the room. How would she ever explain their conversation without raising her parents' hopes?

Maybe it had been a bad idea to agree to Nathan's request. But how could she have refused the plea in those piercing blue eyes of his? The answer was simple. She couldn't.

Chapter 8

I really enjoyed your preaching, Brother Pierce." The woman's gap-toothed grin reminded Nathan of the jack-o'-lanterns he had carved as a child. "We been needing a good preaching. There's folk here what turned from God and is going to burn in hell when they die."

He was sure her words were meant to encourage him, but they had the opposite effect. He felt the weight of responsibility settle firmly on his shoulders. If he was not effective in explaining God's Word, others would pay the ultimate price. "Thank you, ma'am."

A sigh filled him before he turned his attention to the last few people waiting to greet him. Doubt seemed to chase after him each day on his circuit. Was he doing the right thing? Was he bringing converts into the fold? Was he good enough to preach God's message of salvation and forgiveness? If he told these people what he'd done, would they turn from him in shock and disgust? He didn't know the answers to the questions that dogged him. And no matter how hard he prayed for answers, God remained stubbornly silent.

The day was growing warm, and his coat was beginning to itch. Nathan promised himself a quick bath in the nearby stream before getting back on his horse and heading for the next town. But before he could enjoy that, he would have to see what these people needed. He smiled at the couple, a man about his own age and a pretty young woman who looked about five years younger. "What can I do for you?"

The man rolled the brim of his hat between his hands as though he was nervous. "We. . .uh. . .we was hoping you could marry us, Preacher. We been waiting for someone to come by who could say the words over us and make everything all legal-like. My name's Frank Horton and this is Abigail, the woman I love more'n anything."

Of course she looked nothing like the LeGrands' daughter, but Nathan couldn't stop his mind from conjuring up a picture of the engaging woman he'd danced with on his last evening in Natchez. The girl in front of him was dressed in a plain shift that had been mended many times. Her eye color was much lighter than his Abigail's ebony gaze.

His thoughts halted. *His Abigail?* Where had that come from? Abigail LeGrand did not belong to anyone, least of all a traveling preacher with a shameful past.

171

He dragged his wandering thoughts back to the couple. "I would be happy to do so." He smiled at them, opened his *Book of Common Prayer*. " 'Dearly beloved: We have come together. . .'" The words flowed around them, timeless and wonderful.

When he finished, he closed his eyes and bowed his head, waiting a moment to make sure the couple followed his lead. "Lord, here I stand next to Frank and Abigail, who present themselves humbly before You and ask that You bless their union. They have deep feelings of commitment and love for each other and pledge that they will always cling to You first and each other second. Please guide and direct them, keep their hearts tender one to the other, and may their union bring glory and honor to Your name above all else. In the name of Your precious Son, Jesus, the one who died so that all of us might have eternal life, amen."

"Amen and thank you, Preacher." The man put his crumpled hat back on his head and shook Nathan's hand with enthusiasm before turning back to Abigail. "I guess we need to get back to your ma's house. She's gonna need you to help with the young'uns."

Nathan walked with them to the edge of the meadow, where he'd tethered his horse. "I'll stop in at the county courthouse on my way out of town and ask them to record your names."

They nodded and thanked him once again before walking away hand-in-hand. He watched them for a moment, surprised by the yearning in his heart as Frank pulled his new bride close and planted a gentle kiss on her cheek.

What would it feel like to fall in love and marry? He had once believed he loved Iris Landon, and he had even wondered if he loved Margaret Coleridge. But that had been before he murdered a man. The stain on his soul because of that terrible deed would likely prevent him from ever really falling in love. And it would certainly stop any self-respecting young lady from wanting to marry him.

Nathan tucked his Bible into his saddlebag and removed his coat. The sooner he got that through his thick skull, the better. Maybe soaking it in the creek would help clear his head. He certainly hoped so.

❊

"It must be here somewhere." Abigail could hear the frustration in Deborah's voice.

She put a hand on her friend's shoulder. "Don't worry, we're going to find it. It's probably been mislaid."

Having arrived at the orphanage late, Abigail had been surprised to find the children barely controlled by Sheba, the young black woman who cooked and helped care for the orphans. Deborah, she had explained, wouldn't come out of her bedroom.

Concerned that the capable administrator was sick, Abigail had gone upstairs and found a scene of chaos in Deborah's usually orderly room. The rocking chair had been pushed away from its corner, the padded cushion dangling from one corner of the seat. Blankets and pillows made a pile next to the bureau. Clothing hung haphazardly from the drawers suspended at precarious angles, and Deborah's water pitcher and bowl were upside down. The hand-knotted rug Abigail had helped her make had been rolled up and leaned against the wall between the pair of windows overlooking the street. Even the drapes had not been spared—they had been pulled down and now lay in heaps like discarded rags.

"I know I'm being silly about an inexpensive piece of gaudy jewelry, but that bracelet is the only reminder I have of my mother. It has no intrinsic value. I know I left it somewhere in my room last Sunday after the service." The distraught woman jerked the drawer out of the bureau and dumped the entire contents on the bed, grunting with the effort.

Abigail helped her comb through gloves, handkerchiefs, and cotton pantaloons. Something glimmered in the light from the window. "Is that it?"

"Where?" Deborah pounced at the spot Abigail indicated. "No." She lifted a shiny button up. "This came off of my walking dress and I have not had time to sew it back on."

"Your bracelet doesn't seem to be in here." Abigail surveyed the bedroom. She had never seen Deborah's room in such a state of chaos. "Perhaps you laid it down somewhere else because one of the children interrupted you. Wait and see. As soon as we discover it, you will remember what happened."

Deborah tossed the contents back into the drawer without folding them. "I hope you're right."

After helping her slide the drawer back into the bureau, Abigail sat down on the rumpled bed. "Have you looked anywhere else?"

"No, I cannot imagine it would be anywhere else. I always send the children up to change out of their Sunday clothes, and I do the same. That's when I take the bracelet off and put it away." Deborah covered her face with her hands.

Abigail got up and put her arms around the distraught woman. She pushed back her concern about finding the bracelet. Now was not the time to voice her doubt. Deborah needed comfort. "Never fear. We will find it if it's anywhere in the house. Have you talked to Sheba? Maybe she has seen it."

Deborah shook her head. "I have not said anything about it. I'm sure they wonder if I've lost my senses, but I'd rather they think that than to feel accused of thievery."

"Only a guilty conscience would make someone feel accused." Abigail squeezed Deborah's shoulders before stepping back and pointing to the bed. "Why don't you sit down over there while I straighten up the room a little? Who knows? Maybe I'll find the bracelet as I put your things away."

She bustled about putting order to the room while Deborah followed her suggestion. As she worked, Abigail tried to come up with other locations where her friend might have left the bracelet, but every suggestion she made was answered with a breathy no or a shake of the head. By the time she finished tidying the room, her list of possibilities had been exhausted.

"I don't see any way around asking the others if they have seen your jewelry. I understand your reservations, but it must be done." She perched beside Deborah and handed her a handkerchief. "Would you rather I asked? That way you can place the blame on me if anyone's feelings are bruised."

"No, I'll do it." Deborah scrubbed at her face with the square of lace. "I had to make sure it wasn't in here first. In all the years I've been here, nothing has ever been stolen. But I suppose I'm going to have to face facts. Someone in this house is a thief."

"Let's not jump to conclusions. I am still hoping we will find it in the kitchen or lying on the hall table." She met Deborah's forlorn gaze with a smile she hoped was comforting. "Let's check, and if we do not find it, we'll move forward from there."

The children were finishing their breakfast as the two women went downstairs and looked around for the piece of jewelry. When they still could not find it, they called the children and Sheba together and explained what had happened. Being very careful to avoid accusing anyone, Deborah asked if her bracelet had been seen. Worried stares and shakes of the head answered her. No one knew where it could be.

"I'll bet the ghost took it," said one of the older boys.

Fear radiated from the younger children, and even one or two of the older ones looked over their shoulders or shuffled their feet.

"Don't be silly." Abigail stood up to get their attention. "Ghosts don't exist."

Mia nodded her head. "Yes, they do. We hear them at night, Miss Abigail. They pull chains around in the attic and moan like the wind."

"And they walk around in the halls sometimes," another girl added in solemn tones. "But I hide under my covers so they won't see me and take me away."

A little boy began to cry at her gloomy words.

Deborah clapped her hands. "That's enough. All of you know better than to frighten each other. We are a family in this house, and families don't scare each other with tales of imaginary spirits." She opened her arms to the little boy who was crying. He ran to her and buried his head against her shoulder. "Don't worry, Timmy. Everything's going to be all right." She gathered him up and walked out of the parlor, murmuring comforting words in his ear.

Abigail frowned at the older children. "Miss Deborah's bracelet is the thing we need to worry about. I want each of you to keep a sharp eye out for it. As for the other matter, when we find out what is making all the odd noises, some of you are going to feel quite foolish that you let yourselves be tricked into believing such nonsense."

Sheba had not said anything during the meeting, but as the scolded children began to file out of the room, she came to where Abigail stood. "I don't hear those sounds on account of I go home at night, Miss Abigail, but the children sure do talk about it a lot. And I'm wondering now if it's not some homeless varmint hiding out up there and coming down when he thinks it is safe."

Abigail rested her chin on one finger as she considered the maid's words. "Do you think it's a runaway?"

Sheba shrugged. "I don't know about that, but it wouldn't surprise me none."

"Perhaps I need to have Papa and some of the men from the plantation come over here and check it out. If it is a runaway, they'll help the poor soul get away safely."

"And if it's not?" Sheba's eyes grew wide as she voiced the question.

Abigail dropped her hand to her hip. "No matter who it is, I'm sure Papa can take care of it." She infused her voice with all the confidence she could muster. It would not help anyone to see how doubtful she really felt.

❀

"Squirrels?" Abigail could not keep the disbelief out of her voice.

Her father had gone to town this morning to check on the orphanage while she and her mother stayed home to wash linens. She would have much preferred to go with him, but she had not been able to desert her mother. After hours stirring heavy sheets with a long stick, she was more than willing to take a break and listen to her father's report.

"That's right." Her father nodded his head for emphasis. "We found two nests in the attic, so I can understand why the children heard noises."

"How did they get inside the orphanage?"

"They're crafty animals." He frowned. "It doesn't take much of an opening. And they can do a great deal of damage once they manage to get inside."

"How will you make certain they don't come back?"

"That's easy. Susannah Hughes told me last week that her cat has weaned a litter of kittens. I sent her a message to send one over to the orphanage." His chuckle drew an answering smile from her. "I think that will be one well-groomed cat if the children have anything to say about it."

Her mother came back from the clothesline with an empty basket. "What are you two laughing about?"

"Cats and squirrels." Her father caught his wife up in a hug and swung her around. The basket slipped out of her hands and bounced toward the back porch. He explained about his morning discoveries as he dropped a series of quick kisses from her ear to her mouth.

Abigail rolled her eyes at her parents' antics. "You two act more like newlyweds than a staid, married couple."

"It's your papa's fault." Her mother giggled as the man holding her pressed one last kiss on the back of her neck. "He shouldn't be such a romantic man."

"And your mama shouldn't be so beautiful."

"Okay, okay." Abigail put her hands on her hips. "Papa, can you quit nuzzling my mother long enough to tell me if you found Deborah's bracelet?"

Mama's cheeks were flushed. When Papa released her, she rescued the laundry basket and turned to face him.

He sighed and shook his head. "No, we didn't. And I must say squirrels don't usually show interest in shiny objects. That would be more like a bird, although I can't imagine a bird strong enough to fly off with a piece as large as a bracelet."

"That's too bad." Her mother pulled a sheet from the rinse water and wrung it out. "Maybe we can find one like it to give to Deborah."

"I don't know." Abigail returned to her stirring. "It belonged to her mother. We'll have to keep praying it will turn up. I cannot believe anyone at the orphanage would take it."

"It's beginning to look like that's the only reasonable explanation." Her father leaned against a tree and watched them work. "But perhaps it will show up yet."

Mama dropped the sheet into her basket and grabbed another one. "You could help us instead of watching."

"I believe that's my cue to check on the stables." Papa pushed himself away from the tree and sauntered away. "You two seem to have the wash well in hand."

Abigail didn't even try to hide her snort. "So much for togetherness."

She and her mother continued working with Jemma until all the wash was hanging on the clothesline. They would have to come back out before dusk to bring the dry linens in for ironing tomorrow. At least that job wouldn't make her eyes water like the lye fumes had this morning. And climbing into a bed of fresh linens tomorrow night would be worth all of their hard work.

Chapter 9

Coming back to the cottage at Magnolia already felt like coming home. Nathan knew how lucky he was to have such a luxurious place to live in. Most traveling pastors had little besides a bedroll and a Bible.

Early morning sunlight cascaded onto the marble floor as he walked through the foyer. After a week on the road, he should have been able to stay abed this morning, but the birdsong outside his window had called to him.

He rubbed his chin as he walked along the shaded path toward the bluff overlooking the Mississippi River. Perhaps he should have taken the time to shave, but he had wanted to enjoy the morning before anyone else was up. His destination this morning was a large wooden bench on the LeGrands' front lawn that commanded a wide view of the river. Mr. and Mrs. LeGrand talked about enjoying the sunset from the bench, but he wanted to enjoy the vista as the day awoke. Following the pathway, he caught a glimpse of a yearling picking its way through the undergrowth some distance away.

He emerged from the pathway onto the grounds and took a moment to study the plantation home. It was a graceful building with tall white columns and a deep porch that faced the river. In front of the house, old oak trees stood watch over a small pond, whose surface rippled under the invisible brush of a spring breeze. He wondered if Abigail had ever waded at the water's edge or attempted to climb the gnarled limbs of the overhanging trees. It wasn't hard to imagine her being so daring.

Turning to the bench, he was surprised to see it was already occupied. Who else had been called out so early? His eyes narrowed as he tried to make out the person's identity. He did not want to bother anyone, but his curiosity took him several steps closer. A woman. Abigail. Something was wrong. She sat hunched forward, her shoulders shaking and her head in her hands. Was she crying? Concern propelled Nathan forward. "Are you okay?"

Her head jerked upward and that's when he realized her hair was loose as it flew around her. "What are you doing here?" A white towel fluttered to the ground.

"I'm sorry. I didn't mean to startle you, Abigail." He realized his mistake when he searched her face for signs of tears. "I saw you sitting here and I thought you might be in distress and need someone to talk to."

"Distress?" She reached back with both hands and grabbed her hair, struggling to keep it under control. "You frightened me out of my wits. Yes, I'm stressed. You've caught me practically undressed."

At first he thought she was really upset, and his chest tightened in response. He opened his mouth to apologize yet again, but then he saw the gleam in her midnight black eyes. She was teasing him. His chest eased and a smile turned up the corners of his mouth. "Don't put it up on my account."

She stopped trying to twist the damp strands into a bun. "I suppose you will think I am some kind of wanton female, but I washed it this morning and decided to sit out here and let the wind blow it dry." As soon as she let go of the bundle, it fell down again around her shoulders. "I cannot abide the fragrance of lye soap, so I always wash my hair after Mama and I launder the linens."

Nathan took a deep breath to still the sudden pounding of his heart. She looked so vulnerable standing on the far side of the bench. He pushed aside the longing that crept into him. He had no business thinking about running his fingers through her soft tresses. Only her husband would have that right.

Abigail did not seem aware of the effect she was having on him. She beckoned him forward and sat down once more facing the bluff. "I didn't realize you had returned."

Instead of sitting next to her, he leaned against the trunk of a pine tree that stood next to her bench. "I came in yesterday evening."

"I trust your trip was successful." She turned her dark gaze on him. "Did you win more hearts for the Lord?"

He shook his head. "I cannot take credit. I am only a laborer in the field. Jesus is the one who harvests."

"Well said, Nathan. All of us should share your humility." She glanced up at him. "It is one of your most admirable traits."

She thought he had admirable traits? Nathan wanted to ask her to list them, but he supposed that would contradict the humility she attributed to him. He glanced to the river, watching as a flatboat cut an angle across the wide bend below them. Perhaps he would do better to focus on her. "What has been going on here since my departure?"

"Much the same as what was happening while you were here." She brushed at a pine straw that had landed on the bench next to her. "Although we have solved the mystery of the odd sounds at the orphanage."

"Is that so?" Nathan looked back toward her. As she explained about squirrels and kittens he watched the expressions cross her face. The more he was around Abigail LeGrand, the more he found to admire about her. Strong and courageous, she was the type of woman who would meet all of life's challenges with a resolute spirit.

He wondered about the source of her strength. Was it because she had grown up in the lap of luxury? That did not make sense to him. Most people who grew up that way became self-absorbed boors with no idea that they should work on behalf of others.

Which led him back to his question—from where did she draw her strength? Her values? One thing was for certain—her contradictions intrigued him. He had never met anyone like Abigail LeGrand.

❀

Abigail straightened and looked across the strawberry patch, where she and her mother were working once again. They had already gathered some of the succulent fruits a few weeks earlier, and this would likely be their last harvest for this year. "You're supposed to pick the berries, not eat all of them, Mama."

Her mother's guilty look made Abigail laugh out loud. "Did you think I wouldn't see you?"

"They're too sweet for me to resist." Mama pulled her bonnet forward and bent to gather more of the red fruit.

Abigail dropped another handful into her basket, palming one to pop into her mouth. "You make an excellent point."

Laughter filled the air.

"I think we have enough for now." Mama started for the kitchen, her basket piled high.

Abigail grabbed her basket with both hands and followed. "I saw a new recipe in the *Natchez Free Trader* last week."

"Was it a cake recipe?" The older woman emptied her basket into a vat of water that had been drawn earlier. "I think I remember seeing it."

"We also need to make some preserves. I love strawberry preserves on your fresh bread."

"That's a wonderful idea, daughter. We'll take it with us on our trip."

Abigail removed her bonnet. "What trip?"

"A big church conference is going to be held in Jackson in two weeks, and your papa and I have decided to go."

"I thought we were going to Gatlin's Camp Ground like last year." Abigail was shocked at her mother's pronouncement. Her parents usually consulted her before making their plans. It wasn't that she had anything against traveling to the capital city. She had never visited Jackson before.

"We'll probably go there, too." Mama swirled the strawberries vigorously enough to wash them clean. "But we thought it would be nice to visit with the elders in Jackson. We were also thinking about asking Brother Pierce to travel with us."

Abigail's mouth dropped open. "Why would you want to do that? We never took Brother Harris with us to Gatlin's Camp Ground when he was the pastor, much less to Jackson."

A secret smile teased her mother's lips. "But this is a different situation."

"Mamaaa." She drew out the last syllable to indicate her objection to the idea. "You have got to stop interfering in my life. I am not interested in Nath—Brother Pierce. And he's not interested in me."

Her mother put down the spoon and rested her hands on her hips.

"Abigail, I love you dearly, but you have got to realize that not everything going on in this household revolves around you."

The words struck home. She sat down hard in a convenient rocking chair. "I didn't. . ."

Mama leaned over her and put a hand on Abigail's cheek. "I'm sorry, dear. But you are jumping to the wrong conclusion. We were thinking about Brother Pierce. He's all alone and new to the area. If he doesn't go with us, he'd likely have to go by horseback and sleep out in the open. This way, he can go with us on the steamship to Vicksburg and then overland on the stagecoach to Jackson."

"Have you talked to Brother Pierce about your plans?" Abigail got up from the rocker and started pulling strawberries from the water and capping them with a sharp knife.

"Now when would I have talked to Brother Pierce? Your pa and I only decided that we'd make the trip a few days ago, and he hasn't returned from his circuit." Her mother glanced at her for a moment. "Or has he?"

Abigail's cheeks turned as red as the fruit in her hand. "I believe so. He. . . I saw him early this morning on the bluff."

"I see." Her mother took the topped fruits from Abigail and began cutting them into slices to go into preserves and marmalades. Others would be crushed to add to strawberry cakes and pies, while still others would be left whole and served as a dessert with fresh cream from their dairy cows. "What did he have to say about his travels?"

"Not much." Abigail shrugged and concentrated on her work. "He is very humble and credited his successes to God's abilities rather than his talents."

"He is a good man."

Abigail didn't feel like her mother's statement needed confirmation. Anyone could see Nathan Pierce was a good man. Why wouldn't he be? He was a preacher, after all. And preachers had to be good to be effective. Didn't they?

She continued pondering that question until they had all the strawberries ready to go to the kitchen. All the preachers she'd ever met were good men, some more humble than others, some more commanding behind the pulpit. But it did not necessarily follow that she should marry him—them.

She tied a cloth around her head and poured sliced strawberries into a pot on the hot stove. Mama and the cook discussed recipes and preparations, but Abigail let her thoughts wander back to her discussion with Nathan that morning.

He had been so considerate when he thought she was upset, and she had been unable to resist teasing him a little. But she would have to be careful to be more circumspect with him for two reasons. The first had to do with raising false hopes in her parents' minds. No matter what Mama said, she would like to see Abigail married with a house full of children. The second reason was that she did not want to mislead Nathan himself. She was not going to get married and try to make herself into some man's idea of the perfect spouse. The very idea was abhorrent to her.

Her mind made up, Abigail decided she would avoid Nathan Pierce. She nodded. While that might not be particularly easy to do if they were traveling by carriage, on a steamboat cruiser it ought to be a snap.

Chapter 10

I don't think I can fit even one more item into this trunk." Abigail's mother tried to force the lid down over the stack of clothing. "Come over here and see if you can close the latches."

Abigail complied, tugging and grunting as she tried to get the leather straps cinched. "You lack at least an inch."

"Oof." Mama sat down on the lid and bounced. "How about now?"

Abigail pulled so hard on the straps that she worried they might break. "I'm sorry, but this is not going to work." She sat back on her heels. "I can probably squeeze a few things into my trunk."

"Could you?" Her mother looked at her over one shoulder. "I don't know why it takes so many outfits. Your father would chastise me for my excess if he knew what trouble I'm having with this trunk."

"That's only because he's a man. Women require more space. It's a wonder we don't need two or three trunks each. We have to have outfits for the morning and different ones for evening wear"—Abigail ticked off each category of clothing on a different finger—"walking dresses and riding habits, sleepwear and toiletries."

"Perhaps we shouldn't go to Jackson, after all. It seemed much simpler when we were going to the campground." Mama stood up, and the lid of the trunk popped back open. "Let's see what I can store in your trunk."

Soon they had the excess items neatly stowed away in Abigail's trunk.

"Are you two done?" Papa called to them from the base of the stairs. "Nathan is here, and we're ready to load everything onto the wagon."

Abigail picked up her yellow bonnet and tied its wide white ribbon under her chin as her mother walked to the head of the stairs. She glanced in the mirror and sighed. Part of her wished to be considered beautiful, but that description had always been out of reach. She grimaced at her reflection. At least her hair was neat today, not blowing loose in the wind.

Butterflies took wing in her stomach as she considered the trip ahead. The boat ride was sure to be fun, and she was looking forward to seeing the attractions in Jackson, but what she anticipated most were the open-air church meetings. They always strengthened her faith and left her feeling rejuvenated and restored. Optimism buoyed her, and she left her bedroom with a new spring in her step.

❀

The crew did most of the work involved with loading the LeGrands' luggage onto the *Sierra Queen*, the stern-wheeler Nathan and the LeGrand family would be traveling on for the next twenty-four hours. Nathan tried to help, but he was pushed aside as the experienced men lifted the heavy trunks to their shoulders and strode to the boat. Mrs. LeGrand and her daughter would be staying in one stateroom, while he shared another with Mr. LeGrand.

Once again, Nathan marveled over their generosity. If not for their insistence, he would have had a much more arduous and lengthy trip.

"Come on, Nathan." Mr. LeGrand's voice drew his attention to the carriage. "Would you give Abigail a hand while I help my wife onto the boat?"

"Of course, sir." Nathan smiled at both of the ladies and offered an arm to the younger. "Watch your step."

Rough boards spanned the distance between the bank and the boat's deck, making a gangway for passengers. As soon as the two of them reached the center point, he could feel the wood bending slightly. Abigail's hand, which had been resting on his arm, clenched tightly. "Don't be afraid. You're safe."

"You must think me quite the ninny." Her voice was strained.

"Why would I think such a silly thing? Because you have sense enough to be cautious?" He placed his free hand over the one gripping his arm. "Once we get on the boat, you will feel differently."

She nodded and swallowed hard.

"Don't look down, Abigail. Look at me instead." He caught her gaze and held it as they crossed the rushing water. Something happened. He seemed to fall into her ebony eyes. Eyes that had gone from fear to admiration.

He felt strong enough to vanquish anything. His chest expanded, and his smile curved upward. They stepped as one onto the deck of the boat and stopped, still staring into each other's eyes. It might have been a few seconds or a few hours before he once again became aware of the activity around them.

"Thank you, Nathan." She whispered the words before pulling her hand free and walking away, the scarf on her bonnet floating back toward him as if giving him a jaunty wave. He wondered if he'd ever seen anything half so enchanting.

Somehow Nathan knew nothing would ever be the same again.

❀

"That was an excellent meal." Abigail's mother looked up at the waiter standing at her elbow.

"Thank you, ma'am." The man nodded his head as he removed her plate, piling it atop the other empty plates on the wooden tray balanced on his arm.

Papa leaned back in the mahogany chair and patted his flat stomach. "I would be in trouble if I ate like this all the time."

Everyone at the table laughed at his pained expression.

"I agree with you, Mr. LeGrand." Nathan put his napkin on the table. "All of the courses nearly overwhelmed my senses. Soup, salad, two entrées, half-a-dozen side dishes, and fresh fruit for dessert. Perhaps we should take a stroll about the boat to stretch our legs."

"What a grand idea." Abigail sent him an approving smile and gathered her shawl. She and Mama had spent their time changing into proper attire for a formal dinner. Although their cabin was adequate, she was ready to do some exploring. She stood, bringing both men to their feet. "Please say you want to go, Mama."

"I suppose so." Her mother rolled her eyes. "But I don't plan to stay up all night traipsing about. The next few days are going to be filled with all sorts of activities, and we will all need our rest if we are going to take full advantage of them."

"I know you're right, dearest, but the sun has barely gone down." Papa held out his elbow and Mama tucked her hand under it.

"Don't blame me if you fall asleep while talking to Bishop Ross." Her smile softened the words.

Abigail felt Nathan's gaze and looked up at him. His blue eyes were warm—almost a caress. A lock of thick blond hair fell forward across his brow, and her fingers itched to reach up and smooth it back into place. She pulled at her shawl instead.

Nathan was so tall, towering over her like a veritable giant. She felt small in contrast, small and feminine. How did he manage to do that? Abigail had never felt this way before. How many other ladies had he charmed without saying even a word? Her smile slipped a notch, and she sighed. The answer would probably shock her.

He held out his arm. "Shall we join your parents?"

Still feeling the sting of her thoughts, Abigail ignored his gesture and stalked to the door. She would not be his next conquest.

When she caught up with her parents, they were talking to the captain. She joined them without a word, listening as he described the movement of the engine and how it pushed the large wheel at the end of his boat. Captain Rogers was a slender man of average height, who held himself with the stiff posture of a former military man. From the tip of his shiny bald head to the pointed toes of his gleaming boots, he was all business.

One of the crewmen scurried up and whispered something to the captain.

"Please excuse me. I must see to something." He sketched a quick bow and strode toward the wide stairs leading to the pilothouse on the topmost level of the boat.

"I hope nothing is wrong." Nathan's voice startled Abigail.

A shiver like a bead of icy springwater trickled down her spine. Why had he followed them out here? The unchristian thought shamed her immediately. Where else was Nathan going to go? Her parents had invited him along. She was the real problem. She needed to think of him as a brother. After all, as an only child she had often wished for a sibling.

"Captain Rogers has a great deal of experience on the Mississippi River." Her father answered Nathan's comment. "I'm sure he has everything under control."

One side of the hallway they were standing in was formed by the wall that housed the engine. A waist-high wooden rail formed the other side. Looking past it, she could make out the gray green foliage lining the desolate bank. "Does anyone live on the river between Natchez and Vicksburg?"

"Not many." Nathan answered her question. "But I suspect that one day soon there will be homes and businesses built out here. The river is a conduit of enterprise. It helps us move goods from one place to another."

Papa stepped to the rail. "Transportation was much more difficult before Captain Shreve removed the snags choking the river. I can remember back when steamboats first started traveling up the river. It seemed snags were sinking them almost every day. It's much safer now."

"Come along, Jeremiah." Mama tugged at his arm. "These young people don't want to hear how life was when you were their age. And I need an escort to my cabin."

"I'll come with you, Mama." Abigail took a step toward her before being waved away.

"Your father and I need to talk about a few things, honey. Why don't you young people stay out here and enjoy the river's beauty?"

"Yes, ma'am." She wondered if her mother was matchmaking once more. But even if she was, this was Abigail's chance to prove that she could control her attraction to the handsome pastor. She turned back to the rail where he stood.

"I don't know what I've done to offend you, Miss LeGrand."

"Nothing at all until you forgot my given name." She put both hands on the rail and squeezed hard.

"I'm sorry. . .Abigail."

Abigail nodded. Silence surrounded them, broken only by intermittent splashes from unseen wildlife. Damp air made her shiver slightly and let go of the rail to pull her shawl tighter.

"Are you cold?" His voice sounded concerned, kind.

Before she could answer, laughter erupted from the dining room they had left earlier.

He was standing so close she could feel when he twisted around to look over his shoulder. Did he wish to be elsewhere? And here she'd been attributing his thoughtful actions to romantic impulses. "It sounds like they're having a party. I'm sure you'd rather join them than attend me. I assure you I'll be fine out here. I will seek my cabin in a few minutes."

"If this boat is like others on the Mississippi, I imagine some of the passengers have begun a game of chance." He put a hand on her arm. "Abigail, please tell me what I've done to offend you so."

Her heart fluttered like a trapped bird at his touch. How could she explain her feelings when she didn't understand them herself? All she knew was that she had to erect a barrier between them or suffer grave consequences. She glanced up at him. "I...there's nothing wrong, Nathan. I'm...I've been a little preoccupied."

"What is troubling you?"

Why couldn't the man take a hint? Why must he persist in asking her questions? Perhaps if she asked him a question or two about his past she could take his attention off of her. Over the years, she had found this to be an effective stratagem. "Actually you are right. You trouble me greatly, Nathan."

His warm hand left her arm as he took a step back. He acted like she had slapped him. "Please tell me how I can rectify myself."

"Ever since you came to Natchez, I have wondered about your background." She ignored the little voice that whispered caution in her mind. "Yet each time I have tried to find out something more than the basics of where you were born and raised, you deflect my questions. I have begun to wonder if you are hiding some heinous background. Were you a bank robber? An escaped felon? Did you waylay the real Nathan Pierce and assume his identity for some nefarious purpose?"

The scrape of a floating snag distracted her for a moment. She watched the branches slide past, their brittle fingers reaching out as if to snatch at her skirt.

"Be careful, Abigail." He pulled her back from the rail. "I don't want you to be pulled overboard."

Surprised by his move, she fell back against his hard chest. He wrapped both arms around her to steady her, and for a moment she wanted to do nothing more than melt against him. All thoughts of keeping this strong man at arm's length dissipated like shadows fleeing from the rising sun. She would be foolish to deny the delicious emotions swirling through her because of his nearness.

"My past life has nothing to do with the present." His voice in her ear sent shivers running up and down her spine.

Reality collided with fantasy. The truth washed over her like the river rushing past the bow of this boat. She struggled to break his hold on her. "Let go of me."

He complied so quickly she almost fell flat on her face. As soon as she was steady, she turned to face him. "The truth must be pretty awful if you take such pains to hide it."

Sadness crossed his features, but she refused to be drawn in again. She pointed an accusing finger at his square chin. "You're a preacher, so you should be familiar with the warning of Moses in the book of Numbers: *'And be sure your sin will find you out.'*"

She dropped her hand and marched away from him, fighting against looking back with every step. She was right. She knew it. But sometimes being right was a very hard thing.

Chapter 11

Nathan rubbed at his eyes again and shook his head to clear it. He had gotten up and dressed before the sun rose to avoid waking Mr. LeGrand.

Outside, he walked from one end of the steamboat to the other. The only other people he saw were busy crewmen who were tending their duties in the boiler room, the galley, and the pilothouse. He knew the other passengers would be up and about soon, and he needed to find some tranquility before facing anyone.

If only Abigail's words had not kept rolling around in his head all night long. They had carried so much authority. *"Your sin will find you out."* He could have snatched more sleep if his conscience had allowed it. Or if he had not relived those harrowing moments again and again during the night. The struggle, the fear, the sickening feeling of the knife entering Ira Watson's body. Over and over again, he saw the man's shocked face loosen into a death mask. How could he ever ask for forgiveness? He didn't deserve it.

Because of that, he knew he did not deserve any woman's consideration, especially not a woman like Abigail LeGrand. So why had he lowered his defenses? The answer to that question was easy. He was beginning to care for her. He thought back to his feelings for Iris Landon, which were a mere shadow of what he felt for Abigail. And his attraction to Margaret had never grown past friendship. Abigail was so different—so complex and invigorating. He liked being with her, talking to her, teasing her.

How had he gone so quickly from one extreme to the other? For a moment or two yesterday afternoon as they crossed the gangway together, he had thought she was the other part of him, the best part of him, the part God had fashioned only for him.

Maybe if he hadn't taken advantage of her misstep last night when they were alone. . .but she had felt so right in his arms. And he would have sworn she was comfortable there, too. Then she had turned into a wildcat. Her attack might not have left visible scars on him, but her words had surely cleaved his heart.

He wondered how she would act today. What would he say to her? Should he apologize? Or act as though nothing had happened last evening? If only he could turn to someone for answers. But he'd had no one since his parents' death. Uncle Richard, the man who had raised him, had never been much of a role model—a fact proven for good when the man was arrested for kidnapping.

He had friends back in Chattanooga, but no one in whom he could confide. A feeling of homesickness washed over him. But had he ever really had a home? Had God singled him out to live his life without the comforts of hearth and home? So what was this longing inside him for something more?

The sun rose over the tops of the trees, washing the eastern side of the steamboat with buttery color. Mist rose from the dark water and dissipated as sunlight warmed it. Reed-strewn banks slipped past him.

Nathan took one last turn on the deck before returning to his cabin. It was time to face whatever the coming day held.

❀

The low, mournful whistle of the steamboat called people to the water's edge as their steamboat began preparations to dock. Abigail stepped outside for her first full view of the town of Vicksburg. Even though it was bordered by the same river, this city looked very different from Natchez. Instead of featuring ramshackle saloons and ladies of ill repute, the docks here were crowded with warehouses and all sorts of businesses connected to the traffic on the river. Instead of the steep bluffs of Natchez, the bank here climbed a gentle slope to the top of the hill. Houses dotted the side of the hill, and more businesses were perched atop it.

Mama joined her at the rail and pointed. "Look, you can see a church from here."

Abigail spotted the crenellated tower and nodded. "Vicksburg looks like a growing town."

"Yes," her mother answered. "But I doubt it will ever be as busy as Natchez. Our proximity to New Orleans is part of the reason. Natchez has been around a lot longer. When I came down the river with your grandmother nearly twenty-five years ago, Vicksburg was only a bend in the river with a few homes, and Natchez was already the territorial capital."

"I remember reading about when Vicksburg finally became a town. I must have been fifteen or so." Abigail pressed a finger against her cheekbone. "I seem to remember it was named after a minister who objected to the American Revolution."

"Yes, that's right. His name was Newitt Vick. Most of his children still live here. Your aunt and uncle have visited with his daughter, Martha, at her home here. She is—"

"Here are my girls." Papa put one arm around Mama and the other around her. "Are you packed?"

Abigail stood on tiptoe and placed a kiss on his cheek. "Of course not, Papa. We were going to let you do it for us."

As they laughed at her joke, the steamboat bumped up against the dock.

Immediately men began scurrying back and forth to secure it to the large wooden posts that would keep it from drifting back into the river's current.

Mama watched them for a moment. "Perhaps we should go into the dining room to wait until it's time to disembark."

"Good idea." Papa strode to the entrance and held the door open for them to enter.

They sat at the nearest empty table and watched through the wide windows as the crewmen secured the boat. Abigail would have liked to watch them more closely, but she knew it was better to stay out of the way. A waiter came over to their table and asked if they would care for refreshments. Abigail shook her head. She was much too excited to be able to eat or drink.

After he dismissed the waiter, Papa turned back to her. "Have you seen our preacher this morning, Abigail?"

Her excitement ebbed. "No, sir." She frowned at him. "Is he not still in your cabin?"

"He was gone before I awoke this morning." Papa leaned back in his chair and crossed his legs at the ankles. "I was concerned that he may have jumped overboard after your walk last night."

Abigail spluttered. "I. . .I don't know what you mean."

Her mother raised an eyebrow as she glanced toward her daughter. "Although I don't remember your looking particularly guilty last night, I also cannot remember you giving me a reason for your early return to our cabin."

"I'm afraid I am the reason for her discomfort." Nathan's voice startled Abigail.

When had he come into the room? Why hadn't she kept a better eye on the door? Why had the room grown so small? Hot blood burned her neck and cheeks. She could feel all their gazes on her. She wished she could simply melt into the wooden planks at her feet and float away in the water beneath the boat.

"It was nothing." She cleared her throat. "I. . .a tree. . .um. . .a tree scraped against the boat and I almost fell. . .and Na—Brother Pierce pulled me away from the edge."

"I see." Her mother's voice brimmed with mirth.

Her father uncrossed his ankles and stood. "I owe you my thanks, sir. I appreciate your saving my daughter."

"It was nothing." Nathan took the hand her father offered. "I only regret upsetting her." He turned those deep blue eyes to Abigail. This morning they reminded her of a favorite velvet dress she'd worn when she was younger. "Please accept my apologies, Miss LeGrand."

What? He was apologizing to her? Abigail closed her mouth with an audible snap when she realized it was hanging open. The accusations she had flung at him last night came back to her with sterling clarity. "I'm afraid I acted much worse than you, sir."

A choked sound to her right was likely her mama trying to hide her laughter. Abigail's embarrassment deepened.

Nathan bowed to her. "Let's put the whole incident behind us."

"Well said, Brother Pierce." Her father was beaming at the man.

Abigail wanted to stomp her foot. Papa, too? Was her whole family turning against her? It seemed Nathan had won both their hearts. But losing her temper would do nothing to advance her case, so she pinned a smile on her face and nodded agreement.

She would show him. She would be so kind to Brother Pierce it would be like heaping coals of shame on his head. Then he would show his true colors and maybe her parents would realize he wasn't the perfect man they imagined him to be.

❁

Bridgeport Road, the stagecoach route between Vicksburg and Jackson, was a narrow lane with a surfeit of potholes and ruts. Abigail clasped her hands on her lap and tried to keep from touching the passengers on either side of her. She should have known this was a bad idea when she first caught sight of the driver.

His face was dark from a combination of sun and dirt. Even though it was quite warm, he wore a faded knit cap on his grizzled hair. His clothing was rumpled and faded, and his manner was gruff. He did not help her or her mother climb into his coach.

She glanced toward Nathan out of the corner of her eye. He was lucky enough to be sitting next to the window and seemed enthralled by the countryside they were passing through. His shoulders blocked most of her view, although she could see the tops of large pine trees and an occasional horseman.

"Mississippi is so different from Tennessee. No mountains. No waterfalls. Only an endless sea of trees." Nathan turned his serious blue gaze on her.

Would she be overstepping his boundaries by asking about his home? He was so secretive about his past. Yet his comment seemed like an invitation.

Before Abigail could formulate a question that would not seem like it was prying into his past, her mother spoke up from her position on the opposite seat. "I lived for a while in Nashville, but I understand it is nothing like Chattanooga."

"When I was a young boy, many of those living in the area were Cherokee. Ross's Landing, across the river from us, was the first outpost and was built by John Ross, the chief of the Cherokee."

Papa frowned at his words. "I thought you lived in Chattanooga."

"Yes, sir, but we didn't call it that until a few years ago. In fact, my store is actually located in Daisy. It's right close to Chattanooga. If Chattanooga keeps on growing like it has in the past few years, it'll probably swallow Daisy whole."

No one said anything for a few minutes. The stagecoach hit a rut and lurched. Abigail held herself as well as she could manage. Nathan swayed with the motion of the conveyance and their shoulders rubbed together for a few moments. The contact set off a covey of birds in her stomach. She jerked away from him, bumping into the poor woman on her left.

Nathan glanced toward her, then away. He cleared his throat and spoke to her parents. "I don't know exactly what to expect when we get to Jackson."

"I don't either, Papa. Will it be like when we go to Gatlin's Camp Ground later this month?"

"No." Papa shook his head. "This is going to be a meeting of the church leaders, the men who will decide the appropriate path for our denomination over the next year."

Her mother hid a yawn behind her hand. "We probably won't even be part of the meeting, Abigail. We'll be expected to help everything go smoothly, from the meals to the care of the children."

That was not fair. She'd much rather attend the meeting than be stuck washing dishes and changing diapers.

Conversation dwindled as the interior of the coach warmed under the June sun. Mama dozed, her head on Papa's shoulder. He had pulled out a small book and was reading it with great concentration. Abigail was able to watch the scenery since Nathan had shifted his position. Dense forests eventually gave way to sparsely populated areas. She saw a man working to fell a tree next to a log cabin. A garden farther down the road was being worked by a woman in a straw bonnet, her children at her side.

Then the houses grew closer together, signaling that they were nearing town. She could hear dogs barking as they chased the stagecoach. The vehicle came to a stop at a busy corner. Abigail could barely contain her excitement.

Her mother sat up and blinked rapidly. "Have we arrived?"

"Yes, dear." Papa smiled gently down at her.

Abigail could not help the warm feeling in her chest. It was so wonderful to see the love her parents still held for each other. She knew it was founded on their mutual love for God and Christ, faith that kept them strong in the face of adversity and kept them stable during times of prosperity. She wondered if she would ever feel the same for any man.

Nathan swung open the door and jumped down. Then he turned and offered his hand to Abigail. She hesitated a moment before putting her hand in his. What if the same combustible reaction occurred? Not wanting to take the chance, she gathered her skirts and stood up, bending over slightly because of the low ceiling. She was very aware of the gazes of the other passengers as she began her descent.

Abigail almost made it to the ground when one of the dogs came running up, barking loudly. Startled, she lost her balance with one foot on the mounting block. She dropped her skirts and windmilled her arms to keep herself from falling. Her heart stuttered as she realized she would not be able to stop her headlong plunge. A muscular arm snaked around her waist before she hit the ground. Abigail was once again pulled up to Nathan's chest, but today she was facing him. Her nose rubbed against one of the buttons on his coat, and she breathed in the fresh, manly scent of him.

"Are you okay?" His voice was deep, with a gruff edge. As though he'd been frightened, too.

Her father exited the coach quickly. "Are you all right, Abigail?"

No was the answer she wanted to give to both of them. Her pride was in tatters, and her heart was beating so quickly she thought it might burst through her bodice. She pushed against Nathan's hard chest, relieved to find she could stand on her own two feet. "Yes, thank you both for your concern."

The stagecoach had stopped in front of an inn, but she had no idea if it was the place they were staying or not. It was big—five-stories high—and busy. The grounds around them looked more like a market than anything else. Pigs rooted in one corner while chickens scooted between the booted feet of the stablemen.

Abigail felt somewhat overwhelmed by the noise, smells, and activity surging around her. Perhaps she should not have been in such a rush to leave the protection of Nathan's arms. An arresting thought struck her. Was God showing her that independence had its drawbacks?

Chapter 12

I t's about time for you to wake up, daughter." Mama's voice interrupted her dream.

Abigail groaned and rolled over, trying to pull the quilt up over her eyes. "Please don't tell me it's already morning."

"Yes." Mama whipped the quilt away. She must have already pulled back the draperies from the room's east-facing window because sunlight flooded the room. "If we don't hurry, your papa will be finished with his breakfast before we get downstairs."

Another groan slipped from Abigail's lips as she sat up. "I feel like someone whipped me during the night."

Mama put a cool hand on her forehead. "Are you sick?"

Yellow fever was a constant fear, especially in the spring and summer months. "No, ma'am. I'm only sore from all the bouncing of that stagecoach."

She could see the relief in her mother's expression and determined not to complain further about her minor aches and pains. They would fade anyway, once she was up and about. Taking her wrapper from the foot of the bed, she cleaned her face and hands with water from the inn's pitcher while her mother pulled out Abigail's plainest dress of drab brown homespun. "Are we going to be cleaning today?"

Mama nodded as she shook out the skirts. "And cooking." She glanced down at her own gray homespun. "At least that is what your papa says."

Abigail almost protested. She would much rather join the gentlemen in their meetings. But she knew it was impossible. Her parents were lenient with her at home, but here they would wish for her to be circumspect.

As soon as Abigail was dressed and her hair had been pulled into a neat bun at the base of her neck, the two women went downstairs to the dining room. Nathan and Papa were drinking coffee and talking quietly as they entered.

Nathan saw them first and came to his feet. "Good morning, ladies. I trust you slept well."

Her father also stood and beckoned them to the table as they exchanged greetings. As soon as they were seated, a servant brought several bowls of food— eggs, sausage, biscuits, and grits—to be passed among the diners.

She noticed an odd expression on Nathan's face as he accepted the bowl of grits from her father. "Have you never eaten grits before?"

Nathan shook his head. "What are they?"

"They're grits. Do you mean to tell me you don't have any grit trees in Tennessee?" She bit the inside of her cheek to keep from laughing at the look on his face.

"No, I don't think so." His voice was hesitant. "What do they look like?"

"In the springtime, when they flower, the trees are covered with lots of grits. People put out baskets and wait for all the grits to fall into them. Of course, sometimes their children climb into the trees and shake the limbs to get the grits to fall off faster. You probably saw some of them on your way to Mississippi."

The look on his face was priceless. Nathan had no idea whether to believe her or not. He glanced toward her parents, who were studiously avoiding his gaze. Abigail put a hand to her mouth to hold in the laughter, but a giggle escaped. That was enough to set off her parents' laughter.

She put her hand down, and her laughter joined theirs. At first she wasn't sure if the pastor was going to take offense at being the target of her teasing. Then his lips turned up, and soon he was laughing with them. It was exactly what was needed to ease the tension between all of them.

Mama finally took pity on the pastor and explained that grits were nothing more than ground corn. He piled some on his plate and added butter at her urging.

The talk turned general, and Abigail delved into a newspaper article that caught her attention. She nibbled at a biscuit and shook her head over the story about a slave uprising in Alabama.

"What has brought such a dark frown to you on this lovely morning?" The question came from Nathan.

She shrugged her shoulders and folded the paper. "I don't know why our fellow Southerners cling so firmly to slavery."

Her father nodded. "That's an issue that is bound to come up this weekend. Our church leaders need to speak out more openly in favor of abolition. It would help so many to see the truth."

As her mother expressed her approval of Papa's statement, Abigail glanced at Nathan. Would he speak his own beliefs or keep them to himself? A part of her wished he would express his ideas in front of her parents for two reasons: They would no longer think him such a perfect paragon of virtue and intelligence, and they would immediately begin to try to show him the error of his thinking.

But he remained silent, listening as her papa talked about the importance of treating every person with Christian kindness and how easy it was to make a living even without using slave labor. She had heard his speech many times in the past but hoped some of his points would sink into Nathan's mind and begin to work a change.

"I know how it is to believe slavery is not evil." Her mother's words got her attention. This was something she'd not heard before. "My parents owned slaves even before I was born, so I thought nothing of the matter." She reached out for her husband's hand. "But once I met you, I learned the error of my ways. I began to see Jemma and the others as people with talents as important as mine."

Papa shook his head. "It was your faith that led you to the truth."

"Perhaps so, but I seem to remember a fiery young man who was determined to rebel against everyone to prove his beliefs."

Their love was so touching to see. Abigail glanced toward Nathan and wondered what was going through his mind. Was he embarrassed by her parents' obvious affection for each other? Defensiveness filled her. If he dared to even hint at disdain, she would give him a tongue-lashing he'd not soon forget.

Nathan looked away from her parents and met her gaze. For a moment it was as if she could see past the bright blue of his eyes and into his very soul. The longing she saw there made her want to reach out to him. She wanted to hold him close and reassure him that God loved him no matter what. But as quickly as it had appeared, the pain vanished, replaced by his usual calm expression. Had she only imagined the emotion in his gaze, or had it been real?

Abigail's unkind thoughts melted away, replaced by sympathy. What kind of life had this man experienced before coming to Mississippi? Was the profound grief she thought she had seen a few seconds earlier the reason he didn't want to talk about the past? And more importantly, what kind of future did he anticipate for himself?

❀

"Abigail, would you melt some butter in that pan on the stove?" Mrs. Gail Ross, the wife of Bishop Bill Ross, handed her some freshly churned butter before turning back to supervise two young girls who were layering peaches into a cast-iron dutch oven. "That's right, Gabrielle, add some sugar now, and we'll see about rolling out a crust."

The kitchen was a hive of activity as the women worked to feed the church elders who would soon be through with their meeting. Wonderful aromas of fried chicken, stew, and collard greens filled the warm room.

Abigail dropped the butter into the hot pan and stirred it with a spoon. "What am I making?"

Her mother walked over and stirred a pot of collard greens that had been picked earlier that morning. "Creamed corn." Mama's answer made Abigail's mouth water.

She had already helped to make several skillets of cornbread from locally milled grain, and she had peeled enough potatoes to feed an entire army. At first it had been fun to compete with the other young women to see who could produce the longest and thinnest peel, but after the first hour, even that did not distract anyone from the tedium of their task. Once they had peeled every potato, they took them outside and placed them in a huge cauldron of water boiling over an open fire.

Mrs. Ross brought a bowl of brown sugar to the stove and leaned over Abigail's shoulder. "What a good job you're doing. Now take this and stir it in slowly." She walked to the door and called out to the children sitting on the back porch. "Are y'all done shelling that corn yet? We're going to need it right soon."

Abigail was amazed at the energy that kept Mrs. Ross moving from station to station. She was a small woman—about an inch shorter than Abigail—but what she lacked in height, she made up for in enthusiasm and zeal.

As soon as they had arrived a couple of hours earlier, Abigail and her mother had been given aprons and separated from the menfolk. Mrs. Ross and Mama had discussed the menu for a midafternoon feast before parceling out tasks to all the people in the kitchen. It was a good thing Bishop and Mrs. Ross had four children or not everything would have been ready in time.

"Here's the corn." Mrs. Ross brought a large bowl of bright yellow kernels to Abigail and set them down on the counter at her left elbow. "You'll have to keep stirring until the corn is done. Gertrude, go get the cream for Miss LeGrand's corn." Then she was off again, checking one dish or another, waving flies away, and marshaling the younger children to wash dishes while the others continued cooking.

Eventually everything was ready, from the first course—leek soup—to the dessert—deep-dish peach cobbler. The dining-room table had been set, and all they needed was for the men to appear.

Abigail blew out a tired sigh as she pulled off her apron. "I don't think I ever appreciated how much work it takes to feed a large group of people." She plopped down in an empty chair. One of the twin girls—she wasn't sure if it was Gabrielle or Gertrude—handed her a cup of water from the well outside. Its cool moisture was a relief to her parched throat.

"Yes, we so seldom have more than a few people come by for dinner." Her mother sat down beside her at the kitchen table. Abigail tried to hand her the half-empty cup in her hand, but the other twin appeared with a fresh cup. "Thank you, Gabrielle."

Now, how did Mama tell them apart? She glanced at the two girls who wore their aprons like badges of honor. From the braids of their red-blond hair to the tips of their brown leather shoes, they looked identical to her eyes.

"I appreciate all the hard work you ladies did this morning." Mrs. Ross darted back inside after overseeing the dishwashers on the back porch. "It's a delight to have so many willing workers." She smiled at the twins and held out her arms for a hug. "And I cannot wait until we see your father's face when he tries a bite of that peach cobbler."

They giggled as they kissed their mother's cheeks, one on either side. One more hug, and she sent them upstairs to their bedrooms to clean up before the meal, leaving the three older women alone for a minute.

"I wonder why the meeting is taking so long." Mrs. Ross glanced around the kitchen. "They are generally finished by two o'clock."

Her mother shook her head. "We live in chaotic times. I am afraid the issue of slavery is causing a rift in the church."

"How can Christian people truly support such a terrible institution?" Abigail pushed herself up from the table and walked to a large window overlooking several leafy oak trees. Flowers waved gaily under their shade.

"It's not our place to judge them." Mrs. Ross's voice was gentle. "But we have the duty to pray for them."

Her mother laughed. "You sound like Jeremiah. My husband is determined to teach by example and pray for God's intervention. Even during those early days when he was the victim of an evil plot, he refused to do anything more than make certain their plans did not hurt me or his workers."

Abigail listened to the two women discussing the issues, amazed that neither of them felt they should try to change their husbands' minds. She turned to them. "How do you do it? How do you sit back and discuss this without trying to make a difference?"

Mrs. Ross looked confused by the question. "Are you talking about trying to undermine our husbands' decisions?"

Before Abigail could answer, her mother spoke up. "Abigail, we have spoken about this before. The Bible teaches us to submit to our husbands. They are the heads of our households."

"That's right." Mrs. Ross twisted her wedding ring as she hesitated. "My husband and I each have our duties to fulfill. If I tried to usurp his work, or he mine, our family could not function. Bill helps people turn their lives and hearts to Jesus, while my ministry has more to do with their earthly needs."

When Mrs. Ross explained it that way, it made more sense to Abigail. She had seen the same in her own household while growing up, but she had chafed against the restrictions she thought constrained her mother. Had she been that mistaken? "What about suffrage for women?"

Mrs. Ross shrugged. "Mississippi was the first state to recognize the rights of married women to own property separate from their husbands. How much more progressive would you have us be?"

"I would like to be a part of this state's future." Abigail clenched her fist. She had been raised by parents who believed strongly in abolishing slavery. She believed allowing women to vote was almost as important. "I do not want to be treated as though I have no brain for anything beyond housekeeping, motherhood, and clothing fashions."

"Are you saying you think those pursuits have no validity?" Her mother's tones held a note of amusement.

Feeling as though she had been betrayed, Abigail turned to look at her mother. "Of course not. I would not be so foolish. Many women don't aspire to more than keeping an immaculate home and raising their children, but others would like to do something different. Women like Lucretia Mott and Margaret Fuller."

Abigail watched as the two older women exchanged glances. Volumes of information and experience seemed to pass between them. As though they knew something more than she.

Abigail sat back down at the table. Forcing herself to relax, she took a deep, calming breath, and placed her hands in her lap.

Mrs. Ross leaned over and gave her shoulder a pat. "You will understand better once you fall in love. Then you will see the importance of supporting your husband's decisions. Paul's words are not to be ignored lightly. If wives were to try and rule over their husbands, this world would soon be a place of much bitterness and rivalry. Besides, I am sure you will find as much satisfaction in submitting to your husband as I do. When a man truly loves you as Christ loves the Church, you will have no trouble doing so."

Struggling for a moment with the conflicting thoughts in her head, Abigail glanced at her mother and heeded the warning she saw. As someone younger than their hostess as well as an unmarried female, she knew she could not continue to argue the point. Dropping her gaze to her hands, she nodded. "I hope you're right."

"Of course she is." Mama looked relieved. She might have added something more to the conversation, but the sound of male voices in the dining room forestalled her. She stood and held out a hand to Abigail. "Let's go find out what happened in the meeting."

Even though she had great interest in that very thing, Abigail wished she had time to sit quietly and think about what the two women had told her. Was there validity in Paul's instructions to women? Was there an order to things that must be preserved? She did not know the answer, only that she still wanted to plan her own path without having to please some man's arbitrary whim.

Chapter 13

After the Sunday service and a lively meal with the Ross family, Nathan returned to the inn with the LeGrands. The past two days had been filled with so much information he wondered why his head did not explode.

Leaning back against the meager cushions of the rented carriage, he pondered what to do for the afternoon. He wasn't tired, so the idea of an afternoon nap did not appeal. Should he closet himself in his rooms and study his Bible? Perhaps, but this was his first visit to Mississippi's capital city, so he should be able to find an interesting way to spend the rest of the day.

Mrs. LeGrand's voice interrupted his musings. "What do you plan to do this afternoon?"

Nathan raised his head and looked toward her, wondering if she had read his mind. But she was looking toward her daughter, not at him.

Abigail shrugged. "I don't know."

"I have an idea." Mr. LeGrand winked at his daughter. "Why don't you and Brother Pierce explore the city? You could tour the State House. I understand it is quite spectacular in its scope. And Pastor Ross told me the governor's home is nearly complete."

Abigail shook her head. "I don't think—"

"What a wonderful idea!" Her mother's exclamation cut off Abigail's refusal. "The two of you can come back this afternoon and tell us all about it."

"I would not mind seeing the State House." Was that his voice? Had he lost his mind? It was obvious Abigail had no interest in touring with him. He should have demurred. So why was he nodding?

"Good." Mr. LeGrand cleared his throat. "That's settled then. We will let you young people ramble about while we make arrangements for the trip home."

For her part, Abigail said nothing more. But she did not look at him a single time during the rest of the ride to the inn.

Nathan had the idea she was not going to make the best traveling companion, but he did not mind trying to cajole her a little. He would like to return to the easy camaraderie they had shared prior to the steamboat voyage. He liked Abigail very much, possibly a little too much, and he chafed against the polite wall she had erected between them. Perhaps this would give them the opportunity to clear the air between them.

❀

"Right this way, ma'am, sir." A tall, smiling man wearing a fancy coat and tall cravat led the way to the second floor of the State House. "It's so nice to see a young married couple taking an interest in the seat of government."

Abigail's cheeks burned. "But we're not married."

She was surprised at the grin on Nathan's face, which made her cheeks heat up another one hundred degrees or so. What did he find so funny?

"My apologies." The man glanced at both of them. "I guess it's the way the two of you look together, kind of natural like."

What should she make of that comment? After hesitating for a moment, she decided the best way to deal with the situation was to pretend deafness. Nathan proffered his arm but she shook her head slightly. No sense in strengthening their guide's supposition.

Stepping into the main atrium, she was nearly overwhelmed by the size and appointments of the State House. It was definitely a fitting place for decision makers to meet.

Their guide pointed out the gleaming limestone floors and had them look upward some ninety-four feet at the dome above the rotunda. As he led them up a sweeping staircase, he talked about the first, failed architect, John Lawrence, who had been fired when he botched the contracted work for three straight years. His voice warmed considerably as he spoke of William Nichols, the final architect who tore out his predecessor's work and started over in 1835.

They reached the second floor and followed him to the rail that surrounded a large opening overlooking the entry foyer. "As I'm sure you are aware, Mississippi has a bicameral legislature. When they are meeting, the Senate occupies the room to our left, while the House meets in the room to our right."

Abigail looked at the wide doors on either end of the hallway. "You can see from one side all the way to the other."

"What a perceptive young lady you are escorting, sir."

"She is indeed." Nathan's blue gaze swept her face.

The knowing look on the guide's face made Abigail fold her lips in a tight line. He glanced at her and cleared his throat. "Well. . .as I was saying. . .or rather, as you pointed out, miss, the chamber doors allow the presiding officers to see each other. That way the lieutenant governor and the Speaker of the House can begin and end their sessions simultaneously."

"Does the governor have an office in the State House?" Nathan nodded toward the closed doors lined up with military precision along the hallway between the two chambers.

"Yes, he does. And if we're lucky, you may see Governor McNutt during your visit here. His office is on this floor, to one side of the Supreme Court

Chamber directly behind us."

"So all three branches of government are housed in this one building?" Abigail felt her mouth drop open. The building seemed so quiet, yet it must be a beehive of activity at some times of the year.

The guide recaptured her attention. "Let's go up one floor, and I'll show you the galleries where the public can watch the proceedings of the legislature."

"Even ladies?" The question popped out of her mouth before she could stop it.

The guide smiled. "Of course. We in Mississippi revere our women. We would never try to exclude them."

Except from voting or holding office. At least those words stayed inside her mind instead of tripping off her tongue. She had no desire to offend the tour guide, even though he hadn't been very considerate of her feelings. It wasn't his fault women had not been granted suffrage.

They sat in the wooden chairs in the gallery, and she closed her eyes to imagine what the chamber below her must be like while the legislature was meeting. Serious discussions, motions, bills, resolutions. She had read about the legislators' work in the newspaper, but it was so exciting to actually be here. To see the place where they debated and discussed and crafted the laws of the land made her blood pump faster. Perhaps one day she could talk Papa into bringing her back when the legislature was in session.

"Abigail?" Nathan's voice penetrated her thoughts. "Are you ready to go?"

The visions faded along with her excitement. How long had she been daydreaming? Nathan was still sitting next to her, but the guide had returned to the door and was looking at his pocket watch.

"I suppose it's time for us to leave." She picked up her reticule and stood.

The guide put his watch back into the pocket of his waistcoat and led them back down the stairs to the first floor. She and Nathan followed his footsteps like a couple of baby ducklings trailing behind their mama. At the entrance, the guide handed Nathan his hat. "Are the two of you going to see the new governor's home?"

"I had understood it's not complete."

"Almost." The man pointed toward the south. "Visitors are welcome even though many rooms are not furnished. It's election year, you know. I suppose the new governor and first lady will bring their own things with them."

"Thank you for directing us." Nathan pulled a coin from his pocket and offered it to the guide.

"Thank you, sir." He pocketed the coin without glancing at it. "You can take a carriage if necessary, but the mansion is three blocks down Capitol Street."

Abigail felt a bit put out. Why were the two men talking as if she didn't exist? Did her opinion not matter? What if her feet hurt after traipsing all over the State House? Or what if she had no desire to see the mansion? Nathan couldn't know how keen she was to see it. She might have had plans to do something completely different back at the hotel, but did that occur to Nathan? No. He simply held out his arm as if he expected her to fall in with whatever plan he devised. She would not stand for such treatment. "I don't believe I can walk another step."

His head swiveled toward her and his blue eyes narrowed. Was he about to order her to accompany him?

Her chin tilted upward. She would not be cowed by any man.

"What's wrong, Abigail?"

Shame washed through her at the concern in his voice. A sharp thought, however, overrode it. It was about time he considered her opinion. It didn't really matter that she was not overtired. The point was his lack of consideration. His attempt to control her. "I am a bit weary, but please don't let me stop your sightseeing. You go on to the mansion. I'm certain I can manage to find my way back to the hotel."

A frown darkened his brow, turning the sky blue color of his eyes stormy gray. Her chin went up and her spine straightened. She was a grown woman and could take care of herself. She would not cower before any man.

He took her hand and drew her a few steps away from the interested ears of their guide. "I am sorry, but I cannot allow you to do that."

She could feel her eyes narrowing at his statement. "You cannot allow it? I'll have you know I am perfectly capable of managing my own life." She jerked her hand away and turned to descend the steps. If she had to walk every step of the way back to the hotel she would do it.

"Abigail, wait. I'll gladly escort you to your parents if that's your wish. But you should not wander the streets alone. I'm sure pickpockets and thieves abound in such a populous area."

She could hear his footsteps behind her but refused to turn her head. Thank goodness the carriage that had brought them to the State House was still there. She marched straight to it and smiled at the driver as he opened the door for her. She had barely sat down, however, before *he* climbed into the carriage and took the opposite seat.

"I don't know what I've said to set you off this time, Miss LeGrand, but whatever it is, I pray you will explain it to me so I can apologize and we can go on as before."

She raised her chin and looked him straight in the eye. "I have no idea what you mean, Mr. Pierce. It is a pity you do not trust me to take care of myself, but since that is the case, I suppose you shall reap the consequences." Feeling she had put him in his place without uttering a single cross word, Abigail congratulated herself. She turned to gaze at the scenery outside and completely ignored the clamoring voice of her conscience as the carriage retraced the route to their inn.

Chapter 14

Nathan prepared to make the rounds of his circuit once again. Although he would rather have rested a day or two after returning from Jackson, it was probably a good idea for him to maintain a discreet distance between himself and his host's daughter. But before he could go, he would have to take his leave of her. . .them.

Nathan put on his best frock coat and hat and strode to the main house. He knew Mrs. LeGrand entertained guests at this time of the morning. Perhaps her daughter would be out on errands, and he wouldn't even have to see her. That would be best for both of them. He noticed two carriages at the front door, a sure sign of several visitors. So even if Abigail was here, she would likely be preoccupied by other conversations.

Taking the front steps two at a time, he grabbed the brass door knocker and rapped it smartly against the LeGrands' front door.

The housekeeper opened the door and wiped her hands on her checkered apron. "Good mornin', Mr. Pierce." The black woman's drawl was as thick and sweet as honey. "Come on in here. The missus is in the parlor."

The hope that *she* might not be in the parlor died as he heard Abigail's lilting laughter. He took a deep breath before walking into the room. Mrs. LeGrand and her daughter shared the sofa, each talking to a different visitor. Mrs. LeGrand left off talking to her friend Mrs. Hughes and greeted him, but Abigail smiled briefly before returning her attention to Silas Ward, the man sitting in a chair next to her end of the sofa.

A sick feeling invaded his stomach at the sight of the man's hand brushing her arm as he put down his china cup. No one else seemed to notice the familiar way he was acting, so Nathan averted his gaze and tried to concentrate on Mrs. LeGrand.

"Why don't you sit here, Nathan?" She indicated a spot on the sofa. If he took it, he would be sitting between her and her daughter. "I was telling Susannah about our trip to Jackson. Perhaps you can tell her about the meeting with the church elders."

Nathan eased onto the sofa, careful to avoid touching Abigail. Mrs. LeGrand poured tea into a delicate china cup, added a sugar cube at his nod, and stirred it delicately before handing it to him. "We talked about abolition mostly."

Susannah sipped from her teacup and nodded. "I assume some of our local pastors do not like the church's support of abolition."

"That's right." He wondered if Abigail was listening to their conversation. "I have to admit I didn't understand much about the whole issue of slavery until I came to Mississippi."

"In the part of Tennessee where Nathan lived, they don't have many slaves." Mrs. LeGrand touched his hand lightly. "But we've been praying for his eyes to be opened to the true evil of owning another person, isn't that right Abigail?"

"What?" The girl sitting on his other side looked past him toward her mother. "I'm afraid I wasn't paying attention. Mr. Ward has been telling me about his latest visit to the orphanage."

Mrs. LeGrand repeated her statement.

Abigail shrugged. "Anyone with half a brain could see for himself. I'm sure you don't support the institution of slavery, do you, Mr. Ward?"

The man shivered. "No. My uncle and I hired help over the years, but I cannot imagine purchasing another person."

"Where did you grow up, Mr. Ward?" Susannah Hughes asked the question.

His gaze shifted to the floor before he spoke. Nathan wondered if he was marshaling his thoughts or coming up with a falsehood to share with the group. Then he berated himself. Why did he dislike the man so much? Was it because of Mr. Ward's obvious interest in Abigail? Or because she seemed open to his interest?

"To tell the truth, ma'am, we lived all over. My uncle was a bit of a wanderer."

"You poor thing." Abigail leaned forward and put her hand over his. "That's no kind of life for a child."

"No, no. I was lucky to have someone to care for me. Not like the poor orphans back in town who have no family to claim them."

Nathan wanted to roll his eyes at the man's obviously calculated response. But all of the women in the room were nodding. Was he the only one who could see the truth? In that moment he made a decision. He would stay around a day or two and make certain Mr. Ward was not making himself a nuisance in the LeGrand home. Perhaps he would even do some checking and try to find out exactly why the man had come to Natchez.

"Your concern is praiseworthy." Nathan tried to make his tone admiring. At least his statement earned a kind glance from Abigail. But the words stuck in his throat like a clump of mud.

Mrs. LeGrand offered him a lemon cookie from the serving tray. "That reminds me, Nathan, before you came in, Abigail was discussing having a picnic for the orphans. I'm sure you would like to join her."

Nathan started to shake his head. The very thought of having to spend an extended amount of time surrounded by children made him shiver like a fall leaf. Maybe he shouldn't postpone his plans after all. He could always investigate the mysterious Mr. Ward when he returned.

Before he could form the polite refusal, however, Abigail spoke up. "Mama, I'm sure Brother Pierce is much too busy to waste his time with such a frivolous activity."

"Yes, I doubt he would enjoy sitting on the ground with a bunch of children." Mr. Ward tittered. "I'm sure he'd find it far beneath the dignity of a pastor."

"Not at all. I would love to come." Nathan took a bite out of the lemon cookie as silence invaded the room. As its sweetness melted on his tongue, he wondered if he had completely lost his senses.

⚛

"I love you."

The look on Brother Pierce's face was priceless. It reminded Abigail of the time a snake had spooked her horse—the wild-eyed gaze, the way his head swiveled around. She almost expected to see him jump up from the blanket and take off for the woods. Should she intervene? Or let Mia continue to terrorize the man? She decided on the former. "Mia, I need some help washing our dishes in the stream."

The six-year-old sighed. "I wish we could talk some more, Preacher."

Abigail clapped her hands to get the girl's attention. "Mia."

"Yes, ma'am." She got up off the blanket they had used for a table and meandered toward the baskets full of dirty dishes and leftover food where Abigail stood.

"Take these cups to the edge of the water. See the towel I set out to dry them on? We'll be on the strip of sand right next to it. I'll be right behind you with the plates and saucers."

As they passed the blanket, Nathan sent her a thankful glance. She hid her grin. Why had the man decided to come when it was so obvious he did not know how to interact with children? All morning he had been stiff and nontalkative with all but the oldest boys. But she had to admit he'd been good with them, talking about male-oriented topics—hunting, fishing, and horses. With that group, he had been much more popular than poor Mr. Ward, who seemed to know nothing about horseflesh, shooting, or choosing bait.

"Don't you think he's the most handsome man you've ever met?" Mia's blue eyes, so similar in color to Nathan's, had a dreamy quality.

Abigail hid her smile. "I can see you think so. But you should be spending more time playing with the others instead of bothering Brother Pierce."

Mia rinsed out a cup and placed it on the towel Abigail had brought to the stream earlier. "I wish he would 'dopt me."

Settling next to the girl on the sandy bank, Abigail wondered how best to handle the situation. Her heart ached at the poignancy in Mia's voice. Sometimes it was hard not to bring all of them home to live with her and her parents. "You have to remember Brother Pierce is not married. He would not be able to take care of a little girl, especially since he has to travel to other churches so often."

The sounds of the nearby woods enveloped them as the two rinsed the dirty dishes, but it didn't seem to matter to Mia. Her shoulders drooped, and she ran her sleeve across her face. Then Mia's head popped up and her wide eyes searched Abigail's face. "I know what to do. You can marry him! And then the two of you could 'dopt me, and we could make a happy family. I would work really hard every day, and you wouldn't have to do anything 'cept eat cookies and pies."

Abigail's mouth dropped open. She glanced back over her shoulder to see if anyone had heard Mia's outrageous suggestion. She had no doubt she would die of embarrassment if Nathan was listening. But he seemed to be engrossed in the core of an apple he held in his hand. She breathed a prayer of thankfulness and turned to the precocious young girl. "That is out of the question, I'm afraid. I am determined to remain unmarried so I can control my future. When you get a little older, you will begin to understand."

Mia's shoulders sagged once more. She looked down into the clear water. "I guess then"—her voice caught—"I'll have to find another lady to marry him."

The way Abigail's stomach churned at Mia's words, one would think she cared whether or not Nathan married someone else. And she certainly did not care. Not at all.

❁

"You must play blindman's bluff with us, Miss LeGrand." The plea on Silas's face was impossible to resist. They had put away all the food and would soon have to load everyone into the wagon to head back to the orphanage. But she supposed they could play one more game.

The children added their voices to his request. Abigail removed her bonnet and stood, glancing at the blanket where Nathan lounged. "Come along, Brother Pierce. We cannot disappoint the children."

He shook his head. "I am content to watch, and I think you might want to reconsider it yourself now that the day has grown so warm. You are bound to get hot and dirty."

Unaccommodating, overbearing man. How dare he try to dictate what she should do? He could stay in the shade if he wanted to. She would not sit here while the rest of them enjoyed the game. She put her nose up to show her disdain and turned to Silas. "I'll play as long as I don't have to wear the blindfold first."

"Agreed." Silas picked up an unused napkin and rolled it into a serviceable blindfold. "I'll be first." He tied the napkin around his head and held out his hands. "Now where can I find someone to take my place?"

The children scattered about the open area, giggling and whispering to each other as he wandered about with his hands in front of him. His questing fingers finally found one of the older girls, and he pulled off the napkin. "Now it's your turn."

She was in turn teased and taunted by the other players until she grabbed hold of another child's collar. Abigail moved about quickly to avoid capture when she realized that Nathan was no longer sitting on the blanket. Where had he gone? She could not see him at the wagon. Had he wandered off into the woods and gotten lost? Swampy areas in the woods were filled with snakes, poisonous spiders, and even an alligator or two. Distracted by her concern, she failed to notice the blindfolded player near her. When his sticky fingers grabbed her sleeve, she groaned.

The little boy, Evan Jumper, pulled off the blindfold and handed it to her. She started to tie it around her hair when someone's hands came from behind her and took away the piece of linen cloth. She glanced over her shoulder. "Silas."

"Please let me."

Abigail smiled, wishing the preacher was here so he could hear her next comment. "You're such a gentleman, Mr. Ward."

"It's the least I can do since I'm the one who got you involved in the first place."

Abigail raised her eyebrows. "That's right, you did."

"Please allow me to make it up to you." His voice deepened as he slipped the cloth around her head and tied it.

"You could do that by taking my turn," she suggested.

He leaned toward her, his mouth so close she could feel his breath on her cheek. "I have a better idea. Why don't you let me take you to dinner instead?"

Her heart skidded to a stop. Go out in public with him? Yet why not? Her mind raced. He was a much better companion than Nathan Pierce had turned out to be. He understood her and never tried to dictate to her. She took a step away from Silas and put her hands out. "Perhaps I will." Then she threw herself into the game to shut out the voice of caution that somehow mimicked the irritating tones of a certain bossy pastor.

Chapter 15

What was he going to do about his feelings for Abigail? Nathan could barely stand the idea of her going to dinner with Silas. Yet he had absolutely no right to so much as warn her about being too trusting.

Yesterday afternoon he'd returned from getting a drink in the stream when he saw the man tying a blindfold around her head. And leaning forward to whisper in her ear. He wished he'd not been close enough to hear the man's question, but he had. And the words had chased him all through the night and even today as he began to make his round of the area churches. If only he could—

A scream interrupted his thoughts and made Nathan pull up on his horse's reins. Animals in the forest chittered and rustled around him, but that was the only thing he heard. He ran a calming hand on his horse's neck as he waited.

Nothing. Not even raised voices.

Nathan was about to continue on his way when it happened again. Another noise, but this time it sounded more like a moan. Then as he strained his ears, he thought he caught the whistle of a whip. Instinct took over. He tightened his knees and sent his mount into a gallop. Somewhere along this road, someone was in trouble.

As he rounded a bend, a woman came running toward him. He dragged back hard on the reins to keep from running her down. The horse reared and almost unseated him, but after a second or two, Nathan managed to get the frightened animal back under control.

"Please, sir." The woman ran up to him and he saw the tracks of her tears on her dark cheeks. She was dressed in a shapeless black wool shift, a typical dress of slaves in the South. Her eyes were wide with fear and desperation as her hands grabbed hold of his horse's reins. "Please, oh please, sir. You have to help me. He's going to kill my Abram."

"Where?"

She pointed a shaking finger back the way she'd come. "Hurry."

Nathan could not see anything yet, but he set his horse moving once again. The next bend in the road, however, revealed a scene that burned its way deeply into his heart. A large black man had been tied to an oak tree, his back showing wicked stripes from the bite of a whip.

A tall white man with thick shoulders stood behind him, his arm poised to make yet another stripe on the black man's back. He looked back as Nathan galloped up but turned back to face the black man almost immediately.

"Stop!" Nathan brought his horse up short and dismounted. "What do you think you're doing?"

"Nothing that concerns you." The man brought the whip up.

Nathan strode up to him and grabbed his hand. "Yes, it does concern me. You are killing that man."

"He's not a man. He's my property. I can treat him any way I want to." He sneered at Nathan and jerked his hand free. "Now get on your way before I take exception to your interference."

Shaking his head, Nathan pointed at the bound man, who was moaning and trying desperately to free himself. His shirt hung in tatters from his waist. Blood oozed from several of the stripes across his broad back. "I cannot."

The slave owner dropped his whip and reached for his waist. At first Nathan thought he was going to pull a gun, but then he saw the wicked edge and sharp point of a blade. Immediately he was taken back in time. The forest faded away, becoming the main room at Poe's in Chattanooga.

Nathan froze. His heart stuttered. He could not—must not—kill again. He took a step back and raised his hands. "Let's be reasonable."

"The only reasonable thing to do is move on."

"Please, Master, please." The black woman who had first alerted him to the situation ran up to them. She fell to her knees at the white man's feet. "My Abram didn't mean no harm. He wanted to bring me some flowers. He wasn't trying to run away. I swear it." She threw both arms around the man's legs.

As Nathan watched, the maddened look faded from the slave owner's face. He looked at the whip on the ground, back to the male slave's bleeding back, and finally down to the woman kneeling before him. "I suppose he's learned his lesson."

"Oh yes, Master." The woman looked up, her plea for lenience evident in every line of her body. "Abram done learned it good. I promise he won't do it no more." She let go of his legs but didn't make any move to regain her feet.

Nathan felt sick to the core of his being. He had never realized the true horror of slavery. Had never thought about the control slave owners had over the lives of their property. Property! As if one human had the right to own another.

This was the reason slavery should be outlawed. It was wrong, and he knew it, knew it as surely as he knew that he was a coward. No wonder he had earned Abigail's scorn. He wanted to go to her and apologize.

He watched as the white man cut the bonds on his slave and walked away, never looking back. He jumped on the horse that Nathan had not even realized was tethered nearby. Before he galloped away, however, he did turn back to where the woman was supporting Abram. "Leah, I'll expect to see him in the fields at first light."

"Yes, sir." Leah nodded as she wrapped Abram's arm around her shoulders. "Come along. We've got to get back quick."

Nathan's throat choked as he watched their struggle. The beaten man must outweigh her by at least fifty pounds. He had no idea how far away their home was, but it was evident they would never make it without his intervention.

"Let me help." He grabbed the large man by the waist, trying to avoid the ugly slashes on his back. "We'll get him up on my horse and get the two of you out of here."

Leah's large eyes filled with tears again. "Thank you so much, sir. I don't know what we'd've done if the good Lord hadn't sent you."

"You're the one who saved him."

She shook her head and put a hand on his arm. "I had already begged for him to take pity on my husband, but he didn't pay me no mind. Not till you came by."

Feeling unworthy of the admiration in her gaze, Nathan said nothing. But he knew better. If he'd been any kind of man, he would have wrested the knife away from their master and overcome him. He should have stopped the vicious beating. But he had not been able to do it. He had been silent in the face of his fear. He didn't deserve anyone's admiration.

❀

Nathan's heart broke as he listened to Leah crooning to Abram while dabbing the angry red stripes across his back. These people were being treated like animals—no rights, no hopes, no future. He had never considered what it must be like to live this way.

It had grown quiet in the small cabin. He looked up to see Leah, her shoulders bowed, moving to a shelf on one side of the room. "How is he doing?"

She picked up a jar and carefully poured a small amount of green powder into her palm. "My Abram is strong. He's suffered a lot in his life. He's gonna git through this hurt, too."

"Is there something I can do to help?"

Leah pursed her lips. "You can take this bowl outside and empty it. There's a spring right at the edge of the woods where we get our fresh water."

Nathan emptied and refilled the bowl as directed. As he walked back toward the little circle of slave cabins, he realized he was the center of attention. Dark faces peered at him from the doorways while children who had been playing outside stopped to watch him. These people obviously had little experience with white men who cared about their needs. Someone had started a cook fire in the open space at the center of the slave quarters. A rough framework of tree limbs next to the dancing flames probably served as a spit for roasting their meat.

Leah and Abram's home was made of weathered gray wood. It had one door, one window, and a dirt floor. It was smaller than some of the other cabins, and he wondered if that was because the couple seemed to have no children.

As he reentered the single room, Leah looked up with a warm smile. She was kneeling next to Abram and had a hand on his forehead. "He has no fever. Your prayers are strong."

Nathan was humbled by the faith shining in her face. It made him feel grasping and greedy to bemoan his trials when he witnessed this woman's gratitude even though she had so few blessings in her life. "I'm glad."

He handed her the bowl and watched as she poured a little of the water into a wooden cup, added the green powder, and stirred briskly before lathering the paste she'd made onto Abram's back. "This will ease his pain and help him to sleep the night so he will be strong enough to work in the fields tomorrow."

As the afternoon sun dipped below the horizon, the adult workers began returning to the slave quarters. A few of the women came by and spoke in low tones to Leah, bringing food for her and her husband to share. Apparently word had spread to them about the events of the day. They looked in Nathan's direction and bobbed their heads. He nodded in return, feeling very small in the face of their thanks.

"Are you hungry?" Leah held out a bowl of stew.

Nathan shook his head. "Abram needs it more than I." He could feel his stomach rumbling. But he had provisions with him—dried berries and strips of salted beef—that he would eat once he made camp.

Kneeling beside the mat where her husband lay, Leah coaxed him to swallow a little of the stew while Nathan watched. Her tenderness and patience with the wounded man raised a yearning within his heart. Although this couple had so little, they still had each other.

How he wished someone special was waiting for him at home. Someone who would shed a tear of empathy when he was hurt and rejoice with him when triumphs came his way. Someone who challenged him to think and yet loved him in spite of his faults.

Leah finished feeding her husband and returned to the handmade table where Nathan sat. "How came you to be on that road today?"

"I travel about, visiting the communities and spreading the Word of the Gospel." Nathan's hands felt empty suddenly. He had left his Bible in his saddlebags.

Her face broke into a wide smile. "You're a preacher man?"

He nodded, even though he felt unworthy of the wonder in her voice. "I am."

"Could you tell me a story from your Bible?" Her hands pressed together. "I used to go by the church on Sunday and stand in the door so I'd hear the preacher, but then Master said he didn't want us hanging 'bout and told us to stay home. So it's been awhile since I heared anything."

Verses from Luke's Gospel filled his mind, the words of Jesus as He spoke to the multitudes of followers. It was as if God was reaching down from His throne in heaven and inspiring him. " 'Blessed be ye poor: for yours is the kingdom of God. Blessed are ye that hunger now: for ye shall be filled.' " Nathan could feel the comfort in those words flowing through him. His voice grew stronger as he continued. ' "Blessed are ye that weep now: for ye shall laugh. Blessed are ye, when men shall hate you, and when they shall separate you from their company, and shall reproach you, and cast out your name as evil, for the Son of man's sake. Rejoice ye in that day, and leap for joy: for, behold, your reward is great in heaven. . . .' "

Leah clapped her hands. "I see why you're a preacher."

From the other side of the room, Abram shifted on his pallet. "Them's some good words."

Nathan hadn't even realized the man was conscious, much less that he could absorb the meaning of the words in spite of his pain. He got up from the table and walked over to the corner where Abram lay. "May God's embrace comfort you and His Word give you the strength to overcome the evil of this world." He put his hand on the black man's thick shoulder, careful not to touch his back, bowed his head, and took a deep breath. "Lord, please look down on this man, Abram, and heal him. May he and his wife, Leah, find favor in Your sight. Please grant them freedom. Give them hope for tomorrow and bless them with Your mighty blessings. We know, Lord, that You gave Yourself for our sins, and we thank You most humbly. Amen."

"Amen." Both Abram and Leah repeated the word after him.

"Thank you, Preacher." Leah's voice recalled him from the tumult in his heart.

Nathan felt both diminished and strengthened by what was happening in the meager slave quarters. Never before had he felt so strongly the power of the Lord. Never before had he been swept away by awe and wonder. Never before had God seemed so real to him. The sermons and prayers he'd spoken in the past seemed but a pale version of what had taken place here.

He wanted time alone to consider the ramifications, so he took his leave with promises to return. He also made a promise to himself to do something to help these two escape their bondage. Nathan knew he didn't have enough money to purchase their papers, but he also was beginning to realize God could give him whatever was necessary.

Nathan collected his horse and left the plantation behind. When he found a place to make camp, he gathered pine needles for a bed and settled down. He gazed up into the starlit sky. Was God looking down on him right now? A sense of peace covered him like a warm blanket, and Nathan understood that his question was answered. No matter what had happened in his past, God was still there for him.

His unworthiness brought the sting of tears to his eyes. Nathan drifted to sleep somewhere between regret and thankfulness.

Chapter 16

I saw her." Deborah put down her glass of lemonade with a clatter. "I know how ridiculous it sounds, Abigail, but I saw Mrs. Aucoin."

"You're telling me you saw a ghost?"

A nod answered her. "She was dressed in a white flowing robe and carrying a lantern." Deborah reached out and grabbed Abigail's arm. "It had the same green glow the children saw a few weeks ago."

Abigail was dumbfounded. Deborah was not given to flights of fancy. She had been raised in the orphanage and had raised dozens of other children in her turn. She was as practical and capable a person as any Abigail had ever met. And now she was claiming to have seen a ghost.

"I know you remember the story. Robert Aucoin was a pirate who sailed the river and attacked merchants and visitors making their way down to New Orleans. He was caught and hung somewhere around Memphis. When the local authorities came to his wife and told her what had happened, she refused to believe it. She ran from the room, screaming that her husband was a good man who would return to her."

A shiver teased its way down Abigail's spine. She had heard the tales about the poor, crazy woman who walked along the bluff out back, looking for her husband, losing her grasp on sanity when year after year passed without his reappearance. Poor, mad Vanessa Aucoin. Abigail shook herself. "While I'm aware Robert and Vanessa Aucoin were real people who once lived here, no one above the age of twelve really believes they haunt this house. They are only stories children tell because of some ghoulish enjoyment they get from frightening one another."

"I thought so, too, until last week." Deborah let go of her arm and leaned back against the sofa. "I've not been sleeping well, what with the noises the children keep hearing and the lights moving back and forth."

"That must be the explanation." Abigail felt better. Her friend was not becoming unbalanced. "You probably thought you were awake. It's very understandable. What we need to do is hire an assistant for you, someone who can help you with the responsibilities you carry. I come over as often as I can manage, but you need someone else who lives here with you and the children. Then you can get some well-deserved rest."

Deborah shook her head. "I'm sure of what I saw. It was a woman dressed

213

in white. And she had to be a ghost because while I was watching, *poof*"—Deborah clapped her hands for emphasis—"she disappeared like a puff of smoke."

Abigail cast about for some logical explanation. "Perhaps one of the older girls was walking outside."

"No, I checked. For once, all of the children were sleeping peacefully right where they should be." She held up one hand. "And before you suggest one of the neighbors, remember that she disappeared without warning. How could she have done that if she was a real person? The drop down to the river is one hundred feet or more. No one could survive such a fall."

"I don't know, Deborah. But there must be a mundane answer."

"There is. The ghost of Mrs. Aucoin."

Abigail blew out a breath. "I would have to meet her face-to-face before I'd believe that."

"I'd probably feel the same way if you told me the story I've told you, but I know what I saw." She sighed. "Enough of my problems. Why don't you tell me what's been going on with you the past few days?"

The change of subject was abrupt, but Abigail allowed it. She would mention the problem to her parents. They needed to know something odd was going on here. Perhaps they could get to the bottom of the situation.

Abigail sipped at her lemonade as she considered what topic might get Deborah's mind off of her problems. After a moment, she knew what subject to broach. It was sure to remove all thought of apparitions. "I am going to dinner with Mr. Ward on Friday."

That did the trick. Deborah's mouth dropped open. "Mr. Ward has secured your attention? I never would have thought it possible."

"Why do you say that? Mr. Ward is a nice man. He works hard, has an accommodating disposition, and is very considerate of my feelings."

"But I thought your parents had hoped for a match between you and Brother Pierce."

Abigail almost choked on her drink. "Nathan? I cannot think of a worse idea. Brother Pierce is proslavery, antichildren, and very domineering."

"Oh my. Well, that would never do." Deborah summoned a weak smile. "But please be careful when you are with Mr. Ward."

"Why do you say that?" Abigail's hand crept up to her throat. "Do you know something unsavory about Mr. Ward?"

"Unsavory?" Deborah looked at a point directly above Abigail's left shoulder. "I wouldn't say that. But there is something about him, something familiar. Yet when I try to pin down the feeling, it slips away from me. I keep thinking I know him, but I know it's impossible." She turned her focus back to Abigail's face. "I wish you hadn't agreed to see him."

Abigail shrugged. "I thank you for your advice, but I am committed for a dinner. If it makes you feel any better, I will be on my guard."

"I'm certain everything will be fine." Deborah's smile wobbled a bit. "It's probably one more sign I am slipping over the edge of sanity."

"Don't be silly. I'm sure it's a matter of getting enough sleep and relieving your mind of some of the pressures it is under. Once we find someone to assist you, I'm certain you'll feel better in no time."

❀

Silas put down his spoon and looked across the linen-covered table. "Is your gumbo tasty?" Abigail brushed her mouth with a starched napkin and nodded. "It's a bit spicy, but I like it that way."

"That's good." He picked up his spoon and dipped it into his bowl once more.

At this rate, dinner was going to be a very long meal. Abigail wondered what topic she could bring up. They had already covered the weather—warm—the number of people dining out nowadays—dozens—and the broad variety of items available at the local mercantile—amazing.

She glanced at Silas and thought that he was at least a well-mannered diner. He did not slurp from his spoon or put his elbows on the dinner table. But other than that, she could not say many favorable things about him. Silas had a knack of agreeing with every statement she uttered. While that should make her feel as though her ideas were correct, Abigail wondered if he might agree even if she now switched her position to the opposite point of view.

"I had a most interesting visitor this morning."

This sounded like the start of a good topic. "Who was that?"

"William Johnson. He said he wanted to meet me and tell me about his shop around the corner from my office."

A spark of interest flared. Abigail looked at Silas with more enthusiasm. Her father had once patronized William Johnson's barbershop. "He is quite famous in this area."

A nod answered her. "He told me a little of his background. How he was freed as a child and learned his trade before purchasing a building downtown and opening his shop. He said he's the barber for many of the landowners in Natchez."

"Yes, his business acumen is extraordinary, but did you know that he himself owns slaves?"

Silas's eyebrows climbed toward his hairline. "Is that so? How odd. One would think that, having been a slave himself, he would oppose slavery."

"Yes, it is shocking to me, too." Abigail sighed. "Papa says it's because of Mr. Johnson's desire for higher social status."

"Your father is very perceptive." Silas leaned forward. "Mr. Johnson wanted to know if I planned to take part in the Fourth of July festivities."

"What did you tell him?"

When his lips curved upward, she tried to convince herself the man sitting on the opposite side of the table was attractive. Some would describe him as dashing, with his dark hair and eyes, but she found his intense gaze a bit off-putting. As he hesitated before giving her an answer, Abigail found herself comparing him to the tall, blond-haired, blue-eyed minister. Somehow, Nathan seemed much more appealing.

"I'm not certain." His voice cut through her wandering thoughts.

Perhaps it was guilt over not giving him her full attention that shaped her answer. "Oh, you must. We have great fun."

"Sometimes they can be quite tedious with speeches from self-serving politicians and ill-mannered children allowed to run loose like heathens."

Abigail's initial excitement faded in response to his words. Doubt brought her eyebrows together. She thought Silas enjoyed being around children. It was Nathan who was uncomfortable. Or had Silas only been pretending to enjoy the orphans' company for his own reasons?

Tucking the question away for later consideration, she consciously smoothed her expression before answering. "Besides the speeches, we have games, tasting competitions, and boat races along the river. Then everyone gets together to eat watermelon and watch the incredible fireworks display."

His gaze sharpened on her face. He leaned forward slightly. "Will you be attending?"

"Of course." Abigail sat back in her chair, her hand resting next to her empty bowl of gumbo. "My family always goes. Mama's pickled pears usually win the competition for canned fruits, and she's been experimenting with a special recipe to enter into the pie contest this year."

"I may have to sign up to be a judge then." He reached across the table and put his hand on top of hers. "All of a sudden, listening to a few long-winded politicos seems a small price to pay."

Tugging her hand out from under his, Abigail hid it in her lap. "I usually enjoy their speeches, but perhaps I am too dim-witted to give an opinion."

Now it was Silas's turn to furrow his eyebrows. "Please forgive me. I didn't mean to insult you or your celebration. I'm certain it will be an outstanding day. I cannot wait to take part."

Feeling a little foolish for her discomfort, Abigail nodded. "I apologize for my snappish remark. But you should take into consideration that this is my home. I love Natchez, and I hate to hear newcomers disparage our customs."

Their waiter came to their table as she finished speaking, his tray laden with food. Abigail could tell Silas wanted to say something more, but he folded his lips into a tight line and waited as they were served the main course—roast lamb.

"Is there something else I can bring you?" The man smiled at something on the other side of the room.

Abigail shook her head.

"No, thank you." Silas answered for both of them.

As soon as he walked away, Silas's dark gaze returned to her face. "I hope you'll forgive me, Abigail. The thought of losing your friendship is shredding my heart." He put his hand on his chest. "I won't be able to enjoy a single morsel of this dinner unless you accept my apology."

How melodramatic the man was. He ought to be a thespian. He had obviously missed a successful career on the stage. Promising herself to never again be put in a similar situation, Abigail nodded.

Silas stretched his hand out, his fingers beckoning her to put her hand in his.

Abigail would have liked nothing more than to leave the table and take herself home, but she knew it was impossible. So she held onto her temper and forced a smile. "Really, Silas. Please don't make a scene. I accept your apology. You may consider yourself completely forgiven and this whole conversation forgotten."

She ignored his hand and pushed her meat around her plate. Would this evening never end?

Chapter 17

Nathan heard the singing before he reached Gatlin Camp Ground. It seemed to carry on the wind, like the voices of angels, and he felt hope lifting his spirit as he moved forward.

In the week since he'd left Abram and Leah, his mind had poked and prodded at his long-held acceptance of enslavement. He felt like a man who had lived his whole life in a dark cave—a cavern whose walls were indifference and ignorance. How could he have ever been so blind?

Nathan tightened his knees on his horse's saddle as he began singing along with the unseen worshipers. Crossing the clear waters of Topisaw Creek, he followed a well-marked path to an open area. Several wood cabins clustered together at the far edge of the campground, their backs to the dense woods of pine trees wider around than Nathan was tall. A large structure rose from the ground to his right, its walls nothing more than poles driven into the ground. A crowd of people sat under the interlaced saplings and tree limbs that formed the roof.

Wondering if he should try to stow his gear first or join the others under the brush arbor, Nathan dismounted and led his horse to the corral. He removed his saddle and bags, stacking them to one side of the fence for later retrieval.

"Well, would you look at who's finally come riding in." The lilting voice made his heart race and brought a smile to Nathan's face.

"It's good to see you, Abigail." He took off his hat and bowed to her.

"We got here yesterday." She scuffed at a patch of grass. "It's going to be a great week."

"Yes." Nathan stared at the top of her head, his fingers itching to loosen her chignon. He wanted to wrap his arms around her and kiss her. Thoughts of pressing his lips against her soft mouth robbed him of the ability to speak.

Moments passed until she finally turned her dark gaze up to his face. His feelings must have been apparent on his face because her cheeks reddened. She glanced back toward where the others were still singing. "I'd better get back to the meeting. It looks like Bishop Ross is about to begin his sermon."

"Don't go." The two words shot from his mouth with the velocity of a rifle blast. "I. . .I've been thinking about you a lot. Wondering if you've kept busy." He wanted to bite off his tongue as soon as the words escaped. Would she be able to tell how jealous he'd been? The thought of her being entertained by the officious Silas Ward had stolen several nights of slumber. He squared his shoulders. "I mean, I know how much. . .how many. . ."

A smile teased her mouth. She reached up and pushed the errant lock of hair behind one ear. "Yesterday Mama and I were discussing how quiet it's been at Magnolia lately."

His heartbeat galloped at her words. Was she admitting she'd missed him? Excitement raised the corners of his mouth in an answering smile. "I have something important to tell you and your family."

Her brows drew together. "What is that?"

"I've realized how right you are."

"It's about time." A grin replaced the concern on her face. "Tell me more."

He held out a hand to her. After a moment's hesitation, she placed her own smaller hand in his. Together they walked back to the creek he and his horse had recently crossed.

Nathan led her over to a fallen tree and helped her sit down. He stepped back and took a deep breath. "Slavery is a diabolical practice that has to be eradicated."

Delight caused her dark eyes to glow. "What happened?"

Nathan told her briefly about Abram and Leah.

When he finished, she clapped her hands together. "Praise God for opening your eyes."

"Yes." Nathan picked up a rock and tossed it into the creek. "I cannot believe how blind I was. But that's over now."

Abigail stood up and brushed off her skirt. "I am so glad to hear you've come to your senses."

He nodded. "I'm ashamed of my blindness."

"You're not to blame." She put a hand on his arm. "Our experiences form our opinions. In fact, you're to be commended for refusing to be bound by your preconceptions."

Nathan felt at least twenty feet tall—taller than the trees surrounding them. He looked down at Abigail's earnest face. Should he express his feelings now or wait? Was this the right time? The right place?

She turned away, and he realized his hesitation had cost him the opportunity to speak. Maybe that was best. He had absolutely no idea how to form the right words to win her affection.

"We need to get back to the others." Abigail took a step toward the brush arbor. "My parents will come looking for me if I don't return soon."

He nodded, relieved and yet disappointed the decision had been taken from him. He caught up with her as they reached the campground. "Do you think they'll mind if I don't take time to wash?"

She turned back and looked him over, her gaze serious as it slid from his sweat-dampened hair to his wrinkled shirt. "It's up to you."

Wavering for a moment as the desire to be near her warred with his need to clean off the dirt of travel, Nathan finally shook his head. "It won't take me long."

Her gaze returned to his face. Was that disappointment he saw? His heartbeat quickened. He took a step forward.

"The cabin at the end of the row is for the single men's use."

Her dismissive words stopped him from reaching for her hand. Hope leeched out of him as she walked away. With a sigh, Nathan picked up his gear and made his way to the cabin Abigail had indicated, as she disappeared into the crowd of worshipers.

The door creaked as he pushed it open. "Is anyone here?" His question met silence.

Wooden bunks filled the room, some with blankets and bags on them, others empty of anything except a thin mattress. He chose one of the latter, sitting down and placing his bags at his feet. After a quick search, he took out a sliver of Colgate soap and a fresh shirt before retracing his steps to the creek. Although he would have enjoyed a full soak in the cool water, he settled for an abbreviated bath before combing his wet hair and tucking the clean white shirt into the waist of his trousers.

Nathan walked back to the brush arbor and tried to slip quietly onto a bench, but the bishop smiled and beckoned him forward. An air of expectation filled the arbor as if the Lord was in this place.

He glanced around the arbor at the smiling faces. Their peace was almost tangible enough to touch. And then he saw Abigail, her face so pure, so radiant, so filled with adoration for the Lord. In that moment, Nathan knew he must become like the people before him. He had to find the same relationship for himself.

❀

"The poem is called 'Just As I Am,' and it has a powerful message, one I'd like to share with all of you this evening." Brother Oliver Smith had taken the podium for the final evening of the revival. " 'Just as I am without one plea. . .' "

At first mesmerized by the reading of the powerful poem, Abigail found herself glancing toward Nathan sitting next to her. He had been so serious this week. He'd spent hours talking to the bishop and her father, reading his Bible, and even teaching parables to the children. She would have liked to spend more time talking to him, but with so much going on, it had been impossible. It seemed the only time they sat near each other was under the arbor where they could not talk.

He seemed to have won the admiration of everyone here, especially the ladies. And why not? She admired the firm angle of his jaw, his pronounced cheekbones, blue eyes, and thick blond hair. A man ought not be so handsome. Add to that his nice manners, kindness, and consideration of the feelings of others. Who could resist him?

" 'Here for a season, then above, O Lamb of God, I come, I come!'" The preacher's voice rang out, drawing her attention back where it belonged. She hoped no one noticed how red her cheeks had become.

"Jesus is waiting to claim you as His own. He doesn't want to wait until you get your life all straightened out. No, sir. He wants you to come to Him just as you are. I'm going to talk to you tonight about the first time I heard someone reading these powerful words. They changed me. Made me a different man than the one you see standing up here tonight."

The emotion of the preacher's voice pulled on Abigail. She listened to his story about being a thief, a robber who preyed on travelers along the Natchez Trace. As he spoke, she could feel the Lord's presence with them.

"One of my victims was a Christian man. He prayed for me even when I took his money. Even though I laughed at his weakness, this man continued asking for Jesus to forgive me. I wish I could tell you that his faith turned me from my life of crime, but it didn't. I went on my way, certain he was a fool. Then about two weeks later I was visiting my ma up in Jackson, and she talked me into going to her church. While I was there, I heard that poem for the very first time."

He stopped speaking and stood in front of them silently for a moment. " 'Just as I am, and waiting not, to rid my soul of one dark blot.' Now I can tell you I had a lot of dark blots on me and in me. More blots than most." Brother Smith held up the sheet of paper, and Abigail could see the deep creases in it and the stain of what looked like tears. "But I could hear Jesus' voice as though He was standing right there in front of me. His blood cleanses each and every spot. What could I say except, 'O Lamb of God, I come, I come.'"

Tears stung at her eyes, and Abigail reached for her reticule. That's when she realized Nathan was no longer sitting next to her. He had fallen to his knees in front of the bench, his hands clasped in front of him. His head was bowed, his lips were moving. He might be a preacher, but tonight he was meeting the Lord as though for the first time.

Her breath caught and a tear escaped to roll down her cheek. It was not a tear of remorse, but one of joy. What an inspiring thing to see Nathan crossing the line between a man of character to a man of abiding faith.

The preacher ended his sermon with an invitation to everyone to go to the creek for baptisms. Nathan was one of the first ones to meet him in the center of the creek where the water was nearly waist deep, eager to renew his dedication to the Lord with another baptism.

Abigail clasped her hands together under her chin and watched as he submitted to the preacher. Watched as his blond head went under the water. Applauded with the others when he was raised up again, the water sluicing off of him in rivulets. She was standing right at the edge of the water as he waded out, the first to congratulate him.

"Abigail. . .I suppose you're wondering—"

She quieted him with a glance. "Isn't it wonderful to be sure of your place in heaven?"

"Yes." A broad smile creased his face, making him more handsome than ever. "Yes, it is."

Her parents came over then, taking their turns talking to him and congratulating him on renewing his faith. What a wonderful day it had turned out to be, and the perfect way to end a week of revival.

Chapter 18

Nathan accepted Mr. LeGrand's offer to tie his horse to the rear of the wagon and ride back with the family. Even though Abigail had already heard about his change of heart, she listened with attention as he shared the story of Abram and Leah with her parents. He hesitated once when trying to describe the emotions he'd experienced, and she slipped her hand in his.

The squeeze of her fingers almost took his breath away, but he recovered his equilibrium after a moment and continued. "I was arrogant and ignorant, a dangerous combination. Now I want to do something to make up for my wrongheadedness."

"I told him he was to be commended for seeing the truth when he did." Abigail's dark gaze fluttered over him like the gentle touch of a butterfly's wing. She pulled her hand away from his as her father slowed the wagon.

Her mother glanced over her shoulder and smiled at both of them. "She's right. Of course we know that God does not ask us to make reparations, only to do better now that we have been made into new creatures."

As Mr. LeGrand brought the wagon to a full stop, Nathan considered Mrs. LeGrand's statement. He was beginning to realize the truth of her words, and it gave him a feeling of freedom, as though a heavy burden had been lifted from his shoulders. If he held out his arms, he might fly right off the back of the wagon.

"Why are we stopping, Papa?"

Mr. LeGrand pointed toward a glade a few feet away. "This looks like a good place to have our lunch."

Nathan jumped down from the wagon and turned to help Abigail. Then he and Mr. LeGrand spread a blanket on the ground under the shade of an oak tree and waited while the ladies laid out their food. Fried chicken, pickles, and carrots were passed around, followed by a selection of fresh fruits.

As soon as they finished eating, he broached the subject that he felt must be discussed. "I know all of you must wonder about a preacher needing to be baptized."

"Alexandra and I discussed that subject last night after we retired, but we didn't think it was our place to ask about such things." Mr. LeGrand crossed his legs at the ankle and leaned back on one elbow. "Your relationship with the

Lord is a private matter."

"I've heard of people who have been baptized several times." Mrs. LeGrand shrugged. "I told Jeremiah you were probably carried away by the sermon and decided to reaffirm your faith in a public way."

"I suppose that was part of it." Nathan stood and brushed a crumb off his shirtsleeve. "But I have also been guilty of deceit—to myself and to you good people."

"What do you mean?" Abigail shaded her eyes with one hand.

"I am a murderer."

Abigail and her mother gasped.

Mr. LeGrand sat up straight. "What are you talking about?"

"The reason I became a preacher was to make amends for killing someone. I was trying to protect a friend of mine and things got ugly. The attacker and I struggled, and he pulled a knife, but he slipped and fell on the blade." Nathan flexed his hand. "I can still feel the horror of that moment."

Shocked silence greeted him.

Nathan turned away and walked up a slight rise. He wanted to give the LeGrands time to absorb his story and decide whether or not they should continue to offer him their hospitality.

A pond on the other side of the hill reflected the blue, cloudless sky. He meandered toward it, wondering if the LeGrands would forgive him. He could understand if they did not. It had taken him a long time to forgive himself.

He picked up a rock and tossed it in the water. Ripples broke up the smooth surface of the water much like his words had disturbed the peace of his hosts. He sighed and glanced upward. At least he still had the comfort of his Savior. He would lend Nathan the fortitude to saddle his horse and ride back alone. Perhaps he could even be packed up by the time Abigail's family made it home.

A hand touched the small of his back and Nathan whirled around. "Abigail."

"I think you're the bravest man I've ever met." The admiration in her dark gaze warmed him through.

Nathan cleared his throat. "You amaze me, Abigail LeGrand. You have an infinite ability to surprise me. Being around you makes me feel like the most fortunate man alive. I cannot believe you and your family have forgiven me."

"Why not?" She smiled at him. "We can see what kind of man you are. You didn't have to tell us, you know. The very fact that you did proves how honorable you are."

Humility swept through him. This woman believed in him. She was a treasure to him, a miracle. He knew beyond a doubt that she was the only woman he would ever love.

Nathan bent down on one knee and took her hand in his. "Abigail, I once thought I loved a woman, but the feelings I had toward her are nothing but a wisp of smoke when compared to what I feel when I'm around you."

"Get up, Nathan." Abigail tried to pull her hand away. "I don't want to embarrass you, but there's no way I can let you go any further."

When he was a young boy, he'd once strayed into a neighbor's field and been discovered by the man's bull. The aggressive animal had charged him and butted him in the stomach. The pain of that day returned to him in full force as she spoke.

But then he looked up into Abigail's face and saw the sheen of tears in her eyes. Her expression was saying the exact opposite of her words. She cared for him.

"I have to go further, Abigail. This is too important. I have to find out why you're not being honest with me." When he realized how hard she was pulling on her hand, he released it.

She staggered back but caught her balance. "I. . .it's just that I have been raised different from other women." She wiped at the tears that tracked down her cheeks. "I cannot imagine trying to submit to you the way a good wife should."

If she hadn't been crying, he would have laughed out loud. Instead he stood up and closed the distance between them. He put a gentle hand on her shoulder. "Do you think I'm stupid?"

"What?" Her mouth fell open and her tears stopped falling. "Oh. . .of course not."

Nathan let his hand trail from her shoulder to her cheek. "Abigail LeGrand, you are the least submissive woman I've ever met. I love you because of who you are. Your intelligence, your honesty, your unflagging spirit—those are the things I admire about you. The way you always seek to help others. The way you give yourself, heart and soul, to whatever cause inspires you. I don't need some dull, drab female to clean my house and follow my orders. I need a helpmeet. I need you."

Abigail's breath caught, and a look of wonder filled her face. For a moment he thought he'd convinced her, but then the light in her eyes dimmed. She shook her head slowly.

He knew she was about to turn him down. Nathan also knew he could not let her say the words. Once they were spoken, it would be hard for his hardheaded love to retract them. So he put a finger on her lips. "Shhh. I know I've surprised you, but I want you to think about what I've said. Abigail, I want you to pray about it. Take your time. You'll find I am a patient man."

Chapter 19

I 'm ready." Abigail's pink skirt swirled around her feet as she descended the
stairs. She swung her matching parasol from one gloved finger and wondered why she didn't feel more excited about the day ahead. She always
enjoyed the town's Fourth of July celebration. But this year she found herself
pensive about what the day would bring.

It had been nearly two weeks since Nathan had proposed, and she still
didn't know what answer to give him. The question had been uppermost in
her mind no matter what she was doing. The children at the orphanage hadn't
noticed her preoccupation, but Deborah had teased her mercilessly when she
pulled a rose from a vase and tried to write a note with it.

She saw Nathan in the pulpit on Sunday, but he had not been over to visit
her or her parents since they'd gotten back from the revival meeting. Was he
regretting his impulsive proposal? Or giving her time to be certain of whatever
answer she decided to give him?

Nathan's words of love and devotion had awakened a longing in her, and
she was beginning to think the only solution was to accept his proposal. The
idea of submitting to his will had even begun to seem less abhorrent. Perhaps
the bishop's wife had been speaking the truth all those weeks ago in Jackson
when she said it would be easy to submit to a man who loved her as much as
Christ loved the Church.

Mama was waiting at the foot of the stairs. The look she bent on her
daughter made Abigail check with a nervous hand to make sure her coiffure
was straight. "Is something wrong?"

"Why don't you tell me?"

Mama's smile sent color rushing to Abigail's cheeks. "I don't know what
you're talking about."

She walked outside to find her father talking to none other than the
man who had been uppermost on her mind for two whole weeks. He wore
freshly creased trousers, a black coat, and a crisp white shirt. His blond hair
was brushed back from his face, but one lock had rebelled and fallen across his
forehead, giving him a dashing look. His blue eyes shone as though lit from
within, and a warm smile turned his lips up. Odd how a simple glance at him
made her heart speed up. "Nathan. . .I didn't expect to see you."

Papa laughed out loud at her social gaffe as Nathan swept a bow. "Your father asked me to drive one of the wagons. Would you like to ride with me to the orphanage?"

Without a glance for permission from either of her parents, Abigail put out her hand. "I would enjoy that immensely."

As soon as Nathan helped her up, he joined her on the bench. "It's a beautiful day, isn't it?"

"Yes, it's perfect for the celebration." She reached for her parasol and opened it.

"I was worried because of the storms last week."

Abigail watched his strong hands as he handled the reins. "I've been thinking about what you said to me that day."

"I'm glad to hear that." His voice was wry. "I'd hate to think you had forgotten my proposal."

She couldn't help the giggle his words and tone caused. But the laughter fled a moment later when he stopped the wagon. "What are you doing?"

He took her parasol from her hand and closed it. "Something I've regretted not doing that day."

His blue gaze was like a caress. He placed his hands on either side of her face and leaned toward her. His lips brushed hers lightly. . .then with more insistence. His touch was sweeter than a song. It made her feel precious, feminine, beloved. It was the most wonderful thing she had ever experienced in her life. She almost reached out to pull him near again when he ended the kiss.

"I love you, Abigail." His voice shook slightly, as though he was as affected by the kiss as she had been. "Please tell me you'll marry me."

All of her doubts melted away like frost at sunrise. Abigail put a hand over her thundering heart and tried to swallow, but her mouth was dry as dust. She couldn't force out a single syllable. So she nodded.

Nathan gathered her in his arms and hugged her. "You've made me the happiest man on earth." He kissed her again. And again.

Finally she pushed at his chest. "We have to go get the children."

"What children?" He placed a kiss at the base of her neck.

Abigail giggled. "The ones at the orphanage. They're waiting for us."

He sighed and straightened. "I suppose you're right."

All the way into town she drank in his profile and sent silent prayers of gratefulness to God for bringing them together.

❈

"Where's Mia?" Abigail put a hand on her hip. "She was playing jackstraw earlier, but no one has seen her for a while."

Nathan was sitting cross-legged on the ground, playing marbles with some of the boys from the orphanage. She had watched him all afternoon as he talked and played with the children. They all loved him, and he no longer looked as though he was being skinned when they crowded around him. The change in him was one she could definitely live with.

He unfolded his legs and stood up, brushing at the dirt that had accumulated on his pants. "I don't know."

"I'm worried she went back to the orphanage to check on Boots." Mia had pouted when they refused to let her bring the orphanage cat along. Abigail had tried to explain that a kitten would be frightened by all the noise and people, but Mia had refused to budge until Nathan stepped in and convinced her to let Boots take a nap while they went to the festivities. Mia had acted fine once she got to the town square, but she could have slipped off to collect Boots when their backs were turned. "I've already asked around," Abigail continued, "but no one has seen her for the past hour."

Nathan reached for the coat he'd draped over a nearby tree limb. "I'll go to the orphanage and look for her."

"I'll go with you." She looked toward the stable. "Why don't we walk and save the time it would take to get the wagon hitched?"

He held out his arm, and she put her hand on it, blushing slightly at the unexpected tingle caused by his nearness. They walked down the street, smiling and nodding at the people they passed. It seemed everyone in Natchez was here.

Vendors had set up temporary booths selling everything from melons to barbecued ribs. Politicians shook hands and talked about the challenges facing Mississippi. Children shouted and ran through the crowds, playing games of tag or hide-and-seek while their parents looked on from the shade of the large trees ringing the town square. Once the sun set, families would enjoy watching the fireworks before they returned to their homes.

Nathan put his hand over Abigail's. "I may owe Mia my thanks since her disappearance has given me an excuse to be alone with you."

She sliced a glance at him from the corner of her eye. "You're going to make me wonder if it was your idea for her to go back to the orphanage."

His laughter rang out on the still air. "I am crushed to be so misunderstood."

It felt so good when her laugh joined his. Their life together was going to be full of wonderful moments. They walked on in perfect harmony, leaving the crowds behind. If not for her concern about Mia, Abigail would have been content to have their walk last for hours.

"When can we get married?"

The question sizzled through her. "We haven't even told my parents yet."

"We can do that tonight." He raised his eyebrows and waggled them.

Abigail giggled. "I think a Christmas wedding would be romantic."

"Christmas!" He shook his head. "I think July would be much better."

"Let's worry about that once we collect Mia." A frown replaced Abigail's smile as they approached the orphanage. "It doesn't look like anyone is here."

"I think I see a light." Nathan pointed at an odd green glow that seemed to emanate from the backyard.

The ghost! Was it possible? They skirted the outside of the house as the sun dipped below the horizon. The sight that met her eyes made Abigail's blood freeze. A figure in a long white robe moved silently along the edge of the bluff, waving a green-tinted lantern back and forth.

After the first second of disbelief passed, anger swelled inside her. She recognized the arrogant strut of the so-called ghost. What was Silas Ward doing out here? And why was he wearing that robe? Was he using the legend of the pirate's wife for some nefarious purpose? His green-shuttered lantern illuminated a mound in the grass and her breath caught. Mia. With a little cry, she pulled away from Nathan and rushed forward. "What have you done?"

Silas looked up as she ran toward him, his face twisted in a mask of hatred. When Abigail would have knelt to check the little girl, he grabbed her arm and whipped her around so she stood with her back to him. "Where is it?"

"What are you talking about, Silas?" Abigail grimaced as he pushed her arm upward. "Ouch, you're hurting me."

"Let go of her!" Nathan's voice was harsh as he moved toward them.

"Stay back!" Silas pulled a knife from the pocket of his ridiculous robe and pressed it against Abigail's neck.

Nathan stopped abruptly. The blood drained from his face. "What do you want, Silas?"

"I want the treasure. Where is it?" The man holding her sounded crazed.

"What treasure?" She could hear the shock in Nathan's voice.

Silas snorted. "Don't be stupid. This house used to belong to a pirate who hid his treasure here. I've been looking for it, but I haven't found anything...yet."

Abigail kept her head still to avoid the prick of his knife. "How do you know about the treasure?"

"I lived here as a child. One of your father's poor orphans. I used to spend hours exploring, looking for the treasure. But then my cousin came to claim me. He took me away and introduced me to the world of drinking and gambling. What a life...until the money ran out."

His laughter was harsh. "I even thought about marrying you, but that wouldn't work. You may be rich, but your parents have spoiled you far too much. And you're rather plain, too. Besides, I require obedience from my women."

If the moment had not been so serious, she would have laughed at his words. How ironic that she'd thought this man admired her independence. A movement at her feet caught Abigail's attention.

Mia put a hand on her head and moaned. "What happened?" Her voice was groggy.

Abigail hoped the child was not hurt. It was hard to tell in the weird glow of the green lamp. She looked at it closely.

Silas must have realized her confusion. "It's made from green mica. Useful when you need to imitate a spirit. You should have heard that silly matron going on and on about seeing me out here. All I had to do was blow out the lamp and pull off this robe to disappear. Ingenious, isn't it?"

"You were the one scaring the children?"

Silas pulled her away from Mia and the lamp. "Too bad there wasn't much of value inside the orphanage." The knife bit her neck. "Tell me where the treasure is."

"Don't be an idiot. There's no treasure." She put all the conviction she could muster into the words. "We found a sea trunk hidden behind a false wall in the dining room years ago, but it only held letters and a few trinkets."

She could hear the rage in the hiss of his breath at her ear. "You're lying."

A trickle eased down her neck, and Abigail realized she was bleeding. She looked across at Nathan and forced herself to smile. Whether she lived or died tonight, she would always be thankful to have won his love.

Mia picked that moment to push to her feet and run toward Nathan. Silas loosened his hold on her arm. Instead of trying to pull away, Abigail tripped and fell forward, a moan of pain slipping out as her knees made contact with the hard ground.

❀

Nathan froze for an instant before instinct took over. He leaped forward.

Silas started to haul Abigail back to her feet but released her as he saw Nathan barreling toward him. Nathan ducked as the deadly blade slashed the air, but he came up swinging both arms. His first blow made contact with Silas's jaw. The impact shuddered down the length of his arm and made his stomach roil.

The other man's head snapped back, but he didn't lose his footing. His left fist somehow found its way into Nathan's stomach. Nathan's jaw clenched against the pain radiating outward from his midsection, but he knew he could not afford to double over. Silas was lifting the knife above his head now, holding it in both hands as though wielding an axe. Immediately on the defensive, Nathan grabbed Silas's wrists and pushed hard to keep the blade from biting into his shoulder.

Little by little, Nathan realized he was losing the struggle as the blade inched down. He sent a prayer heavenward for the strength to overcome the madman.

He could not win against the downward force of the knife, but Nathan realized he didn't need to. Instead of trying to stop the blade's descent, he relaxed briefly. A triumphant leer of success lit Silas's features when Nathan's grip weakened. But it changed to horror as Nathan twisted to one side. The blade whizzed harmlessly through the air past his shoulder.

Before Silas could recover, Nathan bent down and thrust his shoulder into the other man's abdomen. Silas tumbled backward, arms windmilling as he teetered on the edge of the steep bluff. A shrill scream tore free as he realized he would not be able to save himself, and he disappeared from Nathan's horrified gaze.

It couldn't happen again. He could not break the sixth commandment again. Anguish and remorse filled him.

He didn't even remember Abigail until she flung her arms around him. "I'm so glad you're safe."

Mia ran to them, apparently unharmed. "You did it, Pastor. You saved us. That was a mean man." She hugged him with nearly as much strength as Abigail had.

"Are you two okay?"

They both nodded, looking at him like he was a hero. So why did he feel like a villain? The question went unanswered as wind gusted against his face.

Wait. Had he heard a cry for help?

Nathan disengaged the clinging arms and flung himself to the ground, his head hanging over the edge of the steep bluff. At first he saw nothing in the failing light, but then a movement below made him catch his breath. "Abigail, Mia, go find a rope. Quick."

They ran toward the house as he reached down for Silas's hand. If he could only reach a few more inches. Nathan strained to no avail. "Hold on. We'll help you."

A loud noise brought his head up. A cascade of red sparks lit the sky. The fireworks had begun.

"Why?" The word was tossed up toward him from the man who was hanging on to life by a thread. "Why are you helping me?"

"Because God loves you. He's perfect, and He loves you in spite of the evil you would commit. How can I do less?"

Silence answered him. Nathan closed his eyes and prayed for Silas to live. Tense moments passed—each one like a fading heartbeat. He considered half-a-dozen plans but rejected all of them.

Finally he heard someone running toward him. He turned his head and saw Abigail. She didn't have a rope, but a sheet billowed around her. What a resourceful woman.

She skidded to a stop next to him. "I sent Mia back to the celebration to get Papa and the sheriff." She lay down next to him and dropped one end of the sheet over the edge of the bluff.

Realizing he would need to anchor the material, Nathan grabbed the other end and sat up. He looped the soft cloth around his waist and tied it in a quick knot. "You're going to have to use the sheet like a ladder, Silas."

A jerk told him Silas had grabbed hold. As the pressure around his waist increased, Nathan wondered if he could stop both of them from plunging to their deaths. As Silas climbed upward, Nathan's boots inched closer to the edge.

As if from a distance, he heard Abigail crying and praying and wished he could comfort her. His jaw clenched as one of his boots slid off the grassy edge into nothingness. He gritted his teeth and tried to hold on.

Shouts sounded. He could feel the pounding of heavy footfalls. Then strong hands grabbed him under his arms and pulled back. Help had arrived in the nick of time.

Someone heaved Silas over the edge, and the terrible pressure around Nathan's waist eased. He stood up slowly as the sheriff placed handcuffs on Silas.

Abigail ran to him and threw her arms around his neck. She kissed his cheek, his ear, his other cheek—her lips trembling against his skin. He held her close and thanked God for preserving all three of them.

Mr. LeGrand's voice brought Nathan back to his senses. "I suppose this means your mother was right."

He tried to disengage himself from Abigail's embrace, but she clung to him like a limpet. Finally he looked over her head and smiled at her father. "I hope you will allow me to marry your daughter, sir."

"Don't be silly, Nathan." Abigail smiled up at him, her dark eyes hinting mischief. "Mama and Papa probably knew before we did that we were in love." She pulled his face down and kissed him soundly.

Chapter 20

"I still can't believe Silas Ward was hiding his past and his true reason for coming to Natchez. If only he had told us the truth, so much pain and misery could have been avoided." Abigail shook her head as she guided the buggy toward the orphanage.

"He was the proverbial wolf in sheep's clothing." Nathan's sigh was lengthy and deep. "I'm glad we stopped him before his plans did any more harm."

"Thanks to your efforts." A thrill of pleasure lifted the corners of her mouth at the expression on Nathan's face. He was such a good man. In the weeks since the revival she had seen him guiding others, loving them in spite of their weaknesses, and leading them to Christ by his humble example. How had she ever thought him overbearing or controlling? Christ's love shone through his words and deeds.

This trip to the orphanage was another indication of the changes in this man. He had planned this visit and asked her to join him instead of the other way around. His relationship with several of the children warmed her heart.

As they turned the corner, Nathan pointed toward the orphanage. "We are not the only visitors this morning."

Abigail frowned at the unfamiliar carriage and horses. "It looks like they've come some distance."

Nathan jumped down as soon as she brought the buggy to a halt. "Did your father say anything before you left?"

Tossing the reins to him, she shook her head. "No."

A couple of the boys were chasing each other around the orphanage yard as Nathan helped her dismount, then opened the gate. Before they could make their way to the front porch, the door flew open and Mia appeared with a squeal of delight.

She dashed down the steps and barreled into Nathan, who caught her up in a strong hug. "You seem overly delighted to see me this morning." He planted a kiss on her forehead.

"You'll never believe who has come to us."

Abigail smiled to see the two of them together. They looked so natural.

"I have cousins." Mia's words ended her speculation. "And an aunt and uncle. They've come from Boston to find me." The little girl scrunched up her face for a moment as she gazed at the man holding her. "Is that a long way from Natchez?"

"Yes, it is." Nathan's deep voice carried a hint of sadness. He let Mia slide down as they reached the porch steps. "But I'm sure you'll like it there."

She smiled and ran back inside.

Abigail caught up with Nathan and touched his elbow. "Are you okay?"

A slight grin turned up one side of his mouth. "Of course. I'm thrilled for Mia."

They walked inside together and headed for the parlor, following Mia's excited voice. "And he told me all about how Jesus loves little girls and boys."

Abigail saw Nathan's smile widen. A prayer of thankfulness filled her. They entered the parlor to find a young family inside.

The lady looked much like Mia's mother, petite and fine-boned. Her husband, a shorter, slightly rotund gentleman, was equally well-dressed and wore a pleasant expression as he stood. Their two children, a boy who looked to be a few years older than Mia and a young girl who had to be about her age, sat quietly and listened to their newfound cousin.

Mia performed the introductions—Uncle C. J. and Aunt Dorothy Ogden, and her cousins, Master Patrick and Miss Ruthanne.

"Mia says you are from Boston." Abigail glanced at Nathan, who sat next to her on the sofa.

"Yes." Mrs. Ogden picked at the material of her gown. "I am ashamed to admit that my sister, Mia's mother, and I were estranged almost a decade ago. The reason is not important now, but you can imagine my sorrow at learning of my sister's death. We left when we received the letter telling us about Mia." The warm glance she lavished on the young girl was enough to calm some of Abigail's concerns.

Deborah entered the parlor, a box in her arms. "Hello, Abigail, Brother Nathan. Isn't it a glorious morning?"

The men stood up again, even young Patrick, showing he had been raised properly. The next hour was filled with conversation as they learned everything there was to know about Mia's long-lost relatives. They spoke to Nathan about their church at home and their faith. They talked to Abigail and Deborah about education and a stable home.

By the time the Ogdens readied themselves to leave, Abigail felt reassured about Mia's future. It was still hard to hug Mia for the final time. She would miss the adorable little girl. A glance at Nathan's face told her he also had conflicting feelings.

After Mia finished her good-byes, Miss Ruthanne took her hand. "We're going to have so much fun. You'll love Boston."

Abigail touched Nathan's hand and offered him a smile. "She'll be so much happier."

"Yes, you're right." He brushed a hand across his face, his gesture melting her heart. How wonderful to be in love with someone so caring.

❄

Deborah's sigh broke the silence in the parlor as she picked up a platter of freshly baked sugar cookies. "I highly recommend these, Brother Pierce."

He glanced at the plate of sweets, but his answer was forestalled by Abigail's gasp.

"Is that your bracelet?" Abigail pointed to their hostess's outstretched arm.

"Yes, the sheriff returned it to me." Deborah moved the platter to her other hand and showed them the treasured piece of jewelry. "It seems the vile Mr. Ward must have taken it at some time when he was sneaking about."

Nathan shook his head. "What a shame."

"If not for your bravery, Mr. Ward might never have been stopped." Abigail's voice was filled with admiration.

Nathan tried not to squirm, but it was difficult. God had given him peace over his actions—even if it meant taking another life, he had the responsibility to defend those who needed his help—but he was thankful not to have been the inadvertent cause of yet another man's death. There was still hope for Silas's salvation. "I have visited Mr. Ward twice since that night, and I believe he is coming to the point of listening to God's plan."

The glance from Abigail made him want to squirm even more. He was not worthy of the love he saw in her gaze.

"Isn't it about time for us to go back to Magnolia Plantation?" He hoped she would not see through his bid to distract her.

Abigail raised an eyebrow. "You shouldn't be so modest."

"Don't give him a hard time, Abigail." The laughter in Deborah's voice told him she was not fooled, either. "I wish more men were as humble as Brother Pierce."

Wondering if his ears were as red as they were warm, Nathan led Abigail to the buggy and helped her get settled on the seat before handing her the reins and taking his place beside her.

"Why don't you drive?" She handed him the reins. "I have something much more interesting to do."

He shrugged and guided the horse along the street. "What would that be?"

"Admiring the man I'm going to marry." She tucked her hand around his arm. "Mia is going to be all right, you know."

"Yes." It never ceased to amaze him how perceptive Abigail was. "In the last few days I was wondering if we could adopt her ourselves. But Christ had a better plan in mind."

He loved the way her cheeks reddened. "You are such a special man. I cannot believe how blessed I am to have you in my life."

"And I you." Now it was his turn to blush. "I thank God for you daily."

"I once thought it would be impossible to submit to a man." Her lemony perfume filled his senses as she leaned against his shoulder. "But that was before I knew a man who submitted himself so easily to Christ."

He knew the Scripture she referred to but was curious for her understanding of the subject. "What do you mean?"

"I have always considered myself independent. I thought it a weakness to rely on any man as I've seen so many simpering ladies do."

He couldn't help but interject, "But what about your mother with your father? I wouldn't consider her to be 'simpering.'"

"And neither do I. In fact, it was during a discussion with Mama and Mrs. Ross in Jackson that I really began to see the idea of submitting in a different way. When Mrs. Ross mentioned the words from Paul that I quoted earlier, I began to think that submitting to the right man, the right *godly* man, could indeed be what is intended for a man and wife. Then when I had dinner with Silas, I knew almost immediately I could never submit to him, not even truly respect him."

"So what ultimately changed your mind?"

"You did."

"Me? How?"

"Well, it was actually God working through you. When I witnessed your encounter with God at the campground, I finally understood what Paul meant. I knew I could submit to someone who loved me like Christ loved the Church. You've always wanted only the best for me and have never tried to control me. I love only you and trust you with my heart."

"Hmm, sounds as if we should go camping many more times." He couldn't keep his face serious enough to hide his grin.

Abigail elbowed him in the side. "All right now, where is that Christlike love?"

"Right where you know it to be." He pointed to his chest. "In my heart."

She planted a quick kiss on his cheek. "Same here."

Although he would have liked to bask in the glow of her admiration, Nathan knew it was time to let her see his own weakness. "I didn't start preaching for the right reason."

She sat up and a frown creased her brow. "What are you talking about?"

"Do you remember when I told you and your parents about killing Ira Watson?"

He felt rather than saw her nod.

"I decided the only way to pay for my actions would be to dedicate myself to preaching God's Word. I thought I could earn forgiveness. It wasn't until the night at the campground when I heard that poem about coming to God, 'Just As I Am,' that I realized the truth. No one can earn forgiveness. It's a gift given freely when Christ laid down His life for our sins." The words had come slowly at first, but now they seemed easier. "I thought about quitting. But God kept putting people in front of me, people who seemed to need my help to find their way to Him. People like the slaves I told you about. Even Silas Ward.

People who are hurting and lost. And now that I have turned my life over to God without reservation, I believe He has given me the ability to reach them."

Her hands covered his on the reins, and she pulled the horse to a stop. "I love you, Nathan Pierce. And I know you're right. God has something very special in mind for you."

He glanced around and realized they had not quite reached Magnolia Plantation, so he caught her up in his embrace. "I love you, too, Abigail LeGrand. With your support, I know I'll be able to meet every challenge." He pressed his lips against her softer ones, his heart filling with love and thankfulness to have won the admiration of such a special woman. As their kiss deepened, he made a promise to himself to always treasure her love as much as he did at this moment.

Epilogue

Nathan stood proudly and watched as Jeremiah LeGrand escorted his daughter down the aisle. This was the happiest day of his life.

Abigail stepped close to him, a wide smile on her face. He could barely believe this vibrant woman was about to become his wife. He sent a silent prayer of thanks heavenward. God had blessed him so. She was especially lovely today, her hair piled high on her head, the white skirt of her dress floating around her. All she needed was a pair of wings to qualify as an angel.

Outside the church, the weather was not as sunny as he'd hoped. A storm had blown in as they were getting ready to leave Magnolia Plantation. But at least it had not stopped anyone from attending.

He glanced toward the pews where the children from the orphanage sat. It seemed odd not to see Mia's expressive face among them, but he had received a letter from her describing her new home. She was being well cared for, so he could not be sad. He would have to remember to send her a letter describing the wedding.

Several people in the packed church gasped as lightning flashed outside, almost immediately followed by the boom of thunder. The wind blew against the walls of the church, but inside peace and love filled the air.

Nathan watched Abigail's face as he repeated his vows of loyalty and love. Then it was her turn. Her voice was hesitant at first but gained strength as she continued.

"Ladies and gentlemen, I now present to you the Reverend and Mrs. Nathan Pierce."

Instead of going outside, Abigail and Nathan stood next to each other and greeted their friends and neighbors. By the time they had spoken to all of their well-wishers, the sun had come out once more. Nathan wondered if he would ever get used to the rapid weather changes in this part of the country.

Abigail's father went to the podium to get everyone's attention. "We are going to move this celebration to Magnolia Plantation. We have plenty of food for everyone there."

Nathan escorted Abigail to the carriage as a spattering of raindrops fell on them.

She ducked her head and hurried into the vehicle. "I knew we should wait for cold weather."

Nathan climbed in and sat beside her. "I couldn't wait even one more day for you." Putting an arm around her waist, he pulled her close for a kiss. He still could not quite believe the love flowing between them. God had truly blessed them.

Satisfaction and joy filled her face as she broke free for a moment. "Nor I for you, my love."

As the River Drifts Away

Dedication

To our editors extraordinaire: JoAnne Simmons and Becky Durost Fish. You are wonderful editors who have become our friends. Thanks for giving wings to our dreams. We deeply appreciate the work you put into improving our stories. And for everyone else who wants you to edit their books. . .we call dibs!

Chapter 1

January 1863
Jackson, Mississippi

A bigail, I'm not planning to take you and the girls with me this time." Pa straightened and dusted his hands after tossing a fresh log on the fire. "It's far too dangerous for gadding about."

Ma sighed and pulled her shawl closer about her shoulders. "We're not talking about going on a sightseeing trip, Nathan. And you'll be there to protect us."

Caroline Pierce studied the grooves in the pine floor, wishing she could think of something to say that would bring her parents to agreement. She was eighteen years old, after all. Old enough to find the right words. "Perhaps we sh. . .shouldn't go to Vicksburg." She could feel the pressure of her parents' gazes but refused to look up. Her heart beat a rapid tattoo. Why had she decided to voice her opinion?

"Don't be nonsensical, dearest." Ma reached past the arm of the sofa and patted her knee. "You're not afraid, are you? We'll be much safer with your father than staying here in Jackson all alone."

Ma's tone was gentle, so why couldn't Caroline calm the beating of her heart? She loved her mother and ought to be accustomed to her outspokenness. But she wished just this once that Ma would quietly accept Pa's pronouncement. Then they could turn their attention to some other subject, like yesterday's sermon. She would even welcome a discussion on what color to paint the parlor or whether or not she could mend the tear in her counterpane.

The fireplace logs shifted, and heat from the dancing flames brushed her cheeks. A deep breath seemed to steady her nerves somewhat. Wondering if she'd lost her mind, Caroline opened her mouth to answer. "I'm sorry to disagree with you, Ma. Pa would not make such a decision lightly. We have a duty to listen to him."

"You're quite right, Caroline." Ma's eyes crinkled at the corners as she smiled. "But that does not preclude my discussing the matter with him. Or with you either."

Her hands twisted in her lap. Caroline did not want to "discuss" things. She had already expressed her opinion. But she did not have the courage to argue with her strong-willed parent. Why not accept Pa's bidding? It would make life much easier, and much quieter, in the Pierce home. But Ma was not likely to change, so Caroline folded her lips and remained silent while wondering

243

why they couldn't just go along with Pa. He deserved their respectful acceptance of his decisions.

"If your mother did not challenge me, I'd be certain she was ill." Her father settled on the sofa and placed an arm around her mother's shoulders. "I've never been under any illusion about her timidity."

Caroline wondered if she would ever understand others in her family. Was she a changeling? But that wasn't possible. Even she could see how much she looked like her father. Both of them had blond hair, fair skin, and eyes as blue as a summer sky. But at three inches above five feet, she had not inherited her father's height.

Pa was a well-respected pastor at one of the largest churches in town, but at home he often bowed to the wishes of his wife. Ma and even Tory, Caroline's younger sister, seemed to take delight in disputing many of his decisions.

Perhaps I am the odd one. They didn't suffer from the same malady that twisted Caroline's tongue in knots every time she tried to speak. She nodded and dipped her head once more.

The door to the study opened, and she glanced up to see Tory rushing through the door. Her sister's dark hair fell in thick waves about her shoulders, and excitement brought extra beauty to her face. Grandma said Tory looked like she had when she was younger.

Tory would soon be collecting men's hearts the way some young women collected flowers. Although she was a full four years younger than Caroline, she was already turning heads at church. She was definitely the most beautiful member of the family and the liveliest. But it was her innate kindness that made her irresistible to young people of both sexes. If a group of youngsters was gathered together, Tory was almost certain to be at its center.

"Come quickly." Tory clasped her hands in front of her chest. "A group of soldiers is marching down the street. You have to see them. They are so handsome in their gray uniforms."

"Please tell me you have not been ogling the young men." Pa's sigh was audible.

Ma rose from the sofa. "I'm sure she's done no such thing." Her dark-brown gaze held the same warning as her voice. "Have you, Tory?"

"Of course not." Tory's wide skirts twisted as she turned toward the door to the hallway. "Come along, Caroline. Hurry, or you'll miss them."

Pa stood and offered his arm to Ma. Caroline followed them to the hallway, a smile turning up the corners of her mouth as Pa placed a quick kiss on Ma's cheek. Her love for him was clear in the gaze Ma trained on him as they walked out. Was their love for each other the reason for Pa's tolerance? Caroline worried at the question as her sister flung the front doors wide and a blast of frigid air rushed into the hallway.

"Brr." Her mother's shoulders lifted as the cold surrounded them. "Wait until we've put on our wraps."

"Sorry." Her younger sister closed the doors, a penitent look on her face.

"You allow yourself to get far too excited, Tory." Her mother took her cloak from a hook on the wall. "If you wish to be included in adult gatherings, you'll have to temper your actions with the same good sense your older sister displays."

Caroline felt another blush as she accepted her green wool cloak from her father and wrapped it around her shoulders. She was not comfortable being held up as an example. She had far too many faults.

"I believe we are ready to brave the cold." Pa nodded at Tory. "Let's see these soldiers of yours."

This time when she opened the doors, Tory managed it with a bit more grace. But as Caroline crossed the threshold, her incorrigible sister winked at her, and a giggle threatened to escape. A prime example of why she should not be held up as a model of good behavior.

The street was alive with marching men. Her gaze widened as she stepped to the rail surrounding the deep porch. "Oh my."

Tory grabbed her arm. "Aren't they marvelous?"

A frown brought Caroline's brows together. Marching in formation, five abreast, the sea of gray slouch caps and uniforms filled the dirt road from edge to edge. But as she looked closer, she realized their uniforms were tattered and faded. Sadness and empathy filled her. "Where are they going?"

"Probably to Canton." Her father pointed to the north. "President Davis has ordered General Johnston to keep the Jackson area safe as well as lend support to General Pemberton's troops in Vicksburg."

"Some of them look so young." Ma shook her head. "Younger than you are, Tory. It makes me sad to think of the boys who won't be alive when this war is over."

Tory had leaned over the edge of the rail, but she straightened and looked toward her parents. "Don't say such a terrible thing. Amy Parsons says the South is winning the war. Maybe all our boys will come back unhurt."

Caroline found herself agreeing with her mother. The war had gone on for several years now. Hopes for a quick end had faded as the battles continued to rage, and every day they heard of families who had lost sons, brothers, or fathers.

Pa shook his head. "No matter which side wins, war is a terrible thing. Especially this war between states. I've read in the local newspapers of brothers joining opposite sides and meeting each other on the battlefield."

Caroline's jaw tightened. She hated the idea of siblings as enemies. "We should pray for them." She reached for her father's hand. "And for a quick end to the war."

❦

The first thing Caroline noticed as she disembarked from the carriage was a huge, conical pipe mounted on the nose of a boxy, open-windowed conveyance.

The black smoke belching from the pipe drifted back over the roofs of cargo and passenger cars. "Is that the train we'll be taking?"

Her father nodded and pulled out his pocket watch. "We should be leaving the station within an hour."

"There's another train." Tory stepped up beside her and pointed to a second engine pointed south. "How can you tell which one we should board?"

"That one is going to New Orleans." Pa put away his watch and held out his arm for Ma. "Stay with us, you two. I don't want to have to come looking for you."

Picking up her skirt, Caroline picked her way around bales, barrels, and boxes. She almost fell when an obnoxious businessman pushed past her and was only saved from ending up facedown in a puddle by the quick reflexes of a nearby soldier.

"Careful, ma'am." His hand gripped her arm.

Her breath got stuck in her throat, but Caroline managed to mumble her thanks. He bowed and was quickly lost in the crowd.

"He was handsome." Tory's familiar voice restored her equilibrium.

Caroline rolled her eyes. "You think every man above the age of ten is handsome, especially if he's wearing a uniform."

Tory stuck out her tongue.

"Careful or your expression may get stuck that way." Caroline repeated the warning their mother had often used when she was younger.

"Come along, girls." Ma's voice stopped Tory from answering.

They waited a few feet back as their father spoke briefly with the conductor. Nearby, a farmer made arrangements for livestock to be delivered to his home, his voice sharp as he directed the loading onto a wagon.

"Did you see the size of the lantern on the front of the locomotive?" Tory's voice held a note of awe. "It's almost as large as my bedroom window."

"Yes." Caroline looked toward the large engine. "It must be nearly as bright as moonlight."

Tory nodded. "I wonder why they need it though. That large shovel on the front of the train looks as though it would sweep away any obstacles."

"I've read of Union soldiers pulling up tracks and causing Confederate trains to have wrecks. Perhaps they need the lantern to make sure the track ahead has not been destroyed."

"You young ladies don't have to worry about a thing." The conductor, a tall man with a kindly smile, walked over to them. His reddish-blond hair reminded her of Grandpa back in Natchez. "We'll have you safely to your destination before nightfall."

Tory's face fell, but all Caroline felt was relief at the man's reassurance. She could never be as daring as her younger sister. The conductor indicated the steps with a broad gesture, and she turned to realize their parents had already boarded the train.

She climbed the steps and entered the cabin, feeling her stomach curdle as the floor pitched slightly under the movements of the other travelers. She swallowed hard and moved forward, looking for some sign of her parents. How had they gotten separated so quickly?

"There they are." Tory pointed to a seat at the back, and Caroline breathed a sigh of relief as she recognized them. Ma was already seated next to the window, but Pa was removing his coat and hat. At least he had not begun looking for them.

Tory and Caroline settled themselves on the seat in front of their parents. Tory looked out the window and pointed to a man who was carrying their trunks on his shoulders. "I do hope he doesn't drop my trunk. I cannot imagine how embarrassing it would be to have all my clothing scattered on the ground."

"You have such an imagination." Caroline sometimes wished she had inherited a small portion of Tory's zest for life. . .as well as a large helping of her outspokenness. She sighed and folded her hands in her lap. It was not as though she found life difficult, and she knew the good Lord had created her to have her own strengths, but it would be nice to take pleasure in each day with the wholehearted joy her sister displayed.

Tory continued to remark on all the things that caught her attention as the car filled with passengers. The ring of a brass bell somewhere ahead brought the conductor past them, stopping here or there to help people stow their bags and cloaks.

The train shuddered, and she gripped the edge of her seat, her heart tripping. Caroline twisted her head toward the window and saw the depot moving backward.

Beside her, Tory clapped her hands together. "We're moving."

A second glance out the window proved her sister right. The train, not the depot, was moving, picking up speed with every turn of the metal wheels beneath them. She pried her fingers from the edge of the wooden bench and placed them in her lap once more. Taking a deep breath, she forced a smile to her lips. "So we are."

Tory didn't seem to notice her discomfort, so enthralled was she by the passing scenery. "I wonder if we'll see any Yankees."

"I doubt it." Pa's voice came from the seat behind them. "And I thought I told you not to use that term. You can call them Union or Federal soldiers, but you will be punished if I hear you use that vulgar term again."

"Yes, sir." Tory's voice was penitent.

Caroline hated to see the sheen of tears in her sister's eyes. She reached over and gave Tory's hand a squeeze.

Tory rewarded her with a wobbly smile.

"Look at all the smoke." Caroline indicated the black swirls coming from the engine at the front of the train. "Thankfully it's cool enough in here so that we can keep the windows shut."

While Tory watched the passing scenery, Caroline pulled needlework from her reticule and began stitching. "I don't know how you have such patience." Tory's whisper raised a smile. "And your stitches are so much finer than mine. You will make an excellent wife for some handsome soldier."

Color heated Caroline's cheeks. "Don't be silly. I don't even have a suitor. I'm sure you will marry before anyone makes me an offer."

Tory made a choked sound. "Anyone who gets to know you will never be able to resist your sweetness and feminine abilities. You are the perfect example of the good wife Solomon talks about in the Bible. Why, who knows? He could even be here on this train and watching you sitting here demurely with your stitchery in your lap. He's probably trying to figure out who you are and how to arrange an introduction."

This time the choked sound came from Caroline's throat. "You are being a silly goose." But her heart stumbled. Was it true? She looked around at the passengers she could see. A short, overweight businessman in the seat opposite them had tipped his hat over his face and was apparently sleeping. Up ahead she could see a passably handsome man sitting next to his beautiful wife. A pair of soldiers were laughing and talking as though they had no thought of war or death. Tory's imagination was as vivid as ever but had no basis in reality.

She returned her attention to her needlework. Only God knew what was in store, but she had no doubt He had a bright future in mind for both her and her sister.

Chapter 2

Luke Talbot sawed at the tough slice of beef and wished for the time before the war, the days when good meat was readily available at restaurants. The days when he could expect a decent meal to complement the beautiful young lady seated opposite him. Why had he let Gram talk him into coming to Vicksburg, anyway?

For a wife.

He glanced toward Marianna Lister, the young lady sitting across from him. Glossy black hair framed her beautiful face. Miss Lister's complexion was flawless, as was her genteel conversation and fashionable attire. Yet when he compared her to the woman who had stolen his heart and then betrayed it—

Luke shook his head to stop that train of thought. No need to compare her to Amelia Montgomery. No female would ever outshine her memory. Even though Amelia's lies and subterfuges had probably cost him his chance to become a general in the Confederate army, she would always be the first woman he'd ever loved. It didn't matter that she had betrayed the South and then had the effrontery to choose Jared Stuart instead of him; Amelia had claimed the better part of Luke's heart.

"It is so delightful to spend an evening away from my family." Miss Lister ignored the meat on her plate and nibbled at a biscuit. "Papa always drones on and on about the war. It scares my poor mother half to death. You would think Yankees were standing on our very doorstep if you listened to him."

"Your father is probably right to be concerned." Luke finally managed to separate a bite of meat from the serving on his plate. "Lincoln has made it very plain he would love to capture the city of Vicksburg."

Marianna dabbed at her mouth with her napkin. "That may be so, but it's most unlikely. General Grant will soon realize he cannot prevail and will leave us alone. He's already tried three times to take the city, but our troops have outwitted him at every turn."

"I have the feeling the general is not yet ready to admit defeat."

"Let him come." The young lady opposite him raised her chin in a defiant gesture. "I refuse to cower like some child who is afraid of an imaginary hobgoblin."

Luke smiled. He had to admire the young lady's courage. In fact, there was much to admire about Miss Lister. A very fine example of a true Southern belle, Marianna was beautiful and intelligent. She was also proving herself to be an entertaining companion. She was the best of the crop his grandmother had paraded in front of him since his arrival in Mississippi before Christmas.

"I can almost see you running off a whole platoon of Yankees with a broom and a parasol."

"I suppose you're making a joke at my expense. But I'll do whatever is necessary to protect my home and family."

"Pardon me, Miss Lister." Luke hid his smile. He hadn't meant to insult her. "I didn't mean to make light of your words. I have no doubt you would do a wonderful job of running those Yankees off. I only wish the ladies back in Tennessee had half of your fervor. When we men go off to fight, it's comforting to know we've left our homes in the capable, courageous hands of ladies such as yourself."

Her smile was as wide as the Mississippi River and as bright as sunlight. He ought to tell her that, but he didn't want to rush into anything. There would be time for him to get to know Miss Lister better before he began spouting effusive compliments. Instead he satisfied himself with returning her attractive smile.

Luke reached for his goblet of water at the same time she did, and their knuckles brushed. Her eyes widened slightly in surprise, and a faint flush colored her cheeks. In that moment, he thought he might be able to bury his feelings for Amelia after all. Perhaps Marianna Lister could fill the hole Amelia had left behind.

As their dinner continued, he discovered Marianna's talents ranged from music to watercolors. She also volunteered with the Southern Ladies Relief Society, where she distributed tracts to wounded soldiers. Of course, she also found time to attend balls and visit friends. On Sundays, she worshipped at a local church, and she even rolled bandages for the local hospital on Sunday afternoons.

"I don't know how you do it, Miss Lister." Luke put his fork down next to his empty plate and signaled the waiter to bring the bill. "How do you ever find time for your beauty rest?"

"It's not difficult. I find sufficient time, especially now that the war has curtailed many of the social engagements we would normally enjoy. Mother says it is a shame I have come of age during this beastly war. The good Lord knows there are not many eligible men anymore. It's one reason I was so happy when your grandmother wrote to us of your arrival."

Luke was in the process of pulling money out of his pocketbook so he concentrated on that rather than the feeling of being pursued by an experienced hunter. The material of his shirt rubbed at the back of his neck, but he refused to give in to the instinct to scratch it. He ought to realize by now that until he married he would be the target of matchmaking mamas and their eager daughters. He was young, wealthy, and passably good looking. But he could not remember any young lady ever being quite so forthcoming about her goals. He supposed it must be a cultural difference.

He would have to remember to ask Hampton Boothe about it the next time he saw his friend. Hampton had been a fount of information about the mores of the local society, and he could likely tell him whether Miss Lister was ingenuous or predatory. "I see."

The waiter approached the table once again, and Luke handed him several Confederate bills. The man counted the bills and bowed. "Thank you, sir. I hope you will return to dine with us again soon."

Luke nodded, but his stomach clenched at the thought of fighting to slice his way through another piece of meat that had more in common with jerked beef than roast beef. Unless the other eating establishments in Vicksburg had equally poor offerings, he doubted he would be returning any time soon.

He gathered their wraps and escorted Miss Lister to his carriage, tucking a thick fur around her ankles before sitting across from her in the carriage and signaling to the driver they were ready to leave.

The clang of a train's bell made her lean forward and pull back the velvet curtain covering the coach window. "Do you think we could go to the station and watch the people disembark?"

Luke cast a dubious glance at the gathering dusk. "Won't your parents be expecting you to return home soon?"

"I suppose so." Her lips puckered slightly in a charming pout.

Feeling a bit like a heel for denying her request, Luke crossed his arms over his chest. "Perhaps I could escort you to the station in the future when we have more time."

"Could we?" The pout melted into a warm smile. "You are very kind. I know you must think it odd of me, but I enjoy watching people. Their faces inspire my paintings."

"I would consider it my pleasure." The carriage halted, and he found himself torn by conflicting emotions. He felt a desire to please her, make her continue to smile at him in that admiring way. But his conscience warned him to maintain a proper distance or find himself cornered into proposing to her before he knew for certain whether she would make a proper wife.

So he escorted her to the front door and handed her over to the butler with a promise to call on her again soon. Then he made his escape into his carriage. All the way back to the hotel, he thought about the time he'd spent with Marianna. But would she be the right choice to become Mrs. Luke Talbot?

❀

"I'm so glad you agreed to escort me to church, Luke." His grandmother took his hand as she stepped out of the carriage. "I was afraid you might have other plans this evening. . .like visiting with the breathtaking Marianna Lister."

"Not at all. I wouldn't dream of putting another lady ahead of you."

She swatted his arm. "Flatterer. I'm not blind, you know. You've spent nearly every waking hour at her parents' home this week, culminating in your dinner together. You must know the whole town is abuzz with talk of romance."

"You shouldn't listen to gossip, Grandma." He held out his elbow and waited until she grasped it before moving toward the wide church doors. "Besides, you've been talking about the fiery Brother Pierce almost since the day I arrived at Shady Oaks. I am most anxious to hear his learned sermon."

A giggle turned his head to the right where a pair of young women stood whispering to each other. Rays of the setting sun gilded the blond hair of the taller one. She had an arresting face—it spoke to him of sweetness and a shy personality. Her companion had dark hair and a much livelier expression, bringing to mind some of the escapades he'd been involved in when he was a young boy.

The darker one leaned up and whispered something while looking directly at him. He had no idea what she said, but whatever it was caused the willowy, blond girl's cheeks to suffuse with bright color. Her eyes, as blue as the lakes back home, widened when their gazes met, and her mouth formed a perfect O of surprise.

An instant later he was past them, entering the candlelit sanctuary with his grandmother still on his arm. He wanted nothing more than to turn around, go back outside, and introduce himself to the beautiful blond. But he knew he could not. He had a duty to fulfill to his relative. Good manners and good sense made him move forward. He found a seat for them on a half-empty pew and helped his grandmother get comfortable. As soon as he was seated, he twisted around to see if the girl had entered the room.

"Are you looking for Miss Lister?" Grandma's voice brought him back to reality with a thump.

What was he thinking? That he wanted to meet another young lady? She was probably engaged, maybe even married. The idea tightened his chest. She could not be. She was far too innocent. He almost laughed out loud at the thought. How could he possibly know that? He'd not spoken a single word to her. Yet something inside him knew.

"No. I. . .uh. . .I. . ." He tried to gather his thoughts. He could feel his grandmother's gaze on his face. "Do you know the two girls who were standing outside as we entered the church?"

The question in her eyes turned to confusion. "What girls?"

"Didn't you see them? One was a raven-haired lady, girl really. But it was her friend I would really like to meet. Her hair was as bright as sunlight, golden as a field of wheat. She is one of the most striking women I have ever seen."

Grandma looked back over her shoulder, nodding to someone she knew. "I don't know who you're talking about, Luke. I don't see anyone matching your description."

"They'll have to come inside. Why else would they be loitering about the entrance to the church?"

His grandmother shrugged and turned her attention back to the front of the room. "We're bound to see them sooner or later."

Hoping her words were prophetic, Luke straightened and pulled on the sleeves of his frock coat. The dark wool was warm enough, but since the church was heated, he was beginning to wish he'd chosen something a little less scratchy.

Marianna Lister and her family arrived, but the pew he and his grandmother occupied was already crowded, so they spoke briefly before procuring a pew closer to the front.

The pianist struck a chord, and a tall man, accompanied by his wife and family, walked down the aisle to the front of the church. Luke's attention was first centered on the man, who had to be Nathan Pierce. Why did he look so familiar? His gaze fell on the pastor's children, and recognition dawned. The beautiful blond girl. She was the pastor's daughter. Miss Pierce. He settled against the back of the pew. As soon as the sermon was over, he would make sure they were introduced.

Brother Pierce stepped up to the pulpit and opened his Bible. "I'm glad to see so many here this evening. As I look out on all of you, I see some who are hurting, some who are lost, and some who are simply counting the minutes until I am done speaking."

Guilt straightened Luke's spine. He was not here to meet females, no matter how alluring they were. He had come to hear a man share his insight about the heart and mind of God.

" 'Blessed are the poor in spirit: for theirs is the kingdom of heaven.' " The pastor lifted his hands above the pulpit. "This is the promise of Jesus for all of us. But what good does that do me today, Pastor? The kingdom of heaven is not here. I am hurting. I am lost. I don't know how I'm going to survive the pain."

Luke was disappointed. Was this the man who had such a mighty reputation? He should have known the message would be useless. He was not hurt or lost. He was young and strong, and he knew exactly what he was doing. He'd come to Mississippi to help his grandmother keep Shady Oaks running after Grandpa's death. He'd been transferred from Knoxville at his father's request due to the questions surrounding the arrest and escape of a known Union traitor, the notorious Mockingbird.

A sigh filled him once more for the trouble he'd experienced because of Amelia Montgomery's wrongheadedness. If only he'd realized what trouble she would cause him, he never would have allowed himself to become involved in her life.

He glanced at his grandmother from the corner of his eye. She was completely immersed in what the pastor was saying, so he returned to contemplation of his past. Luke's life may have taken some unexpected twists and turns, but he had no doubt he was on the right road. God willing, he would still have a chance to serve the Confederacy and achieve a respectable rank before this war was over. And he would find the right girl to marry, someone whose beliefs were more in line with his own, someone like Marianna Lister.

A smile touched his lips. In a few years, he would be as successful as he'd always dreamed. He would have a house full of children, an adoring wife, and a thriving sugarcane plantation. He would probably have earned several battlefield promotions. Who knew? He might even attain the rank of general one day. No, this sermon had absolutely nothing to do with him.

Luke's attention was brought back to the church service by the sound of women's voices singing "O Worship the King." He glanced toward the pulpit and saw the two girls he'd noticed before. Their voices harmonized, weaving in and out to form a tapestry of images in his mind. He sat enthralled by the performance, saddened when they reached the last note. For a moment, nothing but silence filled the large room, as though all in the congregation were holding their breath.

When Brother Pierce once again took the podium, he bowed his head and spoke in low tones, exhorting God for a quick end to the war and suffering. He mentioned several families by name who had lost fathers, sons, or brothers to the fighting. He went on to call on God to bless those who were far from home, men on both sides of the battle.

Luke felt his shoulders tighten. Should the man be praying for the enemy? It didn't seem right to him. The pastor ought to limit his supplications to the Confederate soldiers. He raised his head and looked around. No one else seemed particularly concerned at the prayer, so he closed his eyes once again and counted to fifty while waiting for the man to utter *Amen*. Luke stood immediately and held out his hand to his grandmother.

"You'll have to wait a minute. These old bones don't move as well as they used to." She gathered her cloak and reticule and leaned forward.

He reached down to help her rise. "Let me help you."

"What's the matter? Is there a fire outside?"

Feeling like a corrected youngster, Luke held his tongue. But he couldn't quite keep his sigh inside his chest.

"Oh, all right." She twisted her arm away from him and grasped the pew in front of her. "I'm coming."

The other churchgoers were now crowding the center aisle, greeting each other and discussing the sermon, the war, or whatever other subject came to mind. Luke would have liked to avoid getting stuck, but it was too late to worry about it now.

"Mr. Talbot, there you are." A hand touched his shoulder.

Luke's frown became a smile as he realized Miss Lister was standing behind him. Perhaps his grandmother's slowness was for the best after all. "Hello. I saw you come in with your family."

"Did you enjoy the sermon?"

What could he say? Did he dare tell a lie in God's house? Would he be struck by lightning? Paralysis? "I know his words must have been comforting for those who have lost loved ones." He was pleased with the answer. It was not a lie. In fact he had no doubt that many of the people here had been touched by the man's words. Just not him.

"Yes, I thought so, too." She gazed up at him, her hazel eyes showing admiration and hope. Her gaze moved past him. "Good evening, Mrs. Darby. Did you enjoy the sermon, too?"

"Of course I did." She cleared her throat. "Brother Pierce is a talented speaker with a prodigious understanding of the Bible. I hope to hear him again before he returns to his church in Jackson."

Miss Lister's parents caught up with them then, and the conversation turned general. Finally they began to move to the front of the church. But Luke's sense of urgency faded away. He doubted he'd get the chance to be introduced to the lovely blond singer. Not while Miss Lister was hanging on his every word.

The pastor was still greeting members of the congregation and receiving their compliments. He was flanked on one side by his wife, an auburn-haired woman whom Luke would describe as striking rather than beautiful. On the pastor's far side stood the two girls. Once again Luke's gaze clashed with that of the blond. What was it about her that drew his attention? Her cheeks reddened, and she looked down toward her feet.

Grandma must have realized something had happened. Her gaze swiveled from him to the pastor's daughter, and her lips tightened into a thin, straight line. "It's time for us to get back to the hotel, Grandson. Say good night to Marianna and her parents." Her grip on his arm tightened enough to resemble a pinch as she stepped past the preacher and his family with a nod. "Words to live by, Pastor." The woman who'd been so slow inside the church practically pulled Luke down the steps to the waiting carriage.

"Good night, Mrs. Darby, Captain Talbot." He heard the wistful note in Marianna's voice and turned to bow to her.

She was standing on the bottom step, directly in front of the blond he'd wanted to meet. Marianna was all poise and sophistication, exactly the type of girl he'd always thought he would one day marry. But next to the simple, self-effacing young lady whose name he had yet to learn, Marianna seemed too polished—almost an imitation of what a real lady should be.

"Come along, Luke." His grandmother's querulous tones pulled him out of his thoughts. She looked out from the carriage and waved to Marianna's mother. "I assume we'll see you at the Lancasters' ball, Georgia."

"Of course," Mrs. Lister answered her. "We wouldn't miss such an important gathering. Dare I hope to see you and Captain Talbot there?"

"I imagine so." Grandma leaned back against the seat. "We'll be here all week to hear Brother Pierce, so there's no reason for us to miss the biggest ball of the new year."

Their attendance was news to Luke, but he supposed he shouldn't mind. It would give him a chance to see all the single young women that Vicksburg had to offer, perhaps even the girl he had missed meeting this evening.

As the driver pulled away from the curb, Luke caught one more glimpse of her. She was looking away from him as though he had not made nearly the impression on her that she had made on him. He could not believe it. Not that he was particularly vain. But females usually fell over themselves to draw his attention. He was definitely going to have to visit the pastor's shy daughter.

Chapter 3

"Ma, did you see that man who was looking at me and Caroline?"

"It's 'Caroline and me,' Tory. I wonder if you learned anything from that private tutor in Jackson." Caroline's mother shook out her napkin before placing it in her lap. "No, I did not see anyone looking at either of you, but then the church was rather crowded."

Caroline took a bowl of creamed potatoes from her father and put some on her plate before handing them off to her younger sister. She bent a warning frown at Tory and shook her head slightly. Casting about for a change of subject, she cleared her throat and turned her attention to her father. "It was crowded because of Pa's sermon."

"I don't know about that." Her father smiled at her. "But what is this about a young man ogling you? Did you notice anything odd?"

The temptation to say no was very strong, but Caroline knew she could not lie. "I wouldn't say odd, but I did see a man who seemed to enjoy our duet."

Tory rolled her eyes. "A very handsome man and very well dressed. He was tall, with flashing black eyes and a mustache. I first noticed him while we were standing out in front of the church. He was escorting an older lady, probably his mother, but he couldn't take his eyes off of us."

A wave of heat rushed up and burned Caroline's cheeks. "I don't know about that."

"Why shouldn't a young man be interested in you?" Ma took a steaming biscuit from a cloth-covered bowl and reached for the dish of butter. "You are beautiful, poised, and talented. The only reason you don't have a bevy of suitors is because your father and I have not been very diligent about attending social occasions. But that is about to change." She glanced toward Pa, who nodded his encouragement. "Your father has received an invitation to a ball at the home of Mr. and Mrs. Lancaster this coming Friday, and we have decided to attend. Of course you will join us."

Caroline's mouth dropped open. A ball? "But you know I don't like those ostentatious parties."

"I'll go with you, Ma." Tory was so excited her voice came out with a squeak.

Pa shook his head. "You're too young to go to a ball. Don't be so anxious to grow up."

A pout replaced Tory's hopeful expression. "It's not fair."

"I'll tell you every detail." Caroline sympathized with her sister's disappointment even though she would have gladly stayed home and let Tory go in her place. "Everything from the decorations to the gowns to the music. You'll feel like you were there with me."

"It won't be the same, though." Tory sat back in her chair, crossed her arms over her chest, and sighed loudly.

"You will get your turn in a few short years." Ma's voice was pragmatic. "As your pa says, you should not be so anxious to take on the responsibilities of adulthood."

Caroline pushed her plate away. "I don't know why anyone wants to have a ball right now anyway. Don't they realize we're at war?"

"Yes, dear." Ma reached for the salt cellar. "It's an attempt to ignore the truth."

Picking up a serving dish of sliced roast, Pa nodded his agreement. "We know things are not going well for the Confederacy. The only hope they ever had was that the North would allow secession after a few token battles. But that has not been the case. The longer the fighting continues, the less likely the South will emerge victorious."

Silence fell as they considered his words. Caroline wished the Confederate leaders understood the situation as clearly as Pa did so they would negotiate a surrender before the death toll rose even higher. How many more families had to lose loved ones before the war was brought to an end?

Ma cleared her throat. "I'll need the carriage for an hour or so tomorrow, Nathan. We are almost completely out of sugar and flour. And we'll need to see if we can find any lace to spruce up Caroline's blue dress."

She allowed her mind to wander as her parents worked out the details of their shopping excursion. Maybe they would even see the stranger from church while they were at the market. Butterflies tickled her stomach at the thought. He was so handsome and as tall as Pa. Her head would probably fit under his chin.

A shiver made its way down her spine as she remembered his pitch-black eyes and the distinguished side-whiskers that gave him an air of authority. The embodiment of every hero she'd ever dreamed of meeting, he might have stepped directly from the pages of a romance novel.

She might not have formally met him, but Caroline felt like she knew so much about the man. He cared about family as evidenced by his escort of his relative. His presence at Pa's service proved he was a man of faith. She had no doubt he was a man she could lean on, someone on whom she could rely, someone who would take care of her and protect her from all harm.

But what was she thinking? Caroline could never draw the admiration of such a hero. He had probably been looking at Tory, the real beauty of the family. Gloom and doubt gathered around her shoulders. Besides, hadn't he been talking to another young lady right before he left? He hadn't made the slightest attempt to introduce himself to her parents, the first step he would have to take if he was interested in meeting her.

Notwithstanding Tory's opinion, it was obvious he had not been attracted to either of them. What did it matter anyway? It was unlikely she'd ever see him again. And if she did, she'd probably discover that he was nothing like she imagined.

He may have already left the city, returning to his home or even to a stint with the army. Her heart thudded against her chest at the thought of his riding into danger.

"Caroline, have you fallen asleep at the table?" Her mother's voice interrupted her melancholy thoughts.

She looked around to find she was the center of attention. "I'm sorry. I guess my attention wandered."

Pa chuckled. "I believe she may be dreaming of Friday's party."

Caroline would have disagreed, but then she would've had to explain what she had been dreaming of. . .or rather whom. So she glanced down at her lap and said nothing at all.

"I cannot wait until I get to be eighteen."

Glad her sister's statement had drawn their parents' attention, Caroline stood and began stacking the plates to take to the kitchen. "You'll be much better at this than I ever will."

Tory picked up the napkins while Ma gathered the silverware. "I don't know why you shouldn't be the center of attention on Friday."

Caroline couldn't imagine an eventuality more frightening than the image her mother's words conjured. The only way she'd ever become the center of attention would be if she did something incredibly clumsy, like trip on the dance floor or spill punch down the front of her dress.

Dread filled her as she carried the dishes to the kitchen. She could only hope her mother's words were not prophetic.

⸎

"You need to get over the girl who broke your heart, Luke." Grandma's voice penetrated the dark cloud around him.

Luke turned to her. "How did you know?"

He felt cold and exposed even though it was warm enough in their private sitting room. The homey sound and smell of a crackling fire filled the room.

Grandma smirked. "It's not very hard to figure out what's going on in that thick head of yours. It's the same thing that goes on in any man's head when a woman has spurned him. But I'm saying this from the wealth of my experience—no woman is worth spending your time mooning over her."

A thought burst into his head with the suddenness of a lightning bolt. "That's really why we came to town, isn't it?"

His grandmother had been looping thread into an intricate weave she called crochet, but now she put the handwork in her lap. "Nonsense. We came because I wanted to hear Nathan Pierce preach. Surely you've seen the flyers posted all over town." She waited for his nod. "One was delivered to me at Shady Oaks. It piqued my interest. So I thought it would be a good idea for both of us to come to Vicksburg. It's as simple as that."

He cocked an eyebrow. Somehow her explanation was a little too glib to be believable. "And my parents didn't write to you about my recent betrothal?"

She tried to hold his gaze, but her eyelids fluttered. She looked down and reached for the hooked needle and yarn. "They might have mentioned something about a girl from back home. But they said you were better off without her."

As he had expected. "So which of you came up with the idea of finding me a wife? I doubt it was Pa."

"Your parents want you to be happy, Luke." Her fingers poked the needle and twisted it deftly. "And so do I."

"What about what I want?" He blew out a disgusted breath. "Did either you or my mother consider the fact that I will most likely be called back into battle? What do you expect me to do? Abandon a new bride on our wedding night?"

"Of course not." She glanced up at him for a moment before concentrating on her hands once more. "No one knows what is going to happen with this war. Perhaps you won't even have to face those Yanks. Perhaps they'll give up and go away."

Luke pushed himself up from his chair and walked to the fireplace. "You cannot believe such drivel. The Unionists are desperate to control the Mississippi River, and capturing Vicksburg will secure their goal. I met with Colonel Autrey this morning. He informed me of a large contingent of enemy soldiers apparently led by General Grant that is still bivouacked only a few dozen miles on the other side of the Mississippi. As soon as the weather allows, they'll probably march on this very town. Pemberton is going to need all the men he can muster. War is coming here sooner rather than later."

"You may be right, but it is not here today, nor is it likely to arrive before the end of the week. Only God is in control of the future. All we can do is work our way through today."

He pushed the toe of his boot against the stack of dry wood to one side of the fireplace. "Exactly what work do you have planned for today?"

Grandma placed her needlework into a basket beside her. "I thought we might pay a visit on the Listers. You and Marianna seem to be getting along fairly well."

"She is a sweet girl." He turned and caught the smile on his grandmother's face. "But don't go posting any notices in the paper yet. I am not ready to declare my interest in her."

"You ought not wait too long, Grandson. Someone will soon snap up a prize like that young lady. She is talented, kind, and quite beautiful. Her family is well received in this area. She would be an excellent choice for you."

"You are partial to her because you are friends with her mother."

"I admit to a certain amount of partiality." Grandma rang for a servant. "But if she were not a good match for you, no amount of friendship with any of her family would sway my opinion."

A quiet knock on the door interrupted their conversation. When his grandmother called for the person to enter, Luke listened while she gave the servant instructions for a carriage to take them on their outing. He was not deeply averse to the idea of finding a bride, in spite of his comments to his relative. And he supposed Miss Lister was as good a candidate as any other. Perhaps he should go ahead and propose. Get it over with. It would please his parents as well as his grandmother. So why try to hold out against the inevitable?

A vision of crystal-blue eyes came to him, and Luke could almost hear the last few chords of the song from the evening before. His heart quickened. Perhaps he should hesitate. Perhaps he should visit Brother Pierce and meet his family before he made an irrevocable decision. After his first failed attempt, it behooved him to be especially careful in selecting the girl to become his wife.

With his mind made up, Luke went to his room to gather his cloak and gloves. He would take Grandma to visit with the Listers, and then he would insist on dropping by to visit the Pierce family. Meeting the girl he'd only seen from a distance would certainly quiet the clamor in his heart.

Chapter 4

Soldiers marched toward them to the *rat-a-tat* of a drumbeat. Caroline tried not to flinch at the mixture of fear and determination she saw in the faces of the men and boys. She wanted to put her arms around all of them. She wanted to gather them up and send them home to their families. They had no business here. If only she could change things. Her shoulders lifted and fell in a heartfelt sigh.

"We'd better get out of the way." Ma nodded toward the mercantile. "Let's see if we can find some sugar. The cook says she has a few sweet potatoes left from the last harvest, and she wants to make a pie."

"I love sweet potato pie." Tory's skirts swayed as she crossed the street in front of them.

"It would be a treat." Caroline took her mother's arm. "But it is getting harder and harder to find supplies."

Ma glanced back at the soldiers. "When most of the menfolk are marching to war instead of planting and harvesting crops, shortages are to be expected."

Tory held the door open until all three of them were inside. "Maybe we'll be lucky today."

"What can I help you ladies with?" A gray-haired man with a round stomach approached them.

Caroline looked around the large room lined with shelves. Empty shelves. It didn't look to her as though he had anything to sell.

The merchant's gaze followed hers around the store. "Yes, things are a bit scarce, but we're doing the best we can. Now that the winter is about to end, maybe we'll be able to get some fresh produce."

"We'll pray so." Her mother stepped forward. "We are on a mission for a five-pound bag of sugar."

The merchant bowed. "Right this way." He turned and led them toward the counter. "I just received a supply last week. But I have to admit it is a bit dear. Hard to get things brought in when the railroads are closed."

Caroline gasped. "The trains are not running?"

Tory's mouth dropped open, and she turned to her mother. "How will we get home next week?"

"I knew we should not have come." Caroline slapped a hand over her mouth, but it was too late. The words had already slipped out.

Ma bent a frown on both of them. "Don't worry. We will manage."

"I didn't mean to frighten you ladies." The man twisted his apron in his hands. "Where are you from?"

"We live in Jackson."

He looked over their heads.

Caroline wanted to turn around to see what he was looking at, but she refrained.

After a moment he refocused on them and smiled. "I was trying to remember what I'd heard about the Vicksburg to Jackson line. I think it's still running, although there may not be many seats left open for civilians."

Tory sniffed. "I don't want to be stuck in Vicksburg."

Ma shot a look at Caroline before turning to the merchant. "We'll need that sugar now, sir. How much is it?"

While Ma bartered with him, Caroline put her arm around Tory. "It's going to be okay. You know God is watching over us. No matter whether we're here or in Jackson, or even back in Natchez, the important thing is that we're together."

"I suppose so." Tory looked up at her, tears swimming in her eyes. "I just want the war to end, Caroline."

"So do I." She hugged her little sister tightly and led her back to the front door. "Let's go outside and watch the soldiers marching. They'll love seeing a pretty girl wave to them."

She was rewarded with a giggle. "Two pretty girls."

The sun was beginning to sink toward the western horizon, and a cold breeze whipped down the street as they waved at the boys in gray. The sidewalk was more crowded now than it had been earlier as the townspeople came out to cheer for the soldiers. Instead of staying on the wooden sidewalk to watch, the sisters stepped onto the street where they could see better.

It almost felt like a Fourth of July celebration with the prancing horses and marching men. Except that it wouldn't be so cold in July. Caroline's lips were beginning to grow numb, and she turned to look back over her shoulder to see if Ma had come out yet.

A loud noise brought her back around to gaze at the street. "What was that? It sounded like gunfire."

Tory shook her head.

A scream sounded from farther down the street, and the soldiers parted as a carriage careened around the corner. To Caroline it seemed the equipage was traveling in slow motion. She saw the eyes of the four horses as they raced to some unknown destination, saw the reins dangling between them, realized that no one sat in the driver's seat. All of this detail she took in instantly. Her heart pounded as she watched the carriage get closer to their side of the road.

She grabbed Tory's shoulders and pushed hard to get her safely back on the sidewalk, but somehow her feet got tangled up in her skirt. Instead of jumping to safety alongside her sister, Caroline lost her footing. She could feel herself falling, careening out of control much like the carriage bearing down on her. The whole world seemed to shake with the pounding of the hooves. She was going to die, and she could do nothing to save herself.

In the last possible instant, something grabbed her. She slammed against something—someone—hard. The thump of a racing heart reverberated in her head. It was so close she felt it rather than heard it. An iron band across her waist stole her ability to breathe, and the flashing glimpse of worried faces whirled like the kaleidoscope her parents had given to her last Christmas.

In the midst of the chaos and danger, Caroline felt safe, treasured—the way she felt in her father's hug. A scent tickled her nose, a mixture of soap and starch—a scent that presaged spring, fresh linens, and new leaves.

Then the iron band slackened its hold, and her feet touched the wooden planks of the sidewalk. Caroline leaned back a little to see the face of her rescuer. Her breath caught. "It's you."

He frowned at her, a concerned look in his obsidian eyes. "Are you hurt?"

"I—No. . .I don't think so."

His face was barely inches away. Except for the men in her family, his face was closer than any man's face had ever been. If he moved even a tiny bit closer, his mustache would brush her cheek.

The thought stole her breath. Caroline thought she might faint from the realization. Bright flashes appeared at the corner of her vision.

"Caroline!" Tory's voice penetrated her awareness. She felt something pulling on her arm. "Unhand my sister!"

The arm slipped away from her instantly. An impulse to throw herself at the handsome stranger washed through her, but her sister's grip on her arm was like an anchor keeping her from straying into dangerous waters.

"I'm sorry, miss." He bowed to Tory. "I meant no harm."

With every second that passed, she was regaining her senses. Caroline shook off her sister's hand. "You saved me from certain death."

He turned back to her and bowed once more, his charming smile lifting the edges of his lips. "I'm glad to have been of service, ma'am."

The door of the mercantile flew open, and her mother descended on them like an angry hornet. "What's going on out here? Caroline? Tory? Are you all right?"

"Yes, Mother." Caroline could not tear her gaze from the stranger's face. A part of her wanted to touch his side-whiskers, trace a finger along the edges of his mouth. Blood rushed to her cheeks. What had come over her? She blinked to break the connection between them.

"Caroline was nearly run down by a driverless carriage." Tory's voice shook with fear. "She shoved me out of the way, but she fell. I thought she was about to die."

"Thanks to the fast actions of this kind man, everything has turned out fine." The words were coming from her mouth, but she had no idea how.

Ma moved closer as though to insert herself between Caroline and the stranger. "It seems I owe you much, sir. I am Abigail Pierce." She held out her hand.

The stranger bowed over it, showing that he was well versed in social graces. "Luke Talbot, at your service, Mrs. Pierce. It's a pleasure to meet you and your lovely daughters."

The wary look on Ma's face faded. She allowed a smile to turn up the corners of her mouth. "The pleasure belongs to me, sir, especially since you saved Caroline from a nasty accident."

Although Ma was standing between them, Caroline could still see his eyes. Their gazes met, and her breath stopped again. She put a hand to her throat.

"I hope you'll allow me to escort you ladies to your home. It would be remiss of me to leave you standing here when it is obvious Miss Pierce is not completely recovered."

Caroline turned her gaze on her mother, her chest filling with hope.

"I suppose that would be acceptable, Mr. Talbot—"

"Captain Talbot, ma'am."

"You're a soldier?" Tory's voice now held more than a hint of hero worship.

He smiled and nodded. "Although I'm on furlough right now, I am pleased to serve the Confederate army."

"I know Mr. Pierce will want to add his thanks to my own, Captain." Ma's voice was firm. Caroline recognized the tone. Captain Pierce would be going back to the hotel with them unless he had a very compelling excuse.

"I'd be delighted to make his acquaintance."

"Excellent." Ma pulled on her gloves. "As soon as the supplies are loaded, we can leave."

Captain Talbot walked out onto the street and said a few words to the soldiers who were still milling about. He pointed an arm, and a couple of them went running in the direction of the driverless carriage. The others shouldered their weapons and marched east toward the outskirts of town.

Caroline was impressed with his capable handling of the situation. From the time he'd arrived on the scene, Captain Talbot had commanded the respect and admiration of all those around him. He was obviously a leader...and obviously well above the type of man she could hope to have for a husband.

Her sigh brought Tory a step closer. "Are you certain you're unhurt? I could not even scream when I saw that runaway carriage hurtling toward you." She took Caroline's hand in her own. "You sacrificed your own safety for me."

"You would have done the same." Caroline shifted slightly. She didn't deserve any praise. She'd only done what came naturally. The one who deserved the praise was the captain. She was not his kin, but he'd risked everything for her safety.

She glanced toward him once again as he strode back over to them and engaged their mother in easy conversation. She would enjoy whatever time and attention he gave her and her family, no matter that the outcome would probably leave her pining for more. Like the woman who petitioned Jesus for help, she would gladly accept the crumbs Captain Talbot let fall while he was near.

Chapter 5

"I can hardly believe the week is nearing an end." Grandma sat in the rocker and pushed at the floor with her foot. "Where has the time gone?"

Luke opened his eyes wide. "We've been inundated with visits from your friends every morning. And shortly after lunch, we have made calls on anyone in town who has a marriageable daughter. Then it's back to the hotel for a quick supper before we go to the church to hear the pastor. I am exhausted by the time I climb into my bed, and it seems my head hardly rests on the pillow before the sun is up and it's time to start all over again."

"If there's one thing I have learned in my life, it is—to quote one of John Heywood's proverbs—'Take time whan time cometh, lest time steale away.'"

"Good advice." Luke walked to the window and stared out at the street below. The townspeople were making for their homes as the sun set on the far side of the river. The activity looked normal, ordinary, as though the war was over. But he knew better. "My furlough will be over by the end of the month."

"All the more reason to find a suitable wife now." The rocker creaked rhythmically behind him. "No one will travel out to Shady Oaks to visit us. The risk of being caught by a Yankee patrol increases daily."

"Perhaps we should cut our visit short." Luke turned away from the window. "I want to make certain the plantation is in good shape before I have to leave you alone."

Grandma waved a dismissive hand. "I was alone before you got here, young man. I can make it on my own if I have to. Besides, if you will settle on one of the young ladies you've met, I won't have to be alone. Your new wife and I will work in tandem to make sure you have a home to return to."

Luke considered her carefully. "I'm not sure you're willing to give over the reins to some young miss."

"You're wrong about that. There's plenty of work to go around. When I married your grandfather and he brought me down to Mississippi, I had no idea how to run a household. His mother was not very welcoming, and I had a hard few years until your mother was born. Even though all of that happened many decades ago, I still remember what it was like. I am especially well qualified to help your wife find her feet."

"That's a relief." He walked to the rocker and bent to place a kiss on his grandmother's cheek. "But what if I choose someone you don't approve of?"

"I cannot imagine your being so foolish. Your parents raised you to be levelheaded and to know your duty." She patted his cheek. "You'll make an excellent choice."

Luke straightened and pulled out his pocket watch. "I suppose it's time for me to change into my dress clothes if we're to make it to the Lancasters' home before midnight."

"Why don't you wear your uniform tonight?"

A frown creased his brow. "I don't think that's proper as long as I'm on furlough."

"Fiddle!" Grandma pushed herself up. "You are an officer of the Confederacy. Are you ashamed to show your true colors?"

Luke straightened his shoulders. "Not at all, I jus—"

"I don't want to hear any excuses," she interrupted him. "The ladies will love it. And I have a yen to see you in it myself."

Swallowing his arguments, Luke bowed to her. "I will do as you wish, Grandmother." He could see how much she wanted him to wear his uniform. He would have to get past his discomfort and put a good face on the matter. It wouldn't do to let any of the townspeople sense discord between them.

❧

The uniform was a bit snugger than it had been the last time he wore it. Luke tugged on the short jacket as he entered the ballroom. He had been far too lazy over the past months. It was time to get back to Shady Oaks and get the plantation in order. He could find a suitable wife when the war was over. Grandma might be anxious to have someone with her during these troubling times, but he didn't think he'd be stationed that far away.

The room was already full. The musicians played in one corner while the older men stood in tight groups in the opposite corner. In between, couples danced under the watchful gazes of their chaperones. Looking at the people here, one would hardly believe a devastating war was taking the lives of their husbands and sons.

The music came to a rousing end, and he spotted Miss Lister being led from the dance floor. Her escort was a slender man with a wide mustache and wavy black hair. Luke frowned as he watched Miss Lister smile up at him.

"Are you jealous she's caught the attention of Major Fontenot?" A hand clapped him on the back.

"Hamp, what are you doing here?" Luke shook hands with the man who'd traveled south at the same time he had come to take over his grandparents' plantation. They'd found out during the long train ride that they were bound for the same area and had become fast friends. Hampton Boothe had a head of carroty-hued hair that curled in spite of the copious amounts of Macassar oil he applied. It was the bane of his existence.

"Thought I'd come see what you might be up to." Hamp grinned at him. "Looks like the rumors are true."

"What rumors?"

"That you've fallen head over heels for the lovely Miss Lister."

Luke punched him on the shoulder. "And what if I have?"

Grabbing his shoulder in mock pain, Hamp made a face. "Nothing, nothing at all. Far be it from me to try and stop a man from hanging a noose around his own neck."

"Matrimony is not a noose. It's a state of endless joy."

Hamp snorted.

"Check the poets if you don't believe me."

"Matrimony could be nice, I suppose, but I don't know that you should be tying yourself to Marianna Lister for life."

All humor left Luke in a rush. "Do you know something detrimental about the lady?"

"Only that her beautiful face may hide a waspish nature."

Luke rolled his eyes. "Do you think I would be ruled by my wife?"

A shrug answered him. "I'm not saying that. But you might want to choose someone a bit more biddable."

"If I cannot rule my household, I deserve to be hen-pecked." Luke turned away with the intention of finding Miss Lister and asking her for a dance, but a commotion at the entrance to the ballroom stopped him.

Everyone was crowding around the tall couple at the door. Wondering what was happening, he took a few steps in that direction before he recognized them. It was Brother Pierce and his wife. Mrs. Pierce caught his gaze and smiled at him before turning to say something to the young lady who had come up on her other side.

Caroline Pierce. His heart skipped a beat. She was a vision of loveliness this evening. He'd thought she was pretty when he saw her at the church, but tonight she was stunning.

"Who is that?" Hamp's voice behind him was full of curiosity and wonder. "I've never seen her before."

"You ought to spend more time in church." Luke threw his answer over his shoulder as he made his way to where she stood.

Miss Pierce looked as scared as she had when he pulled her from the path of the runaway carriage earlier this week. Everything in him wanted to rescue her once again. He bowed to Mrs. Pierce. "May I have the honor of dancing with your daughter?"

"I. . .I don—"

"It's a pleasure to see you again, Captain Talbot." Mrs. Pierce turned to her daughter. "You cannot break a soldier's heart, dearest. You must give him a sweet memory to take with him when he returns to the battlefield."

Although her cheeks had reddened at the gentle scold, Caroline Pierce nodded and held out her hand.

Luke tucked it into the crook of his arm and led her to the edge of the dance floor. "I count myself lucky to secure the first dance with you. I'm sure you will be flooded with offers when I return you to your parents' side."

Her gaze darted upward to meet his. "Are you making fun of me?"

"Not at all." Luke was stunned. Did she have no idea how beautiful she looked? The dark blue of her dress made her eyes glow like sapphires. Her golden hair seemed to radiate under the light of the candles. He wanted to tell her how beautiful she was, but he had the feeling his compliments might frighten her even more.

The orchestra began a waltz, and Luke swept her into his embrace. She fit in his arms as though made for him. He started off slowly to make certain she could keep up with him. She seemed so innocent he would not have been shocked to learn this was her first ball. But if so, she had been well schooled in the art of waltzing. He twirled her faster and faster, but her steps never faltered. It was as though she knew before he did which way he was going to move.

"You are an excellent dancer, Miss Pierce."

"Thank you, Captain Talbot."

A few more measures followed in silence. All he could see of his dance partner was the top of her head and her wide skirts. Her face was hidden from his view as she apparently found his buttons fascinating.

"I find myself very comfortable with you, Miss Pierce. Most of the other young ladies I have danced with seem to feel it is necessary to chatter endlessly about the most obscure things. You, however, are to be commended for your reticence. It is a charming characteristic."

She did not glance up.

He swung her around again. "Is there something wrong with my jacket?"

Caroline shook her head. "Not at all."

He squeezed her hand briefly. "That's a relief. My grandmother asked me to wear this uniform. She felt I was not handsome enough unless I wore something a bit more dashing than evening wear."

She glanced up then, her eyes wide. "But you are the most handsome man here."

"Thank you, Miss Pierce." He smiled at the words. Her tone of voice was matter-of-fact without the slightest hint of flattery. A warm feeling flooded him. Luke wanted to laugh out loud. He wanted to hold Miss Pierce close to his heart. He wanted to get lost in her blue gaze. The thoughts filling his head both intrigued and scared him.

But what did he know about this girl? She could sing. Her father was a well-known pastor. She was willing to sacrifice her safety for the sake of a family member. Those were all points in her favor, but they didn't guarantee she would make a good wife. He needed to know more. "Where did you grow up, Miss Pierce?"

"In Jackson, but I was born in Natchez."

"I see." He looked up to see his grandmother frowning at him. Odd that she was not happy. He was doing what she wanted—talking to a marriageable young lady. "I haven't been to Natchez. Is it the same as Vicksburg?"

Miss Pierce hesitated a moment before shaking her head. "Natchez feels more. . .more staid. Or maybe I feel that way because I know Natchez was settled so long ago."

He chuckled. "Vicksburg has been around for a while, too."

"Yes, that's true. But the homes here have a newer feeling to them. The riverfront is much the same at both towns—high bluffs overlooking the river."

"Do you still have family in Natchez?"

She nodded. "My brother and his family live at Magnolia. He runs the plantation now that my grandparents have gotten older."

Miss Pierce seemed tailor-made for him. She was quiet and biddable, and her family sounded much like his own.

The music came to a close before he could think of other questions, but Luke was impressed with what he'd learned. He took her back to her mother and stood there a moment, talking to both ladies.

"Why, if it isn't the dashing Captain Talbot."

Luke turned to find Miss Lister bearing down on him, her skirts swaying as she managed to plant herself between him and Miss Pierce. It was not the smartest move. Marianna's cream dress was probably more fashionable than the one worn by Miss Pierce, but he had to avert his eyes from the charms she was exhibiting above the low neckline. Instead of being alluring, it made her look a bit tawdry and desperate.

"Good evening, Miss Lister. Have you met Mrs. Pierce and Miss Pierce?"

She raised her chin and attempted to stare down her nose at the two ladies. "I do not believe—Oh, yes, you're the preacher's wife, aren't you?"

"Indeed." Mrs. Pierce's eyes flashed. She drew herself up and looked past Miss Lister. "And I believe I hear my husband calling to us now. Please excuse us."

Her smile seemed a bit forced, but Luke could not blame Mrs. Pierce. He wished he could follow her and Miss Pierce across the room, but Miss Lister had her hand on his arm. He felt a little like a hooked fish as he watched the two women make their way to the far side of the ballroom.

"I have something to confess, Captain Talbot." Miss Lister's voice was as sweet as cane syrup.

Luke brought his attention back to the girl next to him, careful to keep his gaze trained on her face. "I am almost afraid to ask what you wish to tell me."

She snapped open a fan with her free hand and used it to hide the bottom half of her face. "I have been counting the minutes until I could see you once more."

It was only with an effort that he kept his mouth from dropping open. What kind of change had come over Miss Lister? Where was the charming companion who he had thought might become Mrs. Talbot? She had always been a little forward, but he'd never thought her so brash.

He remembered Hamp's warning. What was he to do now? He could not be rude to her.

"You are very kind, Miss Lister."

The musicians had taken a break, but now they began playing once more. He sketched a bow. "Will you honor me with a dance?"

She giggled behind her fan and nodded.

As he led her to the center of the room, he thought it was lucky this was not a waltz. He took his position to her left as prescribed by the polonaise and held her right hand. Then it was bow-step-step, bow-step-step, bow-step-step-change in the slow movements of the dance. Miss Lister smiled and even tried to move a bit closer a couple of times, but Luke always managed to keep the proper distance between them. He didn't know when he'd ever found a dance so interminable. As soon as it ended, he escorted Miss Lister back to her mother and left her side as quickly as possible.

He managed to partner several other young ladies, although he remembered neither their names nor the conversations. But when he saw his redheaded friend chatting with Miss Pierce, he stumbled and had to apologize to his unfortunate partner. When the musicians took yet another break, he looked around for Miss Pierce in her stunning blue dress but could find her nowhere. His heart wilted. He'd wanted more time with her and had planned to ask her to join him at the midnight repast. Had her parents already taken her home?

He sauntered over to the corner where the widows sat together, their fans waving like butterflies in a field of flowers. He sat in a vacant chair next to his grandmother, thinking to escort her to the dining room since Miss Pierce was not available. "Are you having a good time tonight?"

She pierced him with a frown. "Why have you not been paying more attention to Marianna? I thought you had fixed your interest with her."

Her reproachful tone and pointed complaint made blood surge upward, heating his cheeks and his ears. "Many young ladies of good families are in attendance this evening. Did you expect me to ignore them?"

"Of course not, but you have only danced with Miss Lister once. After all the time you have spent with her, you've raised certain hopes. I would hate to see you disappoint her family or yours by letting your head be turned by some pretentious upstart."

Anger started a slow burn in his belly. Even though they were surrounded by people, or maybe because of that fact, Luke decided it was time to take a stand with her. "I do not care for your tone of voice, Grandmother. You seem to have the mistaken belief you can choose my dance partners. You have no say in the matter at all."

He saw the shock in her expression, but he would not back down from his statements. He realized his desire to give his grandmother respect had evolved into a situation where she felt she was in control of him. It was about time to set her straight on that matter. He was a grown man, and she would respect his position of authority.

Grandma's fan fluttered back and forth with some force as she digested his words.

He noticed the ladies sitting nearby had stopped talking to each other and were avidly awaiting her response.

She opened her mouth once and then closed it before swallowing hard. "You are quite right, Luke. I didn't mean to overstate my concern. It's only that I love you so much. You are my only grandson, and the continuation of our family rests solely on your capable shoulders. Please forgive me."

The other ladies went back to the conversation almost as soon as they realized he and Grandma were not going to have a row.

Luke nodded and leaned over to plant a kiss her cheek. "I love you, too. I was about to go get something to eat. Would you care to join me?"

She nodded, so he stood and helped her to her feet. As they approached the dining room, he listened with one ear to her chatter about the number of people in attendance and their social standing in the community.

Luke hoped his earlier words had not hurt her too much, and although he regretted airing the matter in such a public setting, she should not have chastised him so openly. His pride would not allow him to appear too weak to control his own family members.

❀

Caroline knew the moment Captain Talbot entered the dining room. The room seemed to contract until the only thing she could see was his dark hair and dashing gray uniform. Her heart pounded in her chest as she saw him smile down at his companion. His grandmother, she had learned. Wasn't that sweet? And another indication of what a good man he was.

She wished no one was sitting next to her, but her parents were seated on one side of her and Hampton Boothe, a young man she'd just met this evening, had claimed the seat to her left. He seemed a kind and outgoing sort, the type of companion her younger sister would adore. Mr. Boothe was well read, and his lively sense of humor had made her smile several times.

"My friend has been telling me how wonderful your father's sermons are." Mr. Boothe's voice recaptured her attention.

"I believe so." She dipped her spoon into her bowl of oyster stew. "Of course, I may not be an impartial judge of the matter. Pa says he started preaching for the wrong reason, but God had the right reason in mind all along."

"What is the right reason?"

Caroline looked at his earnest face. "Are you a Christian, Mr. Boothe?"

"I suppose so. When I was a boy, one of those traveling preachers came through here and stayed with me and my family. Before he left, he took all of us out back to a creek and baptized us. All I remember was him raising

273

his hand and asking me if I wanted to be forgiven so I could go to heaven. I knew the right answer was yes so that's what I said. Then he prayed to God and dunked me in that water. When he pulled me back up, he said I was a new person."

"Did he ask you if you believed in Christ as the one and only Son of God and the way to salvation?"

Mr. Boothe frowned for a moment before shaking his head. "I don't remember that part. Is it important? Do I need to get baptized again?"

Lord, please give me the right words. "Getting baptized is important, and I know some folks who've done it more than once, but it's not necessary for salvation. It's your belief that makes the difference. The day Jesus was crucified, He wasn't the only one being put to death. Two criminals hung on crosses beside him at Golgotha. One of them scorned Jesus, but the other one recognized Him and asked for forgiveness. Even though he had not been baptized, Jesus told the second man: 'Today shalt thou be with me in paradise.'"

"So it's okay to wait until you're dying to decide whether or not you believe in Jesus."

Caroline forgot all about the food in front of her. She forgot about Captain Talbot. She even forgot to be self-conscious. "Of course not. That would be utter foolishness. First of all, you would miss so many opportunities to live right and so many blessings that the Lord wants to give you. And then what if you die suddenly, before you get the chance to turn to Christ? Do you want to take the risk and end up spending eternity separated from your Maker?"

"Sounds to me like Mr. Pierce is not the only preacher in the family."

Caroline looked over her shoulder to see Captain Talbot standing directly behind Mr. Boothe. Her breath caught. When had he come over? And why hadn't she kept her mouth shut? Now he would think she was too talkative. He'd mentioned how much he prized a female who did not chatter all the time.

Sharing the Gospel is not idle chatter. Her heart settled into a more sedate rhythm at the thought. She felt the warmth of His presence. No matter what it made Captain Talbot think, she would not feel bad for speaking out.

Her dinner companion rolled his eyes. "You're not welcome over here, Luke. Miss Pierce and I are getting along fine without your interruption. I doubt you have anything to add, and I need to hear what she's got to say about faith. We live in uncertain times, and you never know when you might be drawing your last breath."

"What foolishness is this?" Captain Talbot raised one eyebrow. "I'll admit I haven't known you long, Boothe, but this is an obvious ploy to impress Miss Pierce." He turned his warm gaze to her. "He's got a reputation as a freethinker, you know."

Mr. Boothe's mouth dropped open. "I am no such thing."

"Is that so?" Captain Talbot shook his head. "Then why don't you tell us how many of her father's church meetings you have attended this week, Hampton."

"What?" Mr. Boothe spluttered. "I. . .well. . .I. . ."

Caroline felt a little sorry for the man sitting next to her. He was obviously flustered by the question. She was about to answer for him, but the captain forestalled her with a wink.

"See what I mean, Miss Pierce?" His voice was full of triumph. "Don't let him fool you."

Was the handsome captain flirting with her? Caroline thought he might be. A pleasant glow brought a smile to her face. She gave an exaggerated sigh. "I suppose you will have to come to the revival meeting tomorrow afternoon, Mr. Boothe, to prove your sincerity."

Now it was Mr. Boothe who looked pleased. He shot a triumphant glance toward Captain Talbot. "I would love to attend."

Caroline decided to take the middle road. She did not want the serious matter of salvation to be diluted by foolishness. "My family would be happy to see both of you there."

"Might I hope you will also be glad to see me there?" Mr. Boothe touched her hand where it lay on the table between them.

Certain her cheeks were as red as a bowl of strawberries, Caroline pulled her hand away and tucked it in her lap. "How could I not be? All Christians rejoice over the salvation of a lost soul."

"Save me a place up front, if you will, Miss Pierce." Captain Talbot smiled. "I can hardly wait to see how Hampton reacts to Brother Pierce's sermon."

As he walked off, her mother leaned toward Caroline. "What a fine young man that Captain Talbot is, and he seems quite smitten with you, dearest."

Caroline glanced toward Mr. Boothe, glad to see he was chatting with the person on his far side. She put her hands to her cheeks in an attempt to cool them. "You misunderstand, Ma. We were discussing faith and Pa's sermons."

"I'm neither blind nor so old that I cannot see when someone, or even a pair of someones, is interested in my daughter."

Wondering if she could disappear under the table, Caroline shook her head but remained silent. She was certain her mother was mistaken. Neither man had been more than polite. Yet there had been a special gleam in the captain's obsidian eyes. A gleam that made her breath catch.

What if? A tiny smile teased the edges of her mouth. The very idea that either the sweet Mr. Boothe or the debonair Captain Talbot might be interested in her was at the same time terrifying and exhilarating.

Chapter 6

Luke smiled across the table toward Caroline. "I'm glad your parents agreed to let you and your sister attend lunch with my grandmother and me."

"Me, too."

Her blush was endearing. It hinted at her innocence, a refreshing change from the calculated charm he usually encountered from the local belles. Caroline Pierce was different from all of them. Different from any young woman he'd ever met. He admired her quiet competence and the faith shining in her blue eyes.

Was this why he'd been unable to quash his ardent pursuit? It had been only two days since he'd seen her at the Lancasters' ball, but already he had paid a visit to her parents and invited her to today's luncheon.

"Have you seen many battles, Captain Talbot?"

The eager question posed by her younger sister turned his attention to Tory. He nodded. "Far too many."

"It's a shame the Yankees won't just let us alone." Grandma heaped a steaming spoonful of collard greens on top of her cornbread before handing the bowl to Caroline. "Too many men have died already."

A frown crossed Tory's face. "I'll bet those Yankees run whenever they see our handsome soldiers riding toward them on the battlefield."

Luke considered his answer. He didn't want to disillusion the younger Miss Pierce, but there was nothing romantic about war. "It's not like that, Miss Tory. The Union soldiers are as brave as any of our men. We all follow the orders of our commanding officers even if it means death."

He noticed Caroline's shudder and wished he could reach across the square table and squeeze her hand. He wanted to comfort her, but since his grandmother was present, he contented himself with a wide smile.

"Let's talk about something more pleasant, shall we?" Luke accepted the bowl of collards from Tory, but his gaze remained focused on Caroline. "Tell us about growing up in Jackson. Have you ever visited the capitol?"

"Yes, many times. Ma and Pa are very interested in keeping abreast of the political situation." Her answering smile was like sunshine after a week of rain. "They say it's the duty of all Americans to take part in the democratic process on which this country was founded."

"Do they not consider themselves to be Confederate Americans?" Grandma's voice was sharp with disapproval.

Caroline's cheeks reddened. "I suppose so. But they don't approve of slavery."

Luke was surprised at the admission. Abolitionists were not unheard of in Mississippi, but they were few in number. Too many people here relied on slave labor to make their farms and plantations successful.

"I had heard as much." Grandma's right hand played with her fork. "And that your grandparents in Natchez hold even more radical ideas than your parents."

"I suppose you could say that." Caroline seemed so engrossed with the food on her plate that she could not tear her gaze away from it. "Our grandfather freed all of the slaves on his plantation a long time ago and offered them paying jobs."

Luke's mouth dropped open. "I doubt that made him very popular."

"Oh no." Caroline looked at him, her eyes wide. "In fact, the townspeople once tried to burn our grandfather out. Our grandmother risked her reputation and her very life to warn him."

Tory picked up the story. "They stopped the fire. It was a very brave thing to do. If not for her, Magnolia would have burned to the ground with our grandfather inside the main house." In her excitement, Tory made a wide gesture with her hands. Her right hand bumped her glass of lemonade and it teetered. "Oh!"

Luke tried to prevent disaster, but her flailing hand prevented him from reaching the overturning glass.

From the corner of his eye, he saw Caroline cover her mouth with her hand, but then his focus centered on the unfolding disaster as Tory jumped up, her jerky actions further disturbing their table. The surface tilted toward his grandmother, all of its contents sliding inexorably toward her lap.

Grandma's loaded dinner plate was the first missile to land, followed by plates of cornbread, smoked ham, and stewed apples. The bowl of collard greens tumbled toward her, too, but Luke managed to catch the hot vegetables before they reached the edge of the table. He was not so lucky with the butter crock or the salt cellar, both of which crashed to the floor, blasting their contents across his grandmother's dress, face, and hair.

Tory was frozen, her hands covering her mouth, but her sister jumped up and began picking up the remnants of the food and crockery. "I am s–so sorry."

Grandma pulled a handkerchief from the sleeve of her dress and dabbed at the mess on her face. "It's not you who needs to apologize. It wasn't your fault. But I trust your sister will be severely punished for her shenanigans."

Luke opened his mouth to speak up for the young girl who was now crying quietly, but he was forestalled by Caroline. At his grandmother's words, her head went up and the fire of battle entered her blue eyes. "I beg your pardon?"

"You heard me." Grandma sniffed. "In my day she would be restricted to her room with a diet of bread and water for her unspeakable actions."

Tory began crying in earnest now. Caroline turned her back on his grandmother and stalked over to her sister. "Don't worry, dear. It was only an accident." She looked at Luke. "I think we should return to our hotel."

Luke wondered what had happened to the shy preacher's daughter. He'd never expected to see such determination, such righteous indignation. She was as fierce as any soldier in the midst of battle, eager to defend the innocent.

This was a side of Caroline he'd never dreamed existed, a side he had to admire. Would she leap to the defense of anyone she cared about? He rather thought she might. Beneath her quiet exterior lurked a heart of gold—a treasure to be sought by any man who was looking for a suitable woman to marry.

❀

Caroline had never felt such anticipation before a ball. She had dreaded going to the Lancasters'. . .but tonight was different. She grabbed her fan and reticule and headed downstairs to join her parents.

Only Pa was standing in the hallway. "Your mother is already in the carriage." He took her hand and put it on his arm. "You look especially beautiful tonight, Caroline."

She dipped her head but said nothing. Fathers always thought their daughters were beautiful—at least her father did.

Being careful not to lose control of her hoops, Caroline settled into the seat opposite her mother and listened as her parents discussed returning to Jackson before the end of the month. Her heart sank. She would never see Captain Talbot again once they left Vicksburg.

Her mother turned to Caroline. "You're very quiet this evening."

Pa fingered the edge of his cravat. "She's going to be the belle of the ball."

"Not if Miss Lister is in attendance. She is much prettier than I and more accomplished by all accounts." What she didn't say was she still hoped to see Captain Talbot. After the luncheon with him and his grandmother three days prior, she had been unable to banish him from her thoughts. He was such a considerate man. And so handsome she had to remind herself not to stare at him. He was intelligent, too. It was a wonder no female had managed to win his affections. Perhaps it was the Lord's plan. Perhaps he would fall in love with her and—

Caroline halted the thought. It was silly to have such ideas. No one fell in love at first sight. Never mind the way seeing him made her heart throb. She wouldn't be able to stay in Vicksburg long enough for him to develop deep feelings for her. She sighed. Luke Talbot was certain to fall in love with someone else—someone like the beauteous Miss Lister.

The carriage came to a halt, and Caroline leaned forward to catch a glimpse of the Abbot home. It was an imposing mansion perched high on a bluff overlooking a bend in the Mississippi River. Lamps shone in every window of the two-story brick house and lined the circular driveway, lending a fairy-tale appearance to the estate. As she alighted and followed her parents up the wide stairs, Caroline felt like a princess.

The sensation persisted as she smiled at their hosts and complimented them on their home. She was pronounced a lovely young lady and sent inside to break the hearts of all the young men.

Dozens of couples were already dancing to the melodious sounds of the orchestra. Other guests stood in small groups of two or more, renewing acquaintances or discussing whatever topics were popular—the war mostly.

A couple about the same age as Ma and Pa approached them. After introductions, they launched into a discussion of the church's stance on slavery. It was a touchy subject, but one that held little interest for Caroline.

"I hope your sister has recovered from your visit three days ago."

The deep tones made Caroline's breath catch. He was here, and he'd sought her out. She turned to give him her brightest smile. "Yes, Captain. Thank you for asking. She was devastated to have caused such a mess, but youth is resilient."

"Yes, indeed." The look in his eyes brought a flutter to her stomach. "My only regret was that our visit was cut short by her accident. I would have liked to spend more time with you."

Caroline raised her fan to hide her blush. He probably thought she was a poor, dumb provincial. She wished she had more self-control. What kind of woman blushed because someone complimented her?

"Will you dance with me?"

Caroline glanced at her mother for permission and received a nod.

A waltz was playing as they joined the other dancers. Captain Talbot's arm was a warm band around her waist. He was so strong and confident. She made the mistake of meeting his glance. The admiration she saw in his eyes was almost too much to bear. Her heart was galloping faster than a racing horse. In that moment she knew the truth. Love at first sight might not exist, but she had fallen in love with Luke Talbot. The realization made her miss a step, but he held her close and kept her from stumbling. She wished the song would last forever.

When it ended, they were near a pair of doors opening out onto a balcony. "It's a bit warm in here. Would you like to step outside for a moment?"

Caroline's heart skidded to a sudden stop. Dare she go outside with him? She glanced toward her parents, who were deep in conversation. Excitement at her daring coursed through Caroline. "Only for a moment."

He swept her out of the room instantly, his hand resting lightly at the center of her back. "I hope you know the effect you've had on me over the past days." His face was so close she could feel his breath on her cheek.

Had she made a mistake in agreeing to come outside alone with him? Did he think she was brazen? Caroline moved to the balustrade. "Perhaps we should go back inside."

"Please give me a moment. I have something I'd like to say to you."

The air cooled her arms even though they were covered with elbow-length gloves. Caroline rubbed them as she watched him. "Is something wrong?"

He stepped closer and took her hands in his. Then he did something so unexpected that she could not believe her eyes. . . .

He dropped to one knee. "I can't get you out of my mind, Caroline. Since the first time I saw you, I have had eyes for no woman but you. You are beautiful, talented, and so pure. I know we've only known each other a few days, but I hope you'll believe me when I say I don't think I can live the rest of my life unless you're by my side. I wish we had more time, but life is far too uncertain these days. I cannot risk the chance that we'll be separated, so please say you'll do me the honor of becoming my wife."

Tears threatened to overwhelm her. "Luke." This was her dream come true. This was the fairy tale. This was the man God had created for her. And he was asking her to be his wife. He loved her! It was almost too good to be true. Yet there he was, looking up at her, the love evident on his face. How could she turn him down?

"Please say yes, Caroline."

Where she had been cold a few moments earlier, now a fire burned her skin. Luke's words had changed everything. "Yes." She nodded for emphasis. "Yes, Luke. I will marry you, as soon as we get Pa's approval."

He stood up and took her in his arms. "You've made me the happiest man alive. I want to marry you right away." He pressed a kiss on her temple.

Her toes curled, and Caroline thought she might faint. She nodded again as her eyes drifted shut. She had to be dreaming, but the man holding her felt very solid. A small voice warned her that it was too fast, but she suppressed it. She was in love with a man who loved her. What could possibly go wrong?

Chapter 7

I know a secret." Tory's words brought a frown to Caroline's face. She shook her head at her little sister.

"Then you should honor your promise to keep it." Mrs. Pierce plied her needle with measured precision, never looking up from the sock she was darning. "A promise is like an oath. God has many warnings against breaking an oath."

"But I didn't promise to keep it."

"Tory. . ." Caroline heard the plea in her own voice. She didn't want her parents to find out until Luke could be here, too. She glanced at the clock on the mantel. It seemed to have stopped its forward movement. Would the morning never end? His meeting with the major was supposed to be over before lunch. If he didn't arrive soon, it would be too late. She'd never been able to keep anything from her mother. Ma seemed able to read her mind with a single glance.

As if she had already discerned something, Ma looked up, her gaze shifting between her daughters. "Please don't tell me. . . ."

Caroline's head went up. How did she do that? She held her shoulders straight as though about to face a firing squad. Her stomach knotted. "I have nothing to tell you right now."

"Is it about that boy who rescued you? The soldier?" Ma's gaze pierced her. "Have you agreed to marry him?"

Her lips trembled. Why was this so difficult? Why couldn't she simply say the words? Where was her courage? "I. . .p–prefer to w–wait for C–Captain Talbot's arrival." Only eight words, but she was winded.

Ma stood up and moved to the sofa, where she sat next to her sister. "Tory, you are excused."

"But Ma—"

"You heard me. Now go. I need to talk to your sister." Ma didn't say anything else until Tory's lagging footsteps made it to the hallway and the door to the ladies' parlor was closed behind her.

She took the sampler Caroline had been working on and put it on the low table in front of the sofa. Then she gathered Caroline's hands in her own. "Tell me what happened."

Caroline took a quick breath. "I love him, Ma." Not a single stutter.

Perhaps shallow breaths were the answer.

"I know you think you do, but Caroline, you don't know anything about him."

She pulled her hands free and stood. "I know he's a good man. A Christian man who loves me. He's also kind and thoughtful and brave besides being well educated." Caroline was beginning to feel a little lightheaded, so she stopped talking.

"I see you've thought about this." The ticking of the clock was louder than her mother's comment.

Caroline held her hands out to the fire. "Yes, ma'am."

Ma sighed. "Your pa would say I brought this on myself by begging you to stand up for yourself."

From where she stood, Caroline could see through the window overlooking the entrance to their hotel. She watched a carriage pull up, hoping she would see Luke's handsome face, but the lady who got out was a stranger.

She felt rather than heard her mother get up and walk toward her. An arm went around her waist, and her mother pulled her close. "And I guess he would be right."

Their shared laughter eased the tension.

"I love you, Caroline, and I only want the best for you."

"Luke is the best. I never thought I'd find anyone as good as Pa, but he is."

"Time will tell. As soon as we talk to your father, I'll write to your grandparents and ask them if we can have the wedding at Magnolia."

Caroline's mouth fell open. "But—"

"I know!" Her mother clapped her hands together, excitement showing on her face. "We'll have the wedding at Christmas. It's my favorite time of the year. And the plantation looks so nice when it's bedecked in garland and mistletoe."

She should have known it wouldn't be easy. She looked at her mother and considered how to break the bad news to her. "We don't want to wait, Ma."

That stopped her mother in midplan. Her eyes opened wide. "When were you thinking about marrying him?"

"Saturday." The syllables fell into a deep silence. The expressions that crossed her mother's face might have been humorous under other circumstances, but Caroline could not manage to summon up a smile. "We want Pa to perform the ceremony."

"But why the unseemly haste?"

"Luke has to return to duty in two weeks."

"I see." Her mother walked back to the sofa and sat down. "I don't suppose you could wait until after the war?"

Caroline shook her head. "Don't you remember telling me how you knew immediately Pa was right for you? Luke is the right man for me. I've prayed about it, and so has he, and we believe God has given us His blessing."

"Did you ask Him about the timing?" Ma waved her hand before Caroline could form an answer. "I'm sorry. That was uncalled for." She sighed again. "But I'm not sure the two of you are interpreting God correctly, and I'm worried you may be making the worst mistake of your life."

Caroline moved toward the sofa, confidence surging from some deep place inside her, carrying her to unprecedented heights of self-confidence. "Stop worrying, Ma. I know we're doing the right thing."

❀

" 'Wherefore they are no more twain, but one flesh.'" Rev. Pierce recited the words slowly as though testing each one. " 'What therefore God hath joined together, let not man put asunder.' "

The words reverberated in the nearly empty church with authority. There simply had not been time to have a large, lavish wedding. And with the war drawing nearer to the city, those who could afford to were leaving for what they hoped would be safer havens. Even Hampton had not been able to attend, although he had assured both Luke and Caroline that he was not jealous. And then he'd gone to great length to describe the latest lady to catch his attention.

Luke swallowed hard as Caroline's father closed his worn copy of the Bible and looked down on them with a gentle smile. *How has all this come to pass in such a short period of time?* His heart raced a little faster at the thought. He took a deep breath and turned to his bride, lifting her veil with careful movements. This was his first act as a married man, and it signified that the woman in front of him was now his responsibility.

For a moment it felt as though he looked into a stranger's face, but this was Caroline Talbot, née Pierce, the new mistress of Shady Oaks Plantation and the woman who would help him fulfill his responsibility to his family. Where was the calm serenity that had initially drawn him to Caroline? She looked like a frightened child, one who had lost her parent. Her chin quivered slightly, betraying her fear. He squeezed one of her cold hands reassuringly, rewarded by a wan smile that he returned. He could almost feel the tension draining away from her shoulders, and his ability to ease her fears somehow made him feel more confident in his choice.

"Let us pray." Brother Pierce's voice interrupted his thoughts.

Luke bowed his head but did not close his eyes. He had been very attentive to Caroline and her family's beliefs while courting her. But the time for pretense was over. Religious beliefs were reserved for women and children and of course ministers. Luke was well aware of the fact that real men had to make their own way in this world.

He was surprised to catch the warning frown and shake of the reverend's head as the older man cleared his throat before beginning to pray. At first Luke thought the frown had been aimed at him for his lack of piety, but a rustle behind him betrayed the real target to be the irrepressible Tory. Her duties as chaperone for her older sister were now over, but he had the feeling she would continue to be a distraction for all those around her. Another reason he, his bride, and his grandmother should depart as soon as possible.

He would bet Tory was nearly dancing in the aisle behind them with poorly repressed glee at the marriage of her elder sister. And why wouldn't she be excited? Caroline had snagged one of the most eligible bachelors in Warren County, maybe in the whole state. His head dropped a bit closer to his chest at the immodest thought. *But it's true. Even with the privations of this war, Grandma and I are very comfortable. I can afford to provide anything Caroline could possibly need. I only hope things remain the same.*

"And may they serve as a source of love and strength to each other and the focal point of a Christian household. Amen."

Luke looked up and, at a nod from the preacher, turned to his wife. He bent and dropped a kiss on her right cheek before turning with her to face the few people seated behind them—his grandmother and the other two ladies of the Pierce household. Grandma was crying again. She had hardly stopped since he announced his intention to marry Caroline. He noticed Caroline's mother was also dabbing at her eyes with a handkerchief, but her tears seemed joyful rather than cheerless.

He wished he could believe Grandma would soon recover and put a happier face on the situation for his sake and for the sake of his new bride. After all, Grandma was the one who had pushed him to find a wife. She would have to find a way to live with the woman he'd chosen. . .whether it was the one she wanted or not. And that was the real crux of the problem. Grandma had wanted Marianna for a granddaughter-in-law. In her estimation Marianna Lister, the granddaughter of her personal crony, would make a better wife and mother than the girl standing next to him.

He believed he'd made the better choice. Marianna might seem a little more poised, but she was also more spiteful and forward than Caroline. No, it was Caroline's quiet manner and serenity that had drawn him almost from the first time he'd seen her. Luke knew what he was doing. Caroline had the morals and character to make a perfect wife and mother.

Luke pushed back a lock of his hair that had fallen across his forehead before placing his hand over the small one trembling on his arm. "My heart and devotion are yours, dear wife."

She offered a shaky smile at the reminder of her new status. "I can hardly believe it."

He had to lower his head to hear her words, and he could not resist kissing her cheek once again. A hint of lilac tickled his senses as he breathed it in. Like so much else about his new bride, the scent was understated and subtle, only appreciated by those closest to her. She was so different from the other girls he'd met.

A brief pang struck at him as he thought of the girl in Tennessee, but he pushed it aside. He'd made his choice. Amelia was his past, Caroline his future.

His grandmother stopped crying long enough to snap open her fan and ply it with sufficient force to raise a small breeze. "Now that it's done, shall we go back to the hotel for the wedding breakfast? Luke, you know we'll need to get on the road soon if we are to arrive at Shady Oaks before nightfall." She shuddered. "I don't want to be caught on the roads after dark. There's no telling what dangers might overtake us."

"It's a shame you cannot stay in town for a day or two more." Caroline's mother stood and brushed a bit of lint from the flounce of her wide skirt.

"Now Abigail"—Brother Pierce raised an eyebrow—"we have talked about this at great length. Luke needs to go home and settle Caroline and Mrs. Darby before he has to report back to his unit. There is no time to waste since General Grant seems to have his troops on the move once more."

"You're right, of course." Mrs. Pierce reached for her cloak and drew it around her shoulders. She smiled at her husband, her love for him evident on her face. "It's just so difficult to say good-bye to our little girl."

Brother Pierce patted her shoulder. "She's in good hands." He began moving around the large room, blowing out the candles now that the ceremony was finished.

Tory ran up to where Luke and Caroline stood, threw her arms around her sister, and drew her away from Luke's side as they all gathered their wraps. Luke could hear her excited comments about the beauty of the ceremony as he helped Brother Pierce blow out the remaining candles.

"You will be good to my little girl," said his father-in-law, his voice carrying easily across the empty room. "I agreed to this marriage against my better judgment, you know."

"Yes, sir," Luke responded politely. Inside, he was rather surprised. He'd known Brother Pierce had reservations because of the brevity of their courtship and possibly also because of his rather evasive answers to the reverend's probing spiritual questions. Even though he was a Christian, Luke had not spent much time studying the Bible. He was a good man and felt sure he would go to heaven when he died. That was enough, wasn't it? Especially since he had no desire to don a pair of wings and strum a harp in the afterlife. He'd been baptized when the time was right. Wasn't that what Christ demanded of His followers? "I appreciate your allowing us to be married."

"I went to God with my concerns but could not find in my heart any particular reason to refuse my daughter's wishes. She seems to believe you have a good heart, and I pray you will care for her."

Luke bit down on his tongue to keep from giving the man an abrupt answer. He'd always been taught to respect his elders, but what did Brother Pierce think? That he was going to mistreat Caroline? On the contrary, he could offer her more than most husbands, especially now that he was the owner of Shady Oaks. He had a beautiful home, several hundred acres of crops and woodland, a thriving cane mill, and secure social standing. Caroline would never want for anything. Wasn't that enough? What more did Brother

Pierce expect from his son-in-law? "I promise you Caroline will be loved and cared for to the best of my ability." He endured Brother Pierce's direct stare, his chin high.

Finally Brother Pierce nodded and turned toward the carriage where the ladies awaited them.

Luke followed him, feeling somewhat bruised by the older man's inquiry. Apprehension about the future assaulted him, making his heart thump unpleasantly, but Luke pushed it away. He'd made the right choice. His life was finally headed in the right direction. He and Caroline would be a perfect couple—the envy of all who knew them.

Chapter 8

I hope you are not a slugabed." Mrs.—"Grandma Darby" had taken great pleasure in filling their time in the carriage with tales of Shady Oaks Plantation. "Breakfast is served at seven thirty promptly. Anyone who is late will have to wait until noon."

Caroline could not bring herself to say anything, so she nodded her understanding. It was so difficult to think of calling Luke's starchy relative *Grandma*. Calling her Grandmama or Grandmother seemed more fitting. But that is what Luke usually called her, and he insisted she do the same.

"I hope we find everything in order when we get to Shady Oaks." Mrs.—"Grandma Darby" tucked a stray wisp of her graying hair into her chignon. "I told Luke to send a note to the overseer, directing him to have the slaves properly dressed and ready to meet you."

Although she had never been a poor traveler, Caroline was beginning to feel unwell. She had known her new family would own slaves, but she had not considered the reality of treating other human beings like property. She put a hand over her stomach, hoping to calm it.

"You needn't look so disapproving. Your parents have made their abolitionist leanings apparent. I blame people like them for this war." The older woman nodded sharply as though agreeing with herself. "Slaves are a necessary part of running a plantation as large as Shady Oaks. As long as they are not abused, it is a system that benefits both slave and planter. And we take good care of our slaves. They are practically part of the family."

Caroline refused to argue with her grandmother-in-law before arriving at her new home. She thought of her grandfather Jeremiah LeGrand, who had ended slavery at the plantation in Natchez. Maybe her brother, or even Pa, could give her advice on how to convince Luke and his grandmother to free their slaves and still run a successful plantation.

"You're not much of a talker, are you, girl?"

A headshake was answer enough.

"I declare, I don't know what my grandson sees in you."

Caroline sucked in her breath. "I suppose you'll have to talk to him about that."

"She speaks at last." The older woman's smile did nothing to make Caroline feel better. "I was beginning to think you were either mute or an

287

imbecile with a pretty face."

The carriage slowed before making a sharp turn. Grandma Darby turned her attention to the scenery outside the carriage. "It won't be long now. I can hardly wait to lie down in my own bed."

Caroline wondered if the hotel had not offered comfortable accommodations, but she was not going to ask and have to endure a homily on "The Evils of Staying Away from Home." Not after she'd had to listen to other similar lectures for the past three hours.

If only Luke had ridden inside the carriage, everything would have been different. But he'd decided instead to ride his favorite stallion, Spirit.

It had seemed reasonable this morning when he'd suggested that his two favorite ladies could use the time to get better acquainted. Caroline had even agreed with him. What a mistake that had been. It was only by remembering the warnings in Proverbs about the pitfalls of anger that she had managed to endure the pointed barbs of Luke's grandmother. She prayed Grandma Darby would warm to her once they all settled in at Shady Oaks.

The carriage came to a halt, and Caroline got her first glimpse of her new home. Adjectives like huge, grand, and overwhelming came to mind. Ma's family plantation in Natchez would fit in one corner of this enormous estate. The entrance to the house was some twelve feet above the ground, upheld by a ground floor dotted with narrow windows. A pair of graceful, curved staircases reached upward from the ground to the center of a deep, wide porch boasting a row of whitewashed rocking chairs. Square white columns, at least ten in number, soared from the porch to the roof, supporting a balcony on the second floor that was as wide as the porch below it. The balcony, the porch, and the staircases were encased in black iron railing, another example of the opulence of the estate.

"Oh, my." What had she gotten herself into? Suddenly Caroline understood why her parents had begged her to wait before tying herself to Luke. Why had she not listened to their advice? She could not imagine trying to run such an imposing household.

"I suppose I should not be surprised at your reaction." Luke's grandmother gathered her things as she prepared to get out of the carriage. "I'm beginning to think the reason you don't talk much is because you have very little going on in that mind of yours."

The door opened, and Luke peered in at her. "Welcome to your new home."

Caroline wanted to throw her arms around him and beg him to never leave her alone with his grandmother again. Instead she waited her turn to disembark.

Luke continued holding her hand as he led her up the iron staircase. "I know you and Grandma are weary, but it's important for you to meet your staff before retiring."

It felt good to walk, even though Caroline dreaded having to meet the large group of slaves who had formed a line three people deep that stretched from one end of the front porch to the other. Mostly women, they were a veritable wave of white mobcaps, brown dresses, and white aprons. The men were dressed in brown coats, each with a single row of buttons and a detachable white collar. She felt the weight of their shy glances as her husband led her to the housekeeper, recognizable from the ring of keys she wore at her waist. The woman curtsied as Luke called her name. Caroline smiled and nodded her head while wondering how she would ever keep all their names straight, much less direct their various activities.

Luke didn't stumble a single time, however. He moved from one to the next, patiently telling her the slave's name and area of responsibility. At the end of the line waited a couple whose hands were linked. They were standing a little apart from the others. Caroline knew there must be some significance for their separation from the rest of the staff.

Luke indicated the girl with his hand. "This is Dinah. She'll be your personal maid."

Stifling her immediate discomfort at the idea of a personal servant, much less one who was bound in slavery, Caroline hoped their relationship would instead be one of friendship. She would like to think she would have at least one friend here—besides her husband, of course.

Dinah dropped a quick curtsy, a wide smile betraying her sunny disposition. "Whatever you want, missus, you just tell Dinah about it and I'll take care of it."

"Thank you, Dinah." Caroline wondered if Dinah had a stash of courage somewhere in the huge mansion.

"And this is Hezekiah. He is both my manservant and Dinah's husband."

Hezekiah bowed. "God bless you, ma'am."

"Thank you, Hezekiah."

"All right, everyone, it's time to get back inside." Luke's grandmother clapped her hands. Caroline had almost forgotten the older woman was outside. "We will expect our supper at the regular time, Mabel."

Which one was Mabel? Ah yes, the short, round woman who had tied a kerchief on her head instead of wearing a cap. She nodded. "I've been cooking all day, ever since Master Luke sent us a note saying all of you was coming home."

"Good." The two women went inside discussing the menu.

Luke took her hand in his. "Are you all right?"

"Yes." She squeezed his large hand, thankful her introduction to the staff was over. "I cannot believe all of those people are slaves."

"Yes, well, I can understand your surprise, but Shady Oaks would not be successful at all if not for their hard labor."

Hand in hand, they walked to the iron rail that framed the porch. A cold wind blew past leafless oak trees and made her shiver.

"Are you cold?"

Caroline shook her head. She wanted to savor this moment with just the two of them. She could and would conquer her fears. "Do you not suppose the plantation could be profitable if you hired people to work in your fields instead of buying slaves?"

The look he tossed her was as cold as the wind buffeting them. "I never want to hear that kind of abolitionist talk from you again, Caroline. You may not realize how tense everyone already is. If you come in here and start fomenting rebellion, we are liable to have our home burned down while we are still abed."

Eager to see love in his eyes instead of the ice now filling them, she nodded.

"Good. That's settled then. We will never speak of it again." He put an arm around her and drew her head onto his shoulder. "Don't disappoint me, Caroline. I have great faith in you, but you will have to adapt to the way we do things here."

After a while she shivered again, and Luke insisted on taking her inside. He made sure Dinah had a warm bath ready for her before leaving his wife in the hands of Hezekiah's wife.

Chapter 9

Luke knew he was going to have to do something. Caroline and Grandma had not been getting along all week. He steepled his hands on the surface of his grandfather's walnut desk as he considered his options.

Caroline, sitting on the other side of the desk, was staring at her lap, looking as innocent as a newborn child. Pale winter sunlight slanted into the room from one of the two floor-to-ceiling windows and made her hair gleam, giving the appearance of a golden halo hovering above her head. But he knew his wife was neither as innocent nor as angelic as she appeared.

Instead of using the formal dining room, Caroline was pushing for them to eat dinner at a small table in one of the sitting rooms. Grandma had been scandalized and lost no time in belittling the idea. Neither female was completely right.

While Grandma had been quick to criticize his new wife, Caroline was misguided enough to try the patience of a saint. He wondered why her parents had not been more diligent in teaching her how to manage a proper household. They'd certainly taught her to be diligent in her prayer life, so diligent that he wondered if she loved her Bible more than she loved him.

He understood her need to put her own mark on the household, but Caroline was not being considerate of the established way of doing things at Shady Oaks. His wife seemed determined to change everything from the number of times the family had tea to teaching his slaves stories from the Bible and having them memorize verses. He never would have dreamed his shy, gentle wife would be so full of subversive ideas. "What is the problem now?"

She shook her head. "I don't want to waste your time with trivial matters, Luke. I know you have much more important things on your mind."

"Look at me, Caroline." He waited until she raised her head. He frowned at the puffiness of her eyes. She'd obviously been crying. "I appreciate your consideration of my time, but I cannot get anything done when I have to listen to arguments and complaints all the time. Wouldn't it be easier if you would just go along with Grandma's way of doing things?"

"Yes, but—"

His raised hand stopped her words abruptly. "I don't want to know what the latest problem is. I just want you to go to her and tell her you're sorry. Tell her you misunderstood and her way is the right way. Tell her you want to defer to her experience and learn from her. Tell her whatever you need to tell her so that she will not spend another morning talking to me about your lack of consideration."

Her shoulders drooped. Her head hung low.

Luke felt like a beast, but he had to make her understand how to act if he was to get any relief. So many problems awaited his attention. So many solutions had to be worked out before he left, and the time was slipping past him with alarming speed. He did not have time to act as a mediator anymore. His grandmother and his wife were going to have to learn how to live together under the same roof.

"I'm sorry, Luke. I'll try to do as you say." She glanced up at him. "You won't have any more trouble."

He sat back in the leather chair his grandfather had used to conduct business. He wished Grandpa was still around. Of course that would mean he'd never have come south, never taken over the reins of Shady Oaks, and never married Caroline. Who knew his life would become so complicated so quickly? Would things have been easier if he'd chosen the woman his grandmother had wanted him to marry? Possibly, but it was too late now. He'd made his choice, and they would all have to live with it. Luke rose from his chair and walked around to the front of the desk. "I'll hold you to that promise, dear."

He was ready to give her a hug, but Caroline stood up and, avoiding his gaze, slipped out of the room.

Luke returned to his stack of paperwork with a brief shake of his head. Was it his imagination, or was Caroline hiding something from him?

※

"You won't believe this place." Caroline dragged Dinah down the overgrown path she'd discovered yesterday during a long walk. A walk she'd had to take to keep from exploding at Grandma Darby. She pushed away the uncomfortable memory, along with the memory of not telling her husband about her discovery after she returned to the house and received his lecture. But it was his own fault. He'd not wanted to listen to anything she had to say. All she had done was comply with his wishes.

Dinah tripped over a log lying across the path and would have fallen if not for Caroline's steadying hand. "I don't think we should be out here."

"No one has told me not to come here." Caroline lifted her chin and pulled the maid forward. "If someone finds out, I'll be the one to get in trouble." Not that she could stay out of trouble these days. Who would have ever thought marriage would be so difficult?

She was beginning to be more than a little worried about her husband's faith. Not since they'd arrived had he offered to pray with her or even read scripture to her like Pa did every night. Sunday had come and gone without a mention of the Sabbath. It seemed the only time God was remembered at Shady Oaks was at mealtimes when Luke blessed their food. What had happened to the man who attended every one of her father's revival services?

She'd tried to broach the subject of daily prayer and devotion time with him, but Luke had put her off, saying he had too much to do before he left for Vicksburg. While it was true that he worked from sunup to sundown, she wished he would set aside some time for God. She hoped he meant it when he promised things would get better when the war was over.

"Would you look at that!" Dinah's exclamation brought a smile to her face. "It's a whole empty house."

Dinah was the one bright light at Shady Oaks. From their first evening together, they had discovered they were kindred spirits. It had begun when Dinah shared how she had come to be at Shady Oaks. Caroline knew instinctively this was the first time her new friend had shared such intimate details of her life with someone besides Hezekiah. She knew she could trust Dinah to keep any secrets she might need to share.

Dinah was not sure of her exact age because she'd been sold away from her mother when she was only a babe, but she couldn't be more than five years older than Caroline. She spoke of her good fortune in living at Shady Oaks where she was allowed to marry the man she loved and raise their two children. It humbled Caroline to realize how she took her own freedom for granted.

Caroline let go of her friend's arm and pushed her way past a wooden gate that had fallen into partial ruin and entered the weed-strewed courtyard. "Come on. I didn't have enough time to explore the inside yesterday."

Dinah's eyes widened. "Do you think somebody lives here?"

"I doubt it." Caroline marched up the front steps and rapped loudly on the door.

Both of them waited breathlessly for a response, but the house remained quiet. No one peeked through any of the windows, most of which were darkened by grimy layers of dirt.

Caroline leaned against the wooden door but heard no footsteps shuffling toward her. "I don't think anyone's been out here in years." She walked over to one of the windows, rubbing at the dirty surface with the hem of her cloak. "I wonder if the original owner of Shady Oaks had this house built, too. It looks like a miniature version of the main house."

Dinah finally joined her on the porch. "I wonder why no one lives here now."

"It's probably too far from the main house to be practical." She looked at Dinah, her mouth forming a perfect O. "It might be a dowager house. I wish Luke would move Grandma Darby out here so I wouldn't have to listen to her constant complaints about my failure as a wife."

Dinah's eyes widened.

Caroline took a moment to enjoy the thought before shaking her head. "It would be too mean to exile her out here. I will have to keep praying for a way to please her."

"I've never seen her so unhappy." Dinah's sympathetic gaze raked her face. "I'll pray, too, that she'll be kinder to you."

Fighting to hold back the tears that sprang to her eyes, Caroline turned her attention back to the house. "Let's see if we can get inside. We can clean up one or two of the rooms. Wouldn't it be wonderful if we could use it to help runaway slaves?"

Dinah's gaze turned dreamy. "You mean like the Underground Railroad?"

"It'd be perfect." Inspiration struck Caroline with the suddenness of a lightning bolt. "I've got it! You and Hezekiah can be the first family we help to escape to a free state."

Dinah froze for a moment before letting her shoulders droop. She shook her head. "My Hezekiah says God put us here for a reason. He'll never run away, and my place is at my husband's side." A tear slid down one of her cheeks. She brushed it away with a finger. "But it's real nice of you to think of us. We don't have a bad life here at Shady Oaks, you know. We have our own house, and your family gives us clothes and food enough to make do. I only have one great dream that will never come to pass."

"What's that?" Caroline tried to put herself in Dinah's place, but it was impossible. She'd always had the support of loving parents and the freedom to do most anything she wanted.

Dinah walked to the edge of the porch and looked back toward the thick woods they'd come through to get here. "Now and again a preacher used to come to Shady Oaks. Master Darby, your husband's grandpa, used to let us come to the chapel when the preacher was here so we could listen to the stories about Jesus. I loved those times, but there hasn't been a preacher stop by since the war started." She turned around to face Caroline. "I know God's Bible is full of stories like the ones he used to tell. But I can't read them. I wish I could so I could share them with my children and my husband."

A yearning to help her friend achieve her dream overcame Caroline. Her excitement returned as a bold idea occurred to her. "That's what we'll do here. We'll have all the privacy in the world, and I can teach you how to read!" She stepped forward and hugged Dinah close. "Let's get inside, and see if there's a place where we can work."

Chapter 10

I'll be back as soon as I can to check on you." Luke gave his wife one last hug. "You be careful. No wandering about alone."

She emerged from his embrace with pink cheeks. "You need to follow your own advice. I'll be perfectly safe here with your grandmother and the staff." Tears filled her eyes, turning them into twin pools. "You're the one who will be risking his life."

Luke felt the tug to stay, but he knew he had no choice. He really should have left two days ago when his orders arrived, but he'd decided to wait until the last possible moment to join the fighting. He would be stationed with a small group of men on one of the bayous between the Yazoo and Mississippi Rivers. His mission was simple—repel any Federal squads trying to reach Vicksburg. "It's much more likely I'll spend my time huddled around a campfire rather than exchanging fire with Yankees."

They walked downstairs arm in arm. "I don't want you to come outside, my darling. It's far too chilly this early." He dropped a kiss on her forehead. "It wouldn't do for you to become ill."

When she would have protested, he covered her mouth with his own. She clung to him and kissed him back. The poignancy of the moment stole his breath. He was glad he'd married her. Glad he would be coming home to her soon.

He pulled away and stared at her beautiful face for several seconds, memorizing the light in her blue eyes, the curve of her chin, the burnished gleam of her golden hair. "I love you."

"I love you, too." The slight catch in her voice was another detail he would carry with him during their separation.

With a sigh he let her go and strode to the front door. Hezekiah was waiting for him, both their horses saddled. "Are all of the provisions ready?"

"Yes, sir. We're all set."

Luke nodded. "You understand you don't have to go with me."

"Yes, sir." Hezekiah swung himself up onto the smaller horse. "I need to go with you. Someone has to protect the master. Your ladies would never recover if something happened to you."

"Thanks, Hezekiah. I appreciate your loyalty." Luke mounted his stallion, and the two of them headed north. If they made good time, they'd arrive at the rendezvous before lunch.

Caroline took her cloak from a hook near the front door.

"Where do you think you're going?" Grandma Darby's voice made her flinch.

"Oh, you startled me." She almost lost her grip on her cloak. "I thought you were in the dining room."

Dressed in a black morning gown, the frowning woman looked like a harbinger of doom. "I finished breaking my fast nearly an hour ago. Since then I've met with the cook, the housekeeper, and the overseer. But none of that answers my question."

"I thought I'd go for a walk." Caroline waited for Grandma Darby to contradict her. In the week since Luke had left, they'd managed to rub along with only a few disagreements, usually caused when Caroline broke some rule she was unaware of.

Grandma opened the front door and looked out. "I think that's an excellent idea."

Caroline's mouth dropped open. It was the first time Grandma Darby had complimented her choice. After a moment, suspicion wormed its way into her mind. Did she have an ulterior motive?

"I don't think you should go alone, however. Why don't you take Dinah with you?"

Caroline gulped. Had her subterfuge been discovered? Was Luke's grandmother toying with her like a cat with its prey? "Ummm. . .of course. What a good idea." She put her cloak back on the hook. "I'll go find her."

"Don't be silly." Grandma Darby closed the door and moved into the front parlor. "I'll ring for her."

Odd to realize how normal the querulous tone of Luke's grandmother seemed. Her concerns allayed, Caroline hid a smile. She settled on a straight-backed chair in the parlor and waited. A small basket sat at one end of the sofa. She'd never noticed it there before but decided she would follow the adage "Least said, soonest mended."

One of the slaves came running, listened to Grandma Darby's instructions, and hurried off to do her bidding.

A short time later, Dinah stepped into the parlor, an anxious look on her face. She had her cloak draped over one arm.

"Thank you for coming so quickly, Dinah." Caroline ignored Grandma Darby's snort. She was determined to be polite, no matter what the older woman thought. "Shall we get going?"

"I have a favor to ask of you, Caroline."

Grandma Darby's words set her heart thumping once more. She twisted her hands in the folds of her skirt. "What is that?"

"I have a sudden yearning for some sassafras tea, but we don't have any bark in the larder. Do you know what sassafras root looks like?"

Caroline wanted to answer yes, but she could not truthfully do so. "No, ma'am."

Grandma Darby sighed. "Well it's time you do. You'll find a stand of sassafras trees right at the edge of the woods, a few feet to the right of the path that leads to the creek. The roots have a smooth skin, light brown, and very gnarled. You should recognize it by its smell." She turned to glare at Dinah. "You ought to be able to help her."

Dinah's nod eased Caroline's concern. If she knew what a sassafras tree looked like, they could bring Grandma Darby enough roots for a gallon of tea.

Grandma Darby picked up the basket Caroline had noticed earlier. "I asked Cora to ready a basket with a couple of sharp knives. Be careful not to hurt yourself."

As soon as the girls left the house, they began giggling.

Caroline hooked the basket over her arm. "I thought for sure we'd been found out."

"I knew better than that. If Missus Darby found out, she wouldn't have sent word for me to bring my cloak." Dinah's laughter stopped. "I'd more likely be getting a whipping from the overseer."

The very thought made Caroline feel ill. "Maybe we shouldn't go through with this. Maybe I should just teach you the stories. I could read to you. Then you wouldn't be at risk of such a severe punishment."

Dinah planted her feet on the path and both hands on her hips. "Are you saying you don't want to teach me to read?"

"No, no. Not at all." Caroline could hear the strain in her voice. "My only concern is you, Dinah. You're the one who'll have to pay the price if we're ever caught."

"I suppose we'd better not get caught." Dinah resumed walking. "I think the good Lord knows what we're doing and why, and He'll protect us."

Caroline felt humbled by her words. "Sometimes I think you've got more faith than I do."

Dinah shook her head. "We're both God's children, and that's all that matters." She paused at the edge of the woods. "Do you want to pick the sassyfras now or when we're coming back?"

"Let's do it after your lesson. That way the roots will be nice and fresh. I don't want to give Grandma Darby any more reason to complain."

They arrived at the deserted house without incident and settled in for a lesson. Caroline was watching Dinah copy her letters on a piece of stationery. "Yes, that's a—" Her words were cut off by an eerie sound.

"What's that?" Dinah's eyes widened.

"I don't know." Caroline kept her voice to a whisper.

"Sounds like it's coming from out back."

Caroline had her hearing stretched to maximum. "It almost sounds like a baby crying." She got up and crept down the shadowy hallway leading to the back porch. She nearly jumped out of her skin when something touched her arm. Whirling around, she found Dinah right behind her. "You scared me half to death."

"Sorry." Dinah held out one of the knives from Grandma Darby's basket. "I thought we might need these."

"Good idea." Caroline crept forward again. It was quiet for a moment or two, but then the sound returned. It did sound like a baby. But what would a baby be doing out here in the woods? Had someone set up housekeeping?

"It can't be a baby." Dinah held her knife out in front of her.

Caroline had a firm grip on her weapon, but she held it at her side. "What could it be then?"

"Maybe it's a deserter trying to draw us outside where he can rob us. . . ." Her voice faded away into nothingness. "Maybe we ought to leave while we can."

Caroline turned back to look at Dinah. She squared her shoulders and lifted her chin. "I'm not going to run away like a coward." She stopped whispering, but her voice was still a little shaky. "This is my home. As long as Luke isn't here, it's my responsibility to make sure we're protected."

Dinah's eyes were as wide as saucers. "Or we could go back out the front way and get help."

It was tempting to listen to Dinah's suggestion, but Caroline knew in her heart she could not shirk her duty. She might not know much about running a plantation like Shady Oaks, but she ought to be able to scare off a vagrant before he caused any trouble.

Caroline looked at Dinah as she pulled the back door open and stepped out onto the narrow porch. "No, there's no time. But you stay inside. If I don't come back in a few minutes, you run back to the big house and bring the overseer back here as fast as you can manage."

"Stay in here? By myself? While you go out there and get yourself killed. . .or worse? I can't do that."

Caroline didn't answer. Her attention was on the grounds behind the house and the line of trees several yards back. She could see some evidence the area immediately behind the house had been cleared at some point in the past, even noticing the outline of what had to be an old flower garden. Lack of attention, however, had given nature the chance to reclaim most of the yard with weeds, creeping vines, and thorny bushes.

The noise came again, and from where she stood, it sounded even more like a baby crying. She caught a movement from the corner of her eye and whipped her head around to see a dark shape prowling among the trees at the edge of the woods. She held her breath. The figure weaved in and out of the brush, indistinct even in the bright morning light. Finally she made out its shape. It was a large, obviously anxious animal. As she watched, the coal-black shape leaped to a branch that had to be at least ten feet above the ground. Her breath caught at the grace of the smooth move, and she knew it to be a cat. . .a large cat. It made her think of the caged lions she had seen the year her parents had visited a traveling circus in Natchez. Except this animal was as black as midnight.

"Can you see anything yet?" Dinah had joined her on the porch. "What is it? Is it a deserter?"

"Shh. . .no, it's not a deserter. I think it's a cat."

"A cat? Like a housecat?"

"No, more like a lion." She pointed to the shadowy branches where it had taken refuge. "See, up there. Its fur is so black I almost can't make it out, but if you look real close, you can see its green eyes shining."

"It must be a panther." Dinah's voice was calmer now.

"A panther? I've heard about those, but I've never seen one."

"They're secretive."

"This one doesn't seem to be very secretive. I wonder why it's staying so close to the house even though it knows we're here."

"It's come to eat us up, that's what."

"Don't be silly, Dinah. Panthers don't eat people." Caroline's heart sped up a notch. Did they?

"I've heard stories of big cats that can sneak into a baby's room and take him away before anybody knows what's happening. They said it happened a few years back over at the Devereaux place. The next morning, the mother went to get her poor baby and it was gone. The only thing left in the crib was a few drops of blood and a patch of fur as black as night."

Caroline shuddered. She'd never heard of a panther taking a baby, but maybe it happened to people who lived so far from civilization. Just then the noise that had attracted their attention in the first place returned. It was much closer than the panther sitting so quietly on the tree limb. It seemed to come from right beneath her feet.

Dinah must have heard it, too, because she grabbed Caroline's free hand and squeezed it tight.

At least they knew it wasn't a deserter. But Caroline was beginning to wonder if the true answer was going to be even more dangerous. "What do you think is making that noise?"

Dinah looked at her. "Do you think it could be a baby panther?"

She nodded. "That's what I think, too. But I wonder where it is."

"There may be a root cellar. You know, where the missus of this place kept her canned fruits and vegetables."

Caroline glanced around the overgrown yard. What Dinah was saying made sense. A young cub could have somehow managed to get itself trapped, and that would be its mother out there, waiting to see what they were going to do.

"We'll have to find it," Caroline said. "The mother obviously can't help it, so we'll have to free the cub."

"What if it's not a cub at all?" asked Dinah. "What if it's the father panther, and we get eaten up when we find him?"

The noise started again. "I don't see any way that could be a full-grown panther. It's got to be a baby crying for its mother."

Although the look on Dinah's face was still full of doubt and fear, she took a deep breath and nodded her agreement.

"Good." Caroline pointed to her right, away from the area where the panther watched from the woods. "You start over there, and I'll start on this side of the yard. Just be careful to stay away from the woods. We don't want her to feel threatened. I'd hate to try to outrun her."

The two women stepped off the porch and searched quietly in the yard. Several tense moments passed before Caroline spied a pair of old wooden doors that looked like they were lying on the ground. "I think I've found it."

She moved closer and noticed that the wood on the doors was weathered. She could even see a wide gap where one of the boards had rotted away. This must be where the young cub had gotten in trouble. He'd probably just been exploring when the old board gave way underneath him. The space was far too small for the mother panther to get in and rescue her baby.

Caroline could hear the frightened yowls clearly now. She looked over her shoulder in time to see the mother panther standing on the branch, watching every move she made. The animal's wail sent shivers chasing down her spine. Caroline wondered whether the sound was to calm the little one or to warn her away.

Dinah walked over, her face showing a mixture of relief and fear. "Did you hear that?"

"Yes, but she's still out there in the woods. I hope she's trying to calm her cub."

"What do we do now?"

Caroline studied the area around them. "We've got to find a way to open those doors."

The cries from the other side of the doors were louder now and continued without pause. Caroline wondered if they should abandon the cub to its fate. It would certainly be the easier answer. But she knew she couldn't live with herself if she didn't try to do something to help the poor animal. She wanted to send Dinah back inside to safety but knew it was unlikely the other woman would desert her. With a nod to the mother cat, she bent over and grabbed the wooden handle on one of the doors, pulling with all her might. It didn't budge.

"Here, let me help." Dinah leaned over and grabbed the wooden edge just above Caroline's hands.

The two women pulled and strained. Caroline was beginning to believe they would not be able to get the door open when the old hinges groaned and began to give way. With renewed strength, the two women redoubled their efforts and were rewarded when the door opened fully. The second door didn't give them as much trouble, opening as if its hinges had been more faithfully oiled. Or perhaps their renewed hope gave them extra strength.

Dinah took two steps back. "Are you going down in there?"

"Why else did we work so hard to get the doors open?"

"I don't know." Dinah glanced toward the woods. "Maybe we could just leave it like this and let the mother come rescue her cub."

Caroline shook her head. "What if the poor thing is hurt?"

"We can't do anything if it is."

"I cannot stand here and let that baby cry. It could be hours before the mother feels it's safe enough to come this close to the house." Caroline took a step down into the cellar. It was dark, but not nearly as musty or dank as she imagined it might be. In fact, it had a rather pleasant smell, as if someone had used the cellar to dry herbs.

Three steps took her to the well-packed earthen floor, and she waited for her eyes to adjust to the gloom. It was a small room, bare of furniture except for a table and bench in one corner. After a moment she also noticed the shelves lining the other three walls. Most of the shelves were empty, but here and there she could see jars still packed with fruits or vegetables. The panther cub had quieted when she entered the cellar, so Caroline had no idea where to look for the animal.

"Do you see it?" Dinah's voice seemed far away.

Caroline's gaze searched the gloomy room. "No, not yet." She leaned over the bench. Emerald-green eyes peered at her from under the table, eyes as bright as those of its concerned mother outside. "Oh wait, here it is. Come here, little cat. I'm going to take you to your mother." She approached the cub slowly, unsure of its reaction, and held her hand out in what she hoped was an unthreatening gesture.

"Be careful, Miss Caroline."

Caroline jumped at Dinah's hoarse voice. A giggle tried to work its way up her throat, but she fought it. This was no time to get hysterical.

Something wet brushed the fingers she had extended. It took every ounce of determination she had not to jump back as the panther cub sniffed cautiously. Then it rubbed its head against her fingers, and she felt its soft fur tickling her skin.

"There, there. I know you're scared, little fellow." Her voice was calmer than she would have thought possible. It must be the touch of God's grace. Gaining more self-assurance as the animal allowed her to stroke its head and neck, she closed the distance between them. "Why don't you come here and let me help you get back to your ma? I know you must be missing her something awful. And aren't you a smart kitten to make such a noise?"

A low, rumbling sound issued from the young panther's throat, and it butted its head against her hand. She had gained its trust.

"That's it, little fellow." She carefully picked up the cat and held it in the crook of her arm. The cub rubbed its head against her arm, apparently content to let her carry it away from the dark corner where it had taken refuge. She walked back up the stairs and into the daylight.

"Praise the Lord." Dinah's admiration was plain to see. "You got him."

"Can you see the mother cat?" Caroline peered toward the woods.

"She's over there now." Dinah pointed to a clump of bushes and weeds. "She jumped down from her perch about the time you went into the cellar. She hasn't moved any closer to the house, so I hope she's not planning to attack us."

"I rather doubt that, or she would have done it by now." Caroline looked down at the ebony cat. "Look at this little fellow. Isn't he adorable?"

"If you say so, Miss Caroline." Dinah didn't look convinced. "But you'd better put him down before he decides to start crying again. I don't like the idea of you holding a wild animal, especially since its anxious ma is standing right over there."

"I will, but I need to pick a good spot. A place far enough away from us so his mother can come and see about him. And far enough from the cellar doors that he won't get into trouble again." She looked around, remembering the old flower garden. It should be a safe place to set down the adventurous cub. "I'll take you over there, little guy, and then Dinah and I will wait to make sure your ma comes to get you."

While Caroline walked slowly across the yard, Dinah closed the root cellar doors. "I'm going to wait for you on the back porch."

Caroline nodded. She continued petting the cub as if he were a housecat. As she approached the garden area, she could hear movement in the grass behind her. "It's probably your ma come to get you." Her heart pounded, but she kept walking forward with even, measured steps.

When she reached the garden, she carefully placed the cub on the ground and turned around, her breath catching in her throat. The mother panther was only a few yards away. She took a step to her right, hoping the mother would see she had not harmed the cub.

Although the animal was poised as if to spring, she didn't move. Her bright-green gaze followed Caroline's movements until she was a few feet closer to the house. Then she transferred her attention to the cub, which was unhurriedly licking its front paw.

Caroline continued her slow movements backward, praying she would not fall over an obstacle. After what seemed an eternity, she bumped up against the back porch. Safety was within reach. She moved up the stairs, keeping her attention glued to the panthers.

The mother panther walked over to the cub and sniffed him. She put out a large paw and pushed the cub onto his back, sniffing its stomach. Then she used her head to push the cub back onto his feet. Apparently satisfied, she grabbed the cub by the scruff of his neck and began to walk toward the woods.

Caroline breathed a sigh of relief as mother and babe returned to the wilderness where they belonged. She felt a great deal of satisfaction in knowing she could stand her ground. With God's help, she could overcome her fears and doubts, conceive a plan, and make it work. Maybe one day she would be able to take on the duty and responsibility of running Shady Oaks. Perhaps she could even improve things on the plantation. With the grace of God, she could do some good in this little corner of the world.

"Come on inside." Dinah stood at the back door.

"I'll be there in a minute." Caroline wasn't sure why she wanted to remain out here on the porch. The cub was safe. Dinah was safe. She was safe. But she stood caught up in a sense of wonder, watching the powerful, graceful movements of the big cat as she loped away.

Just before the panther disappeared into the woods, she turned, the cub still dangling from her jaws. Those piercing green eyes looked at her, and Caroline felt a chill dance across her skin. For a moment she felt the full force of the panther's stare. Was she grateful to Caroline? It might be a fanciful idea, but in her heart she knew she and the mother panther had connected on some level.

God's hand was in the events of the afternoon. Besides the remarkable coincidence that the cub had picked this day to fall into the root cellar, it amazed her to think that they had been able to hear the cub all the way from the root cellar. And the mother panther had never threatened them, even though she was a fearsome creature with teeth and claws that could have easily torn them to shreds.

God, You are so awesome. You used this encounter to teach me to rely on Your strength. A feeling of tranquility filled her heart, just like the peace beyond man's understanding that Paul promised in his letter to the Philippians. No longer did she feel all alone in facing her problems. Regardless of the circumstances surrounding them, God would see them through each day.

Chapter 11

Luke took a deep breath and raised his left hand. His right held a loaded pistol. His rifle lay beside him on the limb of the cottonwood in which he perched. He waited for the precise moment of attack, every muscle in his body tense as he watched the enemy soldiers mucking their way across the shallow bayou. Closer, closer, closer... With the lethal swiftness of a striking copperhead, his arm fell.

Simultaneously four shots rang out in the predawn gloom. Four Yankees fell into the water, leaving the men behind them, still wading in water above their knees, at a disadvantage. They reached for their weapons, but it was already too late. Luke led the second volley with his rifle. Shouts and screams of confusion and pain filled the area. The icy water of the little river was turning red with the blood of the fallen men.

In between his small troop and the river, some cattails rustled and shook. Luke heard the *whoosh* of a breath and a quiet splash. The pointed snout of an alligator headed for the wounded and dying men, its keen sense of smell leading it unerringly toward a floating body.

When the surviving men in the river saw the gray shape swimming toward them with deadly intent, they broke rank. It was one thing to face the chance of catching a bullet, quite a different danger to become breakfast for a voracious reptile. They pushed each other out of the way in their haste to escape. After a few minutes, the sounds of their retreat had faded into the distance.

Luke reloaded before he signaled to the others to join him on the riverbank. His face was frozen into a grim mask. He hated this—ambushing unsuspecting men, the death, the thrashing of gators as they completed their grisly feeding.

For nearly a month his days had been filled with too much death and destruction. How he longed for a respite, for the sweet smell of fresh earth and the new cane that should have sprouted by now. Even in the swamp, the signs of spring were all around them. The oak trees and hickory trees had put on their new leaves, bringing to mind his grandfather's words about planting various crops. He must have known even then that his grandson would one day need the information. *"The smart farmer plants corn when the leaves of a hickory tree get as big as a squirrel's ear."*

Those days were long gone, the happy memories fading as the horrors of war filled Luke's heart and mind. The world had become a wicked place. He hoped Shady Oaks was still untouched. He needed to believe he could one day return to the security of hearth and home. Once again feel the steady gait of his powerful stallion, Spirit, as they toured the fields. Hug his wife and tell her how much he loved her.

Luke stretched his senses to their most sensitive, listening for the return of the Union soldiers. He didn't expect it, but he must remain alert as an officer might manage to turn the troops around and send them back in this direction. He heard nothing but the croak of a bullfrog, the calls of birds, and the slap of water against the bank.

He walked over to where one of the bodies not mangled by the gator lay. Two of them lay lifeless on the riverbank, the blue of their uniforms turning black in the water. His foot flipped the nearest body. The face that stared up at him looked so young, so innocent. Surely this soldier was younger than sixteen. A hollow feeling invaded his stomach. His eyes stung, and his breath came in ragged gasps.

"Look out!" Hamp's urgency broke through the misery.

Hands shoved him hard, and Luke fell to one knee. He twisted and pulled his gun, shooting by instinct. Two blasts rent the air.

The other wounded soldier fell back, dead before his body hit the ground.

Time seemed to stretch as Luke straightened. He felt that he was moving through air as thick as syrup. Horror overtook him when he saw Hampton swaying behind him, staring with some surprise at a dark stain on the front of his uniform.

"I believe you owe me a favor, old man." Hamp sat down on the muddy bank with a thump.

Luke reached out to catch him. "No, no. You can't be hit."

"Sorry to argue with a commanding officer"—Hamp coughed and groaned—"but I rather think I am."

"Hezekiah! Come quick!" Luke jerked the tail of his shirt free of his pants and tore off a wide strip of lawn. With quick motions, he folded it into a square and pressed it against the hole in Hamp's chest.

The large black man splashed across the bayou. "What happened?"

"We've got to get Hamp to town. There'll be a surgeon there."

Hamp coughed. "I—it's too late."

Luke turned back to his friend. "You're going to be okay. You have to be."

"Wrong again."

"Don't argue with me. Save your strength." Luke's voice was rough. He looked up. "Get something to bind the wound. A belt, a piece of rope, anything." He continued applying pressure to the awful wound, even though he could feel the blood seeping through the material.

Hamp's green eyes were dull and seemed fixed on an object behind Luke's shoulder. "It's all right. My soul will be free to join God."

"Amen." Hezekiah handed a frayed rope to Luke. He continued whispering under his breath, and Luke assumed he was praying. He wished he could think of the right words to pray for God to work a miracle.

It was all over in minutes. Luke continued to hold his friend until Hamp's body went limp. Tears of regret, anger, and frustration rolled down his face. When would the senseless killing end?

Gently Hezekiah leaned forward and pulled Hamp's body away from him. "We need to get out of here."

Luke nodded. Any moment the enemy soldiers could return. Then they'd all die. He allowed Hezekiah to lift Hamp's body over his broad shoulder. Luke picked up all the rifles strewed about on the ground, and they made their way across the forest to the camp. After directing the other men to pack up the camp and follow them to Vicksburg, Luke and Hezekiah saddled their horses and left.

The tall spire of a church appeared over the rise of a hill. "They deserve to know Hampton died a hero." Guilt squeezed his chest as he looked back over his shoulder.

"You don't need to feel like that, Master Luke. That Yankee soldier is the one who pulled the trigger."

"But if I'd been paying attention, that soldier wouldn't have had a chance to get a shot off at poor old Hamp."

"Every man's got to die, and it's the good Lord who decides when."

Luke wanted to yell at his slave, but he settled for bitterness. "Don't talk to me about a God who would allow this senseless killing to go on. Hamp was a good man. He didn't deserve to die."

"Maybe God wanted Master Hamp at *His* side." The black man didn't flinch under the heat of Luke's glare.

"All I know is Hamp hasn't even had time to really fall in love or father his own children. Why did Hamp die? Why am I still alive? I'm no better than he is. . .was."

"I don't know what you want to hear, Master Luke. The good Lord is the only One who knows why this one lives and that one dies."

Anger threatened to consume him. It felt like a physical wound, as if he was the one who had been shot. He wanted to kick his stallion to a gallop. The need to feel the wind blowing past him was almost overwhelming. Was he trying to outrun his guilt? Luke didn't know. He only knew that nothing made sense anymore.

❈

Caroline couldn't quell the feeling of unease. Was it the weather? Relentless rain dripped from the eaves of the main house. She and Dinah had not been able to return to the house in the woods for more than a week. Maybe that was the reason for her restlessness. She sighed and put her needlework in the basket at her feet. Rising from the sofa, she drifted toward the window and stared out at the gray afternoon. Summer couldn't come soon enough for her liking.

At least she and Grandma Darby were getting along better. Even though she felt it was silly for the two of them to eat in the spacious dining room at the huge table, she held her tongue and endured the formal meals. It was not too high a price to pay in the name of peace. The Lord had answered her prayers about the stilted relationship between her and Luke's grandmother. Since the day Grandma Darby had asked for sassafras root, things had gotten better. Caroline and Dinah had dug up the gnarled roots and carried them back to Cora. That very afternoon, Grandma Darby had been served sassafras tea made from the pungent roots. Caroline was trying to acquire a taste for it.

A rustle behind her made Caroline turn. "Good afternoon, Grandma Darby."

The older woman frowned. "I don't see what's so good about it. We've had enough rain to drown ducks."

Caroline had a hard time keeping her expression solemn. "Well, I suppose we should give thanks for having such a lovely home to keep us safe and warm."

"And what about the soldiers who are not so blessed?" Grandma Darby stalked to the fireplace and held her hands out to the warmth. "It must be miserable for poor Luke and the others. I pray they have found a warm, dry place for shelter."

Even though she tried to ignore it, the dark feeling of foreboding grew stronger. "I wonder when we will hear from Luke."

The words were no sooner out of her mouth than a clamor started in the central hallway. She turned toward the door. Hope that it was her husband arriving, no matter how unrealistic that might be, replaced the dread in her heart. She looked out the window for sight of Luke or his stallion. Her eyes widened. A group of black men stood on the front lawn, wearing ragged clothing and angry expressions. "Whatever is going on?"

"Who is it?" Grandma Darby came to stand next to her. "Slaves? I don't recognize any of them."

At that moment, the door to the parlor opened and Dinah hurried in. "I'm sorry, missus. There's some men outside, and they're threatening to burn us out if we don't give 'em what they want."

Grandma Darby gasped. "Burn us out?" What little color she'd had in her face drained away. She put a hand to her forehead and swayed.

Caroline slipped a hand around her waist and helped her reach the sofa. "You sit here a moment and. . ." She let her words fade. What was she going to do? Face an angry mob? What would she say? How could she keep them from carrying out their threats?

Stories of violent slave uprisings returned to haunt her. Were they all about to die? She glanced at Dinah, whose eyes were as large as they had been the day they'd rescued the baby panther. The memory of that day steadied her somehow. God had helped her then. He would be faithful to stand by her today.

She took a deep breath and sent a prayer heavenward for courage and wisdom. "I'll be back soon, Grandma Darby. Dinah, why don't you see if you can brew up some of that sassafras tea? By the time I get done with the men out front, we'll probably all need a little refreshment."

Dinah scurried off to do her bidding while Caroline headed toward the main foyer. She could hear the strident yells of the men outside, but so far the Darby slaves had not allowed any of them to come into their home.

She pointed to two of the older footmen. "I need you to stand behind me while I speak with our visitors."

The men glanced at each other before turning to follow her. Good. At least now she could give the appearance of authority. She reached for the front door, but one of the footmen stepped past her and opened it, bowing as she passed through the opening.

The temperature was warmer than she expected, but the dampness seeped into her bones. Ignoring the physical discomfort, she stared out over the group of about twenty men. "I understand you men need some supplies."

"That's right." One man, apparently the leader, stood on the topmost step. "We're on our way to join up with the Union army, and we need food and blankets. If you're not gonna give 'em to us, we're gonna take 'em."

Caroline didn't answer him right away. Instead she looked at the men behind him, allowing time to meet each man's gaze. "So you're going to make war on a couple of women?" She continued to focus on each of the faces, ignoring the leader's growl. Their faces turned from anger to shame as she continued staring.

"Why not?" The leader took a step up, his foot landing squarely on the wooden planks of the front porch. "You got enough to share with us, and then some." He looked her up and down.

Everything in her wanted to turn and run. And she might have done it if her feet had not been nailed to the floor. But she couldn't run. She had to stand up to the man and win out. Squaring her shoulders and raising her chin, she faced him down. "We are more than willing to share with you if you're willing to be calm and respectful. But if you continue to threaten me and my family, I'll see to it that you're run off this property without so much as a biscuit to eat."

His eyes widened in surprise. For a moment, she could sense the struggle within him. She prayed hard for the Lord to protect her, to breathe a spirit of conciliation into the man. His gaze dropped to the floor at his feet, and he nodded. "Yes, ma'am."

Relief swept through her like a spring flood. "That's fine then." She smiled at the group of men, further relieved when one or two of them returned her smile. "Why don't all of you go around to the kitchen. Our cook, Cora, will see to your immediate needs while we gather some fresh clothing and food for you."

She turned on her heel and swept back toward the door without watching to see if they would follow her instructions. Praises filled her mind. She swept inside on a tide of thanksgiving. Disaster had been averted. Wouldn't Ma and Pa be shocked to see how she'd stood up to the unruly group? And Luke. Would he be impressed?

Seeing Mabel, who had probably come after hearing the clamor, Caroline asked her to gather the promised items for the men. She then turned to join Grandma Darby, who met her at the entrance to the parlor.

Pulling her into a tight embrace, Grandma Darby said, "I'm so glad Luke chose you to be his wife. I don't know many women brave enough to confront runaway slaves."

As soon as she emerged from the embrace, Caroline smiled. "It wasn't me, you know. It was God. Without His presence, I wouldn't have known how to act or what to say. God changed the heart of their leader. I saw it happen, Grandma Darby. It was amazing."

"I'm sure it was." Grandma Darby led her to the sofa. Both of them sat down, their hands entwined. "And I don't know what you must think of me. A foolish old lady who was no help at all."

Caroline shook her head. "Don't even think such a thing. You know more about this plantation than I'll ever know. All of the details come naturally to you, but they make my head swim. What I did was nothing in comparison. If I had not been here, you would have managed. On the other hand, I could never manage without your knowledge and guidance."

Tears swam in the older woman's eyes, making them gleam. "I don't know why I've been so blind. Can you ever forgive me, Caroline?"

Leaning forward, she placed a kiss on Grandma Darby's soft cheek. "Only if you'll forgive me for my lack of sense."

Grandma Darby let go of her hands and hugged Caroline once again. "There's nothing to forgive, Granddaughter."

Someone knocked on the door.

"Come in," they said simultaneously. Their gazes met, and they broke into giggles.

Dinah walked in with a laden tray. "Are you ready for some tea?"

Caroline nodded, trying unsuccessfully to stop her giggles. She supposed it was a reaction to her fear. She really should go to the kitchen out back and oversee the provisions being given to the visitors. But she wanted to enjoy the new closeness with her grandmother-in-law.

Grandma Darby looked from the tray to Caroline. "You even thought to order a tray? I think you're going to make a fine mistress of Shady Oaks."

Chapter 12

Luke could not believe he was about to attend a rally for the troops. Call it what they would, he knew it was nothing more than an opportunity for the citizens to enjoy another evening of dancing and flirting. He could list a thousand reasons why he should not. He'd just lost a close friend. Yankee soldiers were closing in on Vicksburg. And the obvious—he was married.

Hezekiah fussed with his cravat. "I don't know about this, Master Luke. What would your grandma say about this?"

He twisted his chin away from the black man's fingers. "She'd probably say I deserved a night of leisure after all I've been through." Even though he was looking away from Hezekiah, Luke could feel the large man's frown. He hunched a shoulder.

"She would think it's honorable for you to be seeing another woman?"

Hezekiah's firm jerk on the cravat made Luke cough and gasp for breath. "Careful."

"I'm sorry, Master Luke." Hezekiah twisted the length of cotton into some complicated design before stepping back. "It's done now."

It might have been the disappointed look in the other man's eyes. Or it might have been the voice of conscience. Either way, it made Luke very uncomfortable and not a little defensive. "Don't raise such smoke over this. It's not like I'm going to be alone with some female. I'm only going to a dance. Everything will be aboveboard and open to public scrutiny. I would never break my vows."

"Christ said we have to stay clean all the way through. It's not good enough to appear to be good. Just thinking about doing something sinful is as bad as actually doing it."

Luke snorted and pushed himself up from his dressing table. "If that were really true, we'd all be lost without hope."

Hezekiah's smile was sad and yet full of wisdom. "That's why we need Christ. Without Him, not even one of us could look forward to everlasting life."

Luke mulled over Hezekiah's words as he finished dressing. It didn't make sense. Why would God make it so impossible for men to get to heaven? Why would He make men so fallible they were sure to fail? "Do you think Hampton is in heaven now?"

"I don't rightly know, Master Luke. Only the good Lord knows what's in a man's soul."

"What about you, Hezekiah? Are you going to go to heaven when you die?"

Hezekiah put down the frock coat he'd been brushing. "Well, yes sir, I am. But I'm not in any special hurry. I love my family, and I'd like to live long enough to see my children placed in good homes."

The gentle tone in Hezekiah's voice awoke something in Luke. It was a yearning. A desire to be like the man who was carefully folding his clothing.

He shook his head to clear it. What was he thinking? He wanted to be like his slave? A man who didn't have any control over his life or the lives of his children? What foolishness. He was a successful man, a man others envied. He had a beautiful wife, a thriving plantation, and an idyllic future. By anyone's standards, he was a man who had everything. "I'm glad you're not in a hurry to get to heaven." He clapped Hezekiah on the back. "I'm not ready for you to leave me behind."

Hezekiah smiled. "Thank you, Master Luke."

Luke checked his reflection in the mirror before leaving his room. He was ready to enjoy an evening of music and dancing.

❊

"I was so glad to see you here, Luke." Marianna's dark eyes gleamed as he whirled her around on the dance floor.

Luke wondered why he hadn't chosen this young lady to be his bride. If only he could go back in time, that's one thing he would change. The other being his failure to stop Hampton from being killed. "I only wish I was here under happier circumstances."

Her mouth turned down at the corners. "I heard about Mr. Boothe. We will miss him terribly."

"Yes." He kept his answer short. No need to go into detail. He wasn't sure he could tell her what had happened without breaking down and making a fool of himself. "What's been going on in Vicksburg since I left?"

Her sad expression disappeared like a discarded mask. "Geraldine Stringer and Phillip Anderson announced their engagement. They will get married in August." Her sly glance was full of mischief. "Not everyone is as anxious as you to tie the knot."

"And rightly so. If I had to do it again. . ." He let the words trail off. Marianna was smart enough to understand his implication.

Her cheeks turned pink, and she looked past his shoulder. "I have been busy myself." The words were spoken in an offhand manner, as though her attention was elsewhere.

A little peeved at her inattention, he swung her around so she would have to focus on him. . .or at least on her dance steps. "Are you still volunteering your time with the soldiers?"

"Yes. It's hard, but rewarding at the same time." Her answer sounded stilted to him. As though she was answering him by rote. She felt stiffer, too. Was she no longer comfortable dancing with him?

Before he could ask if he had offended Marianna in some way, the music ended. He escorted her back to her mother and watched as one of his commanding officers, Major Fontenot, approached.

Swarthy-skinned with a mustache thicker and wider than Luke's, he looked like a pirate of old. All he needed was a black eye patch and an open-throated shirt. "Good evening. I hope you have not turned Miss Lister's head with too many compliments."

Why did the man's voice grate on him? Luke gave him a tight smile. "I don't believe I could."

"*Excusez-moi.* I stand corrected." Major Fontenot raised an eyebrow as he made a show of looking around the crowded ballroom. "How is your lovely bride? I have not seen her this evening."

"She is not here." Luke could feel anger building in his chest. Who did Fontenot think he was?

A married man.

The voice in his head was quiet, but he heard it in spite of the noise around him.

The snap of Marianna's fan opening drew his attention. She smiled at him. "Captain Talbot brought poor Mr. Boothe back to his parents."

Luke could almost hear the other man's questions. Why was he here tonight? Why hadn't he gone home right after meeting with the Boothe family? Why had he chosen to attend a party instead of flying to his wife when he had an opportunity?

Suddenly Luke wondered the same things. What was he doing here?

While he was still lost in contemplation, Fontenot led Marianna to the ballroom floor. He watched them twirl around the room for a few moments, surprised to see how she glowed.

He thought of the way Caroline looked at him. Perhaps he could make a quick trip to Shady Oaks if he got up very early in the morning. He would have to return again tomorrow evening, but being near her for even an hour or two would make the trip worth his effort.

Having made up his mind, Luke took his leave and headed back to his room. He would need to be up before the sun in the morning.

Chapter 13

A re you going walking again?" Grandma Darby's voice stopped Caroline and Dinah at the threshold to the front porch.

Caroline hesitated. She didn't like deceiving the older woman, but it was true they were going to walk to the dowager house. "Yes, ma'am." She hoped God would forgive her for not being any more specific about their plans. She turned back to the parlor to find both Grandma Darby and the housekeeper in the cozy room. "Do you need us to gather anything for you while we're outside?"

"No, I think we have everything we need for the moment." Grandma Darby looked toward Mabel. "You're not aware of anything, are you?"

"No, ma'am."

Grandma Darby nodded, turning her attention back to Caroline. "Please be sure to take Dinah with you. After what happened the other day, we should be doubly careful about not venturing out alone."

Caroline leaned forward and kissed Grandma Darby's cheek. "Don't worry about us. We'll be very careful." It was at times like these she wanted to confess exactly where she and Dinah would be and what they would be doing, but even though her relationship with Luke's grandmother was better, she doubted the woman would understand why she was determined to teach Dinah how to read and write. That was a secret she would have to keep for a very long time.

❀

Luke jumped down from his horse and tossed the reins to one of the stable boys who had come running to the front of the house. He could hardly wait to see Caroline. He had so much to talk to her about. And he wanted to hear every detail of all she had been doing since he left.

Would she have managed a truce with Grandma? Or were the two of them still feuding over insignificant differences? A smile curved his lips. He was almost looking forward to the role of peacemaker.

He took the steps two at a time and pushed open the front door. Pulling off his cloak, he laid it across an ornate bench inside the entry hall. "Caroline? Grandma?" He glanced in the parlor, but it was empty.

A sound from the top of the staircase brought his head up. Expecting to see one or both of the women, he was disappointed to recognize the housekeeper.

"Mabel, where is everyone?"

The woman hurried down the stairs. "Your grandmother is in her room resting, and your wife has gone out walking."

"Walking?" He scratched his head. "Isn't it too cold to be outside?"

A shrug answered his question. "Not for her and her maid, it's not. The two of them usually spend every morning out in the woods. But don't you worry. They'll probably be back before too long. They rarely miss lunch."

Luke's spirits deflated. He'd been so excited about surprising them. All the way home he'd imagined the joy on Caroline's face when he arrived. But now she wasn't even here. He glanced around the open entryway and sighed. What would he do until she appeared? Waiting seemed like an unacceptable pastime.

An idea formed in his head. Maybe he wouldn't have to wait. "Which way did they go?"

Mabel inclined her head over her left shoulder. "They generally use that path on the far side of the smokehouse."

Grabbing his cloak from the bench, Luke nodded. "I bet I know exactly where I'll find them."

❊

Dinah was leaning over a scrap of newspaper, her finger tracing the outline of the next word in the title she was trying to read.

"What is the first letter?" Caroline coaxed her student.

"G. . .G. . .ran. . .t. . .Grant!" She looked up for confirmation.

"That's right. Grant. And the next word?"

"F. . .fails. Ag. . .again. 'Grant Fails Again.'"

"Very good, Dinah. Look at that. You're reading the newspaper."

They were so excited neither of them heard the footsteps on the porch. The first indication they had they were not alone was the sound of a deep voice. "That's a hanging offense."

"Luke!" Caroline jumped up from her seat next to Dinah. Excitement and fear fought for supremacy in her mind. One glance at his face was all it took for the fear to win out. He was angrier than she'd ever seen him. "Luke." The second time she said his name, it was a plea for understanding.

He took off his gray cap and slapped it against the stripe on his pants leg, his dark gaze boring into Dinah's frightened face. He jerked his chin up and slightly back. "Get yourself to the big house. I'll deal with you later."

"Yes, sir." Dinah's wide-eyed glance swung between Caroline and her husband.

Caroline tried to reassure her with a smile, but her lips would not cooperate. A nod was all she could manage.

Luke closed the door behind Dinah, his lips tightly compressed. Eyes blazing, he looked around the room, his gaze taking in all the details of the parlor she and Dinah had made comfortable. He grunted when he noticed the newspaper they had been using for their lesson. "Are you determined to bring us all down to your level, Caroline?"

Caroline opened her mouth to tell him about how she and Dinah had become as close as sisters. Dinah wouldn't cause any trouble. Perhaps she could make him understand. "I'm sorry, Luke. I was—"

"I can see what you were doing. Do you have so little sense? Can you possibly think it is acceptable to teach a slave to read?" He stepped toward her and grasped her by the shoulders. "You've probably ruined Dinah. And if anyone else finds out she's been taught to read, I'll have to hang her. Do you want her death on your conscience?"

A vision of her friend's lifeless body hanging from the thick limb of an oak tree flashed into Caroline's mind. She could almost hear the creak of the rope and the sobs of her husband and children.

"Who knows what ideas you've put in that girl's head?" Luke's thunderous tones pulled her away from the horrible vision. "Ideas that could lead to sedition and insurrection. Can't you understand the danger of a slave uprising? You and my grandmother could be murdered in your beds. Is that what you want?"

"No." Caroline swallowed hard and twisted away from his grasp. She didn't want to hear any more. "Of course not."

She searched for a way to get through Luke's anger and calm him enough so she could explain about Dinah's wish to read from the Bible. Caroline wanted to share with him the joy of watching a new world open up for her friend, a world with endless delights and wonderful possibilities. A world all people, no matter their race, should be able to access.

"Then why did you do this? You had to know it was wrong." His eyebrows lowered even farther. "You brought her out here in secret. You lied to my grandmother about your reason for leaving the house. Is that any way to act?"

Caroline felt the blow of his accusation as her own conscience condemned her. He was right. She had lied or at least obscured the truth. What kind of Christian was she? Her parents would be so disappointed. Tears of conviction threatened, but she was determined to hold them back. She needed to keep calm even though she wanted nothing more than to put her face in her hands and cry her eyes out. How else could she show him she was not a child?

Luke strode to the window, his rigid back to her. "Caroline, I forbid you to teach Dinah or any other slave how to read and write. And you are not to come back out here again, at least not until I return home." He turned around to her once more. The planes of his face were sharp, as hard as granite. "I don't know what to think about you, Caroline. You're not the girl I thought you were. You're as deceitful as Delilah, eager to do anything to get your own way. I seem to only be capable of falling for women who do nothing but deceive me."

Caroline shook her head. He could not be saying what she thought. He could not be telling her he was sorry he had married her. Yes, she had faults. Many of them. And she still had so much to learn about how Luke wanted her to conduct herself.

"I should have listened to Grandma's advice and married Marianna Lister. Maybe I should return to Vicksburg and apologize for not realizing sooner what a paragon she really is." He turned around and shoved his cap back onto his head. "I wish I'd never come."

The pain caused by his words was as sharp as the thrust of a sword. Her heart shattered into a million pieces. Unable to stay in the room with him another minute, she turned and ran from the parlor. Tears streamed down her cheeks. She stuffed her fist in her mouth to keep from bawling like a frightened calf and ran down the steps. It didn't matter where she was headed. Caroline's only thought was to put some distance between them.

Branches slapped at her, but she continued running blindly until her breath came in gasps and her side screamed its pain. It wasn't until she was forced to stop that Caroline realized no matter how fast or far she ran she could not get away from his words. The words she never thought she would hear Luke say. The words no woman should have to live with. Her husband wished he had married another woman.

❀

Caroline dragged herself up the front steps and fell against the door. Looking down, she realized her skirts were dirty and torn from her mad dash through the woods. Her hair was a mess, too. She put up a shaky hand to straighten it but couldn't begin to make herself presentable. Maybe she could slip up to her room without being seen. Dinah would help. . .if Dinah was still allowed to tend to her.

A sob broke past her lips. She turned the cold brass knob and slipped inside the hall she'd once thought cold and formal but now realized had become home to her. Was she about to lose the right to think of Shady Oaks as her home?

"Caroline?" Grandma Darby descended the central staircase, her dark dress swaying around her as she rushed to the first floor. "Where have you been? Where's Luke?"

A seemingly endless supply of tears filled her eyes. "I—I don't know."

"What's happened? Was there an accident? Do I need to send someone for Luke?" She gasped and put a hand over her mouth. "He's not dead, is he?"

Caroline shook her head. "We had a fight. I think he's g–gone."

Grandma Darby's eyes widened. She looked around the foyer and pointed at one of the footmen. "Go get Dinah. Send her to Miss Caroline's room with clean towels and fresh water." She put a supporting arm around Caroline's waist. "Let's get you upstairs. Then you can tell me all about it."

She felt older than the woman helping her up the stairs. As though everything good in her life was behind her, the future unfolded before her weary eyes, bleak and void of happiness. Tears flowed once more.

Grandma Darby pushed open the bedroom door with her free hand. "I don't know what's wrong, Caroline, but I know it can be fixed."

The colorful quilt atop her bed beckoned, but Caroline felt too grimy to yield. Instead she chose the straight-backed chair in front of her writing desk.

Grandma Darby dabbed her handkerchief into the bowl of water on her dresser and used it to clean Caroline's face. "You should not despair. You are a Christian. You know all things are possible for us. Jesus will see us through the hard times."

Another wave of shame engulfed Caroline. She was supposed to be a Christian. So where was her faith? A tiny glimmer of hope appeared in her mind, like a flickering candle in the vastness of the midnight sky. Her tears slowed, and she hiccupped.

A knock on the door brought her head up. "Luke?" Hope and fear mingled in her chest.

The door opened, and Dinah stepped through. "I'm so glad you're back, miss. I worried about you."

Caroline stuffed the hope back down.

Dinah put down her burdens and went to the chest holding Caroline's clothing. "We'd better get you changed."

Grandma Darby and Dinah fussed over her, brushing her hair and removing her dirty clothing. She recounted the argument she had with Luke while they helped her bathe, cleaning the painful scrapes and scratches the forest had inflicted on her.

"If it makes things any easier for you, you don't have to tell me why the two of you have been disappearing into the woods every day." Grandma Darby helped Caroline into a fresh gown. "I've seen the closeness between you, and I know about your background, Caroline—the antislavery leanings of your parents and grandparents. I suspect you've been teaching Dinah to read."

Caroline gasped. "You do?"

Grandma Darby rolled her eyes. "I may be old, but I'm not senile, young lady. I can still reason out a thing or two."

"Of course you can." Caroline leaned back against her pillows. "I'm just surprised you haven't tried to stop us."

"Perhaps I should have, but everything seems to be changing, even the basic rules governing society. I suppose I decided to look the other way because I'm simply no longer certain that I'm right."

Even though she was worried about Luke and their future, a part of Caroline marveled over the change in his grandmother. She had gone from being petty and narrow-minded to a woman who was learning to tolerate, if not embrace, new ideas. "The next thing we'll hear is that you want to set Dinah and the others free."

"Remember the day the runaway slaves appeared on our doorstep?" asked Grandma Darby.

Caroline nodded, too weary to talk.

Grandma Darby fussed with an edge of Caroline's sheet. "I listened to those men talk about their emancipation, and I realized they were as determined as my husband to make their way in the world. It came to me that perhaps they deserved that chance. I'll never forget the way you handled them either. You were wonderful."

Any other time, Caroline might have blushed at the complimentary words, but tonight she was far too weary. She watched as Grandma Darby and Dinah banked the fire in her fireplace. Then they blew out the candles and tiptoed out. She watched the dancing flames until they blurred and dimmed. Her last thought as sleep claimed her was that she had to reach Luke and convince him not to end their marriage.

Chapter 14

Her stomach heaved as Caroline sat up on the side of her bed. She lay back down and pulled her knees up toward her chin. It must be a reaction to all the emotional upheaval caused by Luke's unexpected arrival. How she had hoped she would wake up and discover that the scene was nothing more than a nightmare. A headache pounded between her temples, and her eyes felt raw and swollen—indications that her hope was in vain.

The door opened, and Dinah slipped inside. She filled Caroline's washbasin with fresh water and stoked the fire.

Caroline sat up and tried to summon a smile. "Good morning."

"Good morning, Miss Caroline. I hope you slept well."

"I suppose so. But I feel pretty awful this morning."

Dinah's brown eyes were sad. "I'm so sorry about all of this."

The concerned tone helped Caroline focus on something besides her own misery. She swung her legs over the side of the bed. "It's not your fault. I wanted to teach you to read. But I should have approached it differently."

"How?"

Caroline stood and pulled Dinah to her for a hug. "I don't know. But you don't have to worry about it. I'll make sure you don't suffer because of it." After a momentary stiffness, Dinah relaxed and hugged her back. The contact eased Caroline's grief slightly. She pulled back and wiped a tear from her cheek. "It's going to be okay. I promise you that."

"I believe you." Dinah sniffed and turned away. "Why don't we get you dressed so you can go downstairs and eat?"

Queasiness attacked her again at the thought of food, but Caroline swallowed hard against it. She had to go downstairs and begin mending the scraps of her life. She bathed her face in the warm water Dinah had brought. She chose a pale-blue dress, hoping to lift her spirits. But judging by the heaviness weighing on her shoulders as she descended the stairs, Caroline knew her plan had failed.

"There you are, my dear." Grandma Darby gave her a kind smile.

The smell of fried bacon was usually a pleasant smell to Caroline, but this morning her stomach turned over. She nodded to her grandmother-in-law and slid into her seat, turning down a plate of eggs and bacon. "Just a piece of dry toast."

319

Grandma Darby frowned. "You'd better eat more than that. You're going to need all your strength if we're going to put my plan into action."

Caroline's stomach shifted once more. She needed to turn Grandma Darby's attention to something else. "What plan is that?"

"I was thinking of what you told me last night. If there's one thing I learned in my years of living with Luke's grandfather, it's that a married couple should never let an argument fester. The longer you allow differences to separate you, the harder it will be to bridge the gap. You and Luke have an additional challenge since you are physically separated by his army duty."

Caroline looked at Luke's grandmother with new eyes. The woman had surprised her last night when she'd been so kind and supportive. Now she was talking about the weaknesses in her own marriage. Making herself more vulnerable than Caroline would have ever dreamed possible. "He was so angry—" Her voice broke on the last word. Clenching her hands, she took a deep breath. "I—I don't know when he'll come home."

Grandma Darby dabbed at her mouth with one of the linen napkins. "That's why we need to go to him."

Go to Vicksburg? Caroline's tears dried up. "But we can't travel alone."

"Humbug." Grandma Darby threw her napkin on the table with force, raising her eyebrows in a defiant gesture. "Why not?"

Where should she begin? The dangers of traveling were always high, especially for two women without a male escort. But now those dangers had multiplied. What if they had met the group of fleeing slaves while on their journey? She shuddered. "I can think of many reasons we should not attempt such a journey."

"Start with the first few."

Caroline took a deep breath. "Deserters, escaping slaves, renegade Yankees, and we could find ourselves in the middle of a battle."

"I see." Grandma Darby's put her hands on the table and pushed herself up. "I'm starting to believe you don't think your marriage is worth the risk."

"That's not true."

The look Luke's grandmother tossed at her was a challenge. "I can be packed in an hour. How long will it take you?"

Caroline took a bite out of her toast. Madness. Could they even make it to Vicksburg before nightfall?

Grandma Darby exited the dining room as Caroline considered the possibility. The idea tempted her. But what would Luke say when they arrived? Would he listen to her after letting a few hours pass? Or would he still cling to his anger?

An even worse possibility crept into her mind: *what if he had turned to Marianna Lister for comfort? What if he was even now telling the avid young woman all about their argument? What if he was kissing—*

She broke off the thought before it could take root in her mind. She didn't need to torture herself with implausible scenarios. Luke was an honorable man. He would never break his marriage vows. But like an insidious weed, the image popped back into her head. Caroline pushed her plate away and stood up. Perhaps she could eradicate it by concentrating on readying herself for the trip.

At least her stomach had settled after her breakfast. She moved slowly up the stairs to her bedroom and pulled the cord to summon Dinah. She would have to remember to ask for fresh bread. Otherwise it would be an uncomfortable trip for all of them.

❀

"I still don't quite see why we had to come back to Vicksburg in such an almighty hurry." Hezekiah's face wore a confused frown. "I thought we was going to stay at Shady Oaks overnight."

"I changed my mind. A good thing, too, since I received orders this morning to report to the main headquarters."

Even though the sun was shining down on them, a fog seemed to surround Luke. Was he wrong? Should he have been more gentle with Caroline? He hadn't meant to make her run from him. But he had a duty to stop her from making foolish mistakes. A good husband protected his wife, even if it was from her own self.

What about Marianna Lister? The accusing words made him cringe inside. Well, he was man enough to admit he should not have said anything about Miss Lister.

Luke knew he had lost control. It was one of the reasons he had decided to leave immediately after confronting his wife. He'd been angry, and he had lashed out at her in the harshest way possible, determined to make her as unhappy as he was. Her devastated expression haunted him, but he could do little about it. Perhaps he would pen a note of apology to her this evening. If General Pemberton agreed, he might even be able to take off a few days next week and spend them with her and Grandma.

They entered the main headquarters, Hezekiah falling two paces behind. After looking around for a minute, Luke spotted a group of men studying a large map that had been nailed to the wall. He joined them and listened to the discussion.

"Our cannons will keep the city safe from a river assault." The man speaking was General Pemberton. He nodded to Luke but continued talking to the officers around him. "And we're well fortified here, here, and here." He pointed to several spots north, south, and east of the city. "But those are only a precaution. The Union has never been able to get a toehold on this side of the river, thanks to men like Captain Talbot here."

Caught off guard by the use of his name, Luke saluted. "It hasn't been without cost, sir."

"Yes, that's true." Pemberton turned his attention back to the map. "We

321

all hope and pray the lives lost will not be in vain." He continued outlining the defense preparations of Vicksburg, patiently answering questions and listening to suggestions.

"Our spies tell us Grant is on the march." Pemberton pointed to the far side of the Mississippi River, tracing an inland route to the south. "But he has no way to get his troops across the river because his boats are all bottled up to our north. Unless he has a way to spirit them past my cannons, he will fail to get the support he needs to launch another attack against Vicksburg."

"Perhaps he plans to march to New Orleans." The suggestion came from one of the officers standing next to Luke.

Pemberton frowned. "It is possible, but unlikely. Some of you were here when two boats sailed past our cannons in the middle of the night. I think it is more likely he will try to accomplish a second nighttime run with more of his ships. So we need men over in Louisiana who can set signal fires to backlight any boats that try to get past us." He looked at Luke. "I want you to take a few men across the river. Your mission will be to set up bonfires that can be lit at a moment's notice. As soon as the boats are in sight, you'll have to set the signal fires and sneak back across the river to avoid being targets yourselves."

Luke's chest expanded. He saluted. "Yes, sir." Pemberton would only assign such a mission to someone he trusted. The shadow of his actions in Knoxville had finally lifted. He was accepted as a valuable member of the Confederate army.

If only Caroline would value him as others did. . .

Chapter 15

"Wake up, Caroline." A gentle hand shook her shoulder. "We're in Vicksburg."

Caroline opened her eyes to see Grandma Darby smiling. She sat up and looked out the carriage window, surprised to see that dusk had fallen. "I must have fallen asleep."

"I imagine you didn't sleep very well last night. But now that we are going to face the problem headfirst, you were able to relax and catch up on what you missed."

She hoped Grandma Darby's analysis was correct. It was true she'd felt very foggy this morning, but her mind didn't feel much clearer even after her hours-long nap. The very thought of facing Luke's anger once again made her stomach clench. Could she do it?

The nausea she'd felt back at Shady Oaks returned with suddenness. Choking it down, she watched the older lady gather her things. Something in her behavior seemed odd, as though Grandma Darby was nervous. "What's wrong?"

"I—I don't know how to broach the subject of our accommodations with you."

Dread flitted into her disgruntled stomach, its dark wings spreading fear. In all the months she'd observed Luke's grandmother, she had never heard her stutter. What could be that wrong?

"All of the hotels in town are filled to overflowing. There's no room for us at all tonight."

This was bad news indeed. "What are we going to do?"

"I've sent some of our slaves to make inquiries, but we will have to stay with friends this evening. Unfortunately, many of my friends have fled the city because of the rumors of an impending attack." Grandma Darby stopped talking and pulled at a loose thread on her glove. "Fortunately, I have discovered one family who is still here and has opened their home to us."

"Who?" The single word hung in the thick air of the carriage. Caroline put a hand to her chest in an attempt to quell her heart's flutter.

"Timothy and Georgia Lister. Now before. . ."

Caroline's heart stopped. She could feel her blood congealing, and she missed something Grandma Darby said. With a thump, her heart started again, and she sucked in a deep breath.

"I know this is the last place you want to spend a night, but it simply cannot be helped." Grandma Darby grimaced. "If you are the woman I think you are, you will overcome this hurdle. And tomorrow, as soon as a place has been found, we will take our leave. And we can send a message to Luke at headquarters. He'll likely come right over, and the two of you can reconcile."

Caroline could imagine the scene. Luke would sit on one end of the couch, and she would sit on the other. Marianna would either sit inside the parlor with them or lean against the door so she could hear every word. She shook her head. "Maybe I should visit Luke instead."

If she had not been so heartsick, Caroline would have laughed at the shock on Grandma Darby's face. "At the garrison? That would never do. Your reputation would be irredeemable."

A sigh of resignation filled her as she watched Grandma Darby alight from the coach. She sent up a prayer for strength to survive the evening before following her husband's relative, the one who had once advised him to not marry her.

The front of the Lister house was formidable. It stood three stories high and spread outward from the central entrance like a European castle. If she had not lived for the past months at an even larger, more imposing home, Caroline would have turned and run in the opposite direction. But she had spent time at Shady Oaks, so she lifted her skirts and entered the Lister home with her head held high.

❀

Vicksburg's high bluffs cast deep shadows, and the sky overhead seemed to pull a black cloak over its expanse. The river drifted away to the south, unconcerned with the battles being fought along its length.

Sweat trickled into Luke's eyes as he pushed hard on the pole and silently moved his pirogue, the flat-bottomed boat popular on both sides of the Mississippi, through the swampy reeds lining the riverbank. They were patrolling the water as ordered, looking for any sign the Yankees had decided to test the Confederate cannons tonight.

"Watch that branch." Hezekiah whispered a warning.

Luke ducked and felt the pointed needles of a cypress tree brush the back of his head. "Thanks, that was close." He glanced back at his companion, noticing how Hezekiah's hands clung to both sides of the boat. "Are you worried the river is going to reach up and drag you in?"

Hezekiah's eyes widened. "Don't you tease me, Master Luke. You know how scared I am of the water. I don't want to fall in and drown."

"It'll be okay. We won't be getting out of the boat unless we have to light the signal fires."

Water lapped against the side of the boat, rocking it slightly. Luke strained his eyes, looking for what had caused the wavelets. "Look, what is that?"

"I can't see. . . No, wait. I see it. Something's out there, but I can't tell exactly what it is. It don't look much like a boat to me."

"It must be the Yankees."

"What do we do now?" The fear in Hezekiah's voice was much clearer than the outline of the boat trying to slip past.

"We've got to get to the other side of the river and get those signals lit."

"But we can't go now. Not with all them Yankees just waiting to shoot us out of the water. We'll get run down for sure."

"This would be a good time for you to pray," suggested Luke. He took a moment to send his own request toward heaven, just in case God was listening.

With a grunt, he pushed away from the bank. Earlier he and Hezekiah had wrapped their oars in cloth to muffle the sound they made. Now they dipped the oars slowly to further disguise any telltale noise.

The river rushed around them, trying to push their little boat south toward the Gulf of Mexico. Darkness provided cover for the pirogue as it made slow but steady progress across to the Louisiana side of the river. No moon brightened the sky, a fact that had no doubt influenced the Yankees to choose tonight to move their fleet.

Luke and Hezekiah made it across without incident and landed on the little beach Luke had scouted earlier in the day. "I guess your prayers worked," Luke whispered as they stowed the pirogue. "I sure am glad you and God are so close."

Hezekiah nodded and smiled, his teeth white against the dark skin of his face.

The two men made their way silently along the soft bank until they reached the first pile of firewood and dry brush. Luke withdrew a lucifer from his pocket and started the blaze before moving to the next pile of wood. Five piles, five fires. The two men stood back and watched as the blackness was penetrated by the blazes, providing a backdrop to highlight the positions of the ships on the water. Almost immediately, cannons on the opposite shore began their bombardment.

Luke wiped his grimy hands on his pants. "Let's get back to the pirogue. We're easy targets ourselves as long as we stand in front of this fire."

"Will we be safe down there?"

"I would think so. The Yanks aren't going to be interested in this side of the river. Those cannons will probably sink a great many of them. And the ones that are left will be concentrating their attention on the east shore. I imagine General Grant will think twice before he sends his boats this far south again. He'll probably move them back to Memphis and try to figure out what to do next."

"He's gonna be mighty surprised when his boats don't show up."

Luke nodded. "If we can keep him on this side of the river until General Johnson's troops get here to reinforce Vicksburg, I think everything will be okay. This has to work. We have to keep control of Vicksburg. If we lose

Vicksburg, we lose the whole river and probably the war."

The two men returned to the riverbank, not bothering to hide their progress this time because of the uproar on the water. The Yanks were returning fire, but their bullets could not reach the Confederate cannons located on the high bluffs on the eastern side of the river. And they were taking a pounding because the Confederate soldiers could see them so clearly against the fiery sky. Luke could hear the explosions as cannonballs struck the decks of the ironclads.

As they reached their boat, he winced at the cries of wounded and dying soldiers. He climbed into the front of the boat and turned to face Hezekiah. "There's a creek I noticed just south of here when we came over this afternoon. Do you remember it?"

The slave shook his head. "I wasn't looking at much except all that water underneath us."

Luke allowed his mouth to relax into a smile. "You really are frightened of the water, aren't you?"

A nod answered him.

"The creek you missed looked like it might offer some protection. Maybe we can even find a cave to keep us safe until the morning. There's not much we can do from here, and I don't have the stomach for shooting any of the men who make it to the shore."

"Me neither, Master Luke. That seems like something the good Lord would frown on."

"I agree." Luke untied the rope tethering their boat to the shore and stood up to push them out into the channel. An odd sound, not unlike the buzz of a hornet, filled his ears. An instant later he felt a fire light in his leg.

"Master Luke!"

He heard the scream as if from a distance. Then the oddest thing happened. The river rose up and slapped him in the face. For an instant, the cold water brought him back to clarity. *I've been shot.* He tried to swim to safety, but the powerful currents dragged him away from the bank. As the inky waters closed over his head, Luke heard an ominous splash behind him. He wondered if being eaten by an alligator would be a more unpleasant way to die than drowning.

Chapter 16

Caroline tossed her quilt back and rose from the unfamiliar bed. What had awakened her? The question was answered as the sky outside her bedroom window lit up. A firefight was being waged somewhere nearby. Her hand went to her throat as another volley of cannon fire boomed. Was the city being attacked?

She pulled back the curtains. The street behind the Lister home was quiet, but some distance away she could see people out on the street, carrying torches. Were they Yankee soldiers? Had the city fallen? Caroline closed her eyes and prayed for safety for those in the Lister home, for the soldiers fighting on both sides, and especially for her husband.

Noises in the hallway indicated she was not the only one who had been awakened by the commotion outside. Grabbing her wrapper and pulling it on, Caroline opened the door.

"There's no need to be scared." Marianna was speaking to her younger siblings. The candle she held cast a glow on her face. She looked beautiful even when pulled from her bed in the middle of the night. Combined with her jet-black hair and large eyes, her image put Caroline in mind of paintings of the Madonna.

Marianna's parents appeared at the same time as Grandma Darby, each having the presence of mind to light a candle.

"All of you women stay up here while I go see what is going on." Mr. Lister's dark brows were drawn together in a frown. He had taken time to pull on a pair of trousers, but his nightshirt still hung down to his knees.

Another volley of cannon fire made the younger girls scream and run to their mother. Marianna ran to the balustrade and looked over.

Caroline would have joined her to see what was going on downstairs, but Grandma Darby was looking quite shaken so she walked to her instead. "Are you okay?" Her worried gaze searched the older woman's face.

Grandma Darby's smile was wobbly on her face, but she straightened her shoulders and nodded. Gray hair peeked out from the edges of her crocheted nightcap. "I am worried about Luke."

"I know. I've been praying for him since I woke up."

More cannon fire brought all of the females to the edge of the balustrade. The front door stood open, allowing them to glimpse the street outside.

327

Caroline reached for Grandma Darby's hand. "It sounds like it is coming from the river."

"That would make sense." Marianna looked toward her. "But I wonder if the Yankees are really foolish enough to attack us from the water. They should know by now they will never succeed with that."

Mrs. Lister nodded her agreement with her oldest daughter's statement. "Our bluffs are high enough to hold off any attackers."

Footsteps on the stairs drew their attention to the return of Mr. Lister. His face was calm, relaxed. Seeing his expression made Caroline feel better.

"Don't worry, ladies. There's no cause for alarm. The cannons you hear are ours. A flotilla of Yankee ships are trying to use the darkness to float past us, but we're ready for them." He turned and pointed toward the front door. "See that red glow in the distance?"

Caroline looked to the area where he pointed. An eerie radiance pierced the darkness almost like seeing the sun rise. But unless she was mistaken, she was looking west.

"We've got dozens of signal fires lit on the Louisiana side of the river to backlight the Yankees. Makes their boats clear targets. Our cannons are most likely sending all of them to the bottom of the river."

"You see, girls," Mrs. Lister spoke gently to her younger children, "we have nothing to fear. I would suggest all of us return to our rooms and try to sleep." She herded the children to the nursery.

Marianna talked to her father about what he had seen and heard.

Caroline wanted to listen to the man's answers but knew she needed to support Grandma Darby. Putting an arm around her waist, she walked back toward the other woman's bedroom. "I think Mrs. Lister is right."

"I should not have insisted we come to Vicksburg." Grandma Darby blew out her candle and placed it on the table beside her bed. "It has put both of us in harm's way, and it seems unlikely you'll get to talk to Luke with all of this going on."

Caroline's heart went out to Luke's grandmother. She sounded so weary, so lost. "Don't worry about it. You couldn't know the Union soldiers were about to launch their ships. And you were trying to help me get things sorted out." She stood next to Grandma Darby's bed. "Why don't we say a prayer for Luke's safety before I leave you?"

Grandma Darby nodded. "That's a wonderful idea."

They knelt side by side. Caroline steepled her hands and closed her eyes. "Lord, we come to You with frightened hearts tonight. Please protect Luke. Keep him safe from harm. Please don't let his anger remain. And help me find a way to mend the breach between us." She fell silent as God's Spirit seemed to settle around her. What a wonderful Maker she served. Even in the midst of danger and fear, He was faithful to listen to her and answer her pleas.

Grandma Darby shifted. "Lord, You heal the lame and give sight to the blind. Please watch over my grandson. Wrap him in Your loving arms. Give him strength and cunning. He's not bulletproof, Lord, so please cover him with Your protection. Thank You, Lord. We pray in the precious name of Your Son who died for us. Amen."

Caroline pushed herself up and helped Grandma Darby into bed. After pulling the quilt up, she leaned over and gave the woman's wrinkled cheek a swift kiss. "Sleep well."

"You, too, dearest Caroline."

The words echoed in her head as she made her way slowly back to her bedroom. She was almost too tired to put one foot in front of the other. Now that she knew they were not in immediate danger, she felt like wrung-out laundry, not even removing her wrapper as she crawled back into her bed.

After a little while, she realized the cannon fire had stopped. The battle was over. So why did she feel so uneasy?

A compulsion overcame her to pray. Obedient even though she didn't understand, Caroline got out of the bed once more and sank to her knees. She started by praying once again for her husband's safety, but the words somehow got twisted and lost. Supplication filled her, containing all her pleas, hopes, and dreams for a future with the man she loved.

Time ceased to exist as the prayer continued. Finally, when it was over, she stood once more, surprised to look out the window and see that dawn was quickly approaching. Even though she knew God had heard her prayers, she couldn't completely quiet the whisper of dread trying to envelop her heart.

❀

When Dinah entered her room with a tray, Caroline woke to realize the sun was high in the sky. "Why did you let me sleep for so long?"

"You needed the rest."

"That's what Grandma Darby said yesterday. It seems all I do is sleep these days." Caroline sat up in bed and chose a piece of toast from the tray

"It's only natural since you're in the family way."

Caroline gasped as though doused with a bucket of icy water. "What do you mean?"

"Now, Miss Caroline, you had to notice your dresses have been getting tighter. And then you been getting sick in the early morning. It's only natural after all."

Her face flamed, and Caroline didn't know where to look. She was going to have a baby! How she wished she could tell Ma and Pa the good news. They would be so excited. If not for this beastly war, she could plan a trip to visit with them or at least send them a letter to tell them the good news, but for now she would have to celebrate with her new family. She and Luke were going to be parents. What would he say? How could she even tell him?

She finished the toasted bread and got up so Dinah could help her get dressed in one of the gowns that had indeed seemed to shrink over the past

329

weeks. She had thought it was because of the rich food offered at Shady Oaks. "How long have you known?"

"Nearly a month." Dinah straightened Caroline's skirt with quick motions and stepped back. "But I doubt anybody else knows, exceptin' maybe Missus Darby. You got time to tell Master Luke, but you better do it quick. Now go on while I clean up your room. They're waiting for you in the parlor."

Was Luke here? Her heart beat faster. *Thank You, God.* Had a day ever held such promise?

Caroline practically flew down the steps. Forgetting proper decorum, she burst through the parlor door to find the room full. Grandma Darby, Mr. and Mrs. Lister, Marianna, and a swarthy man she did not recognize. But where was Luke? Her footsteps faltered. Why was Grandma Darby dabbing her face with a handkerchief? Why were the rest of the people in the room looking at her with such sadness?

Caroline wanted to turn and run back upstairs. She needed to get back into her bed. Maybe sleep awhile longer. Anything to postpone this meeting.

She didn't want to step inside the room, but before Caroline could turn away, Marianna jumped up and ran to her. "Oh, my dear, I am so sorry."

Tears pushed at her eyes. "What is it? What's happened?"

The swarthy man had stood at her entrance, and now he bowed to her. "Mrs. Talbot, allow me to introduce myself. I am Major Michel Fontenot."

"Michel—I mean, Major Fontenot—is a friend of the family." Marianna had a death grip on her arm. "He is also Luke's commanding officer." She hesitated for a moment, swallowing hard. "I'm afraid he has some bad news."

Caroline would have covered her ears if not for Marianna's grasp. She knew she didn't want to hear whatever it was this man had to say. It was the news that was making Grandma Darby weep. It would make her weep, too. "No."

Fontenot's dark gaze was sad as he nodded. "Your husband and his slave took part in a very risky venture last night, one that gave us a distinct advantage. They crossed the river and lit signal fires to unveil the ships trying to defeat Vicksburg's defenses. Their actions may have kept the city safe, but sadly, they paid the ultimate price."

"No." It seemed the only word she could say.

Marianna drew her to the sofa. "I am so sorry."

Caroline looked up at her and saw the sympathy in the other woman's gaze. The smell of wood smoke from the fireplace threatened to choke her. The air in the room seemed dense with it.

As if from a distance she could hear the others talking. They were saying things about bravery and courage, concepts that had no meaning in this moment. She coughed and took the handkerchief someone handed her, not knowing whether she was about to cry or lose the contents of her stomach....

Another realization dawned—she was carrying Luke's child. And now she would never be able to share her joy with him. Her dreams of a happy future disappeared in an instant, replaced by grief and despair. How could this have happened? Why did God allow it to happen? How would she ever recover?

Chapter 17

Intense thirst pulled Luke to consciousness. He looked around and realized he was in a cave. The crackling flames from a nearby fire held the damp night air at bay. Every part of his body was racked with pain, but he was relieved to find himself still alive.

A shuffling noise brought his head around to see Hezekiah entering the cave with a skinned rabbit in one hand. "Master Luke? It's good to see you awake."

Luke tried to push himself up, but a shooting pain made his eyes water. The walls of the cave swam dizzily.

"Don't you try to sit up yet, Master Luke. You been shot." Hezekiah draped the rabbit over a nearby rock and helped Luke lie back down.

That must be why he ached so. Luke caught his breath after a few seconds. "What happened? How long have we been here?"

Hezekiah squatted next to him and stirred at the fire. "We been here 'bout a week now, and you been pretty sick."

"What happened?" Luke repeated his first question. "All I remember is coming across the river to light signal fires."

"That's right, Master Luke. And we got those fires all lit up. It'll be a wonder if any of them boats made it past our cannons. You and I was about to hole up until morning, but someone musta' seen us. They started firing, and since you was at the front of the boat, you took a bullet right here." Hezekiah's finger lightly grazed a spot above Luke's knee.

The area he touched was very tender, but that was not what made Luke start. "I remember! I fell into the water, and a gator splashed in after me. I thought I was dead for sure."

Hezekiah's chuckle was deep and rich. "That wasn't no gator. That was me you heard."

"Were you hit, too, then?"

"No."

Luke wished he could sit up, but he was too weak. "You jumped in the water after me?"

Hezekiah nodded and busied himself with readying a spit for their meal.

"But you're afraid of the water. You can't even swim. Why would you do such a thing?"

332

"You told me you got doubts about what you believe—so I knew if you died, your soul would belong to Satan, and he'd torment you for all eternity."

Luke's breath stopped. He could feel his heart thudding in his chest. He didn't know what to say. He'd never realized the depth of the slave's faith. "You risked your life to save me."

Hezekiah shrugged. "You're my neighbor. Jesus says we have to love God first and each other next. I couldn't let you die."

The words were simple but so strong. Warmth spread throughout his body, warmth that had nothing to do with the flames of the nearby fire. It was the whisper of God reaching out to him through Hezekiah's faith and willingness to sacrifice his own life. He was humbled. Tears stung his eyes. Gone was all his arrogance, his belief that God was too distant to care about him. "I want to know this Savior."

"Praise the Lord. He wants to know you, too." A smile relaxed Hezekiah's face. "There must be a big celebration going on in heaven right now. Another sheep is coming to the Father."

Hezekiah talked about his own walk with Christ. His words seemed to flow directly into Luke's soul.

Luke's heart had been a hardened, dry sponge. Now it swelled and softened as the love of Jesus entered. In the flickering light inside the cave, he gave his life to Christ. The Holy Spirit took up residence inside him, and the terrible anguish began to ease.

A spiritual hunger awakened inside him. He wanted to know more. He wanted to follow Christ. "I've been such an idiot. Would you pray with me? I don't know what to say to Jesus."

Hezekiah nodded. "I remember the first time I talked to Him out loud. It was a scary thing. Like you finally realize how big and powerful He is, and you wonder how you can dare to speak to Him."

"Yes, you do understand. When I look back at the things I've done, I wonder how God can forgive me."

"It's a mighty strong God who loves you, Luke. He's ready to forgive you. All you have to do is ask Him to come inside you."

Tears fell from his closed eyes as Luke prayed for Christ to enter his heart. He went from feeling dirty and unworthy to feeling the wonder of a Savior who loved him and who gave His blood to wash away Luke's sins. Faith was more than attending church or reading a Bible. It was a personal relationship with his Maker. When the prayer was finished, Luke knew the rest of his life was going to be different. He had made a lot of mistakes, but Christ did not condemn him.

His mind went to his wife. *Caroline.* As if a veil had been lifted, he realized she was the only woman he had ever really loved. He had fallen once for a beautiful girl back home and had even tried to correct that mistake by courting Marianna Lister, a girl for whom he had no tender feelings. But he thanked God for leading him to Caroline instead.

His heart cracked as he thought of the harsh words he'd thrown at her the last time they had been together. How had she fared after he deserted her? Would she forgive him as quickly as Christ had? He didn't know the answer to the questions, but he did know one thing. If it took him the rest of his life, he would seek her forgiveness and treat her with the love and respect she deserved.

He would return to Vicksburg only long enough to resign his position. Then he would find his wife at Shady Oaks, and with God's help, he would make things right between them.

That is, if Caroline would allow him to. . .

❀

The fever came back the next day. Luke tried not to thrash about, but the fire inside his body made him restless. From time to time, Hezekiah gave him cool water or placed a wet cloth on his face. The relief did not last.

The next time Luke's mind cleared, they were on the move. Hezekiah must have built a travois. It was not an easy ride, but it had to be much harder on his slave to pull the framework holding Luke.

"Hezekiah." His throat was so parched he could barely croak, but the man carrying him heard the sound.

"Yes, Master Luke?" He carefully lowered the travois and offered Luke water from a canteen. "You feeling a little better?"

"You're a miracle, Hezekiah." He coughed.

Hezekiah shook his head. "I'm just a man."

"From this day forward, consider yourself a free man. I can't ever repay the debt I owe you."

"You don't owe me nothing."

"I owe you my life, twice over now."

"That's not why I saved you, Master Luke."

"I know that. You were prompted by a higher desire. You are a true child of God." He reached for the canteen and took another mouthful of water before continuing. "You're also my brother in Christ. Even if I don't make it, you tell Caroline I said to free all of the slaves."

Hezekiah stood and lifted the travois once more. "Don't you go talking like that, Master Luke. I'll get you back to a doctor, and he'll fix you up right quick-like."

Luke barely heard Hezekiah begin to plead with God for Luke's life as he faded from consciousness again.

Chapter 18

It's time to consider going back home." Grandma Darby returned her teacup to the silver service on the table at her elbow. "This hotel is nice, but it's not home. And with all the Yankees in Mississippi right now, I'm worried we'll get back to Shady Oaks to find nothing but a pile of ashes."

Caroline punched her needle downward through the pillowcase. "I'm not giving up on Luke." She had designed a stylized T entwined in oak leaves to decorate the linens, but now the green threads blurred into unrecognizable shapes as tears gathered in her eyes. Her sore nose burned—not surprising since she had spent a large portion of the past week crying. But she clung to the belief that her husband and Hezekiah were still alive. She couldn't explain it to Grandma Darby, or anyone else for that matter, because her hope. . .her belief. . .was not based on any solid evidence. She might be leaning on a spider web, but for now it was the only way she could get through each day.

A feminine scream from somewhere inside the hotel interrupted her thoughts. "Who was that?" Caroline sprang from her chair and rushed to open the parlor door.

Grandma Darby was slower but reached the top of the stairwell not many seconds after Caroline. "It sounds like it's coming from the front entrance."

A small group of people, mostly the hotel workers judging by their aprons and caps, had gathered near the doorway. Someone was lying on the floor. It looked like Dinah. Had she been attacked?

Caroline hurried down the steps, her gaze focused on Dinah's prostrate form. A grizzled black man bent over her, waving his hat above her face. "What happened to Dinah?"

The black man looked up at her, and Caroline's breath caught. "Hezekiah?"

"Yes, ma'am." He stopped fanning his wife and smiled up at Caroline.

One word trembled on her lips. "Luke?" She prayed for the strength to endure whatever answer he gave her.

"He's alive, Miss Caroline, but he's mighty sick."

"Thank You, God." Relief spread through her. "Where is he?"

"I took him to the hospital."

Caroline was already halfway back up the staircase when Dinah recovered from her swoon. She could hear her slave's happy exclamations as she reassured Grandma Darby. They hugged each other, their grateful tears mingling.

Grandma Darby finally pulled away. "Can we visit the hospital at this hour?"

Mopping her face with a sodden handkerchief, Caroline laughed. "No army in the world could keep me out."

❀

The smell of death was strong inside Anchuca, the mansion being used to shelter the wounded. Caroline's heart ached for the rows of groaning men as she followed Hezekiah. Here and there, blood-spattered doctors leaned over their patients, performing rough surgeries in the most daunting of circumstances.

"He's in here." Hezekiah walked through the wide entrance to what had once been a ballroom. Every cot was occupied, as well as most of the oak floor. A breeze slipped through the open windows and doors, cooling the room somewhat.

She barely recognized her husband as the gaunt, bearded man lying in the cot Hezekiah stopped at. Her heart clenched. What she could see of his face looked far too pale in the light of the candles. One of his legs was bandaged, and the tattered remnants of his uniform hung in rags on him. She was shocked to see him brought so low. Where was the healthy, confident man she'd married? Was he still inside somewhere? Then his gaze landed on her face, and her heart filled to overflowing with love. Heedless of the people around her, Caroline sank to her knees and reached for his hand. "Luke. Oh, Luke, my dearest husband. Thank God you're alive."

His expression softened in wonder. "Caroline. Is it really you?"

"Yes, my darling. It's me." She pressed a kiss on the back of his hand. "I'm so glad to see you. We had reports you were dead."

He coughed weakly. "If not for Hezekiah, I would be."

"He told us what happened on the way here. It's nothing short of a miracle."

He nodded. "I have so many things to say." He coughed again.

"Not tonight, dearest. Tonight you must reserve your strength." She raised his hand to her cheek. "Tomorrow will be soon enough."

One of the doctors approached them. "Excuse me, but you'll have to leave, miss. He's very weak and needs plenty of rest." Without another word, he turned on his heel and left the room.

Caroline turned her attention to Luke. She patted his shoulder. "I'll be back tomorrow to check on you again. Please try to get plenty of rest as the doctor ordered."

Luke shook his head and motioned her to lean closer. "Take me home." His gaze, dark as midnight and desperate with need, pierced her heart.

Caroline nodded. She had no idea how they would manage, but she would honor her husband's request.

Chapter 19

Caroline sat in the very back of the wagon next to the pallet holding her husband. "I wonder why so many people are out after dark."

Grandma Darby was seated up front between Hezekiah and Dinah, but she must have heard Caroline's remark. "They are coming in for protection from Yankee soldiers."

Dinah nodded her agreement. "They're saying the Yanks killed thousands of soldiers the night before last."

Caroline had heard the same reports. Champion Hill had been a terrible defeat for the Confederacy. The Union army seemed unstoppable now that they had managed to get across the Mississippi River. They had taken Jackson, the state capitol, a few days earlier and were now reportedly marching ever closer to Vicksburg, gaining momentum with each successful battle. It seemed only a matter of time before the city would be taken.

Caroline noted that once they passed the outskirts of the city, the night closed in around them. "Can you see all right, Hezekiah?"

"Yes, ma'am. But I'm gonna slow down a mite."

The wagon bumped through a series of holes and ruts, causing water to slosh around in the bucket on her far side.

Luke made a sound between a groan and a grunt.

Caroline leaned over him and placed a hand on his brow. "It's all right, darling. I'm right here beside you."

"Where am I?"

"In a wagon on the way back to Shady Oaks. Grandma Darby, Hezekiah, and Dinah are up front, so don't worry. We're going to take very good care of you."

She could scarcely make out his smile, but seeing it renewed her hope she was doing the right thing. It had been the hardest decision of her life, one she knew she would question many times in the days ahead. Would Luke have been better off staying in the hospital? Or would the miasma in that building have carried him off? She put a hand over the bandage on his leg, relieved that it did not feel hot. If only they could cure the infection in his chest. She hated to hear his racking cough. Caroline prayed it stemmed from something easier to combat than consumption.

A gun was fired somewhere not very far away. She felt the wagon grind to a halt as Hezekiah pulled up on the reins. She held her breath and stretched her hearing to its limits. Was someone coming toward them? No torches gleamed through the woods or from the road ahead of them. Finally Hezekiah set the horse in motion once more.

Caroline breathed a sigh of relief and dipped one of the rags she'd brought into the bucket of water before wringing it out and placing it on Luke's forehead. She continued to pray silently as they moved through the night, beseeching God to spare her husband's life and cast His protection over them on their perilous journey. The words of Psalm 23 floated through her mind, bringing her a measure of peace that lasted for nearly an hour.

"Miss Caroline, are you awake?" Hezekiah's whisper pierced the fog that had closed around her.

She shook her head to clear it. "What's wrong?"

"I think we're about to have some company."

Caroline's heart clenched as she heard the thunder of approaching hooves. Her frightened gaze met that of Luke's grandmother. Then another sound claimed her attention. Luke's breathing had grown labored. Was he about to succumb to his illness? David's words seemed to haunt her now. *"Yea, though I walk through the valley of the shadow of death. . ."* Could she be as strong as the psalmist? Could she hold her head high and push away the fear that threatened to consume her?

Then the horses were upon them, rearing up at the last minute as their riders saw the wagon. For a few moments, everything was confusion. Hezekiah fought to keep their horse under control while the wagon rocked. By the time he had quieted the frightened animal, they were surrounded by soldiers— Yankee soldiers.

A tall man who was apparently the commanding officer pointed a gun at Hezekiah. "Who are you? Where are you going?" His voice was clipped and had an odd tone. He was obviously not from the South.

Hezekiah raised his hands to show he had no weapon. "My name is Hezekiah. I'm trying to get my master and his family back home."

"Don't you know there's a war going on?" Some of the men snickered at the leader's question.

"Of course we know that." Caroline swallowed her fear and stood. Several pistols were immediately pointed in her direction, but she ignored them, raising her chin and giving the officer her coldest stare. "But what we didn't know was that President Lincoln's army would stoop to terrorizing women."

That stopped the sly laughter, but it raised the tension in the air.

Now that her eyes had grown accustomed to the gloom of the moonless night, Caroline saw that the horsemen numbered half a dozen, so she assumed they must be advance scouts. "Our journey may seem peculiar to you, but as Hezekiah told you, my husband is very ill. He has expressed a desire to return home, and we're doing our best to get him there. We are no threat to you and ask that you leave us in peace."

She ignored Dinah's gasp of dismay. This was no time to be timid.

The leader brought his horse toward the back of the wagon. "Where is this sick husband of yours?"

Caroline pointed downward. "Right here next to me."

The man brought his animal closer to peer at the floor of the wagon.

"What do you say, Captain?" one of the other men called to him. "Is he the spy we're trying to catch up with?"

"I will fear no evil. . ."

After a moment, the man pulled his horse away. "Nah. He's about half dead from the look of it. Besides, I don't see an extra horse. He's not our quarry."

"For thou art with me. . ." Caroline clung to the promise with all her being as she waited for the soldier to decide whether or not to detain them. *"Thy rod and thy staff they comfort me."*

"Let them pass." The man holstered his pistol and saluted her briefly. "We don't make war on women or the wounded."

"Thank you, Captain."

Hezekiah called to the horse and slapped the reins.

Caroline sat down quickly and watched as the small band of soldiers continued on their quest. *Thank You, God.*

Chapter 20

Grandma Darby entered the bedchamber with a steaming pot balanced on a serving tray. "I think this mint infusion may bring down Luke's fever."

Caroline looked up at her from the rocking chair she had placed next to Luke's bed. Grandma Darby was looking rather frail. The ride home last night had been difficult for all of them. "Thank you."

"How is he?"

"Sometimes lucid, sometimes out of his head." Caroline bathed his face with a cool cloth. "Do you know who Amelia is?"

"No." The older woman put her burden down on the table next to the bed. "Why?"

Caroline sighed. "He's called her name twice this morning. She must be important to him."

"He's never mentioned anyone by that name to me." She paused, and comprehension entered her eyes. "He did tell me one time that he'd given his heart to a young woman in Tennessee who had deceived him. Perhaps that's who he's thinking of."

The afternoon Luke had caught her teaching Dinah to read came back with sudden intensity. He had said something then about deceitful women and his first love. At the time she'd thought he meant Marianna, but he must have meant another girl—a girl who still held his heart in her hands—a girl named Amelia.

Despair blanketed Caroline's heart at the realization. Luke would never love her the way she loved him. She couldn't hurt more if she'd been struck a mortal blow. But through the pain, she felt a movement inside her. The baby!

Caroline's chin lifted. She had one thing this Amelia did not: Luke's family name. And she was carrying Luke's baby. It might not be the marriage she had once dreamed of, but Luke was her husband for better or worse. She would look for blessings in every day they spent together.

"Are you all right, Caroline?" Grandma Darby sounded concerned.

She cleared her throat and summoned a smile. "Yes, I was just thinking."

The older woman pulled a straight-backed chair beside her and took Caroline's hand in her own. "I'm so glad you're the one my grandson married. He chose better than any of us realized."

Caroline's smile became a bit more natural. At least she had won one family member's approval. Together they watched as Luke's chest rose and fell in the quiet bedroom. Even the sound of the mantel clock's rhythmic ticking faded as the mint-scented steam filled the room.

Sleep overtook Caroline, and her head fell forward. The motion startled her back into wakefulness, and Caroline leaned forward in the rocker. Grandma Darby had also succumbed to exhaustion, her head resting against the back of her chair. Caroline debated whether or not to wake her but decided against it.

She stood and checked on her husband, laying her hand on his forehead. Was his skin cooler? She moved her hand to his chest. He was definitely cooler. Happiness flooded her. Caroline wanted to dance about the room. She wanted to shout the news from the rooftop. Luke was getting better.

She checked the teapot. With a lighter heart and a renewed sense of purpose, she picked it up and took it downstairs to be refreshed. Luke was getting better.

❈

"You look especially beautiful this morning. I love the way your dress brings out the blue of your eyes." Luke's admiring gaze set butterflies fluttering in Caroline's stomach.

She bustled about the bedroom, fluffing the pillows on Luke's bed and straightening the books on his bedside table. "Thank you, Luke. You are looking quite dashing yourself this morning."

Luke raked a hand through his dark hair. "I could use a haircut."

She stopped her nervous actions and took a moment to study him, trying to ignore how wonderful he looked sitting in the tall-backed chair next to the fireplace. "I don't know if you'll like the result, but I can try—"

"Oh no." He shook his head. "You may have faced down the Yankee army on my behalf and brought all of us safely to Shady Oaks, but I only trust Hezekiah's steady hand with the hair clippers."

Rolling her eyes, Caroline took the tray from his lap, checking to make certain he had eaten all his breakfast. She treasured the banter between them. It was only one of God's blessings that had come about as her husband recovered from his wounds. He had changed so much—the sometimes arrogant, always self-assured man she had fallen in love with had softened. If only she could be confident that she was the woman he loved.

Several times over the past days his gaze had seemed to declare his love, but Luke remained mute on the subject. When she was with him in this room, all her fears and doubts seemed foolish, the imaginings of an overwrought mind. But the moment she left him to tend to her other duties, the specter of Amelia arose once more. And one question above all others came to the forefront of her erratic thoughts. Whom did he really love?

Why hadn't she told him yet that she was carrying their child? Was she scared of his reaction? Scared that he would express love for her only because of the baby?

At first she had convinced herself to remain silent so he could focus on his own health. As the days wore on, it seemed there were so many other things to talk about. Luke read his Bible daily, and they discussed the meaning of many scriptures. Even though she was a pastor's daughter, Caroline found herself challenged by Luke's insightful questions.

Earlier this week she had listened as he talked about his guilt over the death of his friend Hampton. She prayed with him for the men who fought on both sides of the war. They discussed heaven and the afterlife, the importance of spreading the Gospel and her family's ministry. Yesterday they had even made plans to visit her parents in Jackson and her grandparents in Natchez as soon as travel became safe again. But still she had not been able to tell him about the life growing inside her.

"After Hezekiah finishes, will you come down to the parlor today? It's a bit chilly this morning to sit outside, but Grandma Darby and I would love to have you join us in the front parlor while we work on the mending."

He nodded. "I think it's time for me to rejoin the world."

Caroline pondered her husband's statement as she carried Luke's tray downstairs and searched out Hezekiah. Was Luke referring to life on the plantation? Or did he think he needed to rejoin the Confederate army? She hoped he did not think he was strong enough to return to battle. She walked toward the parlor, smiling at Grandma Darby as she took her place on the sofa and picked up her needle.

"How is our patient today?"

"Stronger than ever. He should be down shortly."

"You've done such a good job caring for him, Caroline."

"We all do our parts, but it is God who deserves the praise. He has mended Luke and given him back to us."

The two of them worked in companionable silence, the only sound in the room the crackle of a cheerful fire that removed the spring chill from the air.

A sound at the door brought her head around. Fully dressed, Luke didn't much resemble the unkempt patient she had seen earlier. His face was brown in comparison to the frothy white cravat showing above the lapels of his blue frock coat. A part of her wished she could halt the forward march of time, even return to the days of Luke's convalescence. Guilt washed through her with the thought. It wasn't that she wished for Luke to be ill again, but she didn't want him to reassume the imperiousness that had made her feel so disconnected from him.

The sound of horses' hooves on the drive outside interrupted her train of thought and made Caroline's heart thump. Had the war come to them at Shady Oaks?

Luke frowned and disappeared into the hall, returning a few moments later with a folded sheet of vellum in one hand.

"What is it, Luke?" Grandma Darby asked the question uppermost in Caroline's mind.

Luke's face was drawn, paler than when he'd first come downstairs. "A soldier has brought me a note from Major Fontenot."

Caroline's heart clenched. "What news is so important it must be delivered by messenger?"

"They need me to return to Vicksburg."

"You can't go." Caroline couldn't stop the objections trembling on her tongue. "You're barely recovered."

"I cannot cower here when my strength and expertise might do some good." He picked up the sock she'd been mending and set it on the arm of the sofa before taking a seat next to her. "I hoped we would have more time together, but it seems that is not to be."

Caroline barely heard Grandma Darby make some excuse and leave them alone. Tears stung her eyes. This was a disaster. Would they never have time to mend their differences? And what about the baby? She had to tell him. It might not be enough to stop him from going, but perhaps it would give him a reason to look forward to returning. They needed to discuss so many things, but when? It seemed this was the only time they would have.

"Do you know how expressive your face is, Caroline?"

The look in his eyes made her heart beat faster. "Th–thank you."

He took her hand in his. "I sometimes forget how lovely you are."

Her gaze drank in every detail of him, from the soft, dark waves of his hair to the polished leather of his boots. "I'm not sure you're strong enough."

His endearing smile appeared, making her breath catch in her throat. Would she ever be able to control his effect on her?

"Yes I am, thanks to you and Grandma." He squeezed her hand before raising it to his lips.

Caroline's arms erupted in gooseflesh. "Hezekiah is the one who did the hardest work. I still marvel at the way he carried you to Vicksburg after you were shot."

"I freed him, you know, before he brought me back. Hezekiah will never have to answer to anyone except God for his decisions."

"I'm so glad."

His smile was warm. "That's only the first of the many improvements I intend to make upon my return."

"I can hardly wait." Her stomach shifted, prompting her to change the subject. "I have something important to tell you."

"Your confession is not important. Not until I tell you something very important."

Caroline's heart sped up. Was he about to declare his love? Why now? Why could he not have said something days earlier?

"I was teasing you earlier, but I want you to know how much I admire the bravery you showed while I was too sick to protect you and Grandma. I'm very proud of the way you stood up to an army of Yanks."

Blood rushed to her cheeks. Caroline tried to pull her hand free, but Luke kept it imprisoned. Where were the words of love she was expecting? "I don't deserve your esteem. I was nearly too frightened to get the first word out."

The whole world seemed to slide away as their glances met. She could not look away. She was lost in the depths of his dark gaze. Silence filled the room, and time ground to a halt.

"You are very courageous, my dear. One of God's many blessings in my life."

Caroline closed her eyes for a moment, a conflict raging inside her as violent as any battlefield. She wanted to revel in the happiness of this moment, but she could not. She might have his admiration now, but did Luke love her? Or was he still in love with the girl from Tennessee? The memory of his words the day he discovered her and Dinah returned, forming a wall between them.

She thought she'd buried her pain. Perhaps she had. . .and watered it, too. Because it had grown into a vine that threatened to strangle their marriage. This time he let her go when she pulled at her hands. Caroline stood and walked to the fireplace.

"What is it?" Luke pushed himself up and came to stand behind her.

Caroline stared blindly at the mantel. How could she think when all she wanted to do was turn around and hide her face against his strong chest? But if she continued to bury her true feelings, could their marriage survive?

After silently debating which course to take, Caroline turned and faced him. "I know I'm not the woman you truly love."

❀

His wife's expression was a mixture of pain and determination. Luke felt like she'd punched him in the stomach. Hadn't he just told her how much he admired her? But after a moment, he realized he needed to bare his past if he hoped to have a future with the woman standing in front of him. "You mean Amelia."

"And Marianna, too, for that matter."

He nodded. This was going to be hard, but it had to be done. He had to convince Caroline that he loved her and her only. He remembered the promise he'd made to God. He would do whatever he could to reassure her, to regain her love and respect. He was the one who needed to confess.

"Amelia Montgomery and I grew up together. Our parents always assumed we would one day marry, and I saw no reason to disagree. She had other ideas, however. I escorted her to Knoxville when her parents sent her to stay with relatives. While there, she got involved with the Underground Railroad and was eventually discovered. I thought my heart was broken by her deceit and her choosing someone else over me, and maybe it was."

A soft cry pulled Luke from the past. He looked down at Caroline, surprised to see the sheen of tears brightening her eyes. Wishing he could submerge himself in the liquid blue, he sighed. "I suppose I was looking for someone more traditionally minded when I came down here to lick my wounds. So I focused on Marianna Lister." He could feel a smile turn up his lips. "I could never imagine someone like the proper Miss Lister getting involved in the Underground Railroad. She is consumed with more mundane concerns—the number of flounces on her skirt or the latest dance steps."

He sighed as he saw a tear spill over and roll down Caroline's cheek. "For a short while, I thought I could live with that, but then I met a golden-haired beauty who was neither too worldly nor too accomplished. A young woman with faith to inspire me to become a better man." Luke knelt in front of her and grasped both of Caroline's hands. "A woman whose quiet example has helped lead me into a closer relationship with Jesus."

Another tear followed the first down her cheek and landed on their clasped hands.

"Please don't cry, dearest. You have my heart. You have the best of both of the women I once considered. When I was lying in that cave, weak and wounded, I asked the Lord into my heart. He resides within me now, and I am no longer the man I once was. That's why I've been asking you so many questions lately about the scriptures. I feel such a need to understand, to absorb all of God's Word."

"That's wonderful, Luke. I guess I didn't realize how far you were from God."

"I was a fool. I thought I was in control of my life, but I have learned otherwise. I am learning to turn that control over to Him. I've read His Word all my life, but now the Bible is personal. Now I understand the sacrifice He made for me even though I was nothing but a worthless sinner. My eyes have been opened, and I can truly appreciate the woman I married."

Caroline sank to the floor in front of him. "I love you, Luke, with all of my heart. I'm sorry for questioning you."

"You had the right." He gathered her close. "I've been so wrong. Can you ever forgive me?"

"Of course I can. It makes it so much easier when I understand your past. Can you forgive me for being secretive?"

"Yes. I have come to realize your desire to help the slaves. I told Hezekiah that I plan to free all of our slaves and help them get started however we can. I trust my decision meets with your approval. . .?"

The light in her eyes was all the answer he needed. Luke leaned toward her, planning to taste the sweetness of her lips, but she ducked before he reached his goal. "What is it, dearest? Is something still bothering you?"

"N–no. Well. . .yes. As a matter of fact, I have some very special news. I've been waiting for what seems an eternity to tell you."

Another problem? He would not allow whatever was worrying her to come between them. "Whatever this problem is, Caroline, we will face it together."

A blush darkened her cheeks, increasing his curiosity. "I have been feeling a bit out of sorts for the past weeks—sick and irritable."

"I would never describe you as irritable, Caroline." He winked at her, hoping to ease her discomfort. "Not since you and Grandma ironed out your differences anyway."

She put a hand on his mouth. "Please don't distract me, Husband, or I will never manage to get to the point."

"All right. Tell me straight out. I'm completely recovered, and we don't have much time. If you're sick, I will make sure someone is here to nurse you as well as you have taken care of me. And when I get back, I'll put cotton in my ears if you're still irritable. That way I'll be spared your complaints."

She giggled. "I'm not sick, not really. It's just that. . .well. . .we're going to have an extra guest at Christmas this year."

He must be dense because he could not make sense of what she was trying to tell him.

Caroline sighed and leaned close enough that he could feel her breath on his cheek. "You're going to be a father."

The whispered words swirled around in his head, shocking him into absolute silence. A father? He was going to be a father? "You're expecting?" His voice broke on the last word. He grabbed her shoulders and pushed her back enough to see her face. The confirmation was there, along with her hesitant joy.

He pulled her close again and dropped quick kisses on her forehead and cheek before claiming her lips. They were going to have a child! What a miracle! She was so soft, so yielding—the mother of his children. Feeling her kiss him back was sweeter than anything he'd ever imagined. A prayer of thanks filled his heart and mind. Luke knew he would spend the rest of his life thanking God for all His blessings.

Epilogue

July 21, 1863

A feeling of homesickness filled Caroline as she looked out over the front lawn. What would Ma and Tory be doing today? Were they okay? It was so hard being separated from them. Had her family escaped to Natchez? Or were they still in Jackson? How she wished for some news, but Shady Oaks was too remote. They were cut off from everyone.

Caroline turned from the window to face Grandma Darby, one hand absently rubbing her slightly rounded stomach. "I think I'll go outside to pick some flowers now that the rain has stopped. The arrangement in the entry hall is sorely in need of replacement."

"Don't wander far from the house, dear." The older woman flipped idly through the pages of a *Godey's Lady's Book* that had to be almost a year old. "The overseer said he saw some drifters yesterday down by the river."

"I won't. I just feel so out of sorts. And the baby has been restless all day long. Maybe a walk will do us both good." Caroline left the older woman, lifting her skirt to avoid a soaking as she headed for the garden shed for shears and a basket.

When she had the necessary implements for her task, Caroline walked to the flower garden and began gathering the fresh blossoms. Hot, golden sunshine poked through the fleeing storm clouds, raising steam from the damp grass and hedges. The air wrapped around her face like a warm sponge as she worked.

Soon her basket was full of fragrant flowers. Caroline straightened and turned to retrace her steps when her gaze fell on two bedraggled strangers walking toward Shady Oaks on the main drive. Her heart thumped unpleasantly. They had been so blessed to remain untouched by the battles waging in the state, and she prayed these men would not threaten their peace. Tales of burned-out homes and crops haunted her, but Caroline pushed them away as she moved to intercept the strangers.

The shade of the towering oaks lining the drive hid their features at their current distance, but she could tell that one of the men was limping. He was white, and his larger companion was a black man. The lame one turned his head to say something, and her breath caught.

She knew that profile. The basket of flowers fell at her feet. "Luke!" Joy replaced her fear as Caroline ran toward them. She reached him and threw her arms around her husband, almost knocking him down in her enthusiasm. "I'm so happy to see you." She tried to hide the catch of worry in her voice. He was thin, far thinner than he'd been when he left for Vicksburg. His uniform hung loose, as though it had been made to fit a giant.

"Until now I don't think I ever fully understood the meaning of the phrase 'You're a sight for sore eyes.'" Luke bent his head and covered her lips with his own.

She melted at the familiar touch, but their baby kicked out, apparently not as pleased by the embrace as his mother. Caroline's cheeks flushed.

Luke held her at arm's length, a look of shock on his face. Then he laughed and wrapped his arms around her more gingerly.

Caroline emerged from her husband's embrace and looked over his shoulder at Hezekiah. "Both of you look exhausted. Let's get you inside. I know Dinah is going to be as excited as I am. I hope the two of you are ready to be pampered and coddled."

She placed her shoulder under her husband's arm to help steady him as they moved down the drive together. "Is it true Vicksburg has fallen to the Yankees?"

Luke nodded. "We held them off in pitched battles, but Grant's siege doomed us to failure. We could not get supplies past them, and we never received any reinforcements. Food disappeared within the first few weeks. People were reduced to eating horse meat and even rats at the end. And the daily barrage of cannon fire destroyed almost everything in the city. People dug tunnels or took shelter in caves along the riverbank."

Imagining the deprivation he had faced made Caroline feel ill. "Why didn't everyone escape down the river?"

"Where would they go? Every settlement from New Orleans to Memphis is under Federal control." He shook his head. "Vicksburg was the final town. General Pemberton's surrender gave the Yankees their final victory. They have a choke hold on the Confederacy. It's only a matter of time until the war will be over."

His words brought her hope. The war couldn't end soon enough for her. They climbed the steps slowly, and she pushed the front door open. "Look who has come home."

Her raised voice brought Grandma Darby to the entry hall as well as the household slaves. Soon they were in the midst of a crying, laughing, chattering group of people. After everyone had a chance to welcome the master home, Caroline sent Cora and her kitchen assistants out back to prepare a special meal to celebrate the heroes' return. The housekeeper, Mabel, shooed the maids upstairs to get the bedchamber refreshed. Dinah dragged Hezekiah outside to their cabin on the far side of the cane fields so she and their children could tend to him.

Luke escorted Grandma Darby to her chair before taking a seat next to Caroline in the parlor. "It's good to be home."

"Yes." Grandma Darby picked up the needlework she'd abandoned earlier. "We're relieved you're safe and sound."

"It's due to God lending us strength and endurance." Luke gazed out one of the windows, but Caroline had the feeling he was not seeing the front lawn. "If not for His faithfulness, we would have perished several times. Once Pemberton surrendered, we were all taken prisoner. Our weapons were confiscated, but we at least were given food to eat. It took some time, but most of my men were furloughed." He stopped for a moment, and his gaze refocused. He looked down at Caroline, his eyes sad. "The ones who didn't die in the siege, that is."

Caroline wished she could ease the pain in his expression. *Lord, please help me do the right thing for my husband.*

After a moment, Luke sighed and continued. "Hezekiah found me as soon as I was released, and we started for home. That was three days ago."

"Praise God." The heartfelt words came from Grandma Darby.

Caroline echoed her sentiment.

Luke shook himself and reached for Caroline's hand. "Enough about me. How are you feeling? How's the baby?"

"I feel wonderful now that you're here. And the baby must be healthy, judging by his activities day in and day out."

Luke put a gentle hand on her stomach. "It's a miracle. I can't wait to see you holding our child in your arms."

A vision of the four of them took root in her mind—she and Grandma Darby nurturing the baby while Luke set the child's feet on the narrow path to deep and abiding faith. And God willing, they would have other children, children who would fill the halls of Shady Oaks with love and laughter. She leaned against the back of the sofa.

"Is something wrong, Caroline?" Luke's voice was filled with concern.

Caroline shook her head. "Everything is very right."

A rustle from the other side of the room indicated Grandma Darby's tactful exit.

Luke released her hand and took her in his arms. "I love you, Caroline. I thought of you so often while I was stuck in Vicksburg."

"I prayed for you every night, dearest."

"Your prayers kept me alive. I could feel God's touch even in the hardest days, even when men and women were dying around me." He feathered kisses on her cheeks and forehead before capturing her lips with his own.

Time stood still as they shared soft words of love and devotion. The war might not quite be over, but at Shady Oaks, peace beyond all understanding flowed strong and true.